THE UNCERTAINTY
PRINCIPLE

Ruth Brandon is the author of a number of innovative and highly acclaimed biographies, including *The Spiritualists*, *The New Women and the Old Men*, *Being Divine: A Biography of Sarah Bernhardt* and *The Life and Many Deaths of Harry Houdini*. She has also written four detective stories. *Tickling the Dragon*, her first mainstream novel, was published in 1995 and is also available in Vintage.

BY RUTH BRANDON

Non-Fiction

Singer and the Sewing Machine:
A Capitalist Romance
The Dollar Princesses
The Spiritualists
The Burning Question
The New Women and the Old Men
Being Divine: A Biography of Sarah Bernhardt
The Life and Many Deaths of Harry Houdini

Fiction

Left, Right and Centre
Out of Body, Out of Mind
Mind Out
The Gorgon's Smile
Tickling the Dragon
The Uncertainty Principle

Ruth Brandon

THE UNCERTAINTY PRINCIPLE

VINTAGE

Published by Vintage 1997

2 4 6 8 10 9 7 5 3 1

First published in Great Britain by
Jonathan Cape Ltd, 1996

Vintage
Random House, 20 Vauxhall Bridge Road, London SW1V 2SA

Random House Australia (Pty) Limited
20 Alfred Street, Milsons Point, Sydney
New South Wales 2061, Australia

Random House New Zealand Limited
18 Poland Road, Glenfield,
Auckland 10, New Zealand

Random House South Africa (Pty) Limited
Endulini, 5A Jubilee Road, Parktown 2193, South Africa

Random House UK Limited Reg. No. 954009

A CIP catalogue record for this book
is available from the British Library

ISBN 0 09 974071 0

Printed and bound in Great Britain by
Cox & Wyman, Reading, Berkshire

for Anna
who liked the beginning

If any reader has lost a loved one,
modern physics says, 'Be comforted,
you and they shall live again.'

Frank Tipler, *The Physics of Immortality*

THE SHOPPING MALL is full. It's the middle of the day, the lunchtime crowds ebb and flow. Between the bodies, through the legs, Helen can still just glimpse the child. The black curls, the red T-shirt. But the seconds drip away, the sightings become more fragmentary. The crowd flows between them. Helen cries: – Laura! Laura! She shouts, she screams. No sound emerges. She's desperate to run, to follow, to catch, but she can't. She's rooted to the spot. Benny's beside her now. Is he similarly afflicted, or will he rescue Laura? But as she turns towards him, his familiar jaunty, stocky figure seems strangely diminished. – Bye, Helen, he says. I'm off. Other worlds for me. He shrinks, recedes. Before her very eyes, he vanishes. She is alone.

Helen forces herself into consciousness. She is drenched in sweat. The California sun reaches into the room, fingers her bed. Must be morning. Thank God. She certainly wouldn't want to risk any more sleep, not after a dream like that. What's happened to her? She isn't usually prone to nightmares. Dreams fade unremembered. Helen keeps her worms in the can, where they belong.

The terror subsides. Now only reality remains. Yesterday's events crowd upon her slowly waking brain. It can't have happened. But it did. How could she be mistaken? It wasn't just some passing resemblance. There was plenty of time for her to look, to make sure she wasn't up to her old tricks. At first she saw it everywhere, round every corner, the small figure, the longed-for face. But that doesn't happen any more. She's got over it, as far as one ever does get over these things. She's absorbed it, it's become part of her consciousness. And then she looked in the shoe-shop window, and there was Laura, trying on some sandals. In every detail, Laura. She should know. She *did* know. And beside her – some other woman. Slight, brown-haired. It might have been a younger version of herself. Helen entered the shoe-shop. Was she going to approach them? What was she going to say? *There's been a mistake, I claim my child*? An assistant approached. – Can I help?

Helen fled.

The sun's low in the sky. The guest-room, which faces east, is full of long shadows. Looking at her watch, Helen sees it's only half past six. Patrick won't be up for hours yet. What's she going to do? She feels an urgent need to talk to someone, to unburden herself. It isn't just the child. She's filled with a separate panic, a sense of impending disaster. Connected, somehow – she steps reluctantly back into that dream – with Benny. On the other side of the world, he needs her. She knows it.

Ridiculous! Helen, the rationalist, is not affected by rubbish of this sort. What could happen to Benny? She spoke to him yesterday and he was fine. So why this sudden concern? Those days are past. Their lives are separate enterprises. Left to himself, Benny doesn't give her a moment's thought. All right, a moment's: twenty-five years leave their mark. But little more. When they're together they're together, and that's fine. And that, now, is about as far as it goes.

Perhaps he's finally decided there's no more point in staying together. Is that the message – that he *doesn't* need her? She's been wondering, herself. What justifies connexion? Vitality, only vitality. Feelings that can't be ignored, whatever their nature. They've learned that lesson more than once. But indifference – ? However painless, however gentle.

Still, she would urgently like to speak to him. To hear his voice, to know he's there, that dreams are merely dreams.

And what could be easier? Telephones exist to fulfil this very whim. There's one beside her bed. What's she waiting for? In London it's – she calculates on her fingers – half past three in the afternoon. A perfectly reasonable time to call. She dials the familiar number, hears the double ring, pictures the bleating machines – one on his desk, one on hers, one in the kitchen, one in the hall, one by the bed – and waits for him to answer. After four rings there's a click: and her own voice reciting the familiar message. What did she expect? Benny's a busy man. He's probably having lunch with somebody. Or in bed with somebody. Who knows? Who (in the normal way of things) cares? That's the arrangement. Out of sight, out of mind. Your life's your own. You're a big girl now.

Helen looks at her watch again. Seven o'clock. She and Patrick usually meet for breakfast by the pool around nine. She's only been here a week, and the routine is already established. This is *work*? – What did you expect? he said, the first morning. – It's lotus-land, darling. Relax. Enjoy. Leave the Protestant ethic behind. There are no Protestants in the film business.

She showers, pulls on a T-shirt, makes her way to the kitchen. She needs comfort food, none of this healthy Californian stuff. A mug of thick chocolate and hot toast to dip in it. But she can whistle for that in Patrick's house. He's too busy keeping himself beautiful for his boys. The fridge is filled with exotic fruits and skimmed milk, juices, yoghourts, salads. Nothing of any use whatever. Then, at the back, she spies a chink in the health-food armour: an open packet of English muffins. Carbohydrate! She toasts two, spreads them reluctantly with margarine (Patrick would sooner cut his wrists than keep butter in the house, it's a quicker way to go), and makes herself some milky coffee with watery skimmed milk. Better than nothing, just about. Don't the people here have any normal cravings? Muffins have no substance, and as for margarine, it's not just disgusting, it's unhealthy in its own right. *Differently* unhealthy, that's all. Nevertheless, she feels slightly better. She returns to her room, makes the bed and sits outside in the little guest-room patio, going over the script on her laptop (but she can't really concentrate) and trying to calm down in the morning sun. That's another thing about California. Nothing but sun whatever your mood. – Isn't it a lovely morning? she said naively to someone the other day. – It's always a lovely morning here, they replied kindly, pityingly. No, I couldn't live in California, thinks Helen.

Nine o'clock finally arrives. The pool's on the other side of the house, landscaped, with oleanders and cypresses and even a couple of marble columns. Or rather, marble substitute – is this not Hollywood? Patrick, in his robe, is juicing an orange. He waves a bronzed arm. – One for you?

Helen sits beside him at the pretty wrought-iron table and accepts an orange-juice. Routine, ordinary, normal. The oddest thing about having breakfast beside a swimming-pool on the other side of the world is that it feels perfectly natural. She wonders, as so often she has wondered: Can this really be me? But yes: this is, indeed and as always, Helen Bartram. And that, inescapably, Patrick Costelloe. The detail varies. Helen's thinner than when first they met; Patrick, squashier. It's warmer, they're older. But unmistakably themselves. – Do you feel at home here? she asked him. – Darling, you know me, he replied. I never feel at home anywhere. Don't know the meaning of the phrase. Home's where the work is, home's where my friends are. You have arrived, ergo I feel at home.

That's nonsense, of course. Patrick's great quality, what impressed her about him from the first, is that he feels at home *every*where. He is universally at ease. Is this because he is never really engaged? He views the fight from above. Among all those nervous, striving youths and maidens, Patrick quizzically, impressively, calmly, reclined: detached, amused. That Buddha-like ease was the source of his glamour, that power they all felt and which, to a greater extent than is usual, he has retained. How many of the golden lads vanished, sank without trace? More than Helen cares to consider.

Benny didn't. But his style was never effortless, that British effortlessness at which Patrick excels. Benny is diligent as well as brilliant. With brief interruptions, his work has always been more interesting to him than anything else. That was the source of *his* power: passion, a single-minded passion for the truth of things. A rationalist, when she first knew him, who accepted nothing without cool appraisal. That's how he still sees himself, though it's clear to everyone that, since Laura died, his heart has entirely ruled – overruled – his head. He denies it. Why argue? Helen gave that up years ago. Words are just words. Only actions count.

– How's the script going? Patrick enquires, slicing a pawpaw.

– I'm afraid I haven't done much to it since yesterday.

– Goodness, why not? We seemed to be getting on so well. You looked all set.

– Something happened yesterday, Helen says, and looks down as, unexpectedly, a lump rises in her throat. Not now, not now. The time for all that has passed. Patrick has not brought me here, at great expense, in order to be lumbered with emotion. She swallows hard. That's better. Take a sip of orange-juice.

– Oh dear, says Patrick, who evidently hopes she will not want to talk about it. No doubt he has quite enough happenings of his own to cope with.

– I saw Laura, says Helen, talking about it anyway. – In that shopping-mall on the way to the freeway. She was trying on shoes. It was her. I couldn't believe it, I looked and looked. It really was her.

– Now don't be silly, Helen. Patrick sounds anxious: he's obviously afraid that she's going to break down on him, lose control – require serious attention. – How could it be Laura? Laura died years ago.

– Nine years ago. Helen nods. She needs no telling. – But it was her. Do you imagine I could possibly make a mistake about a thing like that?

– It must have been some child who looks like her, says Patrick firmly.

– It *was* her.

What more is there to say? No, it could not have been Laura. But it was: the same, the very same. The hair, the face, the build, that way of holding her head which she got from Benny. Trying on shoes.

– Anyhow, it shook me up. I couldn't concentrate. And then last night I dreamed about her. And about Benny. He was – going away from me, he sort of melted. I felt quite panicky. Still do. Maybe I should just go home, she mumbles. The lump in her throat has reasserted itself, and this time it won't go away.

– Helen! says Patrick. – Can I believe my ears? Can this be *me* telling *you* that you can't let your life be ruled by dreams and portents? I can hardly bring myself to say it. But you simply must pull yourself together, darling. You can't have seen Laura, it's impossible, you know that as well as I do. And you can't go rushing off now just because you had a bad dream. We're having lunch with the producers – remember? A presentation. I've worked very hard to fix this up. It'll probably never get anywhere, in fact it's entirely out of our hands – it all depends on *Gurdjy*, and you know how long *that* took to get off the ground. I was doing some sums yesterday. Four years before we could start shooting. Unbelievable. By the time we actually began, one of our original cast had died, the cameraman we wanted was in Japan and all the winter locations had to be shot in midsummer.

Patrick's film *Gurdjy*, about the Russian sage Gurdjieff and the dying Katherine Mansfield, is about to hit the screen. It previews in two weeks at Grauman's. If it fails, so will the project upon which they are now engaged. Even if it succeeds, they won't be sure they're there till the camera starts turning. Until then, it's meta-words about meta-films. Concentrate on the development money, says Patrick. Orson Welles shot whole *films* on development money.

– You never can tell, he says now. – This may be our lucky day. So let's get down to that script. And, he adds, I invited Stefan Kertes to that dinner this evening. I know how bored you get with the money-men. He cancelled something specially to see you.

– Stefan!

Who else? Why should she be surprised? It sometimes seems that no significant juncture of her life is complete without an appearance from Stefan Kertes, generally playing the Demon King.

– I thought you'd be pleased. Patrick sounds hurt. – He's an old friend, isn't he?

– I suppose he's part of Benny's life, not mine. He and I don't overlap much now.

– That's not how he sees it. When he heard you were here, nothing could keep him away.

– I don't go for this big act he puts on these days, Helen says crossly. – You can't open a paper without seeing a double-page spread of him and his damned fiddle. I saw a book of anecdotes about him the other day. All cuddly and human. For Christ's sake! Why shouldn't he be human? He's just an ordinary man who's good at physics. Why can't they leave it at that?

– Because they don't want to, I expect, darling. They all think he's let them off the hook. They're going to go on virtually for ever. They can't get enough of it. Can you believe it, not wanting to die? Personally I often feel I can't wait, but there you are. Anyhow, that's why they're all coming, because I promised them Kertes. And *he's* only agreed because I promised him you. You can't let me down now.

– Oh, Pat! In the end, that's why she loves him. He thinks he's so Machiavellian, but the truth always outs – generally in the next sentence. – So long as he doesn't bring that bloody fiddle.

Helen sighs. She's all psyched up to go: she spent some of that spare time this morning calling the airlines to find out about flights to London. But she'd forgotten about the presentation. Patrick's right: she can't just leave him in the lurch. Maybe, who knows, the project will make it. That would be fun. And even if it only gets as far as the next stage along, that still, as Patrick points out, means money. Without which . . . – Oh well, she says. – You've persuaded me. But you're not to leave me alone with Stefan. He gives me the creeps, to tell you the truth.

– That must be why he's so keen to see you, says Patrick. The one soul he hasn't conquered.

– I doubt it. He and Benny have had some sort of falling-out. I expect he wants to put his side of the story. I don't want any part of it, and I'm not strong enough to face a charm offensive. He can't have my soul however much he wants it.

Patrick looks relieved. – I'll be in constant attendance, he promises. – And there'll be lots of other people there. Though I'm sure you can *more* than hold your own about Benny. At least it's not your body he's after. Isn't that usually the way with those elderly middle Europeans? I was going to reassure you. I'm not being rude, darling – you look wonderful, you really do – but in this town, ladies over thirty don't generally have to worry about getting laid against their will.

Helen gives him her best ironical look. Well, he's entitled to a little light revenge. That must have been a nasty shock she gave him. And Patrick never could resist a little dig. He's catty, always was. Not like Benny, thinks Helen. Which doesn't mean Benny's a nicer man. Patrick's fundamentally kind, and Benny's hard as nails. But you have to study someone to know where they're vulnerable, and Benny isn't interested in that sort of detail. Human beings simply don't engage him, any more (to take another immediate case in point) than they do Stefan Kertes. Who is also not a nice man. Their minds are on other things, much larger or much smaller (or that's the impression they like to give). Ideas, not mundanities. Finely-honed barbs don't interest them.

It's to do with being in the theatre, perhaps. People are Patrick's professional study, as they are Helen's. Though Helen tends to watch rather than speak, while Patrick can never resist an indiscretion. Maybe being gay has something to do with it, too. Watchfulness and insecurity. When he came out, Helen was, somewhat to her surprise, not surprised at all. You'd think a revelation like that would have some effect. In fact it did: it relieved her vanity. Helen is aware – how could she not be? – that Patrick has never fancied her sexually, not for a moment. This has never dented their friendship – on the contrary: it was one less potential source of aggravation. But, considering their closeness, it was slightly surprising. Not that Helen has been to bed with all the men she knows well. But there has generally, at some point, been an understanding that this might be possible: a sort of delightful complicity. With Patrick, never. So that when the news broke, all she could think was: Of course! The bigger surprise was how long he stayed married to Colette. But Colette was always irresistible, to either sex. And then there were the children. Patrick always thought he'd enjoy family life, until he tried it.

– So you'll stay another couple of days?

– All right.

– Why not give Benny a ring? It'll set your mind at rest.

Helen does so – naturally, there's a phone by the pool – but all she gets is the answering-machine again.

– You could try telepathy. Concentrate very hard.

– Now, now, don't be naughty. But the bad spell is broken as they laugh together at Benny's recent eccentricities.

And then it's time to have another go at the script, and lunchtime, and the presentation, which goes well. And dinner is, after all, uneventful, since of course Stefan Kertes has neither horns nor tail but is merely a polite elderly man, which makes Helen feel ashamed of her outburst. And then there's more work to be done on the script; and more meetings and discussions, and even some talk about possible casting, though no-one will really commit themselves until they see how *Gurdjy* does. So that, what with one thing and another, Benny and even Laura are pushed to the back of Helen's mind, and, rather than going home early, her departure is, if anything, slightly delayed: it is not until five days later that she steps out into the gloomy, draughty tunnel leading to Heathrow's teeming concourses.

*

How can these grey familiarities possibly have called her so insistently, so seductively, from sunny California? Even allowing for the effects of a long overnight flight, the contrast is deeply depressing. She longs only to be home. But a cab is no magic carpet, and London is jammed. It would almost have been quicker to walk: much quicker to take the tube. A cab is less tiring, Helen tells herself as the meter ticks on and they move another three feet. She crouches glumly in the back seat, practising zen. After several centuries they attain Nirvana, or, as some call it, Kentish Town.

Fumble for the key; open the door. Helen drops her bag in the hallway, shuts the door behind her, leans against it and inhales the smell of her life: coffee, vacuum-cleaner fluff, apples, books and other unidentified residues. *Parfum maison.* The house is tall and thin, part of a terrace. A narrow hallway: to her right, the door into the big double room lined with books, in the back part of which she works; on the first floor, a sitting-room and Benny's study; bedrooms above; kitchen below. Home at last. – Anyone here? she calls, but no-one answers. On the hall table lie a scatter of letters and a note. There are more letters on the mat: evidently Benny left before the post came this morning. She picks them up and moves to add them to the heap on the table.

Time enough to deal with all that after she's had a bath. She feels light-headed and sticky. The note is addressed in Benny's firm black script: Mrs Martins. Mrs Martins is the cleaning-lady. What's today? Tuesday. Yes, Tuesday is her day. Shouldn't she be here by now? According to Helen's watch, set at Heathrow, it is almost midday.

9

Mrs Martins has been increasingly erratic lately. More and more colds, bad backs, tummyaches, less and less time spent actually cleaning when she does come. It's clear that soon Mrs Martins will appear no more, and Helen will have to find a new cleaning-lady. Easier said than done. Or do it herself. No more kids at home, and a bit of dust never bothered her, much. But she doesn't relish the prospect. Coming home to a clean house – one cleaned by somebody else – is a luxury she's never tired of. Would Benny help? Do pigs fly? Helen sighs. Domestic life engulfs her.

What can Benny have wanted to say to Mrs Martins? Feeling slightly (but only slightly) guilty, Helen opens the note. Mrs M.'s clearly not coming, and she'll see Benny before next week.

It reads: Dear Mrs Martins, Please don't come upstairs. Call the police. Ben Spiro.

Helen stares down at the piece of paper in her hand. Her skin seizes up: it feels terribly taut. She starts to sweat and tremble. Her knees threaten to give way beneath her. Nevertheless, she forces them to carry her up the stairs. What's up there, and where is it?

On the first landing, there is a choice of two doors. The sitting-room faces the street; behind it, Benny's room looks onto the garden. The sitting-room door is open. It's empty: nothing special to be seen. The door to Benny's room is shut. Helen opens it.

Benny is sitting at his desk. He's slumped back in his big leather chair. Is he asleep? Is he drugged? Has someone knocked him over the head? She calls, shrilly: – Benny! But he does not reply.

She goes over to the desk, touches his shoulder. No response. Shakes him. Touches his hand, his cheek. They are cold. There's a half-drunk glass of brandy on the desk in front of him, and also another glass, with some white powdery residue in the bottom. He looks so normal – asleep: that thick head of hair still so black – even at his age, nothing but a few white threads – and full of life. But appearances are deceptive. Life is just what isn't there.

What now? Call the police, as per instructions? Helen sits in the armchair by the window and tries to collect herself. But how? She needs someone she can speak to, someone to share this. Benny. But Benny is no longer an option.

She can't face the thought of the police. Not yet, not for a little while. Who, then? There's only one other possible person. Colette. She goes over to the phone and dials the number.

– Yes? Colette's either in a hurry or a bad temper.

– Colette? It's me, Helen. Thank God you're in.

– Helen? What's up? Are you in LA?

– I was. I'm home. Just got home. And –

– Darling, can I call you back later? I'm in the most frightful rush. Supposed to be meeting someone for lunch, and I'm late already. The phone rang when I was just halfway out the door, I was going to leave it to the machine but then I didn't – you know how it is.

– Colette, you've got to come round. Now. The most – Benny's killed himself.

– What? Why? Are you sure?

– Of course I'm sure.

– Sorry. There is a pause, as Colette resigns herself, reluctantly, to the inevitable. – OK. I'll be round in a minute. Let me just phone the restaurant and leave a message.

Helen sits in the armchair, waiting for Colette. Colette will know what to do. The famous double act. In any circumstance, one of them always knows what to do.

Five minutes later the doorbell rings. Colette lives three doors down. She has a key to Helen's house, just as Helen has a key to hers, but the convention is that these keys are for emergencies only. Not, that is, to be used when the owner is in residence. For a minute the two of them cling together, and then Colette says gently: – Come on. You'd better show me. Are you sure he's dead?

– Pretty certain.

They climb the stairs to Benny's room. Colette views the scene. She's all dressed up: a floaty voile dress in some greenish, mauvish print that brings out the delicacy of her blonde colouring. Must have been meeting a new man. For old acquaintances, Colette wears jeans. Always, invariably, jeans. She even wore them once to a funeral, Helen remembers. Perhaps that's what she'll wear to Benny's funeral. She touches Benny, as Helen did, feels the cold hands, the cold cheek. Takes out, as in so many films, her compact mirror, holds it before his mouth. No mist of life appears. Dead. Truly dead. Colette puts her mirror away. Her hands are trembling so that she fumbles the zip in her bag.

She says: – Have you read the notes?

– What notes?

Colette points. There are two envelopes on the desk, one addressed To whom it may concern, one for Helen. How had she missed them? Evidently, shock induced tunnel vision. Helen stares at these envelopes. She feels no inclination to open either of them. Doesn't really want even to touch them. Doesn't want Benny's excuses. What's done is done: notes are beside the point. She shakes her head. Colette says: – I'll phone the police. Then we'll open them. We'd better know what they say.

She picks up the telephone. Dimly, Helen hears her ask for Police, hears her give the address, hears her say: A friend of mine has committed suicide. His wife found the body. Yes, here. Could you send someone round?

She replaces the phone, picks up the first envelope, opens it, reads, hands the note to Helen.

The envelope is typewritten. The letter, also typewritten, reads: – I have decided to end my life. I have always looked upon suicide as a decent and dignified exit should life become unbearable. There is also the pull of curiosity: my studies over the past few years have indicated that existence does not necessarily end with this life, and I have always been a believer in direct investigations. My affairs are in order. I am truly sorry for any pain or grief my action may cause. Should I have miscalculated so that I am found before I am dead, please do not attempt to revive or resuscitate me. This is not a cry for help, but a considered decision.

Helen gazes at this for a while, then tears open the other envelope. It is addressed, in ink, to *Helen*. My dear Helen, she reads. I don't know quite how you're going to feel about this action of mine. That is, I know it'll be a terrible shock, of course, and for that I'm very very sorry. We haven't been as close recently as once we were, but I'm still closer to you than to anyone else I can think of. Please believe this, and believe, too, that what I'm doing is no reflection on you or on our relationship. I've recently had to face some very hard truths. They're not to do with you, or us, or Tim; they aren't shameful; but, taken all in all, the pain's too much. I haven't the strength to carry on. You've been a better wife than I deserved or hoped for. I hope your life blossoms. In my present mood – and I can't see it ending – I should not help it do so. All my love. I mean that. Benny.

The doorbell rings again. Police. There are two of them: a senior man and a woman constable. They ask questions, they take statements. When did Helen last speak to Benny? Three days ago: she confirmed that her return would be slightly delayed. How did he sound? As usual. Not particularly emotional. Not upset. No hint of anything like this. She describes what she found, what she did. There will have to be an autopsy, an inquest. Formalities. After that, the funeral. The undertakers will know what to do.

The doctor arrives, followed by the undertakers: an invasion of unknown people. Finally they leave, taking Benny with them.

The phone rings, and Colette picks it up. When she speaks, the caller hangs up. Colette, puzzled, looks at the phone, looks at Helen. Replaces the receiver.

It is by now halfway through the afternoon. The policewoman made some tea, hot sweet tea, that's what you need when you're in shock. Helen drank it, but did not feel noticeably better. On the other hand, maybe it stopped her feeling even worse. She's reeling from lack of sleep, as well as everything else. She sits in her kitchen, shaking, while Colette bustles about. The two of them know each other's kitchens almost as well as they know their own. Colette makes Welsh rarebits, opens a bottle of wine. – Got to eat, she says. – And we need a drink. Better not have anything stronger on an empty stomach. Where's Tim? We must let him know what's happened.

– Somewhere in India. He went for the long vac. Term doesn't start for another month.

– Any idea where?

Helen shakes her head. – They're travelling around – we've had some cards.

– Oh, God, says Colette. – Poor Tim.

– Benny never cared about Tim.

– Nonsense, says Colette, but they both know this was true. – Well, let's hope the feeling was mutual. At least it won't be so much

13

of a trauma. Gemma's going to be shattered, she sighs. Gemma is Colette's daughter.

Helen is crying now. Up to this point she has been dry-eyed. Formalities have been dealt with, shocks have been absorbed, nothing has seemed real. But now, with the wine, consciousness begins to seep in. Colette hugs her, awkwardly: they are sitting on the wooden kitchen chairs. – Whatever you feel, she says, – you mustn't feel guilty. There's nothing you could have done.

– Oh, but there is! wails Helen. – There is! You don't know. And she tells what happened in California, that dream, then seeing Laura. If only she'd come back. If only she hadn't let herself be persuaded.

– Helen, don't be silly. What are you trying to say, that he was calling you? You sound like one of those addled women that write letters in green ink. Colette sounds unusually brisk. Perhaps she's trying to convince herself. Generally, she's a great one for this sort of thing. She and Patrick both.

– What else can I think? I don't want to think it, believe me.

– It was a coincidence, that's what you can think. If you'd had that dream and come back to everything as normal, you'd have forgotten about it already. Once in a thousand times you get something like this. How many times have you said it to me? Well, now I'm saying it to you. Me saying this to you – she echoes Patrick – I can hardly believe it.

– I wouldn't have forgotten about Laura.

Colette looks uncomfortable. People do not like to be reminded of other people's tragedies. For Colette, Laura is part of the past; for Helen, of course, this will never be entirely true. Colette shrugs. – There must be millions of little girls who look like Laura. Thousands, anyway.

Helen lets this pass. She sits there thinking, If only, if only. If. Benny's favourite word. How many times has he sat at this table expounding his thesis of the moment? Always beginning the same way. – You see, if . . . She shuts her eyes and sees again that stocky, vital, infuriating figure. That was how she knew at once he was dead. Stillness was unknown to Benny.

Colette pours them both another glass of wine. She glances

surreptitiously at her watch. – Don't you worry about me, Helen says. – I'll be all right.

– I'll have to go quite soon. I don't like leaving you here, though. Won't you come over to our place for a bit?

– No, I'd prefer to stay here, thanks all the same. You working at the moment?

– Opening in something next week at a little theatre in Battersea. You must come. I think it's quite good. New writer. She looks down at her glass, almost coyly. – That's who I was meeting for lunch, actually.

O, how are the mighty fallen! Helen can remember when Colette was the hottest thing in London, stage or screen. When producers and directors queued for her services. Swooned for a pout of those lovely lips. How long ago was that? Not so very. Within living memory. Heads still turn at the sight of her. Look! Isn't that . . . ? The fact of having been a star renders one always to some extent starry. And to the dulled eye of daily acquaintance, she's physically changed very little. A few crows treading lightly round the eyes, a little less transparency to the cheeks. But she's still slim and lithe, still filled with the all-commanding confidence of beauty.

The deceptions of familiarity. A couple of weeks ago, Helen found a cache of old photos. The first night of Patrick's first film, *Wheels*. Afterwards, they all went out to supper. There they all were – Patrick so elegant, flourishing his cigarette, Benny vibrating to the tip of each black curl with life and scepticism, Helen smiling as she rarely did in photographs, unselfconscious, blissful, a little girl content – for had she not recently had her own first play performed? And Colette: she simply shone. Exquisite, a perfect creature. Helen had forgotten quite how gorgeous Colette used to be. How does she feel, now, looking at old photos? Is she happy to have been so lovely, or is there just the pain of loss?

*

Not a breath of wind. Behind the bay an ancient castello nestles, silhouetted amid cypresses. The full moon is rising over the sea, and soon the Milky Way will arch its brilliant band across the sky. In spite of all this, Helen was for eating inside. Mosquitoes abound, and they always seem to find her especially delicious. But Colette wouldn't hear of it. – Mosquitoes! she said. – What do a few mosquitoes matter on a night like this?

Helen wraps up and gives way. On these occasions, what Colette says, goes.

They're at a fish restaurant, with a terrace overlooking the Mediterranean. Colette surveys the terrace. The table to which they've been shown isn't quite to her liking, though to an untrained eye it seems much like the rest. – Can't we be nearer the sea? she says. – What about over there? She points to a table near the terrace rail, clearly marked *Riservato*, and smiles winningly at the maître d', a man with unimaginable bags under his eyes. Great purple bruises cover half his cheeks. Doesn't he ever sleep? Between the end of the evening meal and the opening of the early-morning fish market, perhaps not. Such exhaustion must surely inure him to all charm – even Colette's, wide smile gleaming, blonde hair a-flutter, voile wrap rippling seductively.

It works, of course. It always works. Eager hands shift tables and chairs, create a space where none was before; and they are settled. The eyes of the room are upon them, but that doesn't worry Colette – on the contrary: it's what she's used to; it's what she likes best.

For it isn't only the business with the tables that attracts attention. Diners whisper to each other. Haven't they seen that face before somewhere?

Of course they have! Colette's reputation is international these days. Whenever you forget she's a star – easily done amid the familiarities of domestic life – occasions like this remind you. She appears unaware of the commotion she has caused, or, at any rate, takes no notice of it. It has become part of her life: background music, registered only when it stops.

They sit down. The waiter lights their candles and the mosquito-repellent spiral. The pungent smoke makes them all cough, but doesn't deter the insects. There's one now, whining away. Helen's silk shirt has long sleeves, but they are no match for sharp mosquito teeth. – Benny, do mosquitoes have teeth?

He looks at her as if she were mad. – Of course they don't.

– Then how do they bite?

Benny is about to launch into an explanation when Colette says:–
What d'you think about this table? D'you think we might be better
over there? She nods towards a far corner, a particularly secluded
part of the terrace – one she hadn't noticed until now.

Patrick says, – For Christ's sake, darling, do stop behaving like a
film star. This is dinner, not a ballet.

Colette looks to her friends for support, but none is offered. She
subsides crossly. She *is* a film star, isn't she? For the next ten minutes
she casts longing glances towards the favoured spot. For two pins
she'd move again, flutter her eyelashes at the tired man and assume
(rightly) that the world asks nothing more than to make her happy.
And what would the others do? Sit their ground? Dissociate
themselves? No: they'd trail resignedly in her wake amid the fawning
waiters. They all know that: it's happened too often before. Luckily
the wine arrives and the question of food displaces that of location.

Fame! It's what she always wanted, and, at least for the moment,
it's as wonderful as she always thought it would be. She's even
started to believe all that stuff they keep telling her, if not in so many
words then by the way they behave, the way they pamper her, the
money they pay: that the world revolves around her, that she's
irreplaceable. (And will she be too grand, wonders Helen, to be
interested in my next play?)

Wheels was a triumph for both Colette and Patrick. His first
feature film, and what a debut! The use of effects, the subtly
terrifying forays into magical realism, dazzled everyone. He can pick
his project now. Though that doesn't mean he will repeat his first
success. The insecurity will always be there. He's precisely as
bankable as his last film. Fame means he will henceforth make all his
mistakes in the glare of the limelight. But insecurity has never
worried him. – It's all an accident, he says with a shrug – and only he
knows how literally true that is. Easy come, easy go. Everything's
dispensable.

Even the children?

Ah, but who will ever admit to their true feelings about small
children? The world does not encourage openness on this subject.
Colette, for example, cries: – *This* is the only thing that matters! And

picks up whichever child happens to be within reach, Declan or Gemma or Tim or Laura, and gives it a cuddle.

That's what her voice says, and no doubt her heart, too. But what about her life? Those are the words: now let's look at the actions. What do *they* tell? Why, the old, old story, the story behind a thousand women's pages, a million magazines, a trillion agonized conferences; the story that fills therapists' couches and fuels an infinity of self-serving sermons. *Can she have it all?* She does – that's clear – but should she? Shouldn't she devote her life to her children at this formative instant? Is mere heart, mere love, mere as and when – a mere slicing herself in half – is this *enough*? Shouldn't she, really, drop everything else – *now*?

Even Helen, as she loads and unloads the washing machine for the twentieth time in a week, finds herself, guiltily, thinking these weasel thoughts. She may be – she often is – bored out of her mind, but *her* children have the inestimable benefit of her company. Her very own.

Luckily, Colette has wonderful Monica right there behind her.

Patrick and Colette: here's to them. For this millisecond, the hottest couple in town. Can they keep up the heat, the act, the marriage? They're balanced at the top of the roller coaster, and everyone's waiting for the whoosh and the screams as they hurtle to the dip. Meanwhile they dazzle, apparently without effort.

It's sometimes hard to forgive this, but Benny and Helen console themselves by taking part of the credit. Aren't Patrick and Colette their own creation? – their invention, almost. *They* know the truth. The whole thing's unreal – as unreal as the movies. Wouldn't they rather be who they are – Benny in his lab, Helen with her typewriter and her thoughts? Benny is in no doubt; his work claims him utterly. Money is incidental; perhaps even fame. But Helen is less secure. She would never admit it, but she knows the others suspect her shameful secret. Fame allures her. She may tell herself it doesn't, but it does.

Does this mean men have loftier souls than women? Helen looks at Benny and Patrick and knows that, underneath, they are as eaten by ambition as herself and Colette. Their secret is that they can hide it: they can *pretend* they don't care. Yes, that's what she tells herself as she sits at her desk while the babies sleep.

A waiter comes across, and presents Signorina Bosanquet with a bottle of Asti Spumante, compliments of the management. From the other side of the room, the tired man bows and smiles. Must have seen the film. Colette raises her glass to him. Asti Spumante! There's no escape: they'll have to drink the horrid stuff. Luckily it's been iced till you can't really taste it. They clink glasses. Benny smiles at Colette. Patrick proposes a toast. – To us! Onward and upward.

The main courses have come and gone; now they're eating a wonderful ice-cream, the speciality of the house, liberally doused in brandied fruits. The scent of the sea washes across the table: they can hear the hush of waves on the shingle. Patrick's face has lost its tautness, Benny is leaning back in his chair telling scurrilous jokes, Colette recounts some item of gossip. This is how Helen will remember them in bad times to come. Happy days! But happiness is brittle stuff. You hug it to you: it fragments under your grasp.

Later that evening, the telephone rang. It was a man, for Colette. The house had only one phone, in the living-room where they were all gathered, drinking brandy. Colette retired into a corner with it, but they couldn't help overhearing. Colette, when she realised this, seemed totally composed, even though the caller was clearly a lover, or at any rate a suitor. She smiled gaily at Helen when the call ended, and rejoined the group as though nothing untoward had happened. As, in a sense, it had not. You evolve your own way of being married to a woman like Colette. She and Patrick have presumably reached some understanding. Still, it seems a shame she couldn't leave all that behind for just a few days. Why not play happy families, just for a little while? You never know. If you believe hard enough, your wishes may come true.

*

Helen looks affectionately at Colette, takes her hand across the table.
– I don't know what I'd have done if you hadn't been there.
– Oh, well.
They half-smile at each other.
Colette says, – Have you any idea why he did it?
– You read the notes. You know as much as I do.
– D'you think he really believed – ?

– Maybe he really did.

– You don't know what those troubles were he talked about?

– No.

Colette looks at her watch again. – I've got to go. We're rehearsing in twenty minutes. I shall be late as it is. Will you really be all right, all by yourself here? Is there anyone who could come and keep you company?

– I'll be fine. It's just Tim. I wish I could get hold of him.

– Maybe he'll phone.

– Not very likely. He's been away two months already, and he hasn't phoned yet. I asked Benny when I spoke to him. He doesn't phone, period. Why should he break the habit of a lifetime?

Colette kisses her. – He'll know soon enough. I'll be round tomorrow.

The front door bangs. Helen is alone.

Alone, she thinks. Truly alone. Better get used to it, Helen. This is you, now. This is how things are going to be. Tim's deep in his own life, and Colette has her pressing concerns. And who else is there? Damn you, Benny, she thinks. You've done it again. For this has been a pattern in their joint life. Unalloyed pleasure is not permitted. Never has been. When one's been up, the other's been down. Any triumph invariably balanced by a disaster; Helen's victory by Benny's flaming injustice. And vice versa? Were Benny's pleasures tarnished by Helen's failures? Probably. It seems he was less impervious than she'd thought. Oh God, she thinks wearily. What a dance.

She ought to let people know. Phone people up, tell them what's happened. And not just family and friends. The press, the various societies, learned and not so learned, of which Benny was an ornament. Synchrony. The College. Miss Parrinder, his secretary. Yes, Miss Parrinder, that's a thought. Couldn't she deal with most of this? Her number is taped to the wall by the phone. Helen dials it, explains what's happened. Miss Parrinder is distraught: she's been with Benny seven years now. She sees her livelihood and her life both washed down the drain. What a bastard, Helen thinks again. Grief will presumably hit her sometime soon, but just now she can feel only indignation. She summons her strength to calm Miss Parrinder down. Hopes she'll keep coming in, for the moment at least. There's going to be a lot to do. Beginning with all this letting-know. Perhaps they could start tomorrow. That should be soon enough. He's not going to run off anywhere, is he?

Wearily, she drags herself upstairs to run a bath. She's still wearing the clothes she travelled in. She shucks them off and lowers herself into the hot, scented water. Lying there, Benny's obituaries, as yet unwritten, float through her brain. Distinguished zoologist. New ways of thinking about the mechanisms of evolution. Author of many influential books, of which perhaps the most famous . . . Well, which is the most famous? Not, Helen would bet, any *that* obit would mention. The crazies can't get enough of Benny's distinction in the world of the straights, but the straights can rarely bring themselves even to acknowledge the existence of the crazies. In fact, since Benny jumped over the fence, it's only under duress that they acknowledge his existence at all. They certainly don't mention the eccentricities of his later years, not in the same breath as the classic studies he did earlier. Benny likes – liked – to tease them by pointing out that the eccentricities undoubtedly increased the audience for the straight stuff. How many copies has *Immortality and the New Physics* sold? Miss Parrinder would doubtless know. She should, it pays for her salary, not to mention a great many other good things, and will doubtless go on doing so for years.

Did he believe it, Helen wonders, soaping a foot? Did he really believe all that stuff? Last time she asked him, the reply was not illuminating. – Yes, he said shortly. He sounded almost bad-tempered, which was unusual for him. Was it because he thought the question impertinent, cynical? Or had a sliver of doubt begun to creep in, which he wanted to ignore and which she exacerbated? – But why, she persisted, why? – Read the book, he said. She did: and remained as unenlightened as before. So, *did he believe it*? Really?

The hot water lulls her to the point where, jerking awake, she realises she has been more than half asleep. Drifting, drifting. Is that how they all arrived here, at their present selves, step by inexorable tiny step? Can they hide behind inevitability? Or are they what they have chosen to become? Benny's latest action – his last – indicates that, if so, the choice was not a happy one. But Benny, of all people, always hated the notion of karma, that vacant fatalism that threatened to consume them all during the sixties and seventies. That was one of the things that drew them together, the shared violent certainty that their lives were theirs to mould. You chose one thing, and then you chose another. The possibilities were, literally, endless.

But what of all the paths untaken, the possibilities unexplored? What happened to all those myriad Bennies and Helens, Patricks and Colettes, the ones who might have been? The ones whose paths diverged? Do they exist somewhere, as Benny later proclaimed? What are their worlds like? Is there a world in which Saul of Tarsus, setting out on the road to Damascus, suddenly remembered that his grandparents were coming to visit and he'd promised to stay home? In which all that guilt, all that Pauline angst, simply never happened? All those hang-ups – kaput? All those psychoanalysts out of a job? Is there still a Benny there? Has he really gone, as he said, to investigate? To the virtual reality where we'll all end up?

She gets out of the bath and wanders into the bedroom. The bed still smells of Benny. That'll pass soon enough – at the next wash, to be precise. Perhaps she should keep these sheets as they are, unwashed – put them away so that she can have a sniff when she wants to remind herself of him. His distinctive brand of sweat starts her crying again, and this time the tears won't stop. She's going to miss him.

She lies back, alone in the big bed. Yes, this, too – this is really her. Helen Bartram. Helen Bartram Spiro. Now, once again, plain Helen Bartram.

Would she choose the same life again?

She won't get the chance, so what's the point of asking?

Helen is drifting off to sleep when the telephone goes. Damn, she thinks, I forgot to set the answering machine.

– Hello?

– A Mr Spiro is calling you from Madras, says a voice. Will you pay for the call?

Heart pounding, Helen agrees.

– Mum, is that you?

– *Tim?*

– I was in a bookshop here, he says, and I saw a copy of one of Dad's books. *Immortality*, natch, what else? Couldn't believe it! In

22

India! I looked at this damn book and I thought, A message from your family. Remember your family? You've heard from them, maybe they'd like to hear from you. So I thought I'd call and tell you I'm alive. How about you?

He sounds high. Probably is.

– Yes, I'm alive.

– You sound down, Mum. Anything happened?

– I'm alive but your father's not, says Helen. The bald words are out before she has a chance to think, to substitute something gentler. Though, in the end, what gentle way is there of transmitting this sort of news? Death is death, and the more people who know about it, the more factual, the more definite, it becomes. – He died yesterday or today, I'm not sure exactly when.

– Jesus! marvels Tim, shock, for the moment, blunted by admiration. – A synchronicity! Can you believe it? The old bastard! Maybe there's really something in it after all. But, soon enough, the words, the situation, sink in.

– What happened?

– Suicide. What else is there to say?

The fact that they are thousands of miles apart, connected only by radio waves bouncing off a satellite, seems suddenly enormous, insuperable. – Is anyone there, Mum? He sounds suddenly forlorn. – You're not all by yourself?

– Don't worry, sweetie. Colette's been here. I'm OK.

– I'll be home, Mum. I'll try and get back for the funeral.

– I've no idea when that'll be. There'll have to be an inquest. Just look after yourself, says Helen. – Colette's round the corner. She'll hold my hand.

Colette and Helen: Helen and Colette. Best friends for thirty years. More. Eighteen, they were, when they met. A fortuitous meeting. Without it, where would they be now? Somewhere else. Someone else.

Meeting

Helen Bartram stands, shivering, on the cusp of adulthood. The taxi from the station has just dropped her at Somerville College. Three thirty in the afternoon: it's almost dark, and the temperature hasn't risen above freezing all week. At the porter's lodge they give her a key, a room number, essential directions. Her first interview is in an hour.

She waits in her borrowed room, still shivering. The gas fire pops, but hardly affects the temperature. Someone – the room's regular inhabitant – has left a few books on the shelf, but they are all in Spanish. The curtains are threadbare, the carpet is worn. What has this dingy squalor to do with Oxford, golden buildings, eager youth? It feels more like boarding school (not that Helen has ever been to boarding school).

Well, this is it, she thinks. I'm grown up. For the first time, she is not part of a class, not a player in someone else's game, team, gang, not one of John and Frances's children. Now she's just Helen. Out on her own. She stretches her hands towards the fire.

Today Oxford, tomorrow Cambridge: which will she choose? Where make the friends that will shape her future life? Interviews this evening, more interviews in the morning, spend the night in college, take the train after lunch. A friend once told her she was over-motivated. What did he mean? Is it possible to be too ambitious? Is that question itself the definition? If so, it's hardly her fault. Her sister Polly went to art school, her brother James was never so bright. Helen is the repository of her parents' aspirations.

She will remember for the rest of her life the clothes she wore that day: one of those details that stand out, brightly lit, against the dim screen of memory. A cheap navy skirt and waistcoat from C&A, and a green sweater. And a duffel-coat. That was what students wore then, and no-one ever wished more ardently to become a student.

The candidates eye each other over dinner in Hall. They swop subjects, backgrounds, names. Only the first half of the alphabet is on view tonight. The second half arrives tomorrow. Helen sits opposite a girl called Anderson – Annabel Anderson. She wants to study languages (Helen's subject is English). Her outfit is impeccable: she brims with confidence. Her honey-blonde hair is done up in the neatest, the primmest of knots; her lipstick matches her pink blouse – almost. Wandering, next day, through the frosty Oxford morning (they met in the entrance hall, each with an hour to pass before the next interview), she confides her ambition: to have a boyfriend in every college; to win a first-class degree.

The degree she certainly achieved. As to the boyfriends, who knows? She probably managed them as well. Annabel had her plan, and she stuck to it. Helen disliked her at once, and went on disliking her. They met from time to time. Annabel became a publishing executive in New York. She was the only person Helen ever knew actually to wear all the component parts of one of those many-layered designer outfits you see in Gimbel's window.

Suppose Helen had liked Annabel Anderson. Suppose she had been impressed, had tried to impress in her turn. (Not that she would have succeeeded – not dressed by C&A. But suppose a different Helen, the one her mother tried to urge upon her, a Helen turned out in a good tweed suit.) Annabel was – is – a strong character: it is more likely that she would have influenced Helen, than vice versa. What would have happened to *that* Helen? Would she have met Benny Spiro – could he ever have entered her orbit? Or she his? Inconceivable. A disreputable South African quasi-terrorist? And Jewish. Excuse *me*! Later, of course, things looked a little different. Last time they met, over lunch in New York, Benny was all the rage and Annabel, angling for an invitation.

Does Helen imagine, as she attacks her brown soup and anonymous meat slices, that all around her sit not merely a number of nervous, intelligent girls of her own age (surnames ranging from A to M) but as many possible futures?

Naturally, not.

On the icy platform next day, waiting for the Cambridge train, Annabel stands, immersed in a magazine. Should Helen wave? Should she speak? Among the anonymous waiting faces Annabel is now, after all, an acquaintance. Better, surely, than nothing? Better than nervous silence as the train rattles through the frosty Midlands? On balance Helen does not think so. And maybe the feeling is mutual: Annabel's concentration upon that magazine is suspiciously total. So Helen takes herself down to the other end of the platform. Yes: that was the crucial moment. If either had found the other only slightly less unappealing, Helen's life would have been quite different. Helen and Annabel? Surely not. A polite journey, a relieved parting of ways. But Helen and Colette would not have met. And what did they have in common, at the start, but the fact of that meeting?

Standing nearby, as Helen takes up her new position, is an extremely beautiful blonde girl, with thick, bright, wavy hair cut in a bob, wide cheekbones and long, blue eyes. Like Helen, she is equipped with a small overnight case and a large shoulder-bag.

– Going to Cambridge? she inquires.

They exchange names. Helen Bartram: Colette Bosanquet. – I hate it, says Colette. What a ridiculous name. My mother was passionate about her books. Did you know that wasn't even her real name? It was her father's surname.

Helen cannot share this distaste. Everything about this girl, including her name, seems dazzling and perfect. Helen is amazed and flattered that such a gorgeous person should address her – should take the slightest interest in one so drab and ordinary as herself. But one of Colette's most endearing qualities at this stage in her life (it did not last) was that she appeared unaware of her effect on others. And *was* unaware, more or less: she had spent her schooldays at a convent and her holidays with her family. Neither nuns nor siblings expatiated upon her charms, nor were noticeably sensitive to them.

Helen sees a ravishing beauty full of wit and charm. But Colette feels herself naïve, convent-bound, provincial, devoid of all culture. The avant-garde does not thrive in Geneva, Calvin's city, where her father works for the United Nations. And precious little literature (certainly not the works of her namesake) penetrated the convent. Meanwhile Colette sees a self-possessed sophisticate from the throbbing heart of the metropolis (Helen lives in Hampstead and often goes to concerts or plays, by herself or with friends). But Helen is aware only of lumps, bumps and absence of dazzle.

The train draws in. They seat themselves facing each other, across a grimy table. What now? To converse or to retire into their shells? In order to leave the options open, Helen brings out her book. It is a proof copy of Iris Murdoch's latest novel, not yet out, acquired through a friend of her father's who works in publishing. If evidence of Helen's position at the centre of cultural life were needed it is this: *Iris Murdoch herself* is a friend of this publishing friend, and an introduction was offered when it was learned that Helen was up for interview at Oxford. But Helen, characteristically pusillanimous, declined. What would she do, what could she say, in such a situation? What interest could Iris Murdoch possibly have in Helen Bartram?

Despite this cowardice, of which of course only she is aware, Helen hopes that her possession of this proof copy will enhance her aura of culture: it's a bon-bon to be produced when they ask her (as they all do) what she's reading at the moment. Colette, seeing it, gives a little snort of laughter and produces, from her bag, the self-same article.
– Snap!

Helen stares unbelievingly at the twin proof copies. Didn't Colette say she lived in Geneva? What are English proof copies doing in Switzerland? Are they standard issue, this year, for all aspiring female Oxbridge entrants?

– Twin souls, says Colette. – We were destined to meet. Do you believe in signs and portents?

– Not really. Helen tries to sound less definite than she feels, while still conveying disagreement. In fact she distrusts signs and portents and all who believe in them. Superstition and religion are lumped together in her mind as enemies of clarity, tools of self-deception.

Helen is against self-deception. She doesn't, however, want to seem too cut-and-dried on this issue. She likes Colette, and wants to be liked by her. She knows, too, that the times are against her. Fuzzy thinking abounds; the most unexpected people indulge in it. – Do you?

– Absolutely. The enduring result of a Catholic education. We're twin souls. It's obvious.

Helen laughs uneasily. (She doesn't believe in the existence of the soul.) – Seriously, how did you get hold of it?

– Oh, I'm quite serious, says Colette. – It was destined, I'm sure of it. But the hand of destiny (she giggles, which is a relief) was my aunt's friend. She reviews for the Sunday papers. She thought this might give me an edge.

– Over everyone but me.

This time they both laugh. Colette confides she's going to read history, if she gets in that is, but what she really wants is to act. Given her appearance, this seems an entirely reasonable ambition. What would be the use of wasting all those advantages on history?

– Why don't you go to RADA, then?

– I wanted to, but Daddy nearly died when I suggested it. This way, he can tell himself I'm getting an education, and I can spend my time acting, and everyone'll be happy. D'you know what you're going to do?

Helen would like to write. But when someone asks you, What d'you want to do, you can't just say, Be a writer. Like when they say, What are you interested in? you don't say, People. Replies like that, though possibly true, are lame, feeble, hopeless. The prospect of the interviews they are currently undergoing led her to consider these questions in some detail. So she says, – Journalism, if I can.

– Why not, says Colette. – Look at the fools that do. Why not you? I'm sure you have a thousand times more to say than most of them.

On this happy note they immerse themselves in their books, or book.

They exchange telephone numbers and promise to check on each other's results. But when the eagerly-awaited telegram arrives, and Helen finds she has got into Cambridge (but not Oxford, which was what she really wanted), Colette's aunt's number does not answer.

(Colette did not give her the Geneva number.) And Colette does not call her, either. For a short time Helen is disappointed, then thinks no more about it.

At the start of term the following October, the Newnham first year gathers to be addressed by the principal. A hundred pairs of eyes eagerly search out familiar faces amid the crowd of strangers. Helen can see three girls from her old school, none of them particular friends of hers, and Annabel Anderson, also not a friend. Then, across the room, she espies – Colette! What luck! Somehow she had assumed that they were not, despite Colette's signs and portents, destined to meet again. They wave joyfully. When the gathering breaks up, they adjourn to Colette's room (which is slightly bigger than Helen's).

– Why didn't you call to tell me? I tried your aunt, but she was never in.

– Same here. You were always out.

Happily they pour coffee, help themselves to biscuits, compare timetables, and discuss which of the many undergraduate societies might interest them. A pattern is set. They will spend countless such afternoons together.

– It was fated, says Colette. I said so.

2

BENNY LIES IN his coffin, balanced in front of the curtains. Will there be a final *coup de théâtre*, an ultimate quantum test? Ladies and gentlemen, we present Schrödinger's Corpse: only at the instant of observation do the electrons decide whether it's to be dead or alive.

He's not there. Helen doesn't need to look. She's never felt his absence more entirely. Her life, so precariously rebalanced, has once again been overturned. You bite into the chocolate, and someone's eaten the nuts *again*. Yes, she's been here before: but no, that doesn't make it any easier. Benny leaves his own hole, different from Laura's.

For the thousandth time she asks herself: Why? She hadn't expected it of him: it wasn't in character. Especially not now. After Laura, she wouldn't have been so surprised. But he moved on, even from that. They were happy together, when they were together. He seemed to enjoy his new life. Being a guru was more fun than being a prof, he said. He was fêted, he was rich. He liked that: fun was important to him. And there was less responsibility. He presented himself: people took him or left him, as they pleased. And now he's left them. Death: the ultimate irresponsibility.

Benny extinguished is hard to imagine. If he was right, of course, the extinction is not total. There's another world – many such – where all this is not happening. Where he lives on, where Laura is now a young woman. Where he never went to Synchrony, where the

30

four of them simply continued as before. That's what he thought. But for Helen there is only here. This is the only scenario that counts.

Tim's sitting beside her, looking dazed. She touches his hand, and he puts his arm around her. Last time, Benny sat on his other side. Tim clutched their hands throughout the dreadful, unbelievable ceremony. Does he remember that now? It was a long time ago.

Poor Tim. The phonecall, and the flight home, and now this. She told him he didn't have to come, but he insisted. She knows it's for her, not Benny, and he knows she knows. He looks thin and defenceless. His blond ponytail straggles incongruously over the collar of his only suit, which since he's been away has become too short at the wrists and ankles. Still growing. He towers over her these days. – I don't know where he gets it from, Helen's mother said. – None of us are very tall, and Benny certainly isn't.

– Must be a throwback, said Helen.

Other worlds. Why fantasise them? They exist, here, now. She has hers, Benny had his. One address, two universes.

Benny's sits behind her now, packed into the rows at the back. They look quite normal, though Helen knows they're mad. How did they know where to come? Perhaps they have a newsletter. Or, more probably, Miss Parrinder told them. All that's her department: the SF freaks, UFO kidnappees, mystics, New Agers, desperate seekers after eternity, that constituency of Benny's followers from which Helen has always averted her consciousness. He gave them hope. What we all want to hear: Death is not really death. The irrational in search of a rational explanation, a proof that they are not irrational after all. What Benny provided: what he, like all of them, sought. Helen could understand why he went the way he did. One must survive, *ergo* one must devise strategies. Nevertheless, she disapproved.

But funerals, like weddings, are all-embracing. All one's lives promiscuously mingled. There, just in front of the other-worlders, sits the man who most detests everything they represent: Frank Gallagher, the head of Benny's old lab. How long is it since they met? When *Immortality* was published, relations ceased definitively. By then, of course, they'd been cooling for some time. A book doesn't spring into existence fully-formed, like Venus from her shell. It's preceded by months, years, of thought and (in this case) violent and acrimonious disagreement. And more: that other thing, that hung between them but was never mentioned. That mountain of silence.

Not that Benny's and Frank's had been the calmest of collaborations, even before they fell out. Frank never felt quite happy around Benny, even though of course he employed him in the first place. Benny was brilliant, all right, full of new ideas, a magnet for research money, but even so . . . Frank felt threatened. Naturally. How could he not, with Benny snapping at his heels, threatening to outstrip him? What had been Frank's lab was rapidly becoming Benny's. And then – bingo! – the danger lifted, the rival disappeared. Benny left for the opposite camp. (And perhaps that was it. Perhaps Frank always had his suspicions, always knew Benny was fundamentally unsound.)

Presumably Frank has decided it's safe, now, to let bygones be bygones. After all, when you're dead, you are by definition a bygone. But he's not risking contamination. His gaze is directed rigidly ahead. Not that he's in much danger of catching anything from his neighbours. There's only one other person in his row. Casually Helen's glance moves along. And is fixed, caught, as a rabbit by a snake. Surely it can't be – ?

But, unmistakably, it is. Over Benny's dead body the stand-off continues. The nut-brown pate, the fringe of white fuzz. Last seen two weeks ago in California.

What's Kertes doing here? He didn't say he was coming to Europe.

She doesn't even ask herself how he knew. He has his ways. Kertes knows everything.

Helen shivers.

*

Benny, trying to plumb the mysteries of a chicken's brain-cell with the aid of the electron microscope, senses someone standing behind him. Carefully, unhurriedly, he completes the operation upon which he is engaged and then, not before, turns round.

The intruder is Frank Gallagher. Frank's the head of the lab, perhaps ten years older than Benny. They get on well, although Frank thinks Benny covets his position. Benny would never put things so crudely, but he's right. Almost: for Benny's real feelings, should he divine them (but how could he? Benny doesn't even admit them to himself) would make Frank even more nervous than he actually is. For Benny, Frank's job is by no means an end in itself, but merely a stepping-stone en route to the power and acclaim he is sure he will, one day, achieve. How, is not yet clear. Perhaps he will make some shattering discovery which will change the course of biology; perhaps the route will be more circuitous. Meanwhile he hopes, in an as yet unfocused way, that Frank will soon move on – get bored, get promoted. Die, maybe. No, that would be too extreme. But disappear.

Benny, however, is a complex fellow, and this is only one side of him. Another, the side that revels in Frank's friendship, enjoys his company, respects his work, hopes this will never happen. For Benny is, for the first time in his life, completely happy. He is happy at home (though slightly disturbed by Helen's recent obsessive desire to get pregnant). And happy, O happy, at work. Benny's life these days, his real life, is the life of the mind: the life he shares with Frank Gallagher, the life of analysis, discussion and discovery that occupies almost all their waking thoughts. Even politics, which used to obsess him, are receding into the background.

Some people are serial monogamists: Benny is a serial monomaniac. Life, for him, is a string of passions. Each, while it lasts, occupies him to the exclusion of all else. Love has had its place in the succession, and politics, but zoology is turning out more durable.

So far, these preoccupations have succeeded each other smoothly. Each has led naturally to the one that followed, blended in, become part of it: love, politics, science, love, science. But now love, which slid into marriage, is threatening to burst its bounds.

Why does Helen suddenly want children? For a moment this thought insinuates itself between Benny and his chicken-brain cells, and in doing so reinforces his determination to dissuade her, for the moment at least. Children will distract him – even the prospect of them distracts him – and he can't bear distraction. He had thought Helen was with him in this. She, too, has an absorbing professional life, with which children would only interfere.

But what's the point of being married, Helen asks, if you don't have children?

Lots of points, thinks Benny. Their pretty house, their social life, each other's company. Sex. They are still passionately addicted to sex. And here it is, and there they are, and that's another distraction disposed of. Yes, Benny likes being married. He will be faithful, he will even, sometimes, help with the housework. He is the product of generations of good family men. All he asks is to be spared the upheaval of an actual family.

Frank is holding a piece of paper. He offers it to Benny. – Were you thinking of going to this?

The paper is a flier advertising a public lecture to be given in the college this lunchtime by Stefan Kertes. Kertes has recently been in the news with his theories regarding the beginning of the universe. He's a Big Bang man. The subject of today's lecture is: In the Beginning. Frank says: – He's supposed to be a terrific speaker. Have you heard him?

Benny shakes his head. – Helen's met him, though. He was on one of her shows once. She was impressed. But I can't come. I'm just in the middle of something.

– Go on, it'll all still be there.

Benny lets himself be persuaded.

Stefan Kertes' subject is unimaginable. Frank and Benny deal in the solid, the actual – in *stuff*, however small and elusive. Biology is the science of life. But physics, these days, is another country. Solidity, actuality, are meaningless there. Time is no longer inexorable: simply another dimension, in which one may travel both forwards and back. A particle, which may at the same time be a wave, is also a cloud: it occupies all possible positions before observation pins it down and determines whether it is to have mass or velocity (for it can't have both). The only certainty is Sherlock Holmes's: that when all other possibilities have been eliminated, then what remains, however improbable, must be the truth.

He stands at the podium in a pool of light, a small, rotund figure, bald, his pate thickly fringed by iron-grey fuzz, and holds the audience in the palm of his hand. He could speak for ever, and they would never tire of listening. With most lecturers, an hour is more than enough. You get restive: the pile of pages on the lectern seems inexhaustible. But Kertes uses no notes, and very few slides. As he

34

speaks, the universe focuses into beautiful comprehensibility, tempered by sublime imaginings. His frame of reference takes in literature, music, psychology, religion: a world-picture of beguiling completeness. Equations are juggled, diagrams come and go on the dusty blackboard. Physics, as Kertes expounds it, encompasses the world – and not just this world: all worlds, all time, all universes, all life.

It transpires that the lecture's title, with its biblical overtones, is not merely a convenient phrase with which to begin. Kertes startles his audience by announcing that he intends to discuss the argument from design.

Why didn't Frank and Benny leave at once? That was their inclination, certainly. They glance knowingly at each other, eyebrows raised. The argument from design, forsooth. Back to the last century, back to Darwin and Bishop Wilberforce, old Slippery Sam – a man long since disposed of. They push back their chairs, they're on the point of going. But Kertes disarms them. – I understand, he says, that this college is particularly rich in molecular biologists, and I hope that what I have to say will be of particular interest to them.

How can they leave? They subside, and listen.

Kertes informs them that his subject is mind: control by mind. Subjectivity. This is what is implied by design. – Mind, he says, – enters into our awareness of nature at two separate levels. At the highest level, the level of consciousness, we are somehow aware of the chemical and electrical activity going on in our brains. Some molecular biologists insist that this is the *only* area of subjectivity. For this is the most complex attribute of life, and their tremendous success has been to explain life by reducing it to its simplest components. Cats are more complex than bacteria, bacteria are more complex than DNA molecules. And the lower down the chain of life you go, the more fundamental the component, the more completely mechanistically it behaves.

– But, he continues, – there is a level even lower than this: the sub-atomic level, the quantum level. And here subjectivity re-asserts itself. Sub-atomic events cannot even be formulated without reference to the observer. An electron may have mass *or* velocity; it may be a wave *or* a particle. Which, depends upon the observer. The notion of an electron existing in an objective state independent of the observer is untenable. This is Heisenberg's Uncertainty Principle. Mind is inherent in every electron. Molecular complexes must *choose* between one quantum state and another. There is a beautiful fit between the very highest and very lowest manifestations of mind.

He leans forward: – How, then, can we dismiss mind at the largest level of all? I think we cannot. We may have arrived here by chance, but the idea of chance is only a cover for our ignorance. If the average distance between stars had been two million miles instead of twenty, we could not have survived. That would have been enough to disrupt the orbit of the earth around the sun, and to destroy life on earth, that would have been sufficient. And this is just one of the ways in which the slightest changes would have been enough to make life impossible. Instead, what we have is the universe that actually exists.

– Why should all this be so? I am a scientist of the twentieth century, not the eighteenth. So I do not conclude that we are dealing here with the existence of God. But the architecture of the universe is consistent with the hypothesis that mind plays a part in its functioning.

He stops. The lights are switched on.

– Well, says Frank. – A virtuoso performance.

– You're not convinced, then.

– Hardly! Since we live in the universe, is it surprising that this is a universe it's possible for us to live in?

– Isn't the latest thinking that there may be others? Any number?

– The latest thinking in physics, says Frank, – is precisely what you choose to make it. That's how it always seems to me. Fairy stories. Philosophers' stones. Give me something more tangible. Science isn't about poetic syntheses and creation myths and hearts and minds. That's literature. It's about observation and analysis and taking pains. I feel he's trying to hypnotise me, and I don't like it.

– He's got panache, laughs Benny. – The British don't like it. Tell me something new.

– I'm a Scottish Catholic, says Frank. – I had my bellyful of God when I was at school, thank you very much.

Kertes returns to wherever it was he came from. Frank and Benny return to their lab. Life and work continue as before. But things are not quite the same. There's something about Stefan Kertes that won't let itself be forgotten – the something that fills Frank with distrust; the something that Benny, despite himself, despite his rigour, finds so seductive. It comes between them – a seed of suspicion. Benny begins to think that maybe Frank is a little narrow, a little lacking in the broad imagination from which true innovation springs. While for Frank, Benny no longer entirely inspires confidence. There's something about him that's slightly unsound, that's prone to dazzlement; that would like, in fact, to dazzle in its turn. Frank is no dazzler, and (as Benny pointed out) distrusts those who are.

From time to time, Frank finds himself watching Benny. What for? He couldn't quite say. But, in the end, what you seek, you find.

In extremis, Benny preferred Kertes' world. He found Frank's too unforgiving. And, indeed, it did not forgive him.

*

There's Lesley Collinge sitting in front of Frank. All dressed up in her little Jean Muir number, dark and discreet and very, very expensive. She's looking depressed, and no wonder. Benny was her golden goose. Where would Collinge and Pearson be now without *Immortality and the New Physics*? It's made millions – translated into every language you could imagine, and quite a lot more besides. Stayed on the non-fiction best-seller list *in hardback* for three solid years. She must have been hoping for one or two more from the same stable. One or two? Why should he ever stop? From sheer boredom, in Helen's view. Not that he showed any sign of that. Nor, seemingly, did most of the world. No doubt which Benny *they* preferred.

And Helen?

No doubts there, either. This world's the only world for her. As once it was for him. The man she married, the man she loved. It filled him with excitement. She can remember him explaining about the Evolution program he'd just written, calling it up for her on his computer. Breeding his biomorphs: the successive generations, the side-branches, the huge, extraordinary effects of a cumulation of tiny steps. He was planning to include them in a new book. Another blow for Darwinism, another arrow in the heart of the Grand Designer. That was just before he left for Synchrony, the first time. Then Laura died, and took that Benny with her.

After that, it was never the same. He came back, it's true. But who was he then? She recognised the body, but who was the man inside?

*

Tim's at school. The house is silent. Yesterday was better, yesterday was Mrs Martins' day. Not that they converse, to speak of, but it's someone around the house, a human presence. Today, there's nobody.

She looks at the telephone. It sits on the corner of her desk and sends forth siren whispers. Come on, Helen. Company. Just press a few buttons, and there you are. But she makes the effort and resists. People in offices are busy, they don't welcome phone calls about nothing much. She doesn't want to use up her credit. Oh, God! Not Helen *again*!

What happened to all those friends they used to see five, ten years ago? The people she knew from television? His university colleagues, who were so close? Of course, Benny in his new incarnation is an embarrassment. But it's not just that. Grief frightens people. They can't cope. They cross to the other side of the road. They don't want to intrude. They're afraid it's catching.

Of course, quarantine is not a permanent condition. And it's nearly four years now since Laura died, since Benny left. But social occasions tend to be arranged round couples. And what's she? No longer half a couple, nor yet definitively single. Before, she had any number of presentable selves, but most of them seem to have got mislaid. The playwright. The professor's wife. Tim and Laura's mother. The hostess, the friend. Of that Helen, what now remains? She is Tim's mother. She is still, legally, Benny's wife. They never quarrelled, and she has no other plans. Perhaps she should resolve the uncertainty and get a divorce? Start afresh? But the thought depresses her even more. And anyhow, divorce would require more energy than she's got. She writes, but to order: she rarely entertains. They keep going, she and Tim. That's about it. Friends recommend

Valium, they know a good therapist, but Helen resists. Naturally she's depressed: should she not be depressed? People got through, before therapists, before Valium. She will get through.

In an emergency there's usually Colette, but she's away just now filming some terrible series about rival families of showjumpers. She grumbles that no-one takes her seriously any more. It's a vicious circle. She accepts tacky parts and gets offered – more tacky parts. She didn't get that American soap last year. – Such a relief, she said. – I only went over because Maurice insisted. Maurice is her agent. Actually, she was disappointed. She'd have loved it. But Helen is only too happy to go along with the pretence. It would have meant Colette moving to Los Angeles for six months at least, and what would Helen have done then? – You could come too, Colette said. - Make up the four. Because of course Patrick's there as well. No money for films in Britain any more – he's gone to try his luck among the megabucks while people can still remember the title of his last production.

But she couldn't, as Colette perfectly well knew. Because Benny's there, somewhere in LA, and Helen's what he's there to get away from. If not Helen herself, then the memories she brings with her. She would not wish to give chase.

Fortunately, the circumstances did not arise.

Back to the word-processor. Helen stares glumly at the screen.

The phone rings.

Who can it be? Almost certainly, someone who is either selling or begging. When the caller begins by intoning *Mrs Spiro?* on a rising note, Helen knows the call is to be instantly rejected. Only Helen or Miss Bartram receive interesting communications.

Unless it's Tim's school. Her life is pervaded by terror that something might happen to Tim. She fights it down, forces herself to give him as much freedom as she would have done had Laura – had Laura not –

She lifts the receiver. A voice says – Helen?

– Benny? Is that you?

– Yup.

How long is it since Helen heard from Benny? What's it now – March? It must be six, seven months. More. They spent two weeks together in Baja California last summer – he rented a holiday house. Afterwards, Helen and Tim flew back east to visit old friends on Cape Cod. He looked well, relaxed: the whole thing was as casual as if they'd met yesterday, as if they were still a family. There was a card at Christmas with a cryptic message. *Getting nearer*, it read. What on earth did he mean by that? Anything or nothing.

– I'm at Heathrow.

– Are you on a visit?

– Nope. I'm coming back. If that's all right with you?

– *Coming back*? Why didn't you let me know? You might have given me a bit of warning!

– Sorry. I couldn't face it, long explanations over the phone and all that. I just suddenly felt it was the right time.

That crisp, cut-off South African twang. She listens for a note of uncertainty, of anxiety, underneath it. None is apparent.

Felt it was the right time! California has left its mark, no doubt about that. – For all you know, I might have another man installed here!

– Have you?

– No, actually. But you know what I mean.

– Don't you want me there? I'd understand that. I can go somewhere else.

– No, no. Come. I was teasing.

Sort of.

– Right, I'll be there.

Helen is panic-stricken: paralysed. He'll take – what, an hour? A little more, a little less, depending on the traffic. What should she do in the meantime? *If I'd known you were coming* – Bake a cake? Probably not. Make a bed, more like. But where? Where's he going to sleep? Back with her, as though nothing had happened, as though he hadn't been elsewhere for three and a half years? They slept together in Baja. It was at once odd and entirely familiar. Is that what he wants? Is that what *she* wants? Perhaps she'd better make up the spare bed. On the other hand, mightn't he take that as a statement, a gesture?

Better sit tight and do nothing.

She stares at the screen. Might as well turn it off. If she wasn't doing any good before, she certainly won't now.

She hears the taxi pull up outside, sees Benny get out. He cuts an almost glamorous figure in the grey March street, with his suntan, his California gear, his matched luggage. She runs downstairs and opens the door. The taxi driver helps with the cases. Benny tips him, shuts the door and turns towards her.

Should she kiss him, should she throw her arms around him? That's not what she feels like doing. Her feelings are not so simple. She's pleased – that, certainly – but at the same time awkward. And resentful. Yes, above all resentful. She resents his assumption that, having left, he can blow in again when he feels like it, that after all this time family life will still be waiting for him where he left it. She resents the fact that this assumption seems to be more or less correct. She resents the way he is both a stranger and at the same time part of herself, the way she feels more complete with him around, the way she is pleased to see him. – Well, she says lightly, or as lightly as she can manage, trying to keep the edge out of her voice but not really succeeding. – Welcome home! You must be dead. What would you like, a bath? Something to eat?

He laughs, throws down his coat. – God, Helen, you don't know how wonderful it is to see you. Wonderful to be back.

There's a break in his voice. He can't be crying, surely? What *is* this? She almost says: Then why didn't you come? You could have. Any time. It was up to you. But she doesn't. What does she want, a quarrel? So soon? Mum's the word.

– Where's Tim?

– At school, of course.

– Yeah, of course. Well, that's nice. Just you and me. He puts his arm around her shoulder, looks around the hallway, and kisses her. The kiss feels awkward. Benny seems unfazed, however. – Not much changed around here.

– Why would it change?

They go down to the kitchen, as if he were just back from some conference. Helen makes coffee. Benny seems less tired than she would have imagined. – Travelled first class, he explains. – It takes the pain away.

41

– First class! Who was paying?

– I was. You're talking to a rich man. I've just been offered three quarters of a million for a book. My agent thinks she can get more.

– Pounds?

– Dollars, but it's still not bad, you've got to admit.

– What's it about, this book?

– Physics. It's called *Immortality and the New Physics*. I don't expect you'll like it.

– God's there after all, that kind of thing? Do you really believe all that?

She's never quite managed to ask, until now. Somehow it always sounded too bald, out there in California where it's compulsory to believe everything, where nothing is dismissed out of hand. Scepticism is easier in Kentish Town, in March.

He shrugs. – I wrote it, didn't I? I'm not in the habit of writing stuff I don't believe.

He's back. The same old Benny: at once evasive and reassuring. If she didn't know him, she would have declared such a combination impossible.

Benny reoccupies his study, his half of the bed. He writes his book. It will be translated into twenty languages. As far as straight science is concerned, it will mark his irredeemable descent into untouchability.

He comes and goes. Where? Helen doesn't enquire. They never believed in keeping tabs, and if the last three years have established anything, it is the freedom to come and go. At any rate, go; and, it seems, come back. Perhaps he's away lecturing. Perhaps he spends a week or two at Synchrony. Mostly he's at home.

Tim is pleased to have him back: another piece falls into place in his laborious jigsaw of reconstructed normality. Benny even seems quite pleased to see Tim.

Helen starts a new play. It's about two children who suddenly lose their parents, and the worlds they weave for themselves in order to survive. It's an idea she's had for some time. Now she knows what happens next. She's going to bring their father back. How will they cope then? Will they want him? What is he anyway – a man? A ghost? Why has he suddenly returned? How do they know he's not going to disappear again one day, as suddenly as he materialised?

*

Colette slips into the seat beside Tim. She's wearing a black trouser-suit: no jeans for Benny. Not that he would have cared. – I spoke to Patrick, she says. He couldn't make it. He's terribly sorry, but he's got to be there. There's the pre-release preview of *Gurdjy* tomorrow.

– Yes, of course. Of course he couldn't. I'm sure they're going to love it.

Gurdjy. Sex and death – the unbeatable combination. Liberties have been taken with the truth (whatever that might be) but this is art, and hopefully commerce, too. Four years to set it up, six months to shoot and edit, and here it is at last. The rushes look good, everyone's excited, and on to the next while they still remember his name. What he and Helen were talking about two weeks ago.

Is that possible? Only two weeks?

Gemma is just behind Colette. She looks ill, a Duccio Madonna, bags under her eyes, cheeks a chlorotic green. She and Benny were very close. Colette was hardly ever around, and Patrick, never. A girl needs a father, just as a father needs a daughter. Now she feels abandoned, betrayed. Colette was talking about it yesterday. – She takes it all so personally, Colette said. – You know Gemma.

Yes, he might have thought of Gemma. He thought of everything else, made all his arrangements so meticulously. Why couldn't he leave her a note, at least? He always seemed so attached to her – much more than to Tim. Blood is not necessarily thicker.

Gemma and Tim exchange wan smiles.

Presumably Declan won't appear. The outside world does not penetrate his fastness.

Miss Parrinder's wearing a blue felt hat. Helen suddenly feels panic-stricken. Shouldn't she, too, be wearing a hat? Funerals are a form of theatre. They have their conventions. Miss Parrinder is infallible when it comes to conventions. Helen catches her eye. Miss Parrinder smiles uncertainly: is there a hint of disapproval, or is that merely Helen's projection of guilt? Tomorrow, they're going to go through Benny's papers together. Make a start, anyway. The papers are Miss Parrinder's territory. She'll show Helen around it. She'll be polite, helpful, discreet, as always. She'll hate it. Miss Parrinder loved Benny. With every assertion of widow's rights, her claim upon him is diminished.

A hush falls. Time to begin.

Unreality descends like a blanket. People rise, speak, regain their seats. There is music, there is more music. Helen watches as if from a great distance. It was the same last time, with Laura. She is not present. All this is happening to someone else.

The curtain parts, the coffin begins to move. Down into the pit. The final exit, from this world at least. Though for half the assembled company Benny lives on, via a medium, a wormhole, a rights deal.

Helen regains her body. She stands up, turns round, surveys the congregation. Miss Parrinder said, – We'd better book the larger one, don't you think? – Why? said Helen. Will there be many people? Miss Parrinder stared. She said, – Oh, I think there will. And she was right.

Colette says, – D'you think they're all coming back?

If so, they have undercatered. There are drinks and snacks for about thirty at the house. Helen says, – Let's hope not. Otherwise we'll have to rush round to Sainsbury's.

Friends and acquaintances shake her hand and condole. Polly and James, who couldn't stand Benny, are solidly present, though Helen's mother couldn't face it – she's getting things ready at the house – and Benny's parents, thank God, are dead – had they not been, this would probably have finished them off. Frank Gallagher mutters a few words about 'irreplaceable loss' – as if they didn't both know the loss in question happened at least nine years ago. Lesley Collinge says, – I'll ring you.

Tim and Gemma observe the busy toing and froing. Gemma's crying. Tim has his arm around her shoulder. Gemma says, – Does anyone know why he did it?

– Does anyone know why he ever did anything! He thought he'd throw a spanner into the works and watch what happened from some other universe, says Tim savagely.

– You hated him.

– I tried not to.

– What did he do?

– Do? To me, you mean? Nothing. He was never interested enough. For the first time since Benny's death, Tim feels near to tears. Not for his father, but for a father he never had.

– I loved him, says Gemma. – I'm going to miss him dreadfully.

Tim says nothing. What is there to say? Benny loved Gemma. And Declan, and Laura. Everyone, in fact, except Tim. But that isn't going to come between Tim and Gemma. It never has, and it won't now. Gemma is one of the fixed points in Tim's life. He has always known her. He has always been in love with her. He is in love with her still. He has never said so, but of course she knows. Everyone knows. It's a joke. Little Tim. He'll grow out of it. She's got a boyfriend. He didn't come today, though, thank God.

– What are you thinking? she says now.

– About Laura. That's the last time I was here.

– Can you remember?

– Not really. Everything seemed to stop. That's really what I remember. Like a panto. The curtain came down, and when it went up again it was a different scene. I don't really remember Laura any more. Just her not being there.

– That's a bit what it was like for us, too. Dad went then, definitively.

Tim says: – I always felt guilty after that, after Laura died, as though it was somehow my fault.

– That's not how you feel now, though?

– No, why should I?

Gemma looks uncomfortable. – Well, you know. You're not sorry . . . She can't, somehow, bring herself to say it. *You wanted him dead.*

– Absolutely not. Just the opposite. D'you know how I feel? I suddenly feel, at last, it's OK to be me. He says fiercely: – When I have kids, *if* I do, it won't be like that.

Gemma nods in silent agreement. She says, – Who's that talking to your mum?

45

– That's Stefan Kertes, says Tim. – He runs that place in California Dad used to go to. He's mad.

– Stefan! says Helen, surprised, as always, to find herself addressing a mere human being. – I thought you were in California!

– I was. But now I am here. Stefan Kertes presses her hand tenderly, as always, kisses her carnally, as always. There is, as Helen knows, nothing personal in this. Stefan always behaves this way. Not with Colette, though, not any more. He eyes her nervously, holds out a ceremonious hand: she extends a finger. Colette and Kertes have not been on speaking terms since he tried to rape her after a dinner party. Or so Colette said. Helen believed her, but Benny thought she must be exaggerating. He assured her that this was simply a culture-clash, that Central Europeans of Kertes' vintage always behaved that way. All that was required was a vigorous and unambiguous rebuff.

– I did, said Colette. – I kicked him in the balls.

– Actually, you didn't need to, Benny said. – He's impotent. I have it on the best authority.

– I wasn't interested in finding out, Colette said. – Let him find some other way to work out his problems.

Helen wonders, now, how many people know this about Kertes. Does he know they know? Does he care? Is this his karma, does he just accept it – part of the Grand Design?

– I was in Oxford for a conference, Kertes explains. – I open the paper and there is Benny's obituary! My dear Helen! How can one believe these things? I shall come back to your house, of course.

– Of course.

Slowly, the chapel empties. People mill around in the late September sun. Helen speaks to one, then another. She smiles, she is polite, she remembers names. Once again she feels herself floating. Below her, a middle-aged woman thanks friends for coming, gives instructions about flowers, wonders whether there will be enough food.

At the edge of the crowd, a young woman stands alone. She seems lost in thought. She looks at the group surrounding Helen. She takes a step towards them. Then she turns away and walks quickly in the direction of the exit.

Helen, floating, is transfixed. She's seen this young woman before. Was it in a dream? That dream? No, it was –

The young woman's outside the gate now, walking briskly in the direction of Golders Green station. Helen wants to run after her, stop her, touch her, question her. But how can she? This is a person she has never met. And here is her brother James saying, – Will you come back with us, Helen? We've plenty of room.

Her sister Polly says, – Helen! Are you all right? You look as though you've seen a ghost! Here, you'd better sit down.

And here she is in James's car, driving towards her own house. As they pass the station, she looks for the young woman. Is that her, just disappearing inside? Was she wearing a green coat?

Helen can't really remember what she looks like. She tries in vain to reconstruct her face, her figure, as one reconstructs the features of a person loved and absent. Laura, or Benny. Is that the nose? Was that the smile? What colour, really, were the eyes? No, that's not it. The ensemble dances ahead of her, just out of reach.

Back at the house, the party feels like any party. Conversations begin with Benny – that, after all, is what this party is about – but swiftly move on. Benny is already the past.

People drift away. They must stay in touch, they'll telephone, they'll make a date. They mean it. Maybe they'll do it. If not, she won't hold it against them. She's said the same things too often herself.

James must catch his plane. Polly will drop their mother off. Miss Parrinder will be back in the morning.

In the kitchen, Tim and Gemma are loading the dishwasher. Colette is making coffee. Kertes is tucking in to what's left of the baked meats. His enthusiasm for food is just one aspect of his voracious appetite for life in general. Helen's happy enough to see the food go. She's not going to eat it. She hasn't felt like eating since Benny died. She's going to have to reacquire the habit. Tim's off to university soon, and with him will depart the last vestige of regular meals. If she's not careful she'll suddenly realise it's too late, she's starved to death.

Colette pours the coffee. Everyone sits down. – Well, says Helen. – What now?

Colette sips, looks round the table, puts down her mug. – How about, she says, in that actorish intonation with which all children are familiar from television fairy tales (didn't she once do a stint on

47

Jackanory?) – how about trying a ouija board? D'you remember, we all did it that evening Pat and I first introduced you two?

– But it was us who introduced you!

– Nonsense, I can remember it as if it was yesterday! Patrick lived at that terrible old ex-pub, and so did Benny, and the moment I saw Benny I knew. I said to Patrick, let's have a dinner-party, Benny's simply got to meet my friend Helen. Ask him, he'll tell you. Go on, phone.

Helen says, – Heavens, I'm not going to argue. What does it matter now?

But she remembers the ouija board.

*

They've finished the wine and the hash brownies. Benny offers to make coffee. Everyone is slightly drunk and more than slightly high. Patrick, leaning back in his chair, holding Colette's hand, says: – Time for games. What shall we play? Then he lapses into silence.

What does he have in mind? Bridge? Will he regain his power of speech, his train of thought, in time to tell them before the evening ends? Finally Benny says, – What were you thinking of?

– No idea, says Patrick happily. He's eaten a lot of hash, and drunk a lot of wine. – Charades? We could guess each others' fantasies. He looks at Colette. She smiles and moves slightly closer to him. Helen says, – Too much effort.

Colette says, – Let's tell fortunes. Has anyone got a ouija board?

Benny laughs his high-pitched, mocking giggle. – You don't believe in that stuff?

– Benny's a rationalist, Patrick explains to Colette. – He tries to convert me when we meet in the kitchen. It comes of too much zoology. He OD's on Darwin.

– People make up stories, says Benny, – then they start to believe them, and then they worship them and call it religion. It's the root of all evil. I won't have it in the house.

Colette refuses to rise to this bait. It's a long time since she left the convent. – Come on, she says. – It's just a game. What are you so worried about? You're afraid of being converted! Underneath all that rationalism you're nothing but a believer. She's laughing so hard at her own joke that she can barely bring it out.

– I certainly don't have a ouija board, says Benny firmly.

– We can make one. Colette is set on this new project, and not even hash will deflect her. – D'you have some paper?

Benny can hardly deny it.

She tears the paper into small squares and inscribes them with the letters of the alphabet. These she arranges in a circle on the table. Patrick is sent to the kitchen to find a glass. The candles are stood on the mantelpiece and the window-ledge. The four of them sit around the table; the glass is in the centre of the circle of letters. Each of them rests a finger on it. They wait. Benny giggles again. Nothing happens. Their fingers cast long shadows in the candlelight.

– What are we waiting for? says Helen.

– Eventually the glass ought to move, says Colette. – But nobody's to cheat. You mustn't push it. If it won't, it won't.

– Why don't we ask it some questions? Patrick drawls. – Maybe it just doesn't know what to say.

– What shall we ask?

Helen feels excited in spite of herself. She is sure nothing will happen. What could possibly happen, so long as no-one cheats? This certainty relieves but also disappoints her.

Colette calls: – Is there anybody there?

They sit, fingers on the glass. Nothing. Then, just as Helen is about to suggest they give up, the glass begins to move. Slowly at first, then faster, until it's fairly whizzing across the table, around and around. Someone must be moving it. – Who's doing it? Benny demands. But everyone denies responsibility. Helen knows it's not her. Colette is laughing, Benny looks annoyed, Patrick surprised. Colette, then? But she is too superstitious to cheat. (Not unless she had some ulterior motive. But what motive would she have, here?)

Colette calls out again: – Who are you?

The glass hesitates, slows down, then waveringly moves around the table as though it's trying to locate a particular letter. It hesitates before R, before J, before M: finally it settles on L.

– Your name begins with L, says Colette. – Is that right?

The glass tilts slightly, as if in agreement.

– OK, says Patrick. – Let's have another letter.

They sit: slowly, the glass under their fingers begins to move again. Someone's got to be be moving it. Benny says, – Let's each in turn take off our finger, then we'll see. He lifts his hand. The glass goes on moving. Colette, Patrick, Helen, each in turn lifts a finger. The glass seems unaffected. It gyrates for a while, apparently aimlessly. Then it seems to acquire a purpose. Slowly at first, it slides from one letter to another, once more gathering momentum as it goes.

First an O.

Then an R.

Another R.

An A.

An I.

Benny says: – This is ridiculous. What are we supposed to be playing at? He gets up and walks away from the table. But the others, fascinated, persist.

An N.

And an E.

– Lorraine, says Colette. – Who's Lorraine? Does anyone know a Lorraine?

Benny turns green and rushes to the bathroom.

He must have drunk too much wine, eaten too many hash brownies.

*

– But yes, says Kertes. Why not do it, Helen? It's exactly what Benny would like!

Helen reflects that this is probably true. Unlike last time.

– You surely don't believe in that sort of thing? asks Tim, echoing his late father, did he but know it. He sides with Helen in matters of this sort.

– Believe, not believe – I am interested! If nothing happens, I won't be surprised.

– And if something does happen?

– Then I begin to ask some questions. But first we need a board.

50

– Well, I haven't got one, snaps Helen. Now it's her turn to play echo.

Colette, as on that other ocasion, finds a pad and begins to print the letters of the alphabet.

Tim fetches a glass. But just as he's approaching the table, it falls from his hand and breaks. Helen jumps. – Oh, God!

– I'm terribly sorry, Mum, it was an accident, I'll sweep it up.

Gemma, ever since these preparations began, has been silent, radiating disapproval and non-participation. This is not because she is a sceptic, but because, on the contrary, she is a believer. Gemma's life is ruled by the supernatural. She feels it should be treated with respect, and that this is presently lacking. She says: – I don't think we should be doing this. Don't you see, he doesn't want us to.

Irrationally, this – superstition? sentimentality? – ignites in Helen a determination to go ahead with the superstition already planned.

Kertes bursts out laughing and says: – No, no, that wasn't Benny! It is the Kertes Effect! He waits for someone to ask: What's that? Helen won't play, but Colette can't resist a cue.

– What's that?

– It has become famous. When I am near experimental apparatus, it falls to bits, it breaks for no reason. Once, before the war, I was passing through Göttingen in a train. It happened that a friend of mine, another physicist, was at the station. Naturally we chatted a few minutes while the train stopped there. During those few minutes, a piece of apparatus at the physics lab just broke in pieces. When my friend got back, they were all standing around looking at it and cursing. So then he explained I had been in the town, and everyone knew at once this must be the reason. I have teledestructive powers, he concludes triumphantly.

Another glass is fetched. They place their fingers on it, all except Gemma who will have nothing to do with this, and who droops disapprovingly in her corner. They wait.

Nothing happens.

Benny has made his gesture.

Love

Love at first sight; the *coup de foudre*. Does it really exist?

Yes: science says so. Love is located in the nose, rooted in the rooter. The mysterious ingredient which ensures that one thing will lead rapidly to another, shortly to be followed by total obsession, is a scent-carrying particle called a pheromone. Perfumes mask armpits, pomanders overpower farts. And pheromones, Puck-like, draw masks across acne, sweeten the breath, add inches to dwarves and lop the ears off asses.

Particle power! When Henry VIII espied Mistress Ann Boleyn, the witch with six fingers and three nipples, pheromones changed the course of history. The offspring of this unlikely union was Protestant Elizabeth, Will Shakespeare's Queen. Under Catholic Mary, might we not have been Frenchified? Hispanicised? What hope then for the English Bard? Poetry, that delicate commodity, takes its flavour from the age. So one thing leads to another.

Helen's mother's family is supposed to be related to Ann Boleyn's. In every generation, there is a six-fingered daughter. In Helen's, it is her sister Polly. Other inclinations are perhaps also inherited. Helen certainly seems unusually susceptible to pheromone activity. Every day sees a different name in her diary.

Chris Clay, for example. A Trinity Hall lawyer. They met at a War on Want lunch, stuffing themselves with fresh bread and liver sausage that the hungry might be fed. He's a witty fellow. He's asked her to a smoking concert, where he's performing a sketch. What should she wear? She flicks through her trusty collection of assorted garments. In a black flapper dress, beaded and fringed, bought from a junk-shop, she applauds her beau and laughs at his jokes. But when, at the end of the evening, he puts his arms around her and slides his tongue moistly between her lips, she recoils. She can't help it. The pheromones just aren't there. Doesn't he feel it – or, rather, not feel it?

Suppose things hadn't turned out that way? Suppose the phero- mone message had been an imperative push into his more than willing arms? She's wondered about that more than once. For Chris Clay, like so many of those Cambridge lawyers, went into politics. A Tory, naturally, like all his set. Those acned idiots, running the country? Then it was just a joke: now it's no joking matter. God help us, now it's reality. He started out brightly enough with the rest of them. Doing nicely at the bar, safe seat. Then he disappeared. Caught out in some tricky dealing: all down the drain for five thousand pounds. Dishonest, and stupid with it. Others stole more, much more, and kept it quiet. But suppose she'd married him. Might she have prevented this, urged him to resist whatever temptation it was, preserved him for politics? He was spoken of as a coming man. She might have found herself married to – what? the Home Secretary? Chancellor? Prime Minister, even.

And what would she have become? Not what she did – that's for sure. Writing scurrilous plays – no, thank you. Political wives are meant to steady the keel, not rock the boat. Controversy is not required. The stifling knowledge that everything one says – let alone writes – will be minutely dissected, trawled for possible scandal and indiscretion, would be enough to block anyone. Who could pursue a creative career under such circumstances?

She found that old diary recently, in the back of a cupboard. Most of the names it records evoke no memory at all. Tom Morrison? Who was he? Andrew Burnside? Mike W? Had Mike been distin- guished by a name, a whole name in place of that mere initial, would he now bear a face?

Of the most important meeting of her life, however, there seems to be no record. She has to work it out by default. After a certain point, hardly a day goes by without mention of his name. Benny. Benny. Benny.

In fact her date that evening was with a man named David Lankester. Helen lusted after him. He was tall and fair and sinister. He wore shades and an ancient black leather jacket. (He wears them still: he is Professor of English at a fashionable university, and on his fourth wife.)

One morning, abruptly, after a lecture, he approached. – *Jules et Jim*'s on at the Arts. Like to come?

Would she not! Her favourite of all films. Transfixed, she *became* beautiful, feckless Jeanne Moreau, torn between her two swains, incapable of living in or for anything but the moment. All this – and David Lankester . . . Seven hours to wait. They pass like seven years.

At the appointed time, Helen arrives at the Arts Cinema. David hasn't yet arrived. Helen waits five minutes, ten. Is he going to stand her up?

Suddenly, there he is. Her heart leaps. But he is not alone. Another girl, a frail figure with long fair hair, clings to his black leather arm. He passes Helen without acknowledgement, without any sign of recognition.

Is her lust for David Lankester such that she hallucinated this morning's exchange? Is it pure coincidence that she finds herself here, this evening, to see the object of her dreams sweep past with someone else?

He forgot some lecture notes that afternoon. Running back to fetch them he encountered the blonde girl, who wondered if she might just check something. Pheromones did the rest. He was bewitched, oblivious. Later, they married: this was the first of his many wives.

Helen, unaware that she has perhaps been rescued from yet another unpropitious fate (Mrs Lankester no.1? She would have been willing enough), turns glumly away. What now? She has been stood up; is she to go hungry, too?

At supper she sits beside a friend who's going to the Labour Club. A Minister is booked to address it. Helen decides to tag along.

The room is packed with would-be politicians waiting to hear the Minister: hoping, perhaps, for a laying-on of hands? Helen finds a seat beside a tall, blond Chilean called Max. On Max's other side is a person she doesn't know, a stocky young man with curly black hair and a South African accent. Max introduces them. Helen Bartram. Benny Spiro.

The Minister's speech is unremarkable, a politician's speech. Benny and Max greet it with derision. They are serious about politics in an un-British way. For them it is no abstraction, no mere litany of promises made to be broken in the knowledge that everything will muddle along as usual. In Chile, in South Africa, people like Max and Benny disappear and are not seen again. As indeed will be Max's fate three years later. Benny is less foolhardy: he knows he has left South Africa for good. So what are they doing at the Labour Club, so tame, so parochial? Benny told her later that they came by mistake: they thought it was the Socialist Society, an altogether more revolutionary affair.

Max gets up to leave. Somewhat to his surprise, Benny does not accompany him. Instead, he moves into the seat beside Helen.

The meeting ends. Helen has an essay waiting. Benny suggests a drink. He has full lips, mocking brown eyes. The essay can wait a little longer. They make for a pub. The impersonal hubbub cocoons them in a curious privacy. Walled in by sound, Benny and Helen are alone. His hand, on the table, loosely cupping his glass, brushes her arm from time to time; his gaze is so intense that she can almost feel its heat. She watches his mouth, imagining its feel, its taste.

This delicious anticipation, this greedy consciousness of eyes, mouth, hands, is of course not new to her. She has been here before (though never to such a refined, hypercharged degree). She knows where it will end. The only questions are how and when.

Benny says: – I'm starving, haven't had anything to eat this evening. Come back to my place and help me open a can of beans?

– D'you live in college?

He hoots. – College! No, I got out after the first year. I found a better place. Come and see. His South African accent is clipped, the vowels oddly truncated.

They cycle together through back streets. Street after street of grimy terraced cottages, two up, two down, interspersed with terrible little shops selling dried-out bacon rashers and ancient tins of rice

55

pudding. Benny stops in front of a building rather larger than its neighbours, standing on a corner. Once it was a pub; now it's owned by an enterprising psychologist who lets out rooms and asks no questions. It's called Liberty Hall: a sign, swinging on the old pub bracket, announces its new incarnation. – Home sweet home, says Benny.

His room is not large. There is a chair, a table strewn with papers, a double bed. The whitewashed walls are covered with shelves, loaded with books and records. Despite this sparseness, it is the most intensely inhabited room Helen has ever encountered. Unlike Helen, unlike most of his fellow-undergraduates, whose lives are still partially located under the parental roof, Benny has wholly transferred himself to this room.

He turns to her. – Want some beans?

– Not really.

– Nor do I.

For a moment they stare at each other. Then he puts out his hand and touches her face. The magic touch: at last they are free. While the Minister spoke, while they sat in the pub, as they cycled through the dark streets, their minds were wholly occupied by the possibility of this touch and what would follow it.

The embrace continues, with brief interruptions, for some months. Benny's bed – his double bed, essence of sensuality and sin: who, among her undergraduate friends, has access to a *double bed*? – becomes the focus of their lives.

Helen has never met anyone in whom life is as concentrated as it is in Benny. Everything he does – working, politicking, loving – he does with total application. She feels like some hitherto cold planet which has been drawn into the ambit of a radiant sun. And he is fascinated by her Englishness, her appearance of detachment (so deceptive, so laboriously cultivated). Or so they tell themselves and each other. But this is mere window-dressing. Such details are not what brought them together, not what felled them like sawn trees: instantly horizontal. That's all down to pheromones. Each other's smell, that's what they can't resist. They snuff it up, lick it off each other, sniff their fingers surreptitiously during lectures. Yes – *there it is*! And wait only until they can fall once more into each other's arms.

3

HELEN SITS IN the sky. Back and forth, back and forth, London to Los Angeles, Los Angeles to London. It's getting to be almost a regular commute. Just like Benny. She used to tease him about it. – What a way to spend your life, she'd say, as he left yet again for Heathrow. – Twelve hours in a flying slum in the sky! But she seems to have picked up the baton. And she was right. As commutes go, London – LA is unwieldy to the point of unreality. It therefore blends perfectly with the rest of her life these unreal days.

Patrick's call came just after the funeral.

– Helen? Patrick here. How did it go, darling? How are you feeling?

How is she feeling? It seems to Helen these days that all feeling has left her. Numbly, she goes about the daily round. Eats, washes, sleeps her drugged sleep. She isn't used to sleeping pills: their effect is such that she is never properly awake. Time passes. It seems probable that, soon, she will simply stop. Stop washing, stop eating. She's already stopped writing.

What's done this to her? Benny's absence? What's new in that?

The definitiveness. Before, he was simply away: in extremis, available. Now (though his followers would presumably disagree) she knows this is not true. For Helen, at least, Benny has ceased. He's left – whoever 'he' was. After all this time she thought she knew *that*. But it seems she did not. Truths so hard, pain so great, that they drove him to kill himself? What were they? She knew nothing of them. She's hurt, bewildered – disoriented.

Perhaps, though, she shouldn't be surprised. You live with someone ten, twenty years – a lifetime. You raise children together. And then, discussing some fundamental issue, you realise that this person has no idea what you're talking about. Your words, your emotions, are incomprehensible: at the deepest level, you remain separate. During the years with Benny, there were several such moments. She'd be tearful or angry, for reasons she thought so obvious as not to need explaining. He'd stare, turn away, get on with whatever it was he'd been doing. Why didn't Helen get the message? She assumed they knew each other. But she was wrong.

Patrick is talking about *Gurdjy*. Abstractedly, Helen tunes in: – . . . the most tremendous success. It was amazing. They all stood up and cheered afterwards.

– Oh. Good.

– Helen, darling, I'm so sorry. Here I am running on. *That's* not what I called to tell you. Or not only. Listen, what it means for us is that yours truly is suddenly in *unbelievable* demand. And *that* means that our little story's all set to take off.

– Wonderful! says Helen politely. She tries to project herself back to the extraordinarily distant place and time where Patrick still lives. Can it be true that she, too, inhabited that land only three weeks ago?

– Yes. So you'd better get back here by the next plane. Seriously, can you come tomorrow? The point about this sort of thing is that it's imperative to strike while the iron's sizzling. In another microsecond they'll all be chasing another flavour.

– Tomorrow?

– Today would be even better, but I suppose that might be a bit difficult. We could do it by fax, of course, but it's so much easier and nicer face to face. I don't suppose you're doing much else just now. Think of this as occupational therapy. A nice trip to never-never land. You've got to admit, the timing's perfect.

What a darling he is, after all. She knows he doesn't really need her. On the contrary – he'd almost certainly do much better on his own. She ought at least to let him see she realises this. – D'you really need me? I thought we'd finished the script.

– Not any more. I'll explain when you get here. Let me know when you're arriving.

– So you see, Miss Parrinder, says Helen, – I'm afraid I'm going to have to be away for a bit. I don't expect it will be very long. What d'you think we'd better do? Shall we leave the papers till I get back? You've got your work cut out anyhow, dealing with all that correspondence.

– I could go on sorting through –

– There's not much point, though, if I'm not here, is there?

Miss Parrinder looks mutinous, but what can she say? She obviously regards this as some sort of defection, an act of disrespect to the dead. Helen isn't acting as a widow should – as Miss Parrinder would in her place. Being the relict of a man like Benny ought, she thinks, to be a full-time affair – at least in the immediate aftermath of the decease. Whereas Patrick's call has restored Helen, however momentarily, to something quite like her former self. Amid the wreckage, life goes on. This is what Miss Parrinder senses and resents.

Helen knows nothing about Benny's papers, has never taken any interest in them; Miss Parrinder is intimately acquainted with them, has devoted her life to them for the past seven years. But there it is. Unjust and unsuitable though it may be, the papers belong to Helen now. Miss P. wants to wail, as Tim and Laura so often wailed: It's not *fair*. But, as Helen so often told them, life is unfair. The truth, but no less unsatisfactory for that.

Miss P. could leave, of course, flounce out in a huff. But what would be the point of that? Benny's interests need protecting, now more than ever. Miss Parrinder owes him that.

They are standing in Benny's office, beside his empty desk. Files and boxes fill the room from floor to ceiling. Papers lour over them. Published and unpublished, past, present and pending; the higher up, the less current. From the topmost shelves, dust cascades. And no doubt this is only part of it, thinks Helen. There must be more at Synchrony. A life in paper. Too many words. Why add even more to the existing stock? The question that poses itself every time she enters a library. The question that, since it can never be answered, must never be asked.

With an effort she forces herself into the here and now. Benny's work, his legacy. Of which she latterly disapproved. But she can hardly drop it into a well, can she?

– . . . won't do it, Miss Parrinder is saying.

– Sorry. I was miles away. What were you saying?

– Have you seen the letter from Professor Gallagher? Miss Parrinder enquires sternly.

– From Frank? No, I don't think so. What does he say?

Miss Parrinder hands her the letter. It's typed, formal, on college notepaper. This is the professor speaking, not the friend of twenty years' standing.

My dear Helen,

I have just received a letter from your solicitor reminding me that, under the terms of Benny's will, I am his literary executor. To tell you the truth this was something I had quite forgotten. We both made our wills so long ago, at a time when all the provisions, in fact the whole idea of death, seemed entirely hypothetical. But of course it's true – he was to be my executor, and I, his.

But now it comes to the point, so much sooner than any of us had anticipated, I find myself in some difficulty. You'll guess, I expect, what I'm referring to. I could help in dealing with his earlier work – that is to say, the work he did up until the time when he left this Department. Though even so, I have to say it's a task I would rather be spared. But I find myself so wholly out of sympathy with everything he has done since then, that I feel I am quite the wrong person to deal with that.

I am only too aware that the last thing you need just now is extra worries of this sort . . .

– I must say, Miss Parrinder grumbles, – I think it's highly improper. If you agree to do something like that, then in my opinion you should do it. But I suppose one can't expect more of Professor Gallagher.

Helen says wearily: – Oh, I can see why he feels like that. They had some awful quarrels. It was an old will. Benny made it when the children were born. I don't know why he didn't change it. I suppose he just forgot. Had his mind on other things. It was very simple. All to us. He just added a few codicils.

Two thousand pounds to Miss Parrinder, for example. Added the week before he died. So he must have known, the last time she spoke to him.

Still, it's surprising he left Frank in charge of the works. After all that bitterness. Perhaps it was another of Benny's jokes. Departing as he arrived, with two fingers raised.

Mis Parrinder says: – I think the Professor was the most forgiving man I've ever known. She's referring, of course, to Professor Spiro, not Professor Gallagher.

– Really? What makes you say that?

– I never heard him utter a bad word about Frank Gallagher. When all *he's* done for years is try and destroy the Professor's reputation. He wrote that piece in *Nature*, you know.

– About burning *Immortality*? Yes, I knew that. Well, I suppose he felt betrayed. They'd been colleagues for years.

Miss Parrinder, to Helen's relief, does not pursue the rights and wrongs of Benny's later work. They're not here for a philosophical discussion, after all. The idea is to try and sort out some immediate problems. First things first, but what are the first things? Helen is relying on Miss Parrinder to tell her, and Miss P is nothing if not efficient. She's sitting at the desk now, sorting through a pile of papers she's got in a folder. She hands Helen another letter.

Dear Helen,
I do hope you're feeling a bit better, though I expect that'll take a bit of time. Anyway, if it's any consolation, I thought you might like to know that interest in Benny's work, which of course has never really slackened, has if anything been increased by the news of his death. Quite apart from those people who claim to have been in touch with him since he died (I enclose the letters we have received so far, I'm sure you'll want to see them, even though I know this kind of thing isn't really your cup of tea), we've had translation enquiries from Taiwan, Sweden and Argentina, and I

believe the French, Russian, German and Dutch editions are reprinting.

I wondered what you might think about a new, uniform edition, together with some personal memories and experiences – including, perhaps, some of those mentioned in the enclosed letters?

Perhaps you might like to give me a ring sometime. Maybe we could have lunch and discuss all this?

With very best wishes, Lesley.

– Oh, God.
– I think it's a wonderful idea, Miss Parrinder says reproachfully.
– Oh, absolutely. I'd do it myself, but as you know I never dealt with Benny's professional affairs. I don't really know much about them.

The truth is, Frank's dropped her in it. He doesn't wish to spend his time wading through the morass of Benny's later thinking, any more than she does. Both prefer to remember an earlier Benny.

On the other hand, how can she just abandon all this stuff? Whatever her opinions, she's forced to recognise that the person Benny became spoke to a great many people. He earned more in the last seven years of his life than in all the years preceding. She's only just found out how much more – a figure that left her reeling and slightly horrified. She spent yesterday afternoon at the accountant's. If she never worked again, she wouldn't have to worry.

Miss Parrinder's eyes, fixed upon her, say: *You're happy enough to take it.*

– I'd better give Lesley a ring.
– I could do that, if you like. *And all the rest, as you perfectly well know.*

– Could you? That would be awfully kind. Tell her I'll call her from Los Angeles as soon as I know when I'll be back. We'll have to think of someone to take over. I just don't have time, and I don't expect Benny would think I was very suitable, anyhow.

Helen smiles, placatory, but Miss Parrinder won't be mollified. Helen knows what she's thinking, and Miss P. knows she knows. *Why not me? I could do it better than anyone. Haven't I typed every word of it, and dealt with all the correspondence into the bargain?*

62

– I'll try and think of some names.

– That would be awfully kind. I'll leave things in your capable hands. And if there's anything that needs a decision, you've got my phone number there. Helen looks round the room, trying to think of things she's forgotten. Oh, yes –

– Do you know where the personal files are, Miss Parrinder?

Better make sure there are no lurking time-bombs.

– I'm afraid I don't, Mrs Spiro, Miss Parrinder lies. – All I know about is what I dealt with.

The two women survey each other. It's a standoff.

And exactly what did you deal with, Miss Parrinder?

Ah, wouldn't you just like to know!

Miss Parrinder became Benny's secretary just after his return, when the publication of *Immortality and the New Physics* brought in such floods of correspondence, along with endless requests for lectures and television appearances. He'd left the university definitively by then. So there was no more secretarial back-up from there – and of course, he had to move all his stuff out of the office. How did he find her? Helen can't recall, if she ever knew. Probably through an ad. Benny couldn't believe his luck – she does remember that. Miss Parrinder was efficiency itself, and she adored him. No effort was too great. She came three days a week. She put everything in order. Only what she dealt with? She dealt with everything.

She and Helen must be about the same age, but there has always been a sense that they are of different generations, that a respectable distance must be maintained. She has remained Miss Parrinder throughout. Helen knows her first name, obviously. It's Rosalind. Ros, Rosalinda. Does anyone use it? Benny never did, any more than he was ever addressed otherwise than as Professor – at least in Helen's hearing.

Helen has a fantasy that, when they were by themselves, Benny and Miss Parrinder dropped all formalities, became Benny and Rosalind – and who knows what else? Miss P.'s figure, underneath those sensible clothes, those tailored jackets, those baggy skirts and sweaters, is remarkably good. And when she refreshes her lipstick and takes off her glasses – it's like those old ads: oh, my, suddenly, she's pretty. Why didn't she marry? Why doesn't she have a man?

(For she doesn't: she lives two streets away, with her elderly mother.) Because she prefers women? Not judging by the way she looked at Benny. Looking across at Miss Parrinder's full breasts, at the heavy hair coiled at her nape, the neat ankles demurely crossed, Helen can't imagine he resisted – or met with resistance. Miss P. is so jealous of his memory – so jealous of Helen. Her feelings transcend the secretarial.

Well, thinks Helen, let's hope they had a fling. Why not? She didn't ask, but she assumes Benny was not faithful – certainly not latterly. *Them that asks no questions, Don't get told no lies.* Nor any inconvenient truths. That was part of the deal, their deal, that deal of many parts. Helen always feels like laughing when she hears eager modernisers advocate marriage contracts – as though anything shorter than a telephone directory could possibly summarize the complexity of such an arrangement.

She is stifled by the weight of all this paper, deafened by the sound of axes grinding. Miss Parrinder wants to protect him from misrepresentation. Frank pursues their ancient feud. Helen does not doubt that, like Tim, he attended the funeral on her account, not Benny's. Quite right, too. What does Benny care? Whereas Helen, who always liked Frank, does care, and was touched. Lesley – well, that at least is straightforward. She wants to publish anything publishable. Benny was big business.

And Helen? Somewhat to her surprise, she is suddenly filled with rage. How dare he! *No reflection on you.* Thank you so much. And what's she supposed to do now? Rejoice in this absolution? Pick up the pieces and go bravely on, no questions asked? Helen has always been discreet. It suited them both. But to maintain this discretion indefinitely? That would be super-(or sub-) human. Death breaks the contract.

– Do you have some sort of index system? Where things are, what's in the boxes?

– Not written. I just know.

– So why don't you do a handlist while I'm away? What's where, and what it is. That might be awfully useful.

Miss Parrinder sighs, but she can hardly object.

After she's gone, Helen wanders back into the study and stares around. Somewhere, here, are clues to Benny's life – and therefore, maybe, to his death? She's sure of it. But where? Miss Parrinder knows. Not the details, necessarily, but their likely whereabouts. And she'll be back tomorrow, after Helen's gone – and then they won't be there any more. Helen's sure of that, too. But she can't suddenly sack Miss P. and demand the return of her keys. What could she say, what reason could she give? It would be ridiculous. Hysterical.

She remains convinced, though, that she's right. If she doesn't find the stuff tonight, whatever there may be, she'll have to accept Miss Parrinder's version: that Benny was his facade. Which she doesn't believe. Which, she now realises, she never did believe. She accepted it because, towards the end, that was how their life worked.

Helen sits at Benny's desk and tries to insinuate herself into his head. What's she looking for? All she knows is that it's the kind of thing you don't leave lying around. She pulls out some boxes at random. They're full of maths, diagrams, incomprehensible jottings. She replaces them, opens others: equally opaque. She looks around her, nonplussed.

It won't be to hand. Not convenient for a quick peek.

Helen cranes her neck and gazes at the top shelves. Miles out of reach. You wouldn't put anything up there that you ever wanted to see again. She climbs on a chair: not high enough. You need a stepladder. There's nothing in this room, though – nothing that approximates to library steps. The nearest thing is in the kitchen, that high stool with the steps folded under. What an effort! Surely he didn't do this every time he wanted to file something confidential?

The more she thinks about it, the surer she is that that's probably just what he did do. He wouldn't keep it where anyone might find it. On the other hand, there was no need for obsessive secrecy – safes, hidden drawers, concealed cupboards. Who was going to pry? Not Helen. She wasn't interested enough. She had her own fish to fry.

She fetches the steps. The dusty records of the distant past are level with her forehead.

Each of the boxes has a name scrawled on its back, referring to the project supposedly stored inside. She takes down one or two. They appear to be as labelled. In one of the far corners, however, she notices a box less dusty than the rest, and unmarked. It's out of reach. She moves the steps. Still out of reach. An awkward corner.

Helen moves the steps once more and stands on tiptoe. Now she can just reach to dislodge the box. It flies through her outstretched hands to shower its contents around the floor.

She descends to find herself surrounded by correspondence.

Is this what she was looking for? The letters certainly seem personal, not official. She stoops to gather them up. Now that she's found them, doubts assail her.

She doesn't have to look. There's still time. No need to unravel everything: no compulsion to disinter. She could stuff the letters back, replace them for Miss Parrinder to hide. Dispose of them, even.

But she won't do that. The choice was made when the box flew open, so that she couldn't help seeing its contents.

They're from Lorraine.

Lorraine. The one he always denied. Over for years, finished before he and Helen ever met. Purely political, these days. For Christ's sake, Helen, why should I lie to you? Do I ever lie about that sort of thing?

What could she say? Yes?

The letters aren't dated by year – only the day of the month. There isn't even an address. Just: Venice.

Venice, Italy, or Venice, Ca.? If the latter, then maybe that explains the sudden attraction of Synchrony. She always wondered if there was something more to that than he told her at the time.

Suddenly she feels terribly tired. Too tired to deal with all this. It's hardly urgent, is it? Not any more.

She could take the letters with her. Something to read on the flight tomorrow. But when she tries to fit them into her briefcase, there's no room. It's full of drafts, stuff she wants to show Patrick. One thing at a time. Anyhow, does she want Benny with her in California? Probably not.

So she takes the box to her study, stuffs it into a drawer, locks it, and hides the key behind a row of books. Returns the ladder to the kitchen; and goes to bed, where she dreams of Miss Parrinder, who is furious.

Coincidences. You think of a person you haven't seen for years, and there they are, in the street or on the other end of the telephone. You hear a name, a new word, the title of some obscure book, and next time you go to the library, there it is in front of you. What led her to that particular spot, to that one box among so many? Was it (as he would have insisted, had he been here to insist) Benny again, speaking to her from his obscure corner of the universe (whichever universe that may be)?

Messages, signs, directions from on high. Do the stars really foretell? Colette thinks so, and the world is with her. Millions of people buy Benny's book to read scientific explanations of synchronicities. Glimpses of parallel universes, sudden faults in spacetime. Anything but mere coincidence. Priests, psychotherapists, astrologers, palmists – all satisfy the same fundamental need. They interpret, they decipher. They impose order.

Why this passion for significance, for divine ciphers, hidden messages? Benny the zoologist thought that it was all part of natural selection, that the ability to recognise patterns, sequences, connections, to remember that a particular event portends another, was essential for survival. This presaged food: that, warmth. So we became pattern-seeking creatures. It's inbuilt. We can't resist it – not unless we try. To be random, to reject design, goes against the grain. That was one reason he so enjoyed doing it. Up yours, Watchmaker!

Sitting in the plane, she can hear his voice. But it's his later voice, that siren song. – Relax, Helen, it says. Why always feel you have to resist? Go with the flow. Listen to the voices. Just this once, listen to the voices.

*

In the magic morning calm, after Benny and the children have left the house, Helen stands on a stool in quest of a book marooned on a high shelf. The stool is not quite tall enough: neighbouring books cascade onto the floor. Picking them up, she notices that one is Stefan Kertes' philosophical work *Parallel Minds*. She must have bought it before that television interview. By rights, the book isn't even hers. It should have gone to the BBC library. She must have brought it home and forgotten to return it. 1968, that was: seventeen years ago. The year, the day, are impressed indelibly upon her mind.

She opens it: a cloud of dust makes her sneeze. Helen's allergic to book-dust. Sneezes and sniffles and the glares of fellow-readers accompany her every time she visits a library. Is this the physical expression of a resentment she can't admit to? Subconsciously in revolt against a life buried in words?

Kertes, grinning from the jacket flap, denies all discomfort, allergically or otherwise induced. His whole persona – that ridiculous fringe of hair, that bouncy embonpoint – announce: Here I am! Take me or leave me. Well, she left him – or, rather, didn't take him. Not (if all those stories are true) that the evening would have turned out quite as she supposed.

His hair is doubtless sparser now, and no longer black. But the rest is probably much the same. How clearly she can picture him! Funny how others stay fresh in the mind: it's one's own past selves that are effaced. That day's Helen subsumed in all the other Helens. Only moments, odd details, persist. For instance, the clothes. She can always remember clothes: this occasion marked by yellow earrings, that by a favourite pair of tan buckled shoes. The person dissolves, the covering remains intact. That day, she wore a white cotton dress. It had narrow, long sleeves, a high neck, a skirt cropped at mid-thigh: at that time skirts were the merest pelmets. Inset bands of lace gave tantalising glimpses of the flesh beneath. It strained sometimes at the seams – she put weight on and dropped it off as an onion loses skins. Was that day one of her thinner moments? Was that when she wore her hair tied up in a knot of curls on top of her head? Or had she had it cut? These days it's bobbed – still thick and wavy enough for that – but the first grey hairs are showing. She pulls them out, but they multiply like dragons' teeth. And her thighs! Those staunch allies, those veterans of the micro-mini! The other day, looking at a batch of holiday snaps, she thought: No more photographs in swimsuits. The firm flesh of youth has disappeared without warning. Middle age has settled upon her thighs, and no doubt elsewhere.

She glances through the book, fails to engage with its contents, shuts it, replaces it on the shelf, gets on with her work.

A little later there's a ring at the door. It's the John Lewis van, delivering a load of china. She tears open the boxes. The pieces are wrapped in newspaper: naturally, she begins to read it. And what should catch her eye but a description from some months-old Sunday paper of the Synchrony Institute and its distinguished founder, Professor Kertes. Still, it seems, up on his old hobby-horse. Still trying to relate quantum physics to the real world. *When Einstein first heard about the implications of quantum physics – that, at the very smallest level, if you measure the mass of a sub-atomic particle you cannot determine its position, and that if you know its position, you will never ascertain its mass; the notion that, before the particle's specific position is determined by observation, it occupies every possible position, that it may be both a wave and a particle – he refused to believe them. Even Einstein, who was able imaginatively to break through so many barriers! How can these apparent paradoxes fit with our experience of the world? This problem we try to explore at Synchrony. The reconciliation of the micro with the macro.*

There's even a picture. Not much changed, considering. People attain an equilibrium. They look the same for years. And then one day, all of a sudden they're old. Evidently Stefan Kertes has not yet arrived at that point. He is deeply tanned, his skin turned to brown leather in the California sun. And in sharp contrast, as she had predicted, the fringe of hair springing from that nut-brown pate is now snowy white.

Kertes again! She thinks: I must remember to tell Benny.

She always knows his mood by the sound of his steps as he comes into the house. He gets home around six. At that time, she's usually in the kitchen making dinner. The children have finished watching television and are playing upstairs. Tonight, Colette's two are here as well. She's away on tour, and Patrick is off filming as usual. Not that it would make much difference if he weren't. He and Colette have finally agreed to separate: when he's in London, he has a flat in Notting Hill. They haven't divorced – they seem reluctant to commit themselves to such a final declaration – but he's even less available for day-to-day care than he was. The Costelloe household pivots, as it has for years, around the invaluable Monica. What would Colette do if Monica ever decided that she wanted a life of her own? Luckily (for Colette) there is little prospect of this. After nine years with Colette, Monica has no life of her own. Her life is – in every way – Colette's. Presumably there's plenty of excitement, even if vicarious. Perhaps she finds this preferable to a life with no excitement at all, vicarious or otherwise.

Benny says: – She's in love with her, that's obvious.

Tonight, his step is springy, and he's whistling as he descends the kitchen stairs. – Hi! he says. – That smells good.

Helen is making soup. – It is good. She opens the oven to check on the garlic bread.

– You've got enough there for an army!

– Mass feeding tonight. Gemma and Declan are here.

– So where are they all?

– They'll be at the top of the house.

Benny opens the fridge door. – Want a drink?

– Isn't it a bit early?

– I've got something to celebrate!

Helen turns to face Benny. He's changed less than she has. His round face is rosy and unlined, his hair still dark and thick. He says it's the fresh air of the ivory tower. – Oh, yes?

– I've been offered a job.

– You've got a job!

Benny has recently been appointed to a chair. For the moment, passions are quieted, ambition slaked. But not for long. Benny may live in an ivory tower, but it's got a greasy pole up the middle whose top recedes to infinity. Discontent is a permanent state: no recognition is ever enough. Once, Helen used to lose sleep over Benny's wrongs. No longer. Too many dragons have turned out clawless, too many fatal poisons suddenly been neutralised over the years. Nevertheless, he really should have had a chair years ago. Frank didn't push his case as energetically as he might. Relations between them have cooled recently, but it's hard to know whether this is cause or effect. Benny says Frank is jealous, that his creativity has dried up and he relies on Benny to keep the lab at the cutting edge of research. Frank would doubtless produce some equally convincing tale, not that he'd tell it to Helen. Though she's had the impression when they've met recently that something's on the tip of his tongue, that he has physically to restrain himself, to hold back the words by main force. What is it? If Benny knows, he's not saying. He shrugs and tells Helen she's imagining things. Which she isn't. But it can't be too serious, or Benny never would have got that chair.

He says: – Yes, but this one could be fun. It's –

Suddenly, Helen knows what's coming. – Don't tell me. Stefan Kertes called.

Benny stares at her. – How did you know that?

– He's kind of been in touch. And Helen explains about the morning's little messages.

Benny sits down. – I don't believe it. You know he's got this thing about coincidences? Synchronicities? He thinks they're messages from other universes. Overlappings.

– So I was reading. Do you believe that stuff?

– Me? No. Benny laughs. – But then I'm not a physicist, I'm a biologist. I live in the real world. Anyway, he's offered me a fellowship at his institute. Synchrony. You know?

– And are you going?

– I'm tempted. That would give them something to think about.

– You just want to thumb your nose at Frank! What's going on between you two? He keeps on opening his mouth whenever I see him, and then he remembers something and shuts it again.

– He'd better keep on remembering or he won't know what's hit him, says Benny.

*

In LA, Patrick is waiting. What a relief to see him! She was afraid he'd send his secretary, George. George resents Helen's presence in Patrick's life. It's not that he suspects hanky-panky – even were Patrick more inclined to women, would Helen be the one? At her age? After thirty years? As he was at such pains to point out, in LA there's no lack of available talent. But George needs no such suspicions to fuel his resentment. It is enough, for him, that Helen is a woman. And there's not much she can do about that.

But no, there's Patrick's large, familiar figure at the barrier. He

71

kisses her warmly. – Wonderful of you to come at this short notice, darling. We've got so much to do, you simply won't believe.

As they drive, he explains what's been happening.

The film Patrick and Helen are working on is called *Who Is Joseph Elroy?* It's about a mysterious novelist – the Joseph Elroy of the title. Nothing is known of him except for two novels, ignored when they first appeared, but recently rediscovered and now recognised as masterpieces. Recently, the fragment of another novel has been found in a publisher's archive. A conference of Elroy specialists has been convened. All trace of the man himself is lost. Vain attempts have been made to trace him, to follow up old letters, old addresses, possible acquaintances and lovers. It's assumed he must be dead. But as the film progresses, the suspicion arises that one of the conferees, an elderly academic from an obscure university, may be the mysterious Elroy. Is it true? Does that matter? Whether or not he is Elroy, Elroy he will be henceforth. The film is a subtle meditation upon identity and reality.

– They love it, says Patrick. – We've got all the backing we need.

– Wonderful!

– But they want a few changes. He glances sidelong at Helen.

– Don't tell me. Elroy turns out to be a long-lost millionaire racehorse-owner who disappeared to avoid an importunate mistress.

– Not quite. Patrick laughs, a trifle uneasily. – But he has a daughter. And they want much more emphasis on the chase, the detective-story element. It's the daughter that's the academic. He's been working as a garage mechanic – when his book bombed he didn't want anything more to do with that world. He's put her through college – her mother died of disappointment when she was small. And we need more love-interest. She's going to fall in love with the guy who's organising the conference, and either she'll reveal her dad's secret, or maybe she won't know anything about it, and *he* will find out and reveal it to *her*. And the father, Elroy, they thought maybe Harrison Ford, will turn out to have the remaining half of the fragment. But she'll have to choose between the novel and him. He doesn't want it published, he doesn't want to be Joseph Elroy any more. So you see it's all rather changed.

– But Elroy's *old*! How could he be Harrison Ford?

– Old isn't box-office. He wrote this stuff when he was very young.
– About ten.

Patrick turns sharp left. – I quote.

They're getting near his house now, she recognises the mall – the mall which is exactly like every other mall, the mall of her dreams. Of her dream. In just a few minutes they'll be turning into the driveway. Patrick says: – Look, Helen. This isn't a sensitive art-house movie any more. Accept it. Have some fun. Let go, for once. You've never done that, have you? You like to keep tight hold of yourself all the time. You're a control freak. You're afraid they'll think you're not a serious person.

Where's she heard something like that recently? She says weakly, – But I always thought I was so good at jokes.

– Darling, you know perfectly well what I mean. But what's the point? How many lives do we have, for Christ's sake? Life moves on. Try something new.

He's right, thinks Helen as she lies (and fails to sleep) once more in Patrick's guest-room. She must move on. Leave Benny behind. Easier said than done, though. Twenty-five years is a long time. And that box of letters won't let itself fade away so easily. It's pathetic, but there it is. Just one glimpse of Benny's secret life, and her own is taken over as completely as if he were still alive. Which, for her, therefore, he is. Q.E.D.

*

Helen says, – Isn't this rather a large step to take just because you and Frank happen to have disagreed about something?

She thinks but does not say: Hadn't you better be careful? Benny's colleagues already look askance at him: those excursions into television, those weekly columns, the popularity of those books of his. There's a feeling in some quarters that he's not really *serious* – just a populariser. He dismisses this, says it's all down to jealousy. They won't allow that it's possible to be both serious *and* popular. He's probably right. But does he want to add fuel to that fire? It's obvious what they'll say about Kertes and his institute. However, whether by chance or telepathy, Kertes seems to have picked the right moment to pop his question. It seems Benny can't wait to shake the dust of London from his heels. His professorship, the patient years building up his research base at the lab, apparently count for nothing. They are merely bait. From further up the pole, a rope dangles. Who is he to resist?

– It's more than just disagreement. He's making these wild accusations –

– What wild accusations? I haven't heard anything.

So she was right!

Benny's face is scarlet, he's choking on words he can't bring himself to repeat. – He doesn't dare say it in public. It's – oh, it's really too ridiculous. He's implying that I faked some results in the protein experiments.

Benny was in the news last year for being the first to show how proteins may act on a particular strain of virus. The medical and financial implications are far-reaching. As so often happens, a number of laboratories were working on the same problem. Benny got there first. Others, using other routes to the same result, were pipped at the post. His credentials as a serious researcher were re-established, if they had ever been in question.

– But they've replicated those experiments!

– There's some controversy over the best route. We were all racing to get there, and – d'you know, I still can't believe it. Anyhow, you can imagine it rather poisons the atmosphere. I have to admit, I wouldn't mind a move.

– But you didn't do it, did you?

– What d'you think? *Of course* I didn't!

– Did the promotions committee know about this?

– No idea. You can't go throwing accusations like that around without proof.

– So if he hasn't got proof, what made him think it in the first place?

– Christ only knows! He thinks he saw something. I've told you before. I keep feeling he's watching me.

Frank's accusation hangs in the air between them. Benny's right: it couldn't be more serious. If Frank was right, if he had proof, that would be the end of Benny's career. But, of course, he can't be right. He's jealous. He's been jealous of Benny for years.

– Shouldn't you stand your ground? If you leave now, won't Frank take that as a sort of admission?

He shakes his head. – I only have a certain amount of energy. If you knew what it felt like to go in every day, knowing what may be in people's minds . . .

Surely anyone could see that? Why, then, does Helen persist in her objections? She says: – But isn't Synchrony rather notorious? I thought Kertes was considered seriously eccentric these days.

Benny shakes his head. – It's an interesting place. He's got all sorts of people there, any number of disciplines. It could be a lot of fun. A lot of money, too. I don't know where he gets it, but there it is.

– Better not ask. I expect it's the Pentagon, wanting to explore the weapons possibilities of synchronicity.

Benny says nothing.

Helen stirs her soup. – Am I expected to say yes or no now, just like that?

He takes a deep breath. It's clear he hadn't anticipated an argument. Why has Helen joined the enemy all of a sudden? – Think about it.

The children clatter down the stairs. You can hear them coming like descending thunder. Declan heads the group. He's thirteen now, tall and blond, with that wonderful golden skin he inherited from his father. He's at Westminster, a weekly boarder: Friday nights (as now) he comes home for the weekend. But Monica has weekends off. So when Colette and Patrick are both away, he and Gemma stay with the Spiros. Helping each other out, as Colette so presciently predicted. Declan is charming, polite, slightly remote. He's always had this detached quality: he doesn't care to entrust himself too fully to life. What's going on under there? No-one can say, and Declan isn't telling.

Gemma is eleven, also blonde, but paler. She has long hair, tied in a pony-tail, and she wears glasses. She hates them. When she gets older she'll have contact lenses. Next year she'll have a brace, too. She tries to be philosophical, but it isn't easy. She's very like Colette – like enough for comparison to be inevitable – but not quite so pretty, and not quite so bright, at least in the areas that interest her. This is the overriding fact of her life. Benny, who has a soft spot for Gemma, thinks she could be good at science, but what use is that? She's set her heart upon becoming an actress. Of course, she's still got plenty of time to change her mind.

The twins are eight. Laura is little and bouncy, Timmy, taller and quieter. Laura rushes at Benny, whom she adores and who returns her adoration, and flings herself into his arms. Gemma averts her eyes. The sight of Benny and Laura in this mode makes her uncomfortable: perhaps because she's so attached to Benny herself, perhaps because this is the kind of relationship she's never had with her own father.

Timmy sidles towards the stove and peers inside the pan. – Soup! Yum! I'm starving! He beams at Helen, the source and fount of all good meals. Laura, from the superior elevation of her father's arms, says: – Lentils! Yech! Can I have just bacon?

Benny says, – How would you like to live in California?

The children exchange glances. Declan, stressing detachment and unconcern, says, – Are you going to live there?

– It's possible.

– What would you do?

– I've been offered a job.

– Would we go to school there? Laura wants to know.

– Of course. If we decide to go.

– Can't we, Mum? The twins are instantly allured by this new possibility.

Why doesn't she want to go? Why doesn't she leap at the chance? Isn't it reasonable, what Benny's asking? It needn't be for ever. She could give it a whirl. A year in California – isn't that everybody's dream? The sun, the palm trees, the material plenty. The relaxed life. The kids could find a school there. California's full of bright kids. They'd love it. But Helen doesn't want to. Why is she always so contrary? Given the weight of public opinion, she's going to have to find some good reasons. She says: – *I* haven't been offered a job.

– Oh, but –

Declan and Gemma say nothing. What can they say? This isn't their decision, even though it will affect their lives. They look nervous, slightly cast down. What, Helen wonders, as they seat themselves around the table and she dishes out ladlefuls of lentil and bacon, will happen to them if the Spiros vanish?

Come on, Helen. Isn't this rather clutching at straws? They're not exactly going to be orphaned. And Colette's always going to Los Angeles. They can visit whenever they want. Her family, meanwhile, clearly can't wait to be off. Supposing Mrs Columbus had reacted this way? Sorry, Christopher, you simply cannot leave everything for this crazy voyage. Haven't you got any consideration? Where's your sense of proportion? Or the Pilgrim Mothers – think of them. Are you mad? All on *one ship*? We're very comfortable where we are, thank you.

What does she do – write for the telly? So why can't she do that in California? Lots of people do. That's where they *go* to do that sort of thing.

Helen has established herself, during the past few years, as a television playwright. Her second play, *Conqueror*, caused quite a stir, and since then she's written several more. Recently, she's moved on to serials. She's just finished a six-parter about a woman MP who finds herself caught up in a plot to kill the Prime Minister. Rubbish, of course, but popular rubbish. It hit a national nerve, acted out a national fantasy – catharsis for writer and viewers alike. If you can't fulfil your fantasies in real life, this is the next best thing.

Colette's trying to persuade her into live theatre. She wants to get back to the stage. Why doesn't Helen write her a play? What a combination they'd make! Helen isn't sure, though it's nice to be asked. She prefers television. How many people get to watch a stage play? A few thousand? The average viewing figure for *Treason and Plot* was twelve million. And television has other advantages. It's intimate, its effects are close up. She likes that. Helen is not attracted by theatricality. Effects, yes; stage effects, no. That's one reason coincidences annoy her. They have that stagey feel.

How can she leave all this? In California, she might get onto a soap or do some screenwriting – if she's lucky. But she'd have to be very lucky. That's what half the population's trying to do. And suppose she was successful? American TV is another country indeed.

Another planet. She's heard nothing but horror stories about that kind of factory work.

Benny says: – You wouldn't have to get a job. I told you, Kertes is talking about a lot of money. You could relax by the pool. You could write what you wanted.

She can picture the scene. A Hockney of the swimming-pool period. The pool, the glass of gin, the unfinished meisterwerk in the computer. A wife's life. My wife writes. A friend of hers, also in television (she ran a successful production company), went out a couple of years ago under just these circumstances. *Her* husband was offered something irresistible, and who was she to stand in his way? And how does she spend her time now, this high-powered lady? Makes sculptures to set around the swimming-pool. Otherwise, she'd go mad. She called Helen only the other day. – We rent this huge place, she said. – There's a special room dedicated entirely to empty bottles. Imagine!

Helen can imagine. She doesn't want a swimming-pool. She isn't that bothered about the weather. Above all, she doesn't want to be an expat wife, doing the expat round. Where would Benny be – doing it at her side? Not a chance. He'd be at the Institute, deep in those fascinating discussions he's so looking forward to. Why should Benny lead an expat life? He wouldn't *be* one, any more than he is already. What's London to him? Simply a place where, by chance, he happens to have settled. Even without his present troubles, it's colder than California, with less facilities, less money, less prospects. He'd probably feel instantly at home. What was South Africa – the part he grew up in – but imitation California? Sunshine, suburbia, black servants, dentists making a mint. Plus California's full of big brains – nothing but the best for all those high-powered, high-paying defence industries. How can he turn it down?

A few years ago, the answer would have been: For political reasons. LA's hardly the centre of the anti-apartheid world. This would mean – or would seem to mean – that he'd definitively drop out of politics. Though it crosses Helen's mind that he may be acting, precisely, for political reasons. Perhaps he was warned to be more discreet, to deepen his cover. It occurs to her that this quarrel with Frank may be all, or almost all, a front – a pearl of verisimilitude

78

built up around some tiny speck of substance. Why hasn't she heard all this before? Perhaps Kertes merely provided the out Benny's been waiting for. There have been one or two scares recently at the 'publishing office' where he used to spend so much time – trusty comrades who turned out to be double agents. The office organises long, long chains of people to pass money from hand to hand until, eventually, it reaches its intended destination. That way, it can't be traced – they hope. But there've been some accidents recently, and paranoia is mounting. Helen doesn't know the details. Schooled by years of enforced discretion, she doesn't enquire. If Benny's handling the ubiquitous Moscow gold, then the fewer people that know about it, the better.

But Benny appears less political these days. For whatever reason, the subject of South Africa no longer dominates the conversation. He is, or seems, wholly focused on his work.

Anyhow, all these are Benny's imperatives, not Helen's. His work, his politics.

She says: – I may change my mind, of course. But just now I really don't want to go. It's just the wrong moment for me. To visit, fine, but not to live.

Declan and Gemma look visibly relieved. Everyone else looks furious. Benny says tightly: – I see. You haven't given it much of a chance, have you?

Helen curses the demon king and all his stupid show-off effects. This morning she was a happy woman. Her series was such a success, Benny was so pleased with his chair. The road seemed clear ahead. Then Kertes snaps his fingers, and – abracadabra! – everything changes. With a screech of tyres, their marriage has arrived at a crossroads. No traffic lights, no warning signs; and suddenly, the smell of hot rubber is everywhere.

Laura says, – Oh, Mum*mee*! I want to go to Disneyland!

Yes, for the kids it would probably be paradise.

She shakes her head. No use pretending. Selflessness, however gilded, is not for her. – Sorry. But that's how I feel. Does it have to be for life? Couldn't you just go for a bit? Consult or something? A few months here, a few months there?

79

Benny says: – Maybe. Anyhow, he's asked me over for a week to have a look at the place.

– Fine, says Helen. She collects the soup-plates, puts cheese and a cake on the table. The scene she plays out almost every night of her life. Suddenly it no longer feels quite real. The management has annnounced new plans. The run of this particular play is drawing to a close, and the cast can't pretend they don't know.

Lying beside Benny that night, each silently pretending to be asleep (or maybe Benny really isn't pretending), Helen thinks about Frank's accusation. Benny wouldn't talk about it, even when the children had gone to bed. He said: – It's a figment, there's no point solidifying it by repetition. And, as a loyal wife, she should go along with that. (As a loyal wife she should go along. Period.) But she can't help seeing how it might have arisen. Benny's enthusiasm is so tremendous – it's hard not to be blown along by it. A little detail that doesn't fit – why not ignore it? A number that just needs a nudge – would you notice yourself doing it? He knows where he's heading – it's all so clear – just one little detail – Oh, she can see it! And he was right. That *was* where it was heading.

She mustn't even think such thoughts.

Yes, he sweeps you off your feet. That was always part of the attraction. After all these years, though, she's perfected her resistance techniques. She's had to.

The night before Benny's departure, Helen dreams of a plane crash. Her dream is very detailed. She sees Benny sitting there, but she isn't there herself, and nor are the children. The woman next to Benny looks familiar. She's dark and slim, with long black hair. Lorraine. Someone she hasn't thought of for years.

All these old ghosts, coming back to haunt her. No doubt Lorraine, too, doesn't look like that any more. Only in dreams.

The plane has caught fire. It's going to ditch in the sea. Everyone scrambles desperately for the chutes. But they are mysteriously unattainable. At this point, Helen wakes up.

She does not mention her dream to Benny. They haven't talked about Synchrony, or indeed anything much, since Helen gave the wrong answer to the question of California. Perhaps if they don't mention it the problem will go away, or otherwise miraculously solve itself. Perhaps she'll see reason. Benny clearly can't understand her hesitation. He takes it personally. He feels that she values her separateness above their joint enterprise – as indeed seems to be the case; though the same could just as easily be said of him. But it still seems natural for a wife to up sticks on her husband's behalf. Not that she's asking him to up sticks on hers. On the contrary.

Anyhow, if she starts talking about unpleasant dreams, he'll only think this is part of her effort to dissuade him.

She waves him off, suitcase in hand, as so often recently. The parting doesn't feel particularly momentous. Benny's life these days is a continuous round of conferences here, seminars there. It's amazing he gets any work done at all. She's got a busy day herself: she's meeting a script editor for lunch, then seeing her agent in the afternoon.

At six o'clock, she switches on the news. She feels, to her annoyance, unnaturally tense, braced for the worst. What's she expecting? What's she afraid of? Signs and portents? Synchronicities?

But the demon king's off-duty for once. No air disaster is reported.

Benny: 1961

December 16: midsummer. Johannesburg seethes with idlers and overheated pleasure-seekers. It's a public holiday, the Day of the Covenant, Dingaan's Day, when Afrikaners celebrate the Voortrekkers' victory over Dingaan's Zulu impis at Blood River. So called because its waters, that day, ran red with blood. Civilisation ruled.

After dark, this industrial district is deserted. The shutters are pulled down, the streets full of shadows. Someone – a man, a shadow – slips along the wall of the Post Office and deposits a package. Post early for Christmas, address your parcels clearly.

The time of the blast was recorded on a clock which hung above the post-office counter. It dangled by a wire, its hands fixed at the fatal moment: 10.22 p.m. The inside of the building was wrecked, the main door blown off, and glass from two telephone booths was strewn along the pavement.

*

– A bit further down, says Lorraine. That's it ... Just there ... Gently ... ooooh! Oh, God! Oh, Benny! But Benny is already inside her. Greedily they cling to the last receding ripples of sensation.

– Again?

She shakes her head lazily and touches his cheek. They roll apart, fingers touching across the bed.

– I love you, Lo.

Sunlight stripes them: the shutters are half-closed against the afternoon. How happy I am, thinks Benny. I wish this moment could go on for ever. He runs his finger along Lorraine's sleek side. Like him, she is nineteen; unlike him, tall and slender, with long, straight black hair and small, delicate features. A perfect couple. She will never be so beautiful again, he, never so ardent. He can't imagine he will ever love anyone else as much. (And, with one exception, he will not. Did anyone ever notice how Laura's name echoed Lorraine's?) He will marry Helen, but Lorraine will remain somewhere inside him, undimmed by everyday exigencies.

Is Lorraine as consumed as Benny? It's hard to say. There's always something held back, a resistance to be overcome before she will abandon herself. Benny never feels he truly possesses her: her infinite desirability is magnified by uncertainty. Benny's mother, who does not like Lorraine, declares that this teasing mask conceals precisely nothing, this being the contents of Lorraine's head. Benny hates her when she says this. – She's got you on a string, his mother says. – She likes playing with you, can't you see?

Benny says nothing. As far as he's concerned Lorraine can play with him to her heart's content. He can't get enough of it.

From somewhere in the house, they can hear a radio. Benny is suddenly still, intent. Lorraine senses that she no longer has his full attention.

– What's wrong?

– Shh! I'm trying to listen.

Indistinctly, the newsreader's voice can just be made out through the walls. It is clipped, impersonal. He is talking about last night's bomb attacks in Johannesburg and Port Elizabeth. The targets were public buildings: post offices, electricity substations, the Native Commissioner's building. A police guard has been mounted on all post offices, says the voice. A search is being made for suspicious packages. No-one has yet claimed responsibility for the attack, but there is a suspicion it was mounted by the group calling itself Umkhonto we Sizwe, the Spearhead of the Nation. Printed handbills issued by this organisation were distributed throughout city centres after dark yesterday.

83

The muffled voice ceases. But Benny still seems to be listening for something. Then, with a little grunt, he flops back on the bed.

– Waiting for something?

– Nope. Just listening. But his voice has gone flat.

– You sound all let down. Her voice rises questioningly at the end of the sentence, but she knows he won't answer, just as she knows she shouldn't ask.

He laughs. – With any luck they'll blow up that bastard Verwoerd next.

She looks at him across the sheets. – Are you still going to the Resistance meeting?

– Probably.

– Be careful.

Benny does not reply.

*

At five the next morning there is a loud knocking at the door of Judge Leonard Spiro's house. It is repeated, louder, and accompanied by shouts of Police! The servants, whose day off it was yesterday, have not yet arrived. The judge himself, in pyjamas and dressing-gown, finally opens the door. – What the hell is this all about?

On the doorstep stand two burly policemen. They are young, beer-bellied, moustachioed. One of them is holding a piece of paper. – Good morning, judge, he says, waving it. – We have a warrant to search your house.

– Are you mad? Do you know what time it is?

– We wanted to be sure of finding someone in, sir. You're a busy man.

– And what exactly do you expect to find when you conduct your search?

– Perhaps you can guess.

– Absolutely not.

– You must have heard about those bomb attacks.

– You can't imagine I had anything to do with that! Judge Spiro is genuinely shocked.

– We were given a list of addresses. This was one of them. They shrug. It isn't their responsibility. They are merely the messengers.

The party is in the kitchen now. Policemen don't wait for an invitation. They go methodically through the cupboards. Saucepans, plates, groceries, pile up on the floor and the table. The judge, his wife and Benny watch. Mrs Spiro says, – Now you can put them back.

They snigger. – We don't know where they all go, do we?

After the kitchen, they move on to the judge's study. They go through every room in the house. Whatever it is they're looking for, they can't find it. Every drawer has been pulled out and emptied; floorboards have been lifted, clothes, stores, crockery, minutely examined. Empty-handed and unapologetic, they leave.

By now the Spiros' maid has arrived. Clucking in horror, she begins the business of clearing up. Mrs Spiro, dazed and indignant, helps her. The judge beckons Benny to his study. It's awash with scattered papers. The judge shuts the door.

– So what was all that about? he demands.

Benny shrugs. – Do I know? What they told you, I guess. They're mad. You know that.

– Did you have anything to do with this trouble? No, don't tell me. I'd better not know.

They face each other across the room. The judge absently sorts some papers into piles. He's taller than Benny, less thick-set, but with the same curly hair and sardonic face. The judge's hair, however, is grey. – What about this student resistance movement? You know them?

– I expect so, says Benny calmly. – Everyone knows everyone. This isn't exactly the biggest place in the world.

– Where were you that evening, anyhow?

– At Lorraine's. We had a few beers with friends, then we went back there.

– Did anyone see you there?

– Lo, of course.

– How about her parents?

– We don't exactly seek out their company.

The judge sighs. That much, at least, he can understand. Mr

Lemper, Lorraine's father, is a successful businessman (he owns a chain of furniture stores). He expresses no opinions about the current outrages: opinions are bad for business. He is a vulgarian. And his wife is a fool. Lorraine's a beauty, no doubt about that, but otherwise, like mother like daughter, or he's much mistaken. And the judge is rarely mistaken in these matters.

As it happens, in this case he's wrong. Perhaps emotion clouded his perceptions. Whatever she may or may not be, Lorraine is no fool.

– Have you heard from Cambridge?

– They offered me a place.

– I think you should go, says the judge.

– But supposing I prefer to stay here?

– Listen. What harm can it do you to go to Cambridge? It's the best place for what you're interested in. You could really get somewhere. You don't even have to abandon the struggle. There's plenty you can do from there. Whereas I . . . Don't you see, there's nothing they'd like better than to force me out. You know the words of the sainted B. J. Vorster. The judge assumes a thick Afrikaans accent: – *Liberalism is worse then gommunism beegause liberalism leeeds to gommunism.* Did you know he's tipped for Justice? It's important for people like me to stay. We must. Who else can take them on? But we've got to be absolutely clean. We've got to be above suspicion. If they can ban me or put me in prison, what use am I? And what would your mother do?

Benny shrugs.

– Don't you see, you're compromising my position. And if you're not yet, you will soon, he adds quietly.

– I could find somewhere else to live.

– There's no need for that. But after your exams are over, you should go.

– I'll think about it.

– No, you'll do it. For God's sake, man. I'm not exactly sending you to prison!

Later that day, the radio reports that an unexploded bomb has been found by the Health Board building in Klipstown. The

- 86

assumption is that it was planted at the same time as all the others, but failed to go off.

At his farewell party, Benny's friend Joey Kalms says: – Chickening out, eh, man?

Joey is Benny's oldest friend. They have known each other since kindergarten; they have been friends through school and university.

Benny says: – I'll be back.

Joey stayed on. He wasn't chicken. He was arrested three years later, along with all the other members of the Resistance Movement who had failed to leave the country. He was jailed for fifteen years. He committed suicide in prison. That was the story. Who was to contradict it?

Suppose Benny hadn't left. Suppose he'd stayed, like Joey. He sometimes felt that part of him *had* stayed; that the best part of Benny Spiro was still in Johannesburg. It was certainly the last time he felt all of a piece. Did *that* Benny and Joey manage to escape together? More likely they both ended up in jail. And, as his father said, what use was that?

Did he marry Lorraine, *that* Benny? She, at least, wasn't arrested, wasn't imprisoned. That much he knows. Which was slightly surprising, since she knew all of them, even if she wasn't yet involved herself when Benny knew her. It makes you wonder, these paranoid days.

4

ALL DAY, EVERY day, Patrick and Helen work on *Joseph Elroy*.

They've evolved a routine. Up early, breakfast at seven-thirty, down to work by eight-thirty. Work till eleven-thirty; break for lunch, a swim, a game of tennis. Work again till five or six. Then it's a dinner-party or a cook-out, often with people who will be involved in the production, producers, actors, crew. Pitches to be prepared, comments to be taken on board. The day's work to be discarded. And next day, begin again.

It's a dance, really, an intricate and formal affair, the kind of thing that used to be taught to awkward teenagers in a room over a shop in the high street. The Patrick Costelloe School of Dance. All that's missing is the diagram of interlocking footprints. Eliminate a character here, create one there, strike this scene, insert that, move the beginning to the end, shift the middle to the top, replace deserts with mountains, snow with sunlight, move the action from New York to Mexico City to Chicago and back again. Every time they think they've got it right, the reworked script is shown to a distributor or producer who thinks differently. Today, the hero gains twenty years, yesterday he lost thirty. Tomorrow all this will be reversed. It's become an exercise in logistics. Every change means a thousand other related changes, a forest of loose ends waving. By the time they've finished, no single strand of the original story will remain. – But the germ's still there, says Patrick, confident, reassuring. And so, more importantly, is the finance.

Tonight, for once, they aren't going out. Patrick has grilled some giant prawns, which they dip in garlic mayonnaise. He hasn't stinted on the garlic. – If you knew, darling, how I long for smelly food out here! he complains. – Thank God we're not seeing anyone tonight. Free to stink to our hearts' content.

He's heaped the prawns on a platter, but hasn't yet eaten many himself. The meal, like every aspect of life, is punctuated by the telephone bell. Pat grumbles about it, says he'll leave it to the answering-machine, but when the point comes he can never resist picking it up. Who knows, these fabulous days, what great name, what irresistible offer, may not be at the other end? Helen recognises the syndrome. She's seen it before with Colette, even (on a smaller scale) experienced it herself. And when you're in a trough rather than at the wave's crest, you answer it, too: this may be it, the phone-call that's going to change your life.

– Pat, did you see much of Benny when he was out here?

– A certain amount, says Patrick guardedly. – Our paths didn't cross that often.

The phone rings again. He picks it up with what looks to Helen like relief. She eats a prawn. So, talking away, does Patrick. The call ends. – More wine? Fox've got some script they want me to look at. Doesn't sound very interesting.

– About Benny. D'you know if he was seeing somebody called Lorraine?

– Lorraine, says Patrick. He looks pleased, expansive, as though he's been let off some hook. If he was worried about something, it wasn't this. – The name does ring a bell, he says. – But that's about all I can tell you. Sorry.

What, who, did he have in mind? What name was he expecting? What was the question she failed to ask?

When it turned out that Patrick had been gay all these years, then all the other Patricks she'd known – the unattainable god of their Cambridge youth, the earnest provincial theatre director, the dilettante absentee husband, the weekend father – became subtly different people. What changed? Only the framing. But perception of the foreground varies with the background. Exactly the kind of detail that, if Pat were a character in a film script, she'd have to analyse.

Has her view of her own past life been similarly, subtly skewed? But it's *past*. How can the past change? What happened, happened. How can it be altered now?

Easily, once you begin. The differences are not of facts, but emphasis. What seemed inevitable, fated, turns out to have been merely accidental: one of a thousand possible scenarios.

*

Laura and Tim are in a bad mood. They've been in California. Ten days (a stretched half-term) at Benny's beachside condo. Even in February, it was drink your breakfast orange-juice and straight out onto the sand. They went scuba-diving off Catalina, skate-boarded through the shopping-malls, visited colleagues equipped with swimming-pools, ate take-outs and barbecues.

And now it's back to London in March. Steely clouds and a chilly north-easter deny the possibility of spring. School makes no allowances for jet-lag. Helen is preoccupied with work. Timmy caught a cold at once, and now he's given it to Laura. They sit around the kitchen whining, at each other and at Helen, who is trying to get the supper.

– Can't we have hamburgers?

– No, we had them yesterday.

– Can't we have them again today? With Dad, we had them every day. We grilled them on the barbecue.

– So you've told me a thousand times. You're perfectly welcome to start a barbecue if you want, but I think you'll find it's a little chilly. We're having pasta.

– What with?

– Sauce.

– What sort of sauce?

– Oh, Christ, how do I know what sort of sauce? Whatever I can find in the fridge.

– Not those watery canned tomatoes.

Helen, in the act of taking a can of tomatoes from the shelf, turns and glares. – If you can think of something better, suggest it.

90

Laura says: – I'm really hungry, can I have some crisps to be going on with?

– Look in the cupboard.

– There aren't any, we must have finished them all.

– Then you'll have to do without. Have some bread and butter.

– I don't want bread and butter, I want *crisps*. Can't we go and get some?

– Oh, why not. The Greek shop'll still be open. My purse is on the table. Take a pound. I want change, says Helen sternly.

– Coming, Tim?

The front door bangs. Helen turns the radio on. Not six yet. When Benny's not here, they eat early. The kids are starving when they get home, and this way she gets a longer evening. It's still light, insofar as this grey filter can be called light: the days are drawing out now, the clocks go forward next Sunday.

There's a frantic ringing at the doorbell. Cursing, Helen runs up the stairs. Haven't they got the sense to leave the door on the latch when they go out? But it is latched. What on earth . . . ? She opens the door to find Timmy, alone. He looks terrified. Wordlessly, she takes his hand and they race down the steps, towards the Greek shop. It's on a corner, you have to cross a small road to get to it. At the side of the road is a huddle of people looking down at something. A man is crouching beside some bundle. Helen pushes her way through.

Laura is lying almost in the gutter, limp, on her side, black curls hiding her face. Helen screams – Laura!

The man says, – They've called an ambulance. He nods towards the shop.

– What happened? Helen is cradling Laura's head in her lap. Her face is white, no colour in her cheeks. A trickle of blood is running from her nose.

Timmy says: – We were crossing the road and this car came. Mummy, we did look! But he was going so fast, we just didn't see him till he was there!

– Where is he? Helen looks around, but she can see no car.

A woman says, – He didn't stop. Some people are such bastards.

– Did you see him?

– Not really. Not to speak of. I think it was a black car, wasn't it?

The man who had been crouching over Laura says: – I thought it was red.

Helen says: – Timmy, darling, d'you want to go and see if Colette's in?

– Oh, Mum, I'd rather stay with you.

A woman says: – Would you like me to go?

But before Helen can give directions, the ambulance has arrived. Laura doesn't speak, doesn't move. Helen and Tim climb in the back with her. They sit in the hospital, waiting. Helen doesn't feel good about dragging poor Timmy along, but what else could she do? She hugs him close. They try to comfort each other.

A doctor comes to where they are sitting. – Mrs Spiro?

Helen nods.

The doctor says, – I'm afraid your little girl's died. There was nothing we could do. I'm so sorry.

Helen might have said, – Don't bother with crisps now. Supper's almost ready.

She might have said, – No, you've had enough of that junk. Have an apple.

Laura and Tim might have decided to watch television. Or play with the computer.

They might have reached the junction a minute later, or earlier. They might have stopped to stroke, as they so often did, the neighbour's marmalade cat.

*

Before the children arrived, there was always the saving possibility of suicide. When all else failed, a way out. She used to picture it from time to time, a small flame flickering reassuringly in the distance: not because she felt suicidal, but on the contrary, because the consciousness of it gave her courage. Her one inalienable right. No longer.

Gradually, very gradually, feeling began to creep back. She noticed this at first almost with indignation, as though it were somehow an affront to Laura. But it happened anyway, until one day she realised that she was leading something really quite like a normal life. To speak to, to look at, you would have said the same person as before. Yes, that's what they said. What, after all, did they have to go on? Speech, smiles, frowns: the crudest of indicators. She looks sad, doesn't she? All the time, now. But it's understandable, it'll take time. In time, you get over anything.

People want you to be better so badly (for your sake, but also for theirs) that, quite soon, they let themselves be convinced.

– How are you?

– Fine.

– Yes, you're looking better.

Grief, in its contagious form, is over. Life begins again.

Plunged, now, into the comforting oblivion of work, Helen recognises symptoms of thaw. Concentration claims her, and then the sudden rush of guilt. For of course Benny's death means that the whole ghastly scenario has to be played out again. Desolation: to be endured, faced down, doggedly overcome. Though the devastation, when all is said and done, is not quite so terrible. Laura was visceral: Benny, already semi-detached. Repeated absence has its effect; each separation is in some sense a dress rehearsal for the real, the final thing. Willy-nilly, you construct your own life, worlds into which you may escape.

And the greatest of these is work. The absorption, the intimacy of a joint project. This was something she and Benny never experienced together – other than with the children, that universal exception. Otherwise, only with other people. Benny and Frank; Benny and Stefan; Helen and Patrick; Helen and Colette. That must have been what held Colette and Patrick together, in the early days at Huddersfield. One of the things. The heady sense of a joint undertaking, a common engagement. What else did they have? Helen and Benny had sex. But the Costelloes . . .

Helen once asked Patrick how it felt, having a sex-goddess for a wife. This was when Colette's picture was plastered all over the film mags and colour supplements: the knock-out star of the British cinema. – Don't you get jealous? Helen asked. – Don't you worry what she gets up to?

– Not really, he said. – For one thing, Colette's not that interested in men, except as accessories. I should have thought you knew that.

93

– Me? Why? I'd be the last person.

Patrick gave her that knowing look of his, one eyebrow raised, and Helen suddenly found herself thinking about Monica. The way she looked at Colette sometimes. Longingly, lingeringly, Monica's eyes would follow Colette around the room, rest on her greedily when she thought no-one was looking . . . Patrick never looked at her that way.

– So why did you get married? she heard herself asking.

– Not for the sex, darling, I assure you. Why don't you ask Colette? It was all her idea, really. I always assumed you knew that. You were there, for God's sake. You know what she's like when she gets something into her head. I just went along with it. He paused, considered. – I'm a strange person, Helen. I'm not inside life the way you seem to be. I always feel I'm on the outside looking in. I see other people having feelings, so I know what they're supposed to look like, but I don't seem to be able to do it myself. I don't know how to explain it in any other way. Perhaps I hoped that getting married would get me inside, somehow. You know, having kids, all that human stuff.

– And didn't it?

– Didn't seem to. I'm fond of them, of course. But all those violent emotions I see everyone else going through . . . I just can't do it.

*

Colette wants power. It's the only important thing. But it requires planning.

The means are not in question. Her face is her fortune. She smiles, and they fall. For a while, she couldn't get enough of this new sensation. But she's not a fool – on the contrary, she's very bright, yet another example of the world's unfairness. Nor is she cruel by nature. So the game of ninepins soon palls. It's too easy, and Colette prefers a challenge. She only wants the unobtainable. She's looked around and decided. She's going to get – Patrick Costelloe. Nothing but the best. Costelloe or bust.

And who is Patrick Costelloe?

Quite simply the most beautiful, the most talented, the most

94

modish, the most desired man in Cambridge. Tall, golden, assured, sophisticated. The name on everyone's lips. He's a gifted cartoonist, a red-hot stage director, a daring impresario. And a mythical breaker of hearts. Nobody has succeeded in ensnaring him for longer than a week – but that's exceptional; a night is more general. *If* you're lucky. He doesn't have time for involvement. He's otherwise engaged.

Colette has set her heart upon him, so far to no avail. She talks of little else. Helen is getting rather tired of the subject. She, naturally, would prefer to discuss Benny, at least some of the time. But Colette's preoccupation is total. She will think of nothing but tactics.

Can any man can be worth all this effort? What happens when the unimaginable happens, when finally you get him? Anticlimax is surely inevitable. With so much style, what space remains for passion? And who (Helen thinks longingly of Benny) can live without passion?

The answer, as it happens, is – Colette. Passion really doesn't interest her. She thinks in dynastic rather than emotional terms. For Nefertiti, her brother Pharaoh is the only possible choice.

– I just can't pin him down! Colette complains. – He's always surrounded. He gave me a cigarette last night, though. It was his last one. D'you think that means he's starting to take some notice?

She sprawls on the bed in her skin-tight jeans, and cuts another slice of ginger cake. Colette can consume an entire ginger cake at one sitting: neither her figure nor her complexion is affected by these orgies. Helen confines herself to a single slice, and feels her waistband tighten for the rest of the evening.

What can Helen say? Actually it doesn't much matter, so long as she says *something* to indicate that she's paying attention. Colette constructs her own complex scenarios. It's best for the onlooker to be non-committal. Any extended comment is liable to be seized upon, analysed, and rejected accusingly.

– Does it mean anything much?

– Don't be silly, of course it does. He's never looked at me at all before, not really, not like that. Has he?

How would Helen know? This time she doesn't reply.

– Oh, well, says Colette the stoic. She glances at her watch. – I really ought to get down to that essay soon, or I'm for it. What a bore. Never mind. She throws a sop. – What's been happening with Benny? Am I going to be allowed to meet him sometime?

Helen considers this question. She isn't at all sure how she feels about introducing Benny to Colette. She values this female friendship. There's substance there, affection, a genuine sharing of interests and resources. Could it, though, survive real competition? Over men? If there's one thing they both like even better than women, it's men. Feminism's day is dawning, and it will find no more committed devotees than Helen Bartram and Colette Bosanquet. Each is determined that she will never be, as her mother was, economically dependent upon a man, subordinate to his life. But they don't, like some, see men as the enemy, against whom a united front must always be presented. On the contrary.

Luckily, their social lives overlap hardly at all. Helen's interests are political, Colette's, theatrical. This, in Helen's view, is just as well. Why should Benny be uniquely resistant to Colette's charms? Does Helen really want to expose him to the glow of this social sun? He'd melt, like everyone else. And how could their friendship survive such a catastrophe? Helen isn't at all sure that *she* would survive it.

– Well, you know how it is, she says vaguely. – We must fix something up.

– Where does he live? asks Colette. – You must have told me, but I can't remember. I assume it's not in college, the number of nights you spend out.

In fact Helen never has told her, partly because she didn't ask, partly because of this preference for privacy, separateness in their social affairs. She says: – Oh, it's an old pub in the back of beyond.

Colette looks up with sudden interest. – That wouldn't be Liberty Hall, would it?

– How do you know about Liberty Hall? Helen is thunderstruck.

– Costelloe lives there. Didn't you know? says Colette. Suddenly, the conversation has become interesting again. – I thought everyone knew that. What on earth d'you do there? Surely you can't spend your entire time in bed. You must get up sometimes, to eat or pee. You must have seen him. What a stroke of luck. We must fix something up. How about a dinner party? Just the four of us?

96

She has spoken. There can be no more argument.

Helen says to Benny: – Does Patrick Costelloe live here?

– Yes, says Benny suspiciously. – Why?

– It's not me that's interested, Helen assures him. – It's Colette, the friend I told you about. The beautiful actress. She's been trying to snare him for months, but she can't seem to get near him. Can we fix a dinner-party or something? How well d'you know him?

– We see a bit of each other. But he won't be interested.

– Everyone's interested in Colette. You've got to promise you won't fall for her.

Benny promises. (A promise which, as far as Helen knows, he kept.) He says: – I'll tell you Costelloe's secret. He doesn't really like women. He just won't admit it to himself. That's why he gets through them at the rate he does.

– D'you really think so?

– Sure of it.

– How can you be so sure?

Benny shrugs.

– Colette will change all that, says Helen loyally. – You'll see.

– Will I? When?

– When we have this dinner-party.

– But I don't like dinner-parties! Benny can be very awkward at times.

– Imagine it's your birthday.

– Actually, says Benny, sounding surprised, – it is my birthday. I'd forgotten.

Benny provides the venue; Patrick agrees to attend; Colette and Helen will see to the food. There is, however, a snag. Neither of them can cook. The potential may be there, but it has never been tested. Is this the moment to experiment? Colette dismisses Helen's worries. – Enough wine and some nice candles, she says, – that's all that matters. She buys smoked salmon and avocados and cheese and a cake from Fitzbillies.

The evening goes well. Patrick, now that they've snared him, is witty and affable. His contribution to the evening is a batch of hash brownies. But Colette, radiant with achievement (the first battle is over, the campaign well and truly under way), needs no hashish enhancement. She's abandoned her jeans for once, and is wearing a sort of black velvet robe and long gold earrings. Her heart-shaped face rises like a flower on its slender neck, glimmering in the candlelight. A golden scarab ring (symbol of her dynastic intentions?) shines on her finger. How can anyone resist her?

Patrick, contrary to Benny's predictions, shows no signs of doing so. He noticed the ring at once: he has one just like it. A sign, a portent! He fetches it: he, too, wears it on his little finger. As the evening progresses, he takes her scarabed hand.

*

They've finished the script, for the moment at least, and Patrick is off fixing finance. There's nothing to keep Helen in Los Angeles. But she can't bring herself to get on that plane. In England, desolation waits. October chills will soon give way to long, dark, solitary November nights. Tim is immersed in Oxford, and Miss Parrinder is poised to pounce. Here, the sun shines, and she can use Patrick's guest-room as long as she likes. – Give yourself a nice holiday, darling, he said. – You deserve it.

So what's she doing? Taking herself to Yosemite, to Big Sur, to San Francisco? Looking up acquaintances, going to see the little theatres? Checking out the New York scene with a view to stopping off there on her way back?

No. She hangs around the shoe-shop in the mall and strains for a glimpse of Laura.

This time she won't be paralysed. This time she'll have the strength to speak, to touch, to find out *what's going on*. So far there has been no reappearance. But she can't abandon hope, can't stop looking. For what? The past? The future? This world, the next? If only she knew! She'd like to forget, as one would like to forget a nagging tooth, but when her mind is emptied, the pain rushes back. She has to keep probing.

She's not going there today, though. She's made a bargain with herself: if she can keep away for a while, then perhaps next time . . . Where, then?

If she knew where to look, she could try to find Lorraine. Her married name was Margulies. But there are no Margulies with Venice phone numbers, and no Lempers, either. Perhaps she's remarried, or she doesn't live there any more. Or maybe it was Venice, Italy.

Synchrony, then? Helen's never been there. There were always good reasons not to go. At first it was pique – she resented the place too much, she wasn't interested. Then Synchrony became a refuge where Benny could escape from everything he had been when he was Helen's husband, Laura's father. He could put space between himself and the family man, the no-nonsense objectivist, the enthusiast for absence of design. Why should she seek him out against his will? What had the new Benny to do with her? And then, when he came back to London, Synchrony lost importance. He went there from time to time, but, between Benny and Kertes, something had happened, some curtain dropped, some gate clanged shut. Exactly what, why or how, was never explained, and Helen didn't probe. It had become peripheral.

Is that why she's going there now? To find out, now that it doesn't matter any more?

She buys a street-plan and locates the address, up in the Hollywood hills. She even calls to make an appointment. She wouldn't want to arrive only to find Kertes wasn't there.

– Stefan? It's Helen Spiro. I'm in Los Angeles again. Doing a bit of work. Can I come and see you? I'd like to get a picture of where Benny spent so much time.

– But, my dear Helen, have you really never been here?

– No.

– Then you must come! We shall have lunch together and I will show you our place.

What was she expecting? A modern block? A plasterboard fantasy in the Hollywood style? Not, certainly, what meets her eye. She checks the address again. Yes, this must be it. It's built into a hillside, monumental, a pillared Egyptian palace of textured concrete blocks built in terraces down the canyon, festooned with hanging creepers, shaded by eucalyptus and live oak. The entrance is through a paved court: a key-patterned facade is pierced by a huge temple doorway. A polished plate by the door reads: Synchrony Institute.

What is Synchrony? First and uniquely, Kertes' place. And then? A brainstorming centre, a scientific think-tank? A cultist sham, an Angeleno fungus, a perversion of everything science is about? Take your pick. Kertes is no stranger to controversy. On the contrary. He attracts headlines, publicity – and, inevitably, distrust. Just as Benny did. He's a cosmologist – a profession which seemingly allows infinite rein to the imagination, his own and that of his followers. Speaks seven languages, plays the violin like an angel, is expert in archaeology, modern art, Sanskrit and the stock-market. A tabloid tagged him The Cleverest Man In The World, and he has never publicly (or privately) disagreed.

But Kertes never went as far as Benny, never stepped off the end, over that invisible line which separates the innovator from the eccentric, the visionary from the quack. Stefan Kertes, for all his fiddle-playing populism, is still accepted as a great scientist. He sits on government committees, advises industry, speaks to packed houses at all the leading universities. If the limits of acceptability have moved, it's partly because he's pushed them. Being accepted is important to him, whereas by the end Benny didn't care. Kertes was Benny's salvation. Saved him from despair, set him on the road which became his own road. But then Benny went too far, took a wrong turning.

Helen pushes the heavy door. It swings slowly open. Inside, incongruous in the Egyptian hallway, a receptionist sits at a desk. – May I help you?

– My name's Helen Spiro. I've come to see Dr Kertes.

– Please sit down. She nods towards a chair and picks up her phone.

Helen waits. She's annoyed to notice that her mouth is dry, her palms moist. Even after meeting him so often recently, she still can't shake off the feeling that Kertes is somehow more than human, that there is no corner of her brain he can't penetrate and (should he so wish) control. As he did with Benny. It's as if a lifetime immersed in cosmology has imbued him with extra-terrestrial characteristics. He's become one of those visitors from outer space whose signals he tries to detect.

And then he appears, and as always it's hard to imagine what she was so worked up about. As always, too, he's smaller than she had remembered. What could be intimidating about this plump and genial figure? He holds out his arms, kisses her on both cheeks. He's charming, and she is, as always, charmed, even though she knows charm is merely one of the weapons in his well-stocked armoury. But knowledge does not confer resistance: that is charm's power. – My dear Helen! What a pleasure to see you! Come! and he sets off at top speed into the recesses of the house, towards what is evidently his office. Helen follows, washed along in his wake.

They rush along pillared cloisters and down steps. The place is a curious mixture: once evidently the most elegant and beautiful of houses, but no longer personal or intimate. A door opens, and a group spills out: seven or eight men and women, all ages, arguing furiously among themselves. A chalky blackboard covered with equations sits incongruously along one wall of the room they have left, which is low-ceilinged, with long, deeply recessed windows. Other doors, half-open, reveal similar discrepancies. Low, square armchairs which were clearly designed with the house, sit among PCs and laden, makeshift bookshelves. – Perhaps our building is familiar to you?

– No. It's not at all what I was expecting.

– Ah. As he leads the way through cool rooms shaded by loggias, past geometric pools and paved courtyards, Kertes gestures expansively, in familiar lecturing mode. Conversation isn't really his style. Equality is the basis of conversation, and Stefan Kertes does not expect to meet many equals. – It's by Frank Lloyd Wright. He built several houses around here. This one was falling down, in great disrepair. So we were able to acquire it. Of course, it needed restoration. But, as you see, it was worth it. An historic building. And so suitable for our purposes! You know that Wright, too, tried to combine the spiritual with the physical. Do you know how he defined genius? As a man who understands what others only know about.

Clearly Kertes sees many parallels between himself and the Master.

They emerge into a garden room which looks across the canyon towards the skyscrapers of downtown. Like all the spaces in this house, it is low-ceilinged but grandly proportioned. Wright, who was very short, designed houses with himself in mind. It fits Kertes admirably: a taller man might feel less easy.

Helen says: – I can see spiritual and physical when you're an architect, but when you're a physicist? I've never seen the connection between God and physics. Surely investigation and faith are two different states of mind?

Kertes laughs. – Physicists are obsessed with religion! Who else cares about God these days.

– That's what worries me. Too many large thoughts. If you think about God too much, you're in danger of thinking you are God.

– Is that what Benny thought?

Helen shrugs. – It sometimes seems that's what you think.

– One can't help people who misapply what one says. Perhaps both Benny and I have suffered from this. The danger is to let yourself believe it. This, eventually, is what happened to Benny.

– You mean, you resist? Is that what you're saying?

He touches her shoulder. – Naturally you feel angry. You see that Benny is dead and I am still alive. But yes, I resist.

– Had you any idea how he was feeling? Or why?

– I've been thinking, of course, says Kertes. – There were indicators. If you notice the small things, you may help someone change direction in time to avert larger catastrophes. Last time Benny was here, he was accident-prone. He nearly slipped off the sidewalk in front of a car, he fell down the stairs. It looks like absent-mindedness, but didn't these moments perhaps express an inner desire which couldn't yet be admitted? If you are willing to look, you can read the message. I didn't do that. Should I blame myself? Of course, it's important to see only what's there, not what you want to see.

Perhaps Helen should apply this philosophy to her own life? She's been tripping over things a lot recently, though she put this down to distraction, her eyesight deteriorating perhaps. Middle age: things fall apart. Kertes, however, has no such reservations. He's so sure of himself, so certain he knows how things are. And, while he speaks, you believe him. Everything is illuminated, comprehensible, brilliantly clear. This is his great gift. In many, it induces an apparently insatiable desire to listen, to have him explain life, death and the universe till time itself ends. For a while, Benny was one of these listeners. He even learned the trick of it. But when, eventually, the silence and the fog descend, Helen feels only impatience, as though she has been deflected, against her will, from her own path.

They're in the garden now. It's terraced, with walls of hanging greenery. Another Frank Lloyd Wright dictum: *When all else fails, grow vines*. Evidently he took his own advice even in the event of success.

Helen wanders to the edge of the terrace and stares across at the towers of downtown Los Angeles, misted, as usual, by smog. Kertes talks on, but she isn't listening. She's thinking about turning-points, synchronicities, Benny and Kertes. As it happens, inextricably linked in her mind.

*

– I'm most frightfully sorry, says Richard Potter. He raises his eyebrows in that quizzical expression of helplessness which has become his trademark. The housewives' darling. And Helen's. – But what can I do?

Helen stares miserably into her hock and seltzer. How long has she been looking forward to this evening? Brute calculation says, not long. In fact, a week. He's known for a week that he'll be going to Brighton on this story; and that his wife will be away visiting her parents. Since he told her, she's scarcely been able to think of anything else. Oysters for dinner, a stroll along the seafront, champagne as they watch the sunset. And then! A night – a whole night – of exquisite, luxurious fornication, no questions asked, all expenses paid.

– Alex came back early, he says. – Decided she'd fancy a night in Brighton. Believe me, I'm as fed up about it as you are.

Is this possible? Helen decides that it is not. He gets the dinner, more or less congenial company, the seaside, and sex of some description. She gets the crestfallen return to the flat, explanations to her surprised flatmates, the lamb chop, the telly. And frustration. *She wants to go to bed with him* – now, all the time, but especially this evening.

Richard is a front-man on *Roundabout*, the current-affairs show for which Helen is a researcher-director. He's tall, blond, handsome and intelligent. Conceited, too, naturally, but that's by the bye. If you were going to reject people round here on grounds of conceit . . . Is it surprising she fell eagerly into his arms? The only small drawback was that he was married. But that's a minor consideration. Marriage is not on her agenda. You could almost say she's doing Alex a service. Richard would be unfaithful anyhow, with *someone*, and at least Helen isn't trying to lead him to the divorce court. Heaven forbid! The last thing she wants is to become Mrs Richard – a thankless role, as she well knows.

Sod it, she thinks. I'm through with being somebody's girl. She was Benny's, for a while, and that was wonderful while it lasted. But it came to an end. He left Cambridge a year before she did, and they lost touch. What was the alternative? To languish from a distance? She's her own woman now. Not anybody else's. Not Benny's. And certainly not Richard's.

So this is adultery, she thought, the first time she and Richard went to bed. But it felt just like any other brand of sex.

– That's that, then, isn't it, she says.

– Oh, Helen, don't be like that. Please don't. You can't imagine how much I want you, he mutters. Under the table his hand caresses her bare thigh, and creeps on upward until his thumb –

Helen wriggles out of reach, glancing scandalised around the crowded pub. – Richard, really! Stop it!

He giggles. – Sweetie, you can't wear a pussy-pelmet like that and not expect people to be tempted.

– You sound just like my mother.

Helen has had more than one altercation with Mrs Bartram regarding suitable working attire. Hemlines are high this year, and rising ever higher. Helen, who has excellent legs, wears her skirts so short that toning knickers have become a serious fashion necessity. – Really, darling, says Mrs B. – You can't expect people to take you seriously looking like that. What, then, given her age and the current fashion, is Helen supposed to look like? A two-million-year-old fossil? Is this the price of success?

– We'll have to work out something else, says Richard encouragingly.

– I suppose so. Helen glances at her watch. Weeks of evenings kept free on the off chance stretch bleakly ahead. – I must get back to the office. You coming?

– No, I've got to go into town.

Outside, Shepherd's Bush roars uninvitingly around them in the June sunshine. Richard flags down a cab; Helen picks her way disconsolately across the filthy pavements towards Lime Grove.

The office, as always, hums with urgency. *Roundabout* is a daily magazine show: possibly the most energy-intensive, nerve-destroying form of employment yet devised. Every thought, every action, is infused with breathless immediacy. The day funnels inexorably towards seven o'clock, transmission time. Crises bubble up, burst, are replaced by new crises. Interviewees evaporate, essential stories emerge, and painstakingly arranged features are killed without a second thought. Only time is at a premium: effort, by contrast, is deemed infinitely available. It's a maelstrom, and once sucked in, there's no escape. Where would one escape to? The outside world doesn't exist. Helen doesn't know whether she loves her work or hates it. All she knows is that it occupies every cell of her consciousness (except for those few dedicated to Richard).

She has hardly arrived at her desk when her phone rings. It's Nigel Collins, *Roundabout*'s editor. – I've been trying to get you for hours. Where've you been?

– Lunch.

– Well, never mind, Nigel says impatiently. Helen has never seen him eat, though she has definitely seen him drink. – You're here now. Can you come up a minute?

Out of the corner of her eye Helen watches the monitor in the corner of the room. It's relaying the recording now taking place: today's horoscopes. *Roundabout*'s resident astrologer, Emerald Cosgrove, is a fruity, bead-draped lady. It goes without saying that Helen doesn't believe in all that stuff. She not only knows it's rubbish, she's more than once seen Mrs Cosgrove cobble it together. Nevertheless, it remains horribly compulsive. – Aries, Emerald is saying. Helen listens with half an ear. She's an Aries, her birthday is in March. – Today is a day for decisions. Your planetary configuration, Venus and Mercury in the house of the Sun, indicates that this will be a day of beginnings and endings. Old friendships may come to an end, but new ones will begin. You may go on a journey, possibly to do with work. Contrary to what you may suppose, this will be a propitious day for you.

Propitious! Not so far. And, unfortunately, she can't see its complexion changing. The journey's been cancelled, too. Wrong again, Emerald.

– I'm due in the studio in ten minutes, she tells Nigel.

– What for? He sounds annoyed.

– Interview with Stefan Kertes. For tomorrow.

– Stefan Kertes? Who the hell's he?

– The astronomer.

– We've got one of those already. Doing her bit at this very moment. Don't you ever watch the programme? Nigel enquires testily.

– Not astrologer, astronomer. They're different, remember?

– No need to be sarcastic.

– Sorry. If you want to be exact, says Helen, continuing her tease, since she is perfectly aware that Nigel has not the slightest desire for exactitude, – Kertes is an astrophysicist. He's the one with the new theory of what goes on inside black holes.

– What the hell are they? No, don't tell me.

– I couldn't if I wanted to.

– Thank Christ for that. Look, what do we care about black holes? Drop them. I've got something really important for you.

– Nigel, I can't just drop this. Kertes is on his way. He's probably here already. He's extremely famous and extremely busy. I sweated blood to get him here.

– How long will this take?

– We should be through by – she consults her watch and does a quick sum in her head – three.

– Well, don't hang about, come up as soon as you're finished.

She puts the phone down, and it immediately rings again. – A Mr Curtis for you in reception.

The renowned Professor Kertes is a small, plump man, with wiry black hair springing out around a bald pate. The baldness makes him seem older than he really is: at this time, perhaps in his middle forties. Helen holds out her hand. – Professor Kertes? Helen Bartram. We've spoken on the phone.

He looks her up and down. Perhaps her mother was right about that dress after all. – What a pleasure to meet you, Miss Bartram. He has a strong central European accent faintly overlaid with American.

She shepherds him into the hospitality room, pours him a coffee, resists the temptation to help herself to a brandy and begins to explain what they're going to do. The phrases slip glibly out. The interview will probably be edited down to about three minutes. She hears herself say: – Actually, I know it's hard to believe this, but three minutes is quite a long time on television.

– Set against space and eternity, says Professor Kertes, three minutes or an hour, it makes very little difference. So, I shall give you the three-minute version. He flashes her a cheerful grin. Really, he's charming. She grins back.

– I'm afraid it's all a bit of a circus here.

– And you are the ring-master? Or should I say ring-mistress?

– A performing dog is more what it feels like, she assures him.

She ushers him into the studio, now empty of horoscopes. Sets up the interview, introduces the presenter who will be asking the questions, and hurries up to the gallery. Professor Kertes gives the three-minute account. Black holes, as he sees them. Or as he is beginning to see them. Maybe. How Helen envies him his measured uncertainties, marooned as she is in her island of urgency. In the view of Professor Kertes, black holes are tunnels leading to an infinity of other universes. Every universe that might ever have been, every possibility, has its existence inside these unimaginable densities. – This possibility is particularly delightful to physicists, he says, giving that charming smile, full of pure pleasure, – because it unites the very grand with the very small, the general theory of relativity with the quantum universe in which the behaviour of the very smallest particles stands the laws of classical physics, Newton's laws, on their head. An electron is a particle. But a famous experiment, the double-slit experiment, shows that it is apparently capable of being in at least two places at once. Impossible! But now perhaps we can say: each possible position of a particle exists inside its own universe!

– And will it be possible to visit these other universes sometime, Professor Kertes?

– Unfortunately we should first be torn to shreds by the gravitational forces. Though maybe, one day, it may be possible. Occasionally we perhaps glimpse them, even now. If we see a ghost, if a dream foretells the future – then perhaps we may say that the partition has slipped.

– And has this happened to you?

– Perhaps.

– But we can't be certain?

– Ah, this is the great question. Kertes chuckles. – Perhaps only God can know for certain. Unfortunately, he adds unconvincingly, (he, at least, is not convinced) – I am not God.

Helen descends from the gallery, thanks him, offers to call a taxi. She holds out a hand to say goodbye. He takes it in both his. – Miss Bartram, I have two tickets for the opera this evening, the conductor is an old friend. As it happens the person who was to accompany me is away. Do you perhaps enjoy opera?

For a moment Helen is tempted. He's an amusing fellow, and she could do with a little distraction. She almost asks which opera it is. Why not?

Why not, indeed. The opera – dinner – all this would inevitably be just a prelude. Delightful, possibly, but only half the story. If she accepts, she buys the whole deal. That, or a most undignified end to the evening. Does she want to become Professor Kertes' London friend? She tries to imagine him naked. This leads, by a process of association, to a picture of Richard in the same state. No. No, no, no. Unthinkable. She shakes her head. – It's very kind, I'd have loved it, but I'm afraid I'm not free this evening.

– What a pity, I too should have enjoyed it. You are not by any chance related to Professor John Bartram?

– Yes, he's my father.

– Yes, I thought so – you have a look of him. Well, then, perhaps we shall meet again.

His taxi has arrived. He pats her hand and relinquishes it. He departs.

Helen looks at her watch. Five past three.

Nigel's office is a psychological tip, even if his desk is kept comparatively clear by a band of dedicated secretaries. Panic reigns, lightly veiled. Every day is a formidable mountain, scaled in the knowledge that tomorrow will present only another peak in the same interminable range. Nigel's character is not well suited to his work. What is required is oceanic calm: dormancy, almost. Only such a state could sanely sustain the daily adrenalin input of this job. But Nigel is not calm. As a result he despairs; to the point where, in a year's time, he will jump from a tenth-floor window because he can't take the pressure any more. For the moment, however, he is still in charge.

– What kept you?

– I told you.

– You said three.

– For God's sake, it's only five past.

In the corner, the ubiquitous screen relays the latest news. And news is in plentiful supply this sunny June day. The Vietnam war is in full swing. Southern Africa seethes. Campuses everywhere are in revolt as the young reject the world handed down to them by their elders. On top of all this, a new French revolution appears to be in the offing. The citizens have risen up against General de Gaulle's Fourth Republic. Two million workers are on strike. Factories, public services, even the banks are paralysed. Money is running out: the economy is halted. No metro, no buses: Paris is choked with traffic. The young, meanwhile, reject the education system. Left-wing students have occupied the Sorbonne and the Odéon, where a continuous parallel parliament is being run. There is fighting in the streets between students and riot police. Barricades have been built. Trees have been cut down, iron railings torn up, chairs and tables seized from restaurants, cars overturned and set on fire. The police hurl tear gas at the students, the students lob petrol bombs at the police. They get the petrol from the pierced tanks of parked cars. The fighting moves from the left bank to the right, and back again. In Paris a student has died; in Lyon, a policeman. Right-wingers, including the ageing Josephine Baker, flanked by two paratroopers, have organised their own march in support of General de Gaulle and his government. He, meanwhile, has called a referendum. He spoke to the nation on camera, monumentally apostrophizing them: *Français! Françaises!* He demanded their confidence, enunciating gravely, unmoving as a statue. If they vote No, he will leave office. The outcome is uncertain. The Bourse was set on fire immediately the speech ended. If de Gaulle is rejected, the probable replacements appear to be either the Communists or the army; most likely, one followed swiftly by the other. Open-mouthed, the world watches the spectacle.

The central figure of the student uprising is a tubby redhead of German-Jewish extraction called Daniel Cohn-Bendit. He is known, on account of his politics and his hair, as Danny the Red.

– Cohn-Bendit's on the show tomorrow night, says Nigel. He sounds, for once, triumphant, as well he might. *Everyone* wants to talk to Danny. – We've got a half-hour extension.

– Fantastic! Where are we talking to him? He's not in Paris any more, is he?

– No, he left to spread the word and they wouldn't let him back into France. He's coming here.

– Will our lot let him in?

– I've negotiated a twenty-four-hour visa with the Home Office.

– When does he arrive?

– Four thirty at Heathrow. We'll record tonight, after the show. He'll be met, we'll bring him back here, and we won't let him out of our sight until the recording's finished. There've been death-threats already. After we've finished with him he can do what he likes. Nigel likes to pretend he's a hard man. Perhaps he is.

– Who's meeting him?

– You are.

– Me? But I'm not on this evening.

– You are now. There's no-one else free. Sorry and all that.

Oh, well, thinks Helen. At least I've already said goodbye to my night in Brighton. Perhaps this is the journey Emerald was talking about. She says: – You were lucky to find me here. I was planning to leave straight after the interview. I had something arranged, it's been fixed for ages.

– So?

– It fell through. As it happens.

Nigel is not interested in Helen's private life. If you want to work on *Roundabout*, you are not expected to have a private life. – I expect trouble, he says. – Immigration are bastards, they'll try and stop him even though the Home Office is fixed. I'm going to have to do a lot of talking. As soon as he comes out, I want him in the car and back here. Your job is to go to Heathrow and just wait for him.

– When?

– Now! It's already tight because of your bloody astronomer! Goodbye, and I'll see you back here with the cargo. He waves her away and is on the phone before she's reached the door.

At Heathrow, Helen sits and waits. And waits. Everything is on schedule; the car is poised in a special enclosure; the flight from Frankfurt arrived on time. But of Danny the Red, no sign. As Nigel anticipated, he has not emerged from Immigration. They took his passport and asked him to wait a minute. That was two hours ago. Nigel is here now, as well. First he tried arguing; now he is, as always, on the phone. He talks to the Home Office. He talks to the Director General of the BBC. The D.G. talks to the Home Office. The Home Office talks to Heathrow Immigration. The minutes tick by. Cohn-Bendit's due in studio in an hour. Helen wonders idly how the Kertes piece turned out. A mess, probably, since she wasn't there to edit it.

It's a hot night. She ought to be in Brighton now. Or at the opera, even. But instead she's stuck at bloody Heathrow waiting for a pudgy revolutionary. She must be mad.

Suddenly there's a flurry, and there he is, Danny himself! He's dyed his red hair black for some reason. Otherwise he's just like the photos. Round, cheerful and, unlike all around him, unruffled. A crowd of students, who got wind of his arrival and gathered to meet him, begins to cheer. He waves, and gives them a clenched fist salute. Helen runs forward, waving her BBC identification.

A familiar voice cries, – Helen!

She looks around. Surely it can't be – ? Here?

There are two friends with Danny: a girl and a man. And the man is – Benny! Unchanged, except that maybe he looks a little thinner, a little less kempt. Helen gasps, gives him a cursory wave, and turns to the task in hand. – The car's just waiting, Mr Cohn-Bendit. This way.

The four of them make their way through the lounge. Benny and the girl seem umbilically attached to Danny. The students press in towards them. Helen's entire being is concentrated upon getting her quarry into the car. Benny, meanwhile, keeps trying to ask questions. After the first shock, she wasn't really surprised to see him there. Where else would he be at a time like this?

At last they are in and rolling towards the studio. Helen sits in front with the driver; Danny, Benny and the girl are in the back. Danny chats to the girl. The driver radios that they're on their way. Benny says, – For Christ's sake, Helen! It is Helen, isn't it? Weren't we acquainted once?

– I'm sorry, she says. She feels absurd, cut off here in the front seat, but there wasn't room for four of them in the back. – It's all been a bit tense. What on earth are you doing here?

– Isn't it obvious? I'm with Danny. What are *you*?

– I work for this programme.

They look at each other, and laugh.

*

– The first time I met you, says Helen, you were already talking about synchronicities and multiple universes. You probably don't remember.

– Naturally I remember. It was a television programme. You wore a white dress, very sexy. When I met you again, I remembered at once. At that time, of course, he adds, – the multiple universe theory was quite new. Now it is almost clichéd.

– Doesn't it worry you, that people think you've gone over the top? The people you used to work with?

– They don't, he says gently. – Benny, yes. Not me. Did it worry him?

Helen sighs. – No, he didn't care. That was part of the problem. He didn't care about anything any more.

– Oh, I think you are wrong, Kertes says. They're both leaning against the terrace wall, looking across the smog-filled canyon. – He cared very much.

– What about?

– Power. Fame, money, but really power.

– And you don't care about any of that.

– Naturally, I'm not indifferent to these things. But my position is different. I find the idea of the quantum universe intellectually pleasing. I *like* to be uncertain whether Schrödinger's cat is or isn't dead, whether an electron is a wave or a particle, whether it will have momentum or position. I like this way of looking at the world.

– It's hardly new any more, though, is it?

– It may not be new, but its possibilities are still endless and mostly unexplored. That's what interests me. The point where physics meets other subjects. Psychology, for instance. Niels Bohr, who almost invented the quantum universe, told a story of how he once found that one of his children had done something terrible, but when it came to punishment, he couldn't do it. He said: You can't know someone in the light of love and the light of justice. That's the principle of complementarity. It applies at the visible level as much as the sub-microscopic. Things may seem to contradict each other, but the contradiction is only apparent. In the same way, psychology unites two apparently unrelated sides of us, the physical and the psychical. Dreams and synchronicities – to the psychologist they are symbolic. And also, perhaps, as I have so often said, gaps in the physical curtain. If one could in some way control these glimpses –

– Surely that's not possible?

– Why not? This is what we are working on, now. Nothing is impossible.

Helen shivers.

– Are you frightened by this?

– Yes.

– Why?

Is she going to spill her story to Kertes? Become an object of scientific curiosity? Hardly.

– It's too like religion, she says. – What you're talking about is the kind of power people worship. They're frightened of it. I don't like it when you turn maths into myths. She's thinking of Benny now, the irrational appeal of his books, which she so distrusts (and which are so lucrative). – Maths is transparent. But myths make everything fuzzy. People hide behind them. That always makes me uneasy. What are they hiding? Hitler was a myth, so was Stalin.

He stands before his symbol-filled blackboard as before an altar. Latter-day priest, theologian for the modern world. Behind him his text: the equations. He interprets the secrets of the universe, he alone can parse the Holy Book. What are these big bangs and singularities, these black holes and multiple universes and particles that occupy all possible positions, all possible states? These elaborate constructs of whose existence we are assured, but which we shall never experience? What but a myth for our time? Our creation myth. The physicists cite their proofs. Don't all priests, always? You can't visit a black hole to check it out any more than you could visit Olympus, or Heaven. What are those creationists, whom Benny hated so much? Stupid, misguided, ignorant – but more than anything, out of date. They are fossils (for which they adduce elaborate explanations). Their myths are outdated, but they won't accept change. They have to go. The world moves on.

Kertes says: – You want to demystify. As a scientist, I should support that. But perhaps we need the camouflage of the sacred in a secular world.

– Very Jungian.

Kertes laughs. – I was a patient of Jung. I was in Switzerland studying with Pauli, and I was paralysed. Mentally, that is. No concentration. Pauli was a friend of Jung, and Jung agreed to see me.

– What happened?

– For a long time, nothing. Then he released me from my paralysis. As it happens, with a synchronicity. I'd been fishing. It was the only thing I enjoyed in those days, the calm, the water, time passing. I was lucky for once: I caught a fine big trout. I meant to leave it at my hostess's house, but it was later than I thought, so I went on to Jung's with the fish in its basket.

– When I came into his study, I saw a book on the lectern. It was open at a page with pictures of fish and fish symbols. Then Jung came in. He said, I am making a study of fish symbolism, I have become particularly interested in it. And I see that you, too, have been studying this, in a more concrete form! His daughter, in honour of his current interest, had just presented him with a fish embroidery. He fetched it to show me. He said, Synchronicity has shown us your symbol. Now perhaps we shall get somewhere!

– And did you?

– Yes. From then on, he was able to help me come to terms with my fear.

– Which was?

– Nothing so unusual. My family left behind in Vienna. They died, I survived. I felt guilt, paralysing guilt. But I learned to admit it, to admit what was hidden as well as what was visible. Jung was open to hidden forces. You know the story of his visit to Freud? They disagreed about spiritualism. Freud thought it was nonsense, Jung believed in it. And Jung had this curious sensation, as if his diaphragm was made of iron and was becoming red-hot. At that moment, there was such a loud report in the bookcase next to them that they both jumped up. They were afraid it was going to fall on them. Jung said, There you are, there's an example of a phenomenon. And Freud said, What nonsense. So Jung said, It is not nonsense! I predict that in a moment there will be another loud report just like that! And there was.

– So?

– So, strange things happen.

– You mean, Jung produced these sounds by, I don't know, displaced energy?

– It would seem so.

– And you believe this?

– Why not? Jung was a truthful man, in my experience.

– But there are a thousand ways of getting effects like that!

Kertes is suddenly angry. – You're saying he faked it? Excuse me, but if I have to choose between Jung and you, I choose Jung. You think you're above all that, beyond all that, that you alone can see fraud where no-one else has seen it? That you're the only one without hidden motives? It's what we were talking about before.

Why do these ideas frighten you so much? Ask yourself that! He adds softly, almost to himself: – And even if he did fake it, does that make what he has to say any less valuable?

For the thousandth time, Helen's mind returns to that glimpse of Laura. She hasn't told anyone except Patrick. And he dismissed it, so she said no more. They'd all think the same: that she was hallucinating, having a breakdown. But she wasn't. There must be an explanation. Kertes would say, a rent on the curtain, a glimpse of another universe. But who is the brown-haired woman, that version of herself when young? And what was she doing at the funeral? She says: – Isn't manipulation more probable than magic?

Kertes says tightly: – Don't be so ready to dismiss what you can't explain. It doesn't mean there's no explanation. He looks at his watch – I think we should have some lunch.

They walk back to the house, along one of those cloister-like loggias. A woman is walking towards them. She is tall, slender, with glossy, dark hair cut in a long bob. Helen stares at her, transfixed. She draws level with them.

– Helen, isn't it? She speaks evenly, the crisp South African vowels almost buried but still just discernible. – I hardly recognised you. What are you doing in LA? Just visiting?

But Helen can't reply. Her breath has left her. For a minute, it's as if someone had punched her in the stomach.

It's Lorraine.

5

– BUT YES, SAYS Kertes. Lorraine is our administrator. She has been with us for years. It was she who first suggested we should invite Benny. Didn't he tell you?

Helen is beset by an odd but familiar sensation. She speaks the words, executes the business, but someone else (who?) is pulling the strings. Occasionally a glimpse is afforded: another of those rents in the curtain? At any rate, a sudden revelation of what goes on behind the scenes.

This sensation of powerlessness is only intermittent. Anything more would surely be a definition of insanity. The life she led with Benny and (later) the children was mostly what it seemed: open, visible to all. Naturally, it had its complications. But they were straightforward complications: illnesses, disagreements, social contretemps, financial crises. Psychologists may disagree about the ultimate causes of such occurrences, but, generally speaking, they are not mysterious.

Periodically, though, Benny plunged beneath this surface. A sense of mysterious urgency would descend. There would be unexplained comings and goings. Things had to happen here rather than there, now rather than then. All of a sudden, he wouldn't be back till late, if at all; couldn't go out tomorrow night, talk to the teacher, make the party, see the family. Helen's life – their supposedly joint life – became simply a front for other, more important activities.

– But we arranged it weeks ago!

– Sorry. Not possible.

He raises his hands, shakes his head ruefully, and goes on with whatever he happens to be doing.

Helen fumes. But fumes in silence.

Silence? Why? Shouldn't she express her resentment? Shouldn't they have it out? For if you take the agony-aunt view of life, there can be only one explanation for all this. He's having an affair, and *she* is back in town.

In a sense this was true. But Helen's rival on these occasions was not a person. It was politics. How could she complain at Benny's commitment to a set of principles with which she herself so totally agreed? The struggle in South Africa was part of his baggage. She knew that, had always known it. That, paradoxically, was one of the aspects of Benny she most admired.

She knew, too, that this particular cause was not one in which activism could be lightly undertaken. Brought up on a diet of more or less preposterous espionage fantasies, it's hard for the respectable middle-classes of Europe and America to believe that there really do exist worlds where surveillance, assassination, torture, kidnappings are mere everyday realities. But Benny entered one when he joined the ranks of those fighting the South African government. Offices *were* fire-bombed, activists *were* maimed and killed, routinely inside South Africa, but also outside it. Careless talk *did* cost lives.

Helen was not part of this world. And – first and last rule of clandestine politics – the less you know, the less you can give away. Benny did not volunteer information, and she did not ask for it. But, naturally, there were things she couldn't help being aware of. You can't live with someone for twenty-five years and not have some idea whom they are seeing, where they go, what (more or less) they do when they get there. The knowledge seeps in osmotically, even if it's never directly imparted. And this – the shadowy world of the undivulged – was Lorraine's fiefdom. In the twilight, she reigned. The agony aunts weren't entirely off the mark. Politics were politics, but they had a face: *She* who must be obeyed.

What did Helen know about Lorraine? That she was Benny's girlfriend in Johannesburg. That she was married and divorced. That her father was wealthy. That she was sometimes in London on business. What business? What went on in London between her and Benny? Was she part of the network? If Helen tried to enquire, Benny shook his head and talked about other things. Helen felt reproved. Rightly reproved.

Occasionally, they met. For Helen, these encounters were puzzling and disturbing. She couldn't help feeling that Lorraine was not merely informed about her life, but actually knew more about it than Helen herself. A one-sided arrangement, since of Lorraine, Helen knew virtually nothing.

This sense of being at a disadvantage did not arise from any particular incident or remark. It was more a question of relative positioning – as though Lorraine stood always with her back to the light, while Helen was illuminated in every particular. She had a habit of patronizing through compliments, offering kind advice with un-British frankness. – Helen, she said once, (they'd hardly met, the impertinence of it took Helen's breath away), – you have such a turn of phrase, such a way of saying things. You should try writing. Had you thought of that? You could really make something of yourself. Another time (when the twins were two years old and domestic help scarce, when Helen was continuously on the edge of fury and Benny more than usually absent on tasks of overwhelming importance): – You don't do yourself justice, Helen. You could really get somewhere if you put a bit more effort into your appearance.

Lorraine smiles kindly. Helen meditates murder.

But these chance encounters didn't count. They were part of what was overt, and therefore insignificant. Lorraine's real impact upon Helen's life was managed more appropriately, at a remove, through shadows. And, as was only appropriate, Lorraine herself never knew about it.

*

Helen has left *Roundabout*. She thought, Why am I doing this? and the doing at once became impossible. That life was predicated upon total immersion. The slightest detachment revealed its madness: the driven, overblown television universe within which, like hamsters on a wheel, they raced their lives away. The unrelenting pressure drove Nigel Collins to suicide. He jumped out of a window just before the morning conference. Why? What for? A *television programme*?

So she left; and is now a freelance journalist, selling pieces where she can. Is this any better? Definitely worse, in terms of status and of making a living. But how she enjoys not going to the office, not feeling herself available for infinite use! Yet people fight for the kind of job she's quit. Clearly they're made of different stuff.

What now? Colette's in no doubt. They're approaching thirty: time for reproduction. No sooner said than done. Between two roles she had her first baby, Declan; and, eighteen months later, Gemma. A boy and a girl. Perfect. And now she's free again, equipped with a nanny, snapped back into shape, and just about to start a new film.

The Costelloes live in London now, a few doors from Benny and Helen. Why did they suddenly leave Huddersfield? They won't talk about it, the whole thing is very unclear. It was traumatic, that much is obvious. Patrick's lost a certain nonchalance that used to be one of his great attractions. The golden boy's disappeared, and been replaced by the second drawing in one of those strips that used to promote life insurance, the one with the first few lines on the forehead. He keeps saying how he enjoys the babies, how he's always wanted a real family with lots of kids, but actually he isn't much around the nursery. Or around the house. He's got a job in the BBC drama department. They've given him his head – they're so pleased to have him, they hope he'll bring in lots of bright new writers, just like he did at Huddersfield. He's decided he doesn't like working in studio, and consequently spends most of his time filming in remote locations. Nothing, it seems, can keep him in London. Doesn't he like it? Perhaps that was one reason he went to Huddersfield in the first place. From time to time he reappears, then takes off again. He's just been up in the Western Isles, shooting some crofting epic. Meanwhile the Costelloe household is held together by the nanny, Monica.

Success, success. Everywhere you look, success.

Benny, for example. He's getting very well-known, surprisingly so: one doesn't generally connect zoology with fame. Just recently he's been attracting a lot of attention as a leading warrior in the battle against creationists, those madmen in the Bible Belt who want children taught that the world was literally created by God in seven days. He writes a monthly column in *Science* which has attracted a lot of attention – it's so full of new thinking, so clearly and provocatively written. When the court cases came up, he was one of the first people they approached to testify. Naturally, he jumped at the opportunity. These aren't just any old religious maniacs, any more than Benny is any old common or garden atheist. Benny, who pours his articulate, unanswerable scorn on any world-view tending even mildly to the mystical, hates them with a hatred that is itself almost religious, a hatred so extreme (though couched in terms of unrelenting reason) that even Helen is sometimes shocked.

After that surprising meeting at Heathrow, Benny and Helen fell into each other's arms once more. Now they are married. Fate pointed the way: they had only to follow. Benny, hesitating between politics and academe, decided for scholarship. He took a research job in London.

It's a good marriage. They enjoy each other's company and share each other's views. If their passion is less wild, more muted now (and after six years, isn't that inevitable?), the space is filled by liking: a more durable quality, one less easily come by. He makes her laugh and never, ever bores her. She can only hope he would say the same. One of Helen's many worries just now is that she is becoming dull. Suddenly, her mind is stuck in a single track. For she, too, is trying to get pregnant, but she's not succeeding.

Benny is many things to many people: among them, potential father of Helen's children. This role is at the centre of her current world-view, but (she suspects) peripheral to his. Every time they have sex, she pictures the great race. Get set, you millions of sperm. One, two, three – ecstasy! A waft of orgasmic contractions speeds them on their way. Which is to be the lucky fellow? Which wriggling little creature will be first up the tubes and into that egg, hanging ripely there? While Benny sleeps, Helen lies wakeful, breath bated, wondering. And back comes the report, bang on time, every month, written in red ink. Must try harder. Better luck next time.

O, that red message! Doomed if you don't get it, doomed if you do. In the good old days it signified: Saved again. Then, its non-appearance was what made Helen's blood run cold. Twice she had to take urgent action. Now, though, she greets it with a dull and sinking heart. She wants to suggest that they take advice, perhaps visit a clinic. But she hesitates. Doesn't want to seem neurotic. She can't help suspecting that Benny's priorities, at this moment, are different from hers.

The phone rings. It's him.

– Helen? I'm at the publications office. I'm afraid I'll be late tonight.

From time to time Benny does some work for South African Defence and Aid, an organisation which arranges legal representation for opponents of the regime and support for their families. This work is highly secret and often dangerous. Money must be smuggled across the border; contact must be made with banned families, who are forbidden to receive visitors. These activities are never mentioned over the phone. Defence and Aid also produces publications, a front to cover the real work. Benny won't specify, even to Helen, the exact nature of what he does there. His father is one of the lawyers regularly used by the organisation. Helen finds this admirable, but Benny scoffs.

– Don't waste your sympathy, he's making a packet out of it.

– It's pretty dangerous, even so. Most people wouldn't touch it.

– That's true, but charity begins at home, believe me. If you saw their house, you'd realise.

Helen hasn't seen it, because Benny and Helen do not visit South Africa. For Benny to make such a visit would be highly inadvisable. She's met his parents, of course: they come over to London from time to time. She has to agree that you wouldn't take Mr Spiro for a hero or a revolutionary. He just seems like a clever, prosperous, normally (that is to say, not excessively) liberal Jewish lawyer. And this is exactly what he is. It is a measure of the regime's madness that such a person can be considered threatening.

– How late is late?

– Don't wait dinner.

He rings off. Helen rests her chin on her hands. She ought to pull herself together. Ring a friend, fix something for the evening, get on with an article. This morning the editor of one of her more lucrative, less challenging outlets called. It's a magazine featuring the home lives of current TV stars. He said, – Did you once tell me that Colette Bosanquet's a friend of yours?

– That's right.

– Will you talk to her for us? She's the heroine in the new le Carré serial. A thousand words. Plenty of colour. The house, the kids. You know the kind of thing.

She could have said no. But that's not so easy when you're freelancing. You have to sell an awful lot of pieces to make a decent living. Once you start saying no, they stop calling you. There are plenty of people out there only too happy to say yes.

Anyway, what's so terrible about doing an interview with Colette for *TV Life*?

Helen drifts into a daydream about another world in which it is she, Helen, who is the sought-after interviewee. It is a regular daydream: she is well-acquainted with this alternative Helen. She, too, is a writer, but not of pieces for *TV Life*. She writes plays. Why plays? Helen has never written a play. But that's how she always pictures herself, the ideal Helen, the Helen of her dreams. She sees life in theatrical terms. Scenes present themselves.

So why doesn't she write them? It isn't as if there's some career path she's missed which leads to playwriting. She doesn't have to agonize, if I'd done this instead of that . . . All she need do is – do it.

But, firstly, a scene is not a play. Far from it. And secondly –

Yes, secondly?

Secondly, and thirdly and fourthly, she just can't. She's tried, and she can't. She cannot do it. She sits down in front of the typewriter and nothing happens. Every time the same thing. Nothing.

She dials Colette's number. Monica answers. Colette is out.

– When will she be back?

– I'm not sure.

– I'll call again, then.

Helen resents Monica. Her contacts with Colette these days are always mediated. Monica guards the audience chamber, decides which messages to pass on, who will be admitted, who left dangling. Monica is jealous of her power, and of Helen. There's too much past history there in which she played no part. Her relationship with

Helen is adversarial. Helen hates this sensation, that they are fighting over Colette. She feels it demeans her. She suspects, though, that Colette enjoys it. Another of her power plays. Round every corner, power-mad women.

Helen dropped in at the Defence and Aid office the other day – she happened to be passing. Benny was deep in conversation with an extremely beautiful woman, slender, olive-skinned, with long, shining black hair and that effortless-seeming casual elegance which is really the result of prolonged concentration and unlimited expense. She gave Helen a sharp look, as if Benny was her turf and Helen the intruder. Benny said, – Helen, this is Lorraine Margulies. An old friend from back home. Lorraine, my wife Helen.

They shook hands. *An old friend from back home*. Helen thought, How can I compete? She said: – Are you just visiting or are you here permanently? As nonchalant as she could make it.

– Oh, I come and go. You know how it is.

Lorraine reminds Helen of all the Bennies she doesn't know. What happened to the Paris Benny, the African Benny? Did they fade away or do they still, somewhere, flourish? She has her own hidden selves, of course, but they feel, by contrast, insignificant. She can't imagine Benny being troubled by them. Their existence doesn't cross his mind.

Presumably Lorraine's the reason Benny's going to be late this evening, in her guise of overriding political necessity. He's been living in Europe fourteen years now, but he still looks back longingly to the lost paradises of his youth. The sun, the beaches, the good life. Lorraine is part of that sun-soaked Eden dream. What has mere reality to offer by comparison?

The phone rings. It's Colette. Monica passed on the message for once. Helen explains about the ridiculous *TV Life* commission. Colette is obviously delighted. Being a celebrity pleases her. She says, – Why not come round now and get it over with?

Since the Costelloes moved round the corner, the four of them have become very close again – not just the two women, but Benny and Patrick as well. Odd currents flow back and forth, not necessarily where you might expect them. Between Helen and Patrick there's an absolute sexual indifference, although they are the best of friends. And although Benny ogles Colette, it's probably more a game than anything else. Everyone ogles Colette – why not him? (In the twenty minutes Helen's been in the house, the phone has rung four times, each time with some adoring male at the other end. You can tell by the way Colette talks, as well as by what she says.) But the way Patrick sometimes looks at Benny – and the way Benny meets his look . . . What went on at Liberty Hall when Helen wasn't there – before Benny knew her, or even afterwards? How about the confidence with which he told her: He doesn't like women? How did he *know*? *She* knows, meanwhile, that Benny assumes there was something between herself and Colette. Patrick hints (or so Benny says) that Colette's got quite a reputation in that department. In fact Helen has never been attracted to women, but now, looking at Colette, the piquant profile tenderly turned towards the baby, the long eyes, the thick, fine blonde hair, the curl of a smile at a corner of the long mouth – she can suddenly see how it could happen –

But that is not what she wants. What she wants is friendship, the old equality. Not to be a lover, a poor relation, a supplicant, a friend of the famous. When they're actually together, as now, they fall into the old, easy ways. Sometimes, though, the sense of grievance grows until it threatens to obscure everything else. Is Colette so secure in her multiple fulfilments that she simply doesn't sense the envious darkness that fills Helen's soul? Envy does little for friendship. Helen particularly hates this aspect of her present life.

They sit in Colette's kitchen drinking tea, while Declan bangs around his playpen and Gemma sucks at her bottle.

– Still no luck? Colette says. She is the one person who knows all about Helen's travails with – rather, without – the baby.

Helen shakes her head and shuts her mouth firmly to keep back sudden tears. Colette's offhand kindness, contrasting so cruelly with all that petty resentment, not only shows her up but shows how far she has sunk. If she's not careful, this will fuel yet more resentment, and so interminably on until all friendship, all affection, is used up.

– About this interview, Colette says. – We don't really need to do one, do we? I mean, you know what goes on here as well as I do.

– I think they want quotable quotes.

– Oh, God. Come on, then.

Helen brings out her tape-recorder. Declan, who has been rattling the bars of his cage, at once starts to bawl for attention. Simultaneously, Gemma pushes her bottle away and shouts in counterpoint. Colette says: – She's tired. Hang on, I'll just get her changed and down. Can you keep an eye on Dec? I told Monica she could have the rest of the day off.

Helen is left facing the baby. She doesn't know anything about babies: being the youngest, she never had to hold or play with one. She hasn't the first idea what to do with Declan. Gingerly she approaches the playpen and says, – Hello!

Declan is a beautiful child, blond, blue-eyed, just like his parents. She can suddenly see, with absolute certainty, what he's going to look like in twenty years. Exactly like Patrick when she first knew him. Helen sometimes wonders if Patrick's absences reflect a sense that he's played his part in Colette's scheme of things, and that henceforth he's *de trop*. She's established her career, she's got her babies: she can manage on her own now, thanks all the same.

No, that's unfair. Envy doing its horrid stuff again.

Helen can't think of a thing to say or do. Should she release Declan from the playpen? Will he wreak mayhem? She is immediately and wholly bored at the prospect of having to spend fifteen minutes alone with an almost-two-year-old. She can't help seeing the funny side of it. Here, in the abstract, she pines for a baby – and what happens when faced with one in the actual flesh? She can't wait to be released. People always say: It's different when it's your own. Let's just hope so.

After an eternity, Colette returns. – Everything OK? she says, lifts Declan onto her lap and sniffs him suspiciously. – Oh, God, he needs changing, too. Come on up. You sure you still want a baby?

They climb the stairs to the nursery floor Colette had built at the top of the house: a room for the children, a nanny's room, a tiny bathroom. Helen watches while Colette deftly cleans and changes Declan, pats his small bottom and sets him down on the toy-littered floor. They stand watching as he contentedly hits a toy rabbit with a brick. Colette says, – It's the nape of their neck I think's so wonderful.

– Mm.

Colette giggles. – Every time you feel the blues coming on, all you need do is walk round here and take a look at the real thing. Seriously, though, I've been wanting to have a talk.

– Oh, yes?

– You don't have enough distraction, says Colette. – Now you don't have a proper job, you just sit home moping. It makes you tense. Think how easy it was when you didn't give it a thought, except to hope to God you'd got away with it. One fuck was all it took.

– What do you suggest? Relaxing massage? I really don't think I could bear to go back to television. And I don't think Benny's in the mood to go through hoops to find out if it's him. What good would that do, anyway?

– No, but *TV Life*! Come on! You're so talented, Helen. You've got to start doing something that's worthy of you. The telly job wasn't right, I can see that, but nor's this. Look – what d'you really want to do? What d'you fantasise about?

Helen is touched by this unprecedented abnegation. She didn't think Colette realised other selves existed, these days. She says: – Writing plays. I've told you before.

– So write a play. What's stopping you?

– I sit down at the typewriter and nothing happens.

– Don't you have an idea *before* you sit down?

– I think I do, but then it turns out I don't. The act of sitting seems to evaporate it.

Colette considers this. – Well, she says finally, – why not try and work out a framework. Give yourself some constraints. Why not try a television play? Half an hour, forty-five minutes? Cast of three, four at most. At least you know a director, and an actress.

– What should I write about? Helen asks hopelessly.

– God, I don't know. This is your play, not mine. What's bugging you? Write about what's bugging you. I wouldn't try the state of the nation first off. Look, says Colette, – I'm worried about you. I'm seriously going to take you in hand. In a month's time we'll meet and you've got to have the outline of a play to show me. It needn't be long, and not too many characters. And there's got to be a nice part for me.

What's bugging me? Helen asks herself, as she lets herself and her tape-recorder back into her empty house and starts on her thousand words for *TV Life*. She lists the items on a piece of scrap paper:

1) No baby
2) C's success
3) Lorraine

As usual, she can't see a play there.

She switches on the television, as much for company as for any other reason. It's the nine o'clock news. There's a demo going on outside South Africa House. The cameras pan across the crowd. And there – yes! – is Benny. And, beside him, Lorraine. Helen stares at the screen. It's them. No question about it. And – isn't his arm around her shoulder? She cranes forward. The camera cuts to another shot.

Helen finds she is trembling and sweating. She feels hot and cold. Is it shock? No: it's anger. Blind fury.

Suddenly, she knows exactly what her play's going to be about. It'll be a farce – a farce about a man, his wife and his mistress. The wife wants a baby but can't conceive; the mistress doesn't want one, but finds herself pregnant; and the man doesn't want one at all. The mistress is called Lauren. It may be unwise, but there it is. That's her name. She's going to be a bitch, a clever, funny bitch. It's going to be a wonderful part. Colette will adore it.

When Benny lets himself in long after midnight, she's hard at it, scribbling and shifting pieces of paper around.

– Work, work, work. What's so urgent? He sounds more cheerful than for some time. Is it because he's glad to see her absorbed in work again? Or does she owe this to Lorraine? If so, it's the second service Lorraine's performed for her this evening.

– I'm writing a play. How was the office?

She does not mention seeing him on the news.

– There was a panic, he says shortly. – I'm bushed.

Not long after this incident, there *was* a panic in the publications office. A trusted member of the team turned out to have been a spy, passing on information to the S.A. police. And where there is one spy, may there not be others? Who, in the end, can really be trusted? The old girlfriend, the vamp? What better infiltrator? Unoriginal, maybe, but undeniably effective. How can anyone be certain? Benny worried about unidentified packets in the mail. Helen worried about Lorraine. And then things subsided, and life went on as before.

Helen did not mention her suspicions to Benny. Quite apart from the regular putdown – Look, this is not your bag. You just don't know about this stuff, OK? – there would be all those other undercurrents. Why should Helen suddenly attack Lorraine? Because she's jealous, that's why.

But grateful.

The play was a great success.

*

The old distrust has not subsided.

They are sitting in Lorraine's garden, sipping chilled white wine. It turns out that Lorraine lives at Synchrony – not actually in the house, but in a sort of garden-house, which may or may not have figured in the original plan. At any rate, they grew vines. At a passing glance you wouldn't even realise it was there. And behind it is a tiny courtyard, brick-paved and lushly planted, hidden, private. There's a table, a couple of chairs and a swinging seat. Lorraine swings, one elegant leg folded beneath her, one toe on the ground.

– I somehow thought you lived in Venice.

– I used to. Years ago.

Helen can't think what to say. She was looking for Lorraine, wasn't she? Wasn't that her first idea? But, as so often, now she's where she aimed to be, she finds herself at a loss. It's all too sudden. When Lorraine asked her for a drink, her immediate reaction was to say no. And what sort of reaction was that? Clumsy, boorish, panic-stricken – the very character into which these encounters always seem to thrust her. What could be more normal, more civilised, than this invitation, what ruder, stupider, more cowardly, than its rejection? Helen pulls herself together, smiles, and accepts.

It's a pleasant place. Delightful. Is this where he came? After Laura? Was this his bolt-hole?

*

The most difficult thing to believe is the reality of Laura's non-being. She seems always on the brink of appearance; and then they remember.

Benny says: – We could have another. D'you want to try?

– I'm forty-three, Helen says. Even if I got pregnant at once, I'd be forty-four when it was born. And I wouldn't, it took ages last time. I can't face all that again. I just don't have the energy. She adds: – And it wouldn't bring Laura back.

He shakes his head. – If that's how you feel.

At night they clutch each other, desperate for comfort. Perhaps they'll find it in the warmth of each other's body? But all they can find in each other is loss and grief and anger – the anger each of them feels, can't help feeling, at cruel fate, but also at the other. Helen, who blames herself for Laura's death (*if only, if only*) feels that Benny blames her, too – as, indeed, he does. As she, in her turn, blames him. If he hadn't decided to waltz off to California, if he hadn't been so vain, so ambitious, if they'd just gone on with their old life – that happy, settled life, the life they still had only a year ago – Laura might be with them now. These thoughts torture them, day and night.

Of course, none of this may be said. Over the marmalade, they stare bleakly at each other. Peering across the chasm, they exacerbate each other's grief.

As for Timmy, who can tell what goes on inside his head? He gets on with his life. He goes to school, he sees his friends. He says very little. What is there to say? He asked Helen: – Mummy, d'you think Laura's in heaven? – Sweetie, she said, – there's no such a place as heaven. It's just a story to help people get through times like this. She's dead. She's just stopped, except in our memories.

Benny says: – How can you say that to him? He's only a child. He *needs* stories to help him get through. *I* need them, for Christ's sake.

She can hear the rage in his voice. Benny is consumed with anger these days: it's what keeps him going. At Laura's funeral he said to Patrick: – Christ, I wish I could kill the bastard that did it! I tell you, if I got my hands on him . . .

Patrick flinched. He said: – He probably feels as bad as you do.

Benny said: – I don't think so. One can always hope, I suppose.

For Helen, Timmy is a consolation. She's still got him, at least. But not for Benny. He can't bear the sight of Tim these days. He doesn't say anything, of course. But Helen, and no doubt Tim, can hear the words. They don't have to be spoken out loud. Why couldn't it have been you? Why Laura? Why not you?

One evening she can bear it no longer. She says: – We can't go on like this. Why don't you go back to California? We'll all be happier.

– But what will you do?

– I'll get on with my work.

– D'you think you'll be able to?

Helen has already tried, once or twice, to take up the play she was writing when Laura died, but she can't seem to do anything with it. It's like the old days. She sits at her desk and can't think. Can't bring herself to care what happens to her characters.

– I'll try and get some episodes for a soap. I was talking to someone the other day. That'll ease me back into it.

– Well, says Benny, – if you think you'll really be all right.

It's clear he can't wait to get away, away from this house of memories, back to the sunshine: back to another world.

*

– More wine?

Lorraine leans over, holding the bottle. She's wearing a bright yellow shirt which sets off her olive skin. Helen could never wear that colour, though she's always wanted to.

– Helen, I want to know about Benny. Can you bear to talk about it? He was my oldest friend. We knew each other for ever.

– Yes.

– He comitted suicide, is that right?

– Yes. I found him.

– Oh, God. I'm sorry. That must have been so awful . . . But do you have any idea why? He never seemed suicidal to me. Not recently. Of course I know about Laura, but that was years ago.

– Yes.

– Did he leave a note, or anything?

– Not that explained much.

– And nobody's found out anything?

– No. Well, there was one thing. An accusing note creeps into Helen's voice: she can't help it. – Something about his current scientific interests. I think that was the phrase.

– You sound very hostile.

– I feel hostile. Helen wonders whether Lorraine is aware quite how hostile, and why. – I think it's crap. Absolute crap. I didn't know whether to laugh or cry when I realised what direction he was going. He was always so much the other way – and then all this semi-mystical stuff dressed up as science and intellect. Poor Benny. Caught in his own bind. He found he needed the consolations of religion, and he could hardly admit that, could he? So he had to dress them up as something else. I suppose it was lucky for him in a way that he happened to be working here when it happened.

– Why?

– It offered a ready-made escape-route, didn't it? This stuff of his only started after Laura died.

– You make it sound as though he went soft in the head. But lots of people are interested in what he was thinking about, you know. Lorraine sounds severely disapproving. Helen reminds herself that they are in Southern California, a place where mere parallel universes, mere virtual resurrections, epitomise restraint and sanity.

– So I understand. The words emerge clipped and cold, naked. But what more is there to say?

Sunlight filters through the greenery. Lorraine gently swings herself back and forth, balancing on the tip of a toe. They stare into their glasses of wine, avoiding each other's eyes.

– He must have found it hard when he went back to England. Working in such a hostile environment.

– It was his choice. He didn't have to stay.

– That's true. Lorraine sips thoughtfully, abstractedly. What's she thinking about now? Benny? Helen? In Lorraine's life, what part does Helen play? Once again she feels hijacked, part of someone else's schema.

Behind Lorraine, inside the little house, someone is moving about. Helen says, – Who's that?

Lorraine glances round. – It's the girl that helps with the cleaning.

– Is it easy to find help round here? The universal preoccupation of middle-class women. Helen latches onto it with relief.

– The staff get help from some of the people here.

– What, at Synchrony? In lieu of fees or something?

– Something like that.

– What d'you do here, exactly? Are you a scientist?

– A psychotherapist. I thought you knew that?

– But I thought this was a sort of think-tank. A learned institute.

– I help with the admin. Didn't Stefan tell you? Anyhow, it isn't *just* a think-tank. We get some strange types here. We seem to have become a sort of staging-post on the route to salvation, for some people.

– Can't you choose who comes?

Lorraine shrugs. – Things develop the way they develop. If people want to learn, we try to help them. You have to go with the flow.

– I hate that phrase.

– Maybe that's your problem. What about your son? There was a little boy as well, wasn't there? How's he taking things?

– Not so little, these days. Tim. He's OK. He and Benny were never particularly attached. Perhaps it's something between fathers and daughters.

– Really? I sometimes saw Ben with a friend's son who happened to be over. Declan. Nice-looking boy. They seemed very close. But perhaps it's different with your own.

Declan? Benny never said anything about seeing him here. Not to her. When was Dec in LA? Wasn't it when he was supposed to have vanished? Colette was beside herself. Even through the mists of her own preoccupations, Helen registered that much. And then they found him and brought him back. Helen never knew the exact details.

– Well, there you go, she says uninformatively.

– It's funny, says Lorraine, – I was always so envious of you, with your family life.

Helen is oddly touched by this, perhaps because it's so unexpected. She would never have imagined Lorraine envying anyone. She seems so bullet-proof, so self-sufficient.

– Didn't you ever have children?

– No, I never got round to it. And then it was too late.

Helen shrugs. – They aren't the only thing in life. Thank God.

– No. They're not.

A girl puts her head round the door. – Anything else you need?

– No, that's fine. Lorraine raises a dismissive hand: barely acknowledges the girl. Helen recalls her awkward exchanges with Mrs Martins, so consciously matey, so filled with ambivalence. Evidently Lorraine has none of that pinko guilt around servants. Perhaps this is one of the results of growing up in South Africa. Benny was the same – Helen's mother remarked on it more than once. Helen smiles at the girl. Old habits die hard. Lorraine's face remains expressionless.

– Does Stefan live on the premises too?

– Sometimes. He has an apartment.

Lorraine stands up, stretches, finishes the wine remaining in her glass. Glances at her watch. She's had what she wanted (and what was that?) out of this conversation. – I'd better be getting back. You must come again.

As though she owns the place.

Why didn't Patrick tell her Lorraine was at Synchrony? Had he forgotten? Didn't he know? Driving back, Helen reflects on the unsaid, the unseen, the unperceived. Nothing is solid, nothing is what it seems. The very road beneath her seems to shift and ripple as she drives.

When she gets back, Patrick says: – Did you feel the earthquake?

– What?

– There was an earthquake. Only a small one, he adds reassuringly. – But the big one'll come sooner or later. It's only a matter of time. Better get back to London quick before it happens.

*

Venice, 16 September

Benny dear,

I've been thinking about what you said the other day, and I can't

134

do it. I'm sorry. Part of me would like to, more than anything. But I just can't.

You'll want to know why not. Well, there are an awful lot of reasons. To do with you, to do with me, and, believe it or not, to do with Helen.

Let's take the last first. You know what I feel. But that's how things worked out. By the time we met again it was too late. And whatever I feel, I couldn't want to make her suffer more than she's suffering already. Could you?

Then you. Benny, you've got to find your own way through this. Clinging to fantasy isn't going to do it for you. And under these circumstances, it's not what I'd want. The moment passed. There would always be that shadow hanging over us. What a way to start a new life! It would be all wrong.

It was too late for us one way in London. And it's too late again now. For all sorts of reasons, too late. I don't imagine I need to spell them all out. This is painful enough without that.

That's the story of our life, I guess.

With love from Lorraine.

*

Benny sits on the white chair, looking through vine shadows at Lorraine, who is on the swing. He is holding a glass. He is trying not to cry, and just about succeeding. His hand shakes. Wine spills onto his feet. He says, – How am I going to get through it, Lo? Tell me. I want to know. How am I going to get through? What's the point?

She leans forward, hands on her knees. – Life goes on. It goes on.

– Not necessarily.

– Oh, Benny – don't say that. You mustn't say that.

– Will you help me through?

– Of course. Whatever I can do.

– I don't know what I'd do without you.

– That's hypothetical. You aren't without me. I'm here.

– Perhaps we should finally get married. When I'm through this. Our turn at last. What d'you think?

– I'll think about it.

– Promise?
– Promise.

*

Is that how it was? Helen wonders. The letter lies on the desk before her. She picks it up and reads it once more.
Is that how it was?

Femme Fatale

Benny's at a meeting in the Publications Office. Under discussion are names of those needing support, possible routes for cash, people that must be got out of the country.

He's sitting with his back to the door, talking, when it opens and someone comes in. Absorbed in the point he's making, he doesn't turn round. A space is made, and the new arrival sits down at the table. Only then does he see who it is.

Lorraine! Here in London! He feels his heart turn over in his chest, exactly as the clichés describe. Nobody told him. But then, why should they? For one thing, nobody gossips about comings and goings. For another, why would anyone here know about his adolescent passions thousands of miles away, thousands of years ago?

She hasn't changed much. Not quite so ravishing – she was one of those girls who hit a peak around twenty. But beautiful enough. Tougher, more elegant. He notices all this, registers it; registers, too, that there is no wedding band on her finger.

What's she doing here? Lorraine was never interested in politics. Far from it. She always resented the way they absorbed him, took up time and energy that were rightfully hers, led him to hidden places, from which she was shut out. She wanted him all for herself. Lorraine was never one for sharing: only the whole pie would do.

She used her advantages ruthlessly. That exquisite body, for example, it dazzled him every time. He couldn't believe his luck. Like a child let loose in a sweet shop. All for him! He couldn't get enough of it. Neither of them could.

– But they're in the next room, the door isn't even locked!

– Oh, God, don't stop now, don't stop!

– Jesus, Lo, what'd you do if your mother came in?

But she didn't hear him. Or maybe she did hear him, and didn't care. Maybe it was just the edge she liked. Benny sometimes felt he was nothing but some kind of token in a game Lorraine and her mother were playing between them. No, he wasn't altogether sorry to leave, even though he missed her so much sometimes, it felt as though he'd left a part of himself behind (no prizes for guessing which one). That lessened with time, naturally. Then Helen came along. But with Helen it was different, another thing altogether.

She's introduced as Mrs Margulies, who will be able to help them from time to time. They discuss the various ways in which she may do this: as a link in a chain; as a conduit for information; as an ear to the ground.

Inevitably, when the meeting ends they leave together. Long-lost friends.

Benny says: – This is a surprise. I thought you despised politics?

– Maybe I did. Maybe I don't any more.

– Did you know I'd be here?

– I guess I knew you might be.

What now? So long, see you sometime? After all these years? Hardly.

He looks at her ring finger. – You never married?

– Yes, but not any more. We divorced a couple of years ago. Dicky Margulies. Remember him?

He thinks back. – Vaguely.

She shrugs. – My mother always liked him more than I did. Turns out I was right.

– Any kids?

– No, or I wouldn't be doing this. How about you?

– Am I married, you mean? Yes.

– What's she like, your wife?

He laughs. Still the same high, nervous giggle. – Nice. Clever. She's a journalist. You'd like her.

– I don't expect so.

He raises an eyebrow sarcastically – another thing she remembers, another part of Benny that's lived on inside her head all these years. Don't we forget *anything*? Or is it just Lorraine who's cursed with this seemingly total recall?

– Come on! That was a long time ago.

– Yes. But it's never been the same with anyone else.

They stare at each other, seeking out the remembered Benny, the remembered Lo. Where are they now? Do they look out through these present eyes? The past dissolves in the present, so that memory is instantly all but subsumed.

When Lorraine and Dickie, at her insistence, divorced, his mother said: – I sometimes wonder what you're made of, Lorraine. Have you ever cared for a single creature besides yourself?

How should she know that under Lo's polished-steel surface beat a heart irretrievably broken by love?

Through the eight unsatisfactory years of that marriage (contracted on the rebound), the dream of Benny sustained her. Watching as Dickie pounded his way up through the real-estate business, listening as he snored at night, making discreetly sure that no unwelcome pregnancy should interrupt her studies (nor keep her tied to Dickie – though this, of course, was at first barely admissible even to herself) – she shut her eyes and thought of Benny. He didn't write, but from time to time there were snippets of news. At least he wasn't in prison, or dead: she had to concede that he'd been right to go. When, unknown to Dickie, she made the contacts which brought her, finally, to this room, she experienced the furtive, defiant pleasures of infidelity.

And now fantasy is made flesh. How can it fail to disappoint? Before she entered the room, her knees shook, her hands were cold and clammy, she could scarcely even breathe. She opens the door: and there he is – the man of her dreams. Thirty-three, thicker-set, untidily dressed, in need of a shave. Slightly sour breath. Obviously feeling awkward. Does her heart pound? Would he shine out across a crowded room, as he has shone so often in her mind's eye?

Lorraine wonders: Shall I leave now, at once? Start life afresh? Wouldn't that be something? Worth a trip to London, any day.

But then she hears her mother's voice. *Didn't I always tell you? Didn't I always know that Benny Spiro's not the man for you?* And she thinks: Whose life is this? Did I come all this way just to chicken out at the last minute?

Benny watches her and wonders what to say. This whole thing has caught him off balance. He's a man who thinks of the future rather than the past. Not that Lorraine was wiped from his mind. But it's years since she's played a significant part in his life, real or imagined. Is she really expecting to take up where they left off? It almost seems so. Is that what he wants? He's a different person, and so, he assumes, is she. And yet . . . Here she is, a beautiful woman, and he was once blindly in love with her. Maybe the old chemistry won't work again. Very likely not. But how can he know, until he tries? How can he resist? Why should he?

Remembered ambivalence floods through him: desire fights with prudence. Lorraine was always trouble. Worth it, but trouble. In this respect at least, it seems she is unchanged. Then he thinks of Helen and the threatened babies. Too much emotion: everywhere he turns, complications. It sometimes feels as though his energies are entirely taken up paddling through shoals of distraction. The calm space where his real life will happen is forever just out of reach. (And what will it consist of when, finally, the rapids are behind him? Science, politics? Are these more real than babies, than love? *Love is for man a thing apart, 'Tis woman's whole existence.* Benny's problem in a nutshell.)

Lorraine slides her arm through his: they're in the street now, walking towards a pub. – Well, has it?

– No, different.

She looks annoyed, squeezes his arm reprovingly. Her fingernails dig into his flesh. Men turn to look at her. Benny can't help feeling a proprietorial glow at being associated with someone so spectacular. – Do *you* have kids? she asks.

– No, but we're trying. That's the next item on the agenda, or so I'm led to believe.

– Don't you want any?

– Not really. Helen does, though. There is a pause. He says: What went wrong with your marriage?

– Oh, I don't know. It just didn't work. She dismisses the subject.

– It happens. You're happy, I can see.

– Yes. Yes, we're happy.

– She wasn't here today?

– She doesn't do this. She drops by now and then.

– You always did like to keep things separate.

– She's busy with her own stuff.

– Well. That's that, then.

– That's what?

– That's you and me.

– It doesn't mean we can't see each other from time to time, he hears himself say.

She says: – Good. I'd like that.

6

– I DIDN'T KNOW Declan met Benny in California.

– Didn't you? I suppose I just assumed you did.

Colette and Helen are having a drink together. They've taken to doing that a lot these days. As Colette says, a vodka shared is a vodka halved. – There was so much going on just then, says Colette now, excusing this oversight. – What made you think of it? After all these years he's been at High Leys.

– Lorraine mentioned it. Said she'd seen them together a few times.

– Yes, I believe it was Benny who found him.

– You believe! Don't you know?

– It was always very vague. I suppose I assumed Benny wanted to spare me the ghastly details. I wasn't too bothered. He turned up, that was the only thing that mattered.

– Patrick didn't seem to know anything about it, either. Apparently Benny just arrived with him one day.

– Yes, that's what I understood. Perhaps they ran into each other on the street. One of those lucky chances. You know what they say, the longer someone's disappeared, the harder it is for them to get in touch with home. Like a fence that gets higher and higher. You can see it, can't you? We were lucky, that's all. In a way. At least there isn't that awful uncertainty. You think when they're little that they'll be there for ever. But even when they don't actually die, or disappear, that's not necessarily true.

That, at least, is what Helen thinks she said. By the time she stopped speaking you could hardly hear her, she was just muttering into her glass.

Later, driving through the steep-sided lanes of Oxfordshire, Helen thinks: But only death is as final as – death.

Here she is, after all, on her way to see Declan. He is still here, his body still moves around the planet. Gemma gave her directions. She visits, from time to time. Colette doesn't. He won't see her. As she says, he isn't there for her. Is this some sort of punishment, some indictment he's handing out? You weren't there for me, so now see how it feels.

Gemma said: – That's just her guilt talking. Declan's the only thing that reminds her she can't have it all ways all the time.

– But he won't see her, will he? Helen pointed out. – There must be some reason.

– It's the one bit of him he feels hasn't given in. He did this big thing, ran off, and now here he is, back again. Couldn't even do that properly. I suppose he still feels he's got to assert himself somehow, and this is the only way he can think of.

– That's a bit childish, isn't it?

– But not totally unjustified, said Gemma.

That was always Benny's view, too. – The poor kid doesn't know if he's coming or going, he said. – It's all very well talking about making contact, but who's he supposed to make contact *with*? And it's true that as soon as he was old enough, Colette handed him over, to Monica, to the school, to Helen – to anyone who would take charge. Seen from that angle, his present difficulties – to say nothing of Colette's – may well be no more than a logical consequence of his upbringing.

A convincing hypothesis. Not, however, when put by Benny. Helen could never bring herself to agree with him on this. Couldn't agree? Her feelings on this subject transcended mere disagreement. She resented Benny's line with an almost personal fury, which surprised her, since it wasn't her he was criticising.

Partly, this anger arose from loyalty to Colette. After all (she pointed out), Gemma had the same treatment, and turned out fine – as normal, whatever that is, as easy and sociable, as you could wish.

What was Benny saying? That Colette had no right to pursue her career once she had children? *Benny*? The radical thinker invoking *Kinder, Kirche, Küche* – the feminist's very own KKK – ? So what about all these female role-models we're supposed to be producing for our daughters? And where was Patrick in all this? Gemma and Declan had two parents, remember? Pursuing *his* career, that's where. Which, at that time, was probably less successful than Colette's. Hah. A strong whiff of chauvinism there.

That's the overt reasoning. But there's another, far stronger source of anger, and one which may not be admitted: Benny's dislike of his own son, Helen's cherished boy. He never took to him, never enjoyed his company, never sought him out or played with him, as he did with Laura. The truth was, he much preferred Declan to Tim. Preferred all the other children to Tim. Tim could do nothing right, they could do nothing wrong. Helen's view of Declan was naturally coloured by this preference. In the end, she feels, it's his life. We make our own fate. People are what they're going to be, from the moment they emerge, bloody and bawling, from the first of life's great fights. Watching the children grow, her own and others, she has become daily more convinced of this.

And there's always been something worrying about Declan. His mind was always elsewhere, closed off. Even when he was tiny, he stared at you and went his own way. Helen can remember discussing this unnerving manner of his with Benny when he was very small – four, five, even younger. She always felt there might be something organically amiss – some wire that had not quite connected, so that contact with other people was never entirely within his reach. Something genetic, perhaps. Hearing Patrick describe himself, his sensation of disconnection, Helen thought: It's Declan.

Benny, however, preferred to apportion blame.

Colette said: – I asked him to keep a lookout, when I saw him over there.

Another gobbet of submerged life suddenly surfaces.

– You saw Benny in California? You never told me!

Is that a blush creeping up Colette's cheek? I've caught her out, thinks Helen. More guilt. Colette these days is simply consumed by guilt. Who would have thought it possible? Shamelessness – that was always her line. Helen hopes she will rediscover it. Guilt doesn't suit her: she isn't used to it.

They sip vodka and think of lost children, lost husbands.

*

Colette sits in her hotel room, waiting. In point of fact it isn't strictly a room: it's a bungalow, set in landscaped grounds. She's over to audition for a new soap, and the studio is sparing no expense, even at this stage. She's not sure if she really wants the role – it's a middle-aged harridan. Is this how she will wish to be remembered? The initial run is thirteen episodes, but other related ventures by this studio have taken off and continued into infinity.

Which means that she will spend an awful lot of her life out here filming. She glances bleakly at those strange LA palm-trees with their long long stems and their tiny sprouting heads. Colette doesn't really like LA. She's spent a lot of time here, but never much enjoyed it. But she has her reasons for wanting to be here now. Earlier this year, Declan disappeared. He went out one Monday morning – ostensibly to school – and never came back. Colette, naturally, is beside herself. The apple of her eye. Sweet sixteen, tall and blond. A honeypot. Somewhere, in this teeming world – he is. Where? How can she transport herself to that spot? One terrible scenario after another plays itself out inside her head.

The police weren't much help. All they could say was that no relevant dead bodies had appeared. Yet. Otherwise, nothing: not a sign. Nor did Gemma know anything. She and Declan never got on: even if he'd been the confiding type, he wouldn't have confided in her. His friends were equally uninformative. Nothing was wrong, so far as they were aware: no crisis loomed.

The only thing Colette can think of is that Laura's death tipped him over some edge. Just as Benny loved Declan more than his own son, so Declan loved Laura much more than his own sister. When she died everything changed, for everybody.

First, Patrick disappeared. He'd been semi-detached for years, but essentially available. No longer. For six months, not a word. His excuse was that he was directing a film. But they all knew this was just the proximate reason: if it hadn't been this, it would have been something else. Or nothing at all. It was as if he'd been walking on ice all these years. Then suddenly it shattered, and off he ran, just when he was most needed. First Laura, now Pat. No wonder the children are in a bad way.

Colette was in the middle of shooting a ten-part television adaptation of Proust. She was the Duchesse de Guermantes: her return to the big-time. What was she to do? You can't drop out in the middle of a thing like that, not if you want to get a job ever again. They'd have had to re-take all her previous scenes. It would have cost – out of the question. And if she'd stopped, what good would that have done?

Life sweeps you along, and Declan somehow got left behind.

The air-conditioner rattles. It's driving her mad. She'd like to get out, go for a walk, should such a thing be possible in LA. Failing all else, she'd even go for a drive – a calming drift along the freeways. Who knows, she might even see Declan in the next car. But she can't: she's waiting for a visitor.

The phone rings. It's the reception desk. – Ms Bosanquet? A Dr Spiro is here for you.

She would have preferred to visit Benny. She's always been curious about his other life. Who is he, all by himself out here? Whom does he see, where does he live? Nobody knows, not even (especially not?) Helen. The Benny Helen sees, when she and Tim come out to visit, is a version prepared for public consumption. He can be contacted at the Institute. When the family arrives, he rents a house or a camper van. But Colette's theory is that he has an alter ego, another personality into which he slips when he arrives in LA. How else to explain the bizarre article he's just published? And the word is that he's proposing a book. His London colleagues and friends are mystified and, on the whole, appalled. Ex-colleagues, one should perhaps say. He hasn't been back since Laura died. Officially he's on unpaid leave, but who knows whether they'll want to keep his place warm for him now? They're beginning to feel he's more of an embarrassment than anything else. He hasn't resigned, though, nor does he want a divorce. – Bear with me, he says. I need to know it's all there, but I must get myself sorted out first. Under the circumstances, they can hardly sack him.

He seemed pleased when Colette called him at Synchrony.

– How long are you here?

– I'm not sure. If I get the part, I guess I'll be here a lot. I wanted to come anyhow. Did you know about Declan? He disappeared. Just like that. Went out one morning and no-one's seen him since. Apparently it's possible he may be out here. They think he's with some cult. Though God knows what we can do, if he is. They brainwash them, don't they? Sorry. I'm running on. Getting hysterical. Last time I saw Pat he told me to get a grip on myself. I sometimes feel I'm gripping myself so hard the circulation's cut off altogether. So where are you living?

– Gently, he said. – Gently. It'll work out. Let's go out to dinner. You don't want to come to my place, it's a tip. I'll come and fetch you.

His car pulls up in front of the bungalow. It's a little Japanese convertible, bright blue. He's wearing a white suit, which sets off his deep tan.

– You look well!

– That would be going too far, Benny says. – But I'm feeling better. Finding my way through.

– We've noticed!

He laughs. – The article, you mean. I thought it might ruffle a few feathers. Well, too bad. You evolve. Have to, to stay sane. How about you, though?

– Pretty fragile.

Colette pours drinks: they sit on the veranda and contemplate the hotel's lush verdure, the unnatural blooming of the desert.

– So tell me about Declan.

Colette's voice is steady now. Only her shaking hand betrays her. – He just disappeared one day. Went out in the morning, to school I assumed, and didn't come back. Well, I knew he couldn't be round at Patrick's, because he's gone off, so there isn't that excuse any more. I rang all his friends – he wasn't there. The police couldn't do anything. In the morning I went to the school. Declan? they said. Declan Costelloe? Charming boy. But he left at the end of last term.

They actually had a letter, written on my headed paper, explaining that I'd decided to move him to a sixth-form college.

– He forged it?

– Seems so. I don't expect they check signatures too minutely – schools aren't exactly banks, are they? And they didn't know him very well. He'd only been there a little while. You know he insisted on leaving Westminster.

– So what had he been doing?

– Who knows? He went out every morning and came back in the evening. We just assumed he was going to school.

– What about homework, stuff like that? All those letters schools keep sending home? Didn't you ever wonder?

– You know Dec. It's not easy to keep tabs on him. Anyhow, I contacted some missing persons' organisations, and eventually they picked up a rumour that he'd joined some cult. He'd been seen in the street with some other kids. But when they saw the kids again, he wasn't with them. There's some notion he's at the cult headquarters somewhere near here. But it's all very vague, sighs Colette.

– Any idea where this place is?

– They did give me an address, but no-one really knew whether he was there, or whether it really was Declan they'd seen. I'll check it out, obviously. Not quite sure what I'll do when I get there, though. Knock on the door, d'you think? I mean, I don't expect they'd exactly say Come in. Perhaps I ought to set up camp outside. The trouble is, time. I haven't had a moment since I arrived. And I'm due back in London next week.

– Have you been in touch with Patrick?

– No-one knows where he is, either. Shooting some rafting epic in the Amazon, was the last I heard.

– No, he's in town. He called me the other day.

– Oh. Well, I don't know whether I want to see him or not. What kind of state's he in? I'm not sure I could cope with another nervous wreck, just now.

– What happened?

– It was Laura. Didn't you know? Maybe you'd gone by then. He just went to pieces after the funeral.

– I didn't realise . . .

– Oh, it wasn't *just* Laura, says Colette. There was something else there, too. Something he'd been trying to forget.

What's distance where memory's concerned? They ran away to London, but it wasn't far enough. Where is? Brazil? California? Patrick keeps on running.

*

A mid-November dusk. The trees are dropping their last leaves. In the fading light, colour drains from the golden carpet. The world becomes grey. Minute by minute, it loses definition. Behind the gardens, behind the trees of this suburban road, a few lights appear.

Cars rush past, churning leaves into mush. Women, chatting, push strollers along the pavements. Clouds of older children form and reform around them. In this quiet neighbourhood, children still walk to and from school. They scuffle through the leaves, shouting and laughing. Some boys are kicking a football. An ordinary afternoon.

Mostly, the traffic moves sedately along here. There isn't very much in the middle of the day, but by four o'clock you need to be careful: the rush hour's begun. There's a nasty blind curve there, and the leaves make the surface slippery.

Two children are out in the road. After a ball, maybe, or perhaps hurrying to buy toffees at the corner shop. Did they look? It doesn't make much difference. Even if they looked both ways, right, left, and right again, just as it says in the Highway Code, they couldn't see very far.

A car rounds the curve. It's going much faster than it should. Doing fifty at least. School's out, don't people realise?

There's a bang as it hits something. Is it the football?

No. The ball's just there, rolling along by the kerb.

The child is a small heap of clothes, pushed along like a doll in front of the bumper. With a screaming of brakes and tyres, the car stops.

Too late.

*

– How's Gemma?

– Fine. She seems OK. That's one thing, at least.

– I miss her, says Benny. – Almost more than anyone. She kind of kept me going. I thought, At least Gemma's still there. You'd have thought I might resent, you know, her being there when Laura wasn't.

He doesn't say: It was Tim I resented.

Colette doesn't say: That was one of our problems, Pat being so jealous of you and Gemma.

*

Everyone is invited for dinner at Colette's. Four Costelloes, four Spiros. Just like the old days.

The children are lighting the candles on the Christmas tree. Colette insists on real candles, so beautiful, so romantic – and it's her house, isn't it? So she gets her way, although Patrick, uncharacteristically responsible for once, thinks it's a stupid, dangerous habit. There's a huge heap of presents underneath, which they're checking in detail. Laura's found a package labelled To Laura with lots and lots of love from Colette. – It's soft, she says, squeezing it. I bet it's clothes. I hope it's from Tammy Girl. They've got some cool things there. D'you think we'll be allowed to open some of them tonight? We won't be here on Christmas Day. We've got to go to Grandma Fran's.

– All the best things are in California, says Tim. – It's not fair. Why can't we go and live there with Dad?

Benny spends half his time in California. He does alternating three-month spells: summer over there, autumn in London, winter in Los Angeles, spring in London. Last summer he rented a large house with a pool, and the family joined him for the school holidays. It's December now – nearly Christmas – and he's off again the first week in January. The Institute's in Westwood, not far from the university, and this time he's taking a condo in Santa Monica, near the beach. The kids are green with envy.

– Because your Mum doesn't want to, says Gemma.

– I think it's stupid, says Tim. – All she does is write things. Why can't she do that in California? They've got word-processors there, haven't they?

– We could just go and live with Dad, Laura says wistfully.

– Who'd look after us, silly. He's out all the time.

Declan is examining a small, square, heavy package, To Dec from Pat. He weighs it in his hand. He's hoping for a really good camera. Might this be it? It doesn't seem quite big enough. He shakes it gently, but nothing rattles. He says: – I think it's quite good having parents in two different places. It can be really useful.

– They'll catch you out one of these days, says Gemma.

Declan likes to keep his movements private. He tells Colette he's spending the night at his father's in Notting Hill, while Patrick thinks he's in Kentish Town. Colette tends to believe what he tells her. And Patrick – well, Patrick doesn't seem to worry. He was never on authority's side, and he's not about to change now. He's cool, he's laid-back, he bloweth where he listeth. And he knows what it is to feel shackled by family life. Perhaps he's acting out his own fantasies through Declan. Dec doesn't enquire. He's been all right so far. The odd spot of trouble, the odd dicey friend, but nothing heavy. Yet. And quite often, he does what he's said he was going to do. Just not always.

– So?

– So then they'll make you board full-time, not just weekly.

– I'd run away.

Gemma says: – I saw something in the paper about a boy that's been shooting shot-gun pellets at people on the towpath of the Regent's Canal. They haven't got him yet, but quite a lot of people have seen him.

Tim and Laura are wide-eyed. Tim says: – Have you got a shot-gun?

– Pat has, says Declan, sounding bored. – So what?

– So be careful.

– So why should I take any notice of you? What d'you care what I do? Miss Know-all. Ooh, Mummy, d'you know what Declan's been doing? What's it got to do with you, anyway?

Gemma says, – I hate it, everyone living in different places. I wish it could always be like now.

This evening, they are back in the days before all these complications set in, when Helen and Benny, Patrick and Colette, safely installed in their contiguous houses, visualised an extended family life stretching ahead of them. The silences, the awkwardnesses, the resentments that crowd in when they find themselves marooned in marital isolation, miraculously disperse once they're in company. They seek each other out in a kind of desperation – desperation to hold the demons at bay, desperation to find themselves again as once they were. The venture can't, after all, be said to have failed. The children have grown up together, as everyone hoped they would, albeit mostly in Helen's house. They have all been able to pursue their demanding careers. And who knows but that family life may not yet reassert itself? When they're all together, the magic tapestry is rewoven. Everything seems so simple. California, Notting Hill, might not exist.

The grown-ups are drinking claret while a stew, containing most of a bottle of wine, bubbles on the Aga. Stew is one of Colette's specialities. Like the Aga, it represents a certain vision of family life: spacious and comforting. This was the vision she started out with, before the children came along and when they were little. Since then it's faded somewhat, like an old stage set: holes have appeared, corners are missing. But it's dusted off for occasions such as this.

Colette's house, like Helen's, has its kitchen in what used to be the half-basement. Unlike Helen's, however, the back part, with the big table and the garden door, is double-height: the entrance-hall and front-room have been converted into a sort of gallery. The architect tried to dissuade her: the arrangement would be hard to heat, and did she want a house full of kitchen smells? Colette saw his point, but ignored his advice. Helen's kitchen is cosy, low-ceilinged, cottagey: not Colette's style at all. She hankers for large spaces, for galleries and arches, and she isn't bothered about heating bills. The fact is, she doesn't normally spend much time in the kitchen. The stew, the Aga, are Monica's territory, and Colette is careful not to encroach. Who depends on whom? Relationships evolve. Colette is, in all practical matters, dependent upon Monica. She must be kept happy. Those that don't like this may do the other thing. Helen, for example.

– I never seem to see you these days.

– Oh, well. I've been busy. And Monica –

– What on earth's Monica got to do with it?

But they both know what Monica's got to do with it: that icy welcome, that reluctant admittance. What's Colette to do? Mention it? You must be joking.

– You could come to me.

But they both know that that's not the way it is. That's never been the way. There are visitors and visitees, phoners and phonees. Helen is one of the former, Colette, one of the latter.

However, Colette's not working just now – work's becoming a bit thin on the ground these days, to tell the truth. She could no longer be described as a *jeune première*, and somehow she hasn't quite managed the transition to interesting middle-aged parts. – There just aren't any, she wails. – Helen, darling, why don't you write some for me? So Monica's taken the opportunity to go on a long holiday. She went to Australia for a month, and now she's going on to spend Christmas with her family – there's an old mother near Liverpool, and a sister, too, somewhere. She'll be back in January. Colette's working up a one-woman show, and she's hoping to get it into rehearsal then.

Colette tests the stew. The meat's tender, the little glazed onions bob invitingly. – Ready, everyone! she yells up the stairs.

The children come trooping down, sniffing appreciatively. They're getting so *large*! Their clatter, their exuberance, fill the room. They take over the table, chortling and yelling. Gemma says: – I'm sitting next to Benny, I never see him these days! She gazes up at him adoringly. Gemma loves Benny. He was always her ideal daddy. Her own father has many wonderful qualities, but being an ideal daddy is not among them. Benny puts his arm around her adolescent waist and hugs her. Patrick, across the table, stares at them, inscrutable behind his half-moon spectacles. He pours himself another glass of claret. Declan does likewise. He's allowed a glass of wine, these days. Colette's terrified he'll turn into a drunk, but Patrick insists that it's time to start educating his palate. Over their crystal goblets (nothing but the best tonight) they survey the scene.

Colette moves the candlesticks and plants the stew stage centre. She lifts the lid. A mouthwatering aroma fills the room. Helen cuts some bread that has been warming in the oven. Timmy hands it round. Everyone begins to eat. Patrick says, – I was reading about your friend Stefan Kertes the other day. There was a big piece in one of the papers, I forget which.

Helen says: – The Times, wasn't it?

Patrick says: – Sounds a bit of an unusual scientist. I always thought he was a physicist. But according to this piece, he's mostly interested in the paranormal. Is that right?

– Hardly, Benny says. – That's just what the papers pick up. Stefan's a pukka scientist, all right. But he's become very interested in chance, randomness, that sort of thing.

– He's getting mystical, says Helen. – The argument from design, the uncaused cause. It gets them all in the end. What's wrong with random? We evolved because that was the way things were. End of story. Who cares why? Why should there be a why? I thought you were Mr Random. You'd better be careful it doesn't get to you.

– That's not why I go there.

Helen says: – Why do you go there, then?

– I want to learn about what other people are doing. I want to explore some new ideas. Anything wrong with that?

They glare at each other across the table, taking up their positions for the familiar marital joust. Patrick, however, cuts across it. He says: – The piece I was reading said Kertes was interested in coincidence. Is that all part of the same thing?

– Sort of, says Benny. – Don't get me wrong. I don't go along with everything he does.

– Don't dismiss it, Patrick says. – I think he's maybe onto something important there.

– Could be. Benny isn't committing himself in this company.

Patrick, somewhat ponderously, persists. Is he already a little drunk? Colette's getting quite worried about his drinking these days. – Don't you believe coincidences happen?

– Of course. But I don't think they're meaningful. They just happen.

Patrick doesn't reply at once. He's a one thing at a time man, especially when he's drunk, and the thing just now is stew. He attacks it with concentration, pursues the little onions around the plate with his fork, mops up every drop of juice with his bread. Then he sits back, takes a sip of wine, and says: – Let me tell you something that happened to me the other day. I was at Heathrow, just off to New York for a couple of days, and I was getting a ticket at the parking lot. Well, when I'd got it I went back to my car to take it to its place, but the key wouldn't fit, and then I suddenly realised it wasn't my car at all. It was exactly the same make, same colour, same year, but not mine. Mine was next to it. So when I was getting in, the chap the other car belonged to came along, and we had a laugh. Then when he got to take out his luggage, his case was exactly the same as mine – you know, that green one with the zip. So then we got the minibus to the terminal. Turned out we both wanted Terminal Three.

Declan says: – I bet you were on the same flight.

– Well, we were, exactly that. So then we got talking, and it turns out he's a screenwriter. We spent the flight discussing various projects, and with any luck, I think I may direct one. What d'you think of that?

– Very nice, says Benny.

– You shouldn't be patronising, says Colette. – I've noticed it before with scientists, you just want to dismiss things you can't explain. What you don't know isn't worth knowing. Well, I think there are all sorts of things that can't be explained, not the way you do it, and if your Mr Kertes takes them seriously, so much the better for him.

– Hold on, says Benny. – What have I said?

Helen says: – Coincidences have to happen sometimes, it's the law of averages.

– I don't know about sometimes, says Colette. – They're always happening to me. I dreamed of Gemma last month, I was in Leeds, and when I phoned her the next day it turned out she'd woken up sweating all over at exactly the time I must have been dreaming. You know that awful bout of flu she had. You can't tell me it's just chance.

– What else is it? says Benny. – You'll be telling me you believe in telepathy next. Unknown waves. N-rays. Card-guessing. Do you know how all those Zener card-guessing sessions worked? You could see through the backs of the cards. I was shown a pack once.

– You're essentially destructive, Patrick says. – I've noticed it before. You can't just deny all these things. What I don't understand is why you want to. He lours at Benny, suddenly aggressive. It's always like that with him: you never know when he's going to flip from amiability into something more dangerous. It's one of the sources of his power. He makes people nervous, and they try to please him.

– I wasn't brought up religious. I have no emotional need for unexplained mysteries. I find reality quite extraordinary enough for me. Your trouble, says Benny, – is that you think things become less interesting if you explain them scientifically. You're attracted to coincidences because you think they're magic, because you think science can't explain them. I've never been able to understand why people think *that's* interesting. Explanations make things *more* interesting. In fact there's a perfectly valid, boring statistical explanation for coincidences, but you're not interested in that.

– You think you can explain everything, do you? inquires Patrick.

– Of course not.

– So you just dismiss whatever you can't! cries Colette.

– Benny hasn't dismissed anything, says Helen hotly. – He's not the one that's getting all worked up, you are. Nobody's saying *you* can't believe these things. No-one's denying they happen. It's just, we don't think there's anything to it. So what? Why should you care?

She's shouting now, to make herself heard above Colette's attempted interruptions. Out of the blue, battle has been joined: Costelloes versus Spiros, artistic mystics versus stony sceptics. There's a shrill edge to Helen's voice which only appears when she's fighting to win, deeply engaged. About *coincidence*? Yet the emotions are undeniably there, the fury's real enough. Helen tells herself that it's exhilarating, that she enjoys a good argument. She is not entirely convinced.

156

The children have been silent throughout all this. Now Gemma gives what sounds like a muffled cough. Everyone turns towards her. Tears are spurting from her eyes, great fountains of tears. – I can't bear it, she sobs, and rushes out of the room. Colette rushes after her. The other children say nothing. Tim and Laura are playing some game with the bread, apparently oblivious to all that is taking place. Declan's eyes are bright, darting from one antagonist to the next.

– Well, says Patrick. – I hope you're happy now. He pours himself another glass.

– It was an argument, says Benny. – So what? Can't we have an argument? Gemma's thirteen. She gets over-emotional. She probably thought we were falling out for good. I saw a crow on the roof this afternoon. What does that mean, d'you think? Death in the family?

Helen says: – Benny, shut up.

Gemma returns. Colette's arm is protectively around her. She sits down again, but between her parents, not beside Benny. Everyone moves round to accommodate the new arrangement. Spiros on one side of the table, Costelloes on the other. The stew is removed, the cheese and salad take their place. The flaming pudding is produced. Colette always makes two while she's about it, and they won't be spending Christmas together. Perhaps that's a good thing after all? More wine is poured. Presents are exchanged. No-one mentions coincidences. Calm is restored.

When the evening ends they promise each other, a little more heartily than usual, that they will meet again soon.

They won't. The eight of them will never be together again.

*

Colette says: – Gemma adores you, of course. Always did. But she never was a problem. It was always Declan I worried about.

– How old is he now?

– Sixteen. Colette shakes her head, and her lips begin to tremble.

– And you haven't heard from him at all?

– We found he'd emptied his building society account. And he hasn't been murdered, or if he has the police haven't found him. That's all we know for sure.

– I'll keep an eye out. I may have some contacts.

– Thanks. Another drink?

– We'd better eat, he says gently. – I know a good Chinese place.

Benny's mind is full of what may have happened to Declan. Drugs? There was quite a drugs scene at both his schools. Prostitution? He's such a pretty boy. At least a cult would save him from all that. Give him some sort of reason for living, which he always seemed to lack. Benny does not mention these thoughts to Colette. It's unlikely she needs help constructing horrid possibilities.

She says: – Let's talk about something else. It's the only way I can keep sane. Tell me about yourself. This article. D'you remember that awful argument we all had about coincidence and science? And here you are turning all mystic. What happened?

He laughs and shrugs. – You know as well as I do what happened. It's not irrelevant. I want to find a way of reconciling the different bits of my life, if that's possible. You could put it crudely and say I don't want to believe Laura's dead, and modern physics can convince me intellectually that she isn't. Maybe Stefan'll help me see how to do it. He's assembled quite a group. It's very fluid, people come and go. I like that. It opens you up to new ways of looking at things. That was one of the things I came here for, to look at science in new ways. It's easy to get locked into a way of thinking, but it's much harder to get unlocked.

– Hasn't it rather cut you off from your old friends? (– They can't believe it at the lab, Helen said. – They're convinced he's gone mad. They think it's delusions of grandeur. He knows everything about biology, so now he thinks he can make pronouncements on physics, too. They'll make allowances, in the circumstances, but if he goes on like this I think they'll want to sever their connections. – Is that how you feel, too? Colette asked. – How can I pronounce? said Helen bleakly. It isn't as though this world's up to much, is it? If he wants to invent a more agreeable one, who can blame him? I wish I could do the same.)

– I find I don't much care about that any more. I don't have anything to say to them just now. I expect they feel the same way. People tell you they're moved by intellect not emotion, that they don't have an agenda. Can you believe that? *Everyone's* got an agenda. I suppose what I'm saying is, I've got to the point where I can admit mine. Kertes helped. He's an extraordinary man. You must meet him.

– If I get this part, no doubt I shall. I'd have to be over here a good deal.

– Funny, if you both ended up here, you and Pat!

– That's one reason I quite hope I don't get it.

– You could always turn it down.

– My agent would never forgive me. Do you know how much this kind of thing pays?

They order a sweet-and-sour carp. It arrives whole on its platter. They pick at it with their chopsticks. Its bony remains gape at them. Colette says, – Remember that fish restaurant in Italy?

– Ten years ago, that must have been.

– Don't remind me.

*

Helen says: – Benny, do mosquitoes have teeth?

Benny can't bear it when she puts on this little-girl, ingénue act. It doesn't suit her. Besides, he's preoccupied. Under the table, Colette has slipped off her shoe, and they're playing footsie. That, at least, was how it began. Now they've progressed past anklesie to thighsie and –

– Of course they don't, he snaps.

Benny has always sternly removed thoughts of Colette from his mind. Naturally he finds her desirable. Everyone does. And as though nature's gifts were not enough, there's now the added lustre of her being a film-star. But how can they? Everybody he loves would get hurt, and he's not an unkind man, nor irresponsible, let alone stupid.

But now here's Colette with her foot crawling all over him, and he can't think of anything else.

What an actress she is! You'd never guess. She hardly glances at him, chattering away, the life and soul of the party. Just occasionally there's a small, ravishing grin shot in his direction, hardly there before it's gone.

The tired man sends over his bottle of Asti Spumante, and they clink glasses. Colette's hand brushes Benny's: the touch flashes through his body so violently that it seems impossible the sparks aren't visible. But what are they going to do? Or, rather, *when*? He can't just slip out of Helen's bed and into Colette's and suppose no-one will notice. If there's one situation rather than another in which dalliance is out of the question, this is it, when they're all at such close quarters, living in each other's pockets, the scene cluttered with children, nannies, spouses . . .

Later that evening, there's a phone-call which is obviously from one of Colette's boyfriends. Benny's head is in turmoil (and not just his head). Colette retires to the corner with the phone, but makes no other attempt to keep the call private. It's almost as if she's grateful to whoever it is, as if she wants the room at large to witness what's going on. She smiles at Helen and rolls her eyes complicitously. Patrick seems quite unmoved. And Benny? Is there a message here for Benny?

There is, of course, and he reads it loud and clear. Just fun and games, darling. Nothing to get worked up about.

He's kept his distance, then and ever since.

*

Colette has to make an early start. They ride back to the hotel through the warm night. She's wearing a chiffon dress that floats behind her in the breeze. Once again, he's reminded of that night in Italy.

It would be a lie to say she's as beautiful now as she was then. Yet amid all their calamities, Benny realises he still desires her. Still desires her? *Because* of their calamities, he desires her more than ever. For a few hours, why not forget it all? He's always wanted her, and she's always known it. She always fancied him, too. Even before that night, he knew. But while the four of them were so bound together, it was out of the question. He knew that even while her teasing toe was nearly driving him out of his mind. All that risk, and what for? Undying love? Hardly. A little pleasure – a lot of pleasure, even. But nothing that wasn't available elsewhere. She made that clear enough, and he could only agree. Now, though, what's to prevent it?

He says: – How about a nightcap? And takes her in his arms.

A few days later, driving to the studio along the freeway, Colette is caught in a traffic jam. As they edge along, she glances at the cars on either side. As usual, the first rule of traffic jams is in operation: She's in the wrong queue. On either side cars move past while she remains stationary.

On her right, a truck towers. And on her left, sliding past, is a small blue convertible. It's Benny's: she'd recognise it anywhere. He doesn't notice her. Why would he? Her rented car means nothing to him.

In the seat beside him is a woman. Colette can't see her very well. She gets an impression of dark glasses, long black hair. She feels a twinge of jealousy.

It's ridiculous – they both knew the other night wasn't the start of anything, just unfinished business, what the moment demanded. Probably never to be be repeated. But what is jealousy if not irrational?

*

Helen rounds a corner, and there it is. For the past mile the lane's been following a high wall, obviously the boundary of some big estate. And now, at last, the entrance is revealed. Great wrought-iron gates, beyond which an avenue of horse chestnuts sweeps between meadows towards the distant house. No name, no sign, but this must be it. She looks once more at Gemma's directions, and gets out of the car.

The gates are shut. Helen tries them: not just shut, locked. She notices an entryphone, let into one of the stone pillars. There's a bell at the base. She rings. No answer. And again. She knows they're there, she's not going to be put off. If they're stubborn, so is she. Again, vigorously, and again. Eventually there is a crackle of life.
– Yes?

– I've come to see Declan Costelloe. I wrote. It was all arranged. My name's Helen Spiro.

– Please wait.

Once again, silence. It's cold, waiting out here, even though a thin December sun is shining. She could keep warm in the car. But then how will she hear the entryphone? Helen jumps up and down, swings her arms, curses. Minutes pass. She rings the bell again, furiously and at length. The machine crackles. She yells into it, – I've been waiting here for about twenty minutes. I've come to see Declan Costelloe. It was all arranged. Will someone please open the gates!

There is no reply, but a buzzing noise indicates that something may be happening. Helen pushes the gates, and finds that they have unlatched. Quickly, before anyone can change their mind, she swings them wide and drives through.

The house is built of pale stone. The front facade shows two square wings joined by what must be a gallery, with a doorway below. Around the roofline is a balustrade made of letters. Halfway along the drive Helen stops the car and reads: CONSIDER THE LILIES OF THE FIELD THEY TOIL NOT NEITHER DO THEY SPIN EVEN SOLOMON IN ALL HIS GLORY WAS NOT ARRAYED LIKE ONE OF THESE.

It's a long balustrade.

She continues up the drive and parks in front of the grand doorway. No other vehicle is visible. How do they come and go, in this place? There must be some traffic between here and the outer world. A back entrance somewhere.

She gets out of the car and puts her hand up to ring the bell. But before she can do so, the door swings open.

Helen steps inside, half expecting to find an empty hallway. The place seems like something out of science fiction, or a dream: perfectly functioning, but with no visible inhabitants. But no: on the other side of the door is a person. A woman, about Helen's age, dressed for the country: tweed skirt, blue twinset, brogues. She wears no make-up; her greying hair is cut short. She shuts the door. – Yes?

For the third time, Helen explains herself. – My name is Helen Spiro. I'm here to see Declan Costelloe. It was all arranged. She fumbles in her handbag and produces a typed note: *Mrs Spiro. It will be possible to see Declan Costelloe on 9 December after 10.30 in the morning. Please bring this letter with you.* The paper is headed, *High Leys*, with a line drawing of the house, but there is no signature.

Helen hands the note to the woman, and looks around her. She is standing in an oak-panelled hallway. Ahead of her, wide, shallow oak stairs climb to what must be the gallery. A verdure tapestry hangs on the wall. Beneath their feet is a fine Persian carpet. It's not at all the kind of place she had imagined Declan inhabiting.

The woman peruses the note. She takes it to a table upon which sits a telephone, and lifts the receiver. – Reception here, Leader. There's a person here with a letter that seems to come from you. To see Declan Costelloe.

She listens, nods, replaces the receiver, leads Helen towards the back of the house. They cross a stone-flagged garden room. The woman points ahead, across a lawn. – You see that hedge? You'll find a small doorway in it, straight ahead. Go through and you're in the vegetable garden. That's where you'll find him.

A muddy path leads around the lawn, beside what must in summer be a herbaceous border. Helen walks it, glad that she's wearing her heavy boots, conscious of hidden eyes following her movements. She finds the doorway in the hedge. She goes through.

On the other side, she is confronted by a wide expanse of walled garden, vegetable beds bordered by brick paths. Facing her, a long greenhouse is built against what must be the south wall. Much of the garden is bare earth, as one would expect at this time of the year, although there are gappy rows of winter veg: cabbages, sprouts, leeks and parsnips. Three people, two men and a woman, are trenching in compost. Helen recognises one of the diggers as Declan. She calls his name. The three diggers turn. She waves.

For a moment it seems as though he will ignore her. He looks back at the earth he has been digging, at the heap of compost, at his two companions. He stirs the earth with his spade. Then slowly, reluctantly, each movement heavy, as though made despite great opposing forces, he sets his spade in the bed and comes towards her. After a minute, his companions resume their work.

Helen looks at him, smiles, holds out her arms. But he stops about two feet away and stares, questioning, stony-faced. The smile freezes on her lips: her hands drop to her sides. – Declan! Didn't they tell you I was coming?

He mumbles something that might be Yes, or, I forgot.

Helen is struck by his size. He was still a boy when she saw him last, and now he's become a big man, tall and broad. How many years is it since he ran off? Eight? At least. It was just after Laura's accident.

– Is there somewhere we could go?

He looks around wildly, helplessly, as though this situation is too much for him. Then, with a sideways glance, he indicates the greenhouse. – Over there?

– That'll do fine. Just to get out of the wind. Helen finds herself talking very gently, as if to a small child or a timid animal one wants to reassure.

The greenhouse is surprisingly warm. It smells of loam and damp. The staging is filled with pots of geraniums and orchids, ready to be moved into the house. A mimosa is trained against one wall, its tight little sprays of buds not yet burst.

– It's nice in here, says Helen.

– Yes. Peaceful. He moves towards the geraniums, fiddles with the pots. Anything rather than face life, even in the familiar and unthreatening form of Helen, whom he's known for ever. Who knows what dark forces she represents for him? Family, society, demands, responsibilities, uncertainties?

– Declan, I came because – did you know Benny died?

– Benny?

– I'm sorry. I thought Colette might have told you.

– No. No, I didn't –

– He committed suicide, Helen ploughs on. No way back now. No way of phrasing this benignly. – I don't really know why. I'm trying to find out about him. I can't just let him go, just like that. I'm sure you can see that.

– But I –

– I was in California, Helen continues. – Doing some work. She does not mention that this work was with Declan's father: let's keep this strictly neutral, as far as that's possible – I met Lorraine, from

164

Synchrony. She said Benny brought you round to see her a couple of times.

– He may have. Declan sounds defensive now, the child caught out in some forbidden activity.

– Why not? It seems a perfectly normal thing for him to have done. Dec, it's not you I'm trying to find out about, or Lorraine. It's Benny. You obviously saw him a bit when you were out there. How did he seem to you? Was anything strange going on? I know he couldn't face life after Laura died. None of us could. She stops, suddenly engulfed by tears. After all these years, it still happens. She forces them back. – I can't believe this is to do with that. That was years ago. He must have got past the point where he'd commit suicide because of that.

– I don't really remember, Declan mutters.

– Not anything? You must remember *something*! Helen is growing impatient. She's driven a long way, and she's tired. Declan isn't stupid, let alone retarded. She's known him too long: he can't pull that one on her. He just can't be bothered. – Come on, think, she says sharply. – Who was he seeing? Anyone in particular? Did he seem happy or sad? Try and remember.

She fixes her eyes upon him, throws the whole of her persuasive force into her gaze. She *will* engage him. But he stares past her, at the plants, at the sky, at his feet, at the other two gardeners mistily visible through the panes.

He's hiding something, she's sure of it. He knows something about Benny, but he won't tell her. Why not? Misplaced loyalty of some kind, perhaps?

– Did you promise him you wouldn't say anything, is that it?

He shakes his head. He fidgets, he looks bored. He simply isn't interested. Helen's world, that world of busy inquisition, is a place he has rejected. He wants no part of it.

– Oh, Declan! She feels like kicking him, but at the same time wants to take him in her arms, comfort him, protect him. Just as she would with Tim. Just as she used to when they were all little. What happened? What went wrong?

– Did he hurt you in some way? Benny?

– No, no. Declan shakes his head. – We were friends.

But more he will not say. Nothing, no wiles, no bullying, will draw him out.

– If you really won't tell me anything, I suppose I can't force you.

Declan nods. Without another word, he leaves the greenhouse and returns to his digging. He doesn't look up as Helen makes her way around the garden to the gate in the hedge. She looks back: he digs on.

She re-enters the house by the garden room. The place is filled with silence. Not a creak, not a murmur. No dog barks, no music plays. Is everyone out digging?

As she enters the hallway, the woman reappears. Dead on cue. Helen's progress has not been unobserved amid the silence.

– You found him. Not a question: a statement.

– Yes. I'd like to speak to someone about him.

– How d'you mean?

– I'm worried about him. There's something wrong, that's quite obvious. I'd like to know what's happening, what's being done. Since I'm here. We're very old friends, I've known Declan since he was born.

– I don't quite know what you think this place is, Mrs –

– Spiro. Helen Spiro.

– Mrs Spiro. This isn't a school or an institution. Declan Costelloe is an adult. He's here by choice.

– I never said he wasn't. But I'd still like to speak to someone. As one friend to another. There must be someone in charge here, someone who runs the place. Who was that you spoke to when I arrived?

– The Leader never sees anyone without an appointment. She sounds primly shocked at the very idea.

– Well, I couldn't make an appointment, could I? I didn't know I'd want to see him. And I don't live anywhere near here, so it wouldn't be very easy to come back. Couldn't you see if he's got a minute? I'm quite happy to wait.

The woman hesitates. – I don't know if he's there just now.

– Why not call him and see? Why should he mind? He can always say no.

Once again, Helen tries her hypnotic gaze. Come on, she urges. Pick up that phone. She gives a little half-smile. Go on.

This time it works. With a little flounce, a slight huffiness, Cerberus swallows the cake. – Leader? The woman that came to see Declan Costelloe wants to see you. It's a Mrs –

– Helen Spiro.

– Helen Spiro.

She listens, then puts down the phone. She looks amazed, and rather annoyed.

– He says he'll see you.

She leads the way up the staircase, which turns back upon itself in a grand double sweep. The gallery is hung with a job-lot of ancestors, evidently bought for effect rather than prolonged contemplation. They hurry past crinolined ladies and florid Victorian businessmen. Where the gallery joins one of the wings, a man is waiting. The woman says – Here you are! and Helen is left to face the Leader.

He holds out a hand, smiling cordially. She'd expected something more forbidding, after all that build-up. A man of medium height, thickset, once-blond hair now greying, a round face that might seem bland if the eyes were not so intelligent. Dressed in a suit of expensive hairy tweed that makes Helen itch just looking at it.

Doesn't she know that face from somewhere? It's definitely familiar. She smiles and shakes hands while she tries to remember. It's just there – and just out of reach.

– I'm sure I know you, she says. – But I can't place you. Perhaps I'm going mad.

He laughs, turns and leads the way towards an open door. – Keep trying. It'll come.

It's the voice that does it. She remembers now. Last time they met, the mood was more soulful. Holding her awkwardly, one hand on her breast, the other on her crotch, – Has any man ever held you like this? he asked, and she can hear once again her crushing reply: – Yes, lots! The unwelcome tongue in her mouth. It was very rough, she recalls, pimply-feeling. She can still remember the sensation. Rasping. Her astonished realisation that he did not recognise *how* unwelcome.

– Christopher Clay!

– I wondered if it might be you, he says, ushering her into a

167

panelled room. – In fact I broke one of our strictest rules out of sheer curiosity.

– Oh?

– Residents never receive visitors unless they positively want to see them. And I have to say Declan didn't much want to see you. But in view of everything, I decided to stretch a point.

Same old Christopher. Enjoying the exercise of power, even so tiny a power as this. – I want to go into politics, he confided not long after they met.

– Do you? Why?

She can't remember exactly what he said, perhaps because he was already learning the business, avoiding detail, preferring rotund generalities. Every politician's first lesson: Detail ties you down. But the tendency was clear enough. Why politics? Because politics is the means by which a man of ideas may put those ideas into effect. What ideas, exactly? Betterment, he said vaguely. The betterment of the nation.

And incidentally the betterment of Christopher Clay. Why did he want to go into politics? So that he could make the rules. And so be in a position to break a few, discreetly, from time to time.

– Was it a good visit?

– Not particularly.

Christopher Clay shuts the door and waves her to a chair. It's the study to end all studies: red leather armchairs, Turkish carpet, leather-topped desk, bookshelves filled with sets of matching volumes in half-calf bindings.

– What are you looking for?

– The pipe. In a room like this, there's got to be a pipe.

He frowns. – I never smoked. Surely you remember that?

– It was a joke, she explains lamely. – And it's an awfully long time ago. You might have picked up all sorts of habits since then.

– You were always so cheeky, Helen.

– Yes, I'd never have made a politician's wife.

– Well, as things turned out, I didn't make a politician.

– Yes, I seem to remember . . .

– It was for the best, he declares, and gestures towards the window. Lord of all he surveys. – My work was elsewhere.

– That was really what I wanted to talk to you about. Though of course I didn't know it was *you*. What is this place, exactly?

He leans back dreamily in his chair. Now is the moment when, if he had that pipe, he would light it and begin the endless cycle of puffing, gesturing, tamping, relighting, with which pipe smokers play for time. – Perhaps you've seen our ads. The New Life College.

Helen considers. The name brings to mind closely-printed posters on the walls of the Underground, but she can recall nothing of their contents.

– We offer a philosophy. A way of life.

– Is that here? The college?

– This is what you might call the British Mother House. We have branches worldwide.

– Very monastic. Do all the students live in?

– It's not quite like that. We have a large number of corresponding students. They constitute the main body of the College. We couldn't possibly accommodate them all. We're talking about several thousand people. Mostly we work at a distance, by post and video, with occasional seminars in different places. But for some of our students, that isn't enough. They want to make their life with us. Declan is one of those.

– What brought him here?

– You'd have to ask him. Some come to us by way of the advertisements, but it's usually word of mouth. His eyes meet hers, opaque. Perhaps he doesn't remember. Perhaps he never knew. Whatever, he's not telling. His lips are pressed tightly together. Sealed, as they say in romantic novels.

– I didn't think he seemed at all well. He's terribly withdrawn. Don't you think he should be getting some treatment?

– Treatment's exactly what we offer. The reconciliation of body and mind.

– And what exactly does that mean?

– In a case like Declan's, calm through physical labour. The shedding of the self.

What orotundities! All words and no meaning. He may have changed the frame, but the habits survived intact.

– You don't look as though you do much physical labour! (Or much shedding of the self.)

The Leader looks affronted. – The System works on many levels. He gestures impatiently, and gazes out of the window, perhaps hoping to find inspiration in the landscape. – The aim is to achieve tranquillity through a fusion of body and mind. At first, the body is used to calm the mind. As one moves on, the effort becomes more purely mental. You're right, he continues, leaning forward earnestly, – to think that Declan isn't well. Indeed he isn't. When he came here, he was an ill boy. I think it would be fair to say that, under our treatment, he's making considerable improvement.

– What is the treatment, exactly?

– At the moment, it's body-work.

– You mean, labour?

– In a word.

– How d'you decide who's going to come and live here?

– It's decided on a basis of need.

– And how d'you assess that?

He stares at her blandly. – Need entails sacrifice.

– You mean the neediest are prepared to pay the most?

– The more intensive the treatment, the higher the fees. Naturally.

– So Declan's paying you for the privilege of digging your garden?

– Among other things. It's really not as simple as that. And of course people are fed and housed. He gestures around. – Space is limited, as you see. The fees have to reflect that. Even hospitals charge hotel expenses.

– Quite a business.

– You make it sound very cynical. I can see what you're thinking. You were always so transparent, Helen! You see me here and it's all very pleasant, and you see Declan and his companions out there, and you think it's a nice little racket. Helen, some people just can't deal with the world as you and I can. They need help. They need someone to give them a world they can cope with while they're learning to cope with the world as it is. Would you prefer to see Declan sleeping in doorways? That's the most likely alternative for someone like him. Tea?

He rings a silver bell – all part of the Edwardian fantasy in which he lives, that age when a gentleman could lead a gentleman's life – and a few minutes later a girl arrives bearing a tray lavishly equipped with the correct period properties: silver pots and jugs, anchovy toast, fruitcake, scones. The girl looks vacant, withdrawn. Like Declan. As with Declan, her face is impassive, expressionless. What body-work does she put in, Helen wonders. She sets the tray down on a small table and draws the curtains. Thick, tapestry curtains. It's getting dark.

– Another disciple?

The Leader nods, and takes a piece of toast. He bites into it with obvious relish, and waves towards the plate. – Help yourself.

– Do you have some sort of training, or do you make it up as you go along?

He says placidly: – We run regular seminars with lecturers and theoreticians of the highest quality. Your late husband was a member of our organisation. Didn't you know?

Helen stares at him. – *Benny*?

– Absolutely. He takes another bite of toast, without taking his eyes off her, enjoying her evident astonishment.

– How long – ?

– Six or seven years. Did he never mention us?

– Not to me.

Chris Clay looks genuinely amazed now. – You never read the lectures or saw the videos?

– No. I suppose I didn't really want to know.

– Well, allow me –. He gets up, opens a cupboard in the panelling, and brings out a videotape. On the jacket is a picture of Benny. He hands it to her, and automatically she puts it in her bag. – You ought at least to have copies of what he did. There's more. If you give me your address, I'll see they're sent on.

– Really, you don't need to bother –

– I insist. His death was a great loss to us. I had meant to attend the funeral, but it just wasn't possible.

– It was private. A family affair. The words sound unexpectedly abrupt – almost rude. For some reason, Helen finds the idea of Benny's association with a place like High Leys unsettling, almost shocking.

– But Benny, if you'll allow me to say so, was more than just a private man. He is unruffled by her tone. Does anything shake that monumental calm? Is this an example of what High Leys can achieve, or merely the result of a thick skin? He leans across the table. – Have you coped with his death?

– Not really, not yet. It hasn't been long.

– You've had help, I hope.

– I don't want help, thanks. It's something I'm going to have to get through on my own.

– You think you're self-sufficient, but you're not. Nobody is. You're a very clever woman, Helen, but you seem to think you're superhuman. You're not. You need help. Everyone needs help. And once you've learned to accept help, you can help others.

– What is this? Are you trying to induct me or something?

– Helen, just listen for a change. Concentrate. Put your cup of tea down. What I want to show you, is how you can make the most of Benny's death. It's possible to use situations, to turn things around. For instance, all the energy you used to use up in sex is available now for other things. Had you thought about that?

– Not really.

– Think of it building up inside you there, and then think what you could do with it.

– I find sex makes me feel more energetic, not less.

– We can help there as well. His eyes, unblinking, are fixed on hers. It's really very difficult to tear her gaze away. Has he hypnotised her?

– Helen. He takes the cup from her hand, puts it down, takes the hand in his own. His hand is hot and slightly moist. She thinks of that tongue, and shivers slightly. – I've often thought about you. Our organisation offers such opportunities. I'd like you to come back and find out more. Why don't we fix a time? Give us a day, or even better, two. I can guarantee you won't want to leave.

In spite of herself, Helen feels relaxed, lulled, tempted. She's so alone these days, life is such an effort. To offload her troubles, to decline responsibility, once in a while. What wouldn't she give! The fire flickers in the grate. The curtains hold the night at bay. There is a scent of buttered toast.

– You could stay now. It's a long drive to London, and I'm sure the roads are icy. We could put you up. We could have a good, long talk, just the two of us.

Suddenly Helen remembers. She looks at her watch. The spell is broken. – God! Is that the time?

He looks annoyed. – It's only just gone five.

– I must go, says Helen firmly. – I said I'd meet my son in Oxford at six. I'll be late as it is.

Her heart is beating, as if she's made some narrow escape. She picks up her coat and bag and makes for the door. The Leader does not move. His eyes do not follow her. She finds she's almost running. She can't wait to get away from this place. Its tentacles curl around her, its ripples enclose her. She hurries along the landing, down the stairs. The carpet muffles her footsteps.

What was she expecting? The entrance-hall is empty, the door is not locked. Her car is where she parked it.

Lights are starting to appear behind the house's many windows. Those two tall rectangles, thickly curtained now, are the Leader's red-leather study. Above, under the lettered eaves, some smaller squares are lit. A place for everyone, and everyone in their place.

Could Benny really have been part of all this? Chris Clay seemed to hint he was the guiding light, but that's hard to believe. How scornful he would have been of this setup, how quick to ridicule, to expose. (But apparently was not; did not.)

In the half-light, a figure rounds the corner of the house and begins to walk along the front towards the main door. Helen's hand freezes on the car key: the back of her neck prickles. It's too dark to make out the features, and the light has drained away all colour, but she recognises that figure. The way it moves, hurried, absorbed. It's the brown-haired woman she saw in the mall.

Before Helen can move, the woman opens the house door, slips inside, and closes it after her.

What should Helen do?

Obviously, follow. Isn't this her chance? When will she have another?

But she can't. She can't bear to go back into that house. If those

173

tentacles touched her once more, if those sticky ripples lapped her round, how would she ever break free?

And Tim will be waiting.

Clinging to the thought of Tim, she starts the car and drives to the gates. They are not locked – not from the inside. She opens them and drives through. Doesn't stop to close them.

Doesn't stop until she reaches Oxford.

7

TIM SAID HE'D see her at the Randolph at six-thirty. Her eyes scan the road mechanically, but inside her head there is only the brown-haired young woman, slipping round corners, disappearing into stations. Sitting in shoe-shops: beside her, Laura. If that were possible, which it is not. Who is she? What is she? A ghost, a figment. Sceptical Helen, Our Lady of No Illusions, is being haunted.

At six o'clock a breathless Helen sinks into one of the Randolph's all-devouring armchairs. She ran to get here on time, even though she knows Tim is invariably late. This way, the pleasure of seeing him is in a sense prolonged, since, for her, their meeting has already begun. Meanwhile she's got plenty to think about.

How late would he have to be before she started to worry about him, before an internal cinema of overdoses, drownings, car crashes, began to unreel inside her head? One hour, two? Then he'd stroll in and – she wouldn't say a word. Helen treats her relationship with Tim very delicately. She's terrified he'll realise how appallingly essential his existence is to her own. Such a realisation would horrify him – would frighten him away. So she leaves him to his devices. India, Oxford – she lets him assume that out of sight is out of mind. Which in his case, of course, it is.

It's ten to seven when he shambles in, well inside the permitted limit. He gazes around the foyer. It's full of people, but padding and carpeting ensure that all sound is reduced to a polite murmur. In his pony-tail and threadbare jeans, he looks like some exotic visitor from outer space. How thin he is, and how tall! How solid-seeming, and in fact how transitory, how indescribably destructible. Helen feels the usual spasm of tenderness at the sight of him: what Declan will not allow Colette. Colette's darling, her beautiful boy. Gemma has always been second-best where Colette's concerned. And what does Declan do by way of thanks for this devotion? Forbids her to come near him. Denies her the pleasure of contemplation, even.

Gemma finished art school last year. She gave up acting, didn't try science: now she's a painter, safe from family comparison. She's turned into a plump, pink-and-white, radiantly blooming Renoir girl. Colette can persuade herself she's still a beauty, until pretty Gemma enters the room and, without herself being beautiful, shows what's faded. Since being a beauty has constituted much of Colette's life, this makes her nervous. She behaves badly, hates herself for it, and can do nothing about it. Then she hates herself even more. Last time Helen saw them together, they were at each other's throats as usual. They were in Colette's kitchen, drinking tea. Monica was pottering round the Aga pretending to cook something. Gemma doesn't like Monica, never has, but her dislike is tempered these days by the recognition that Monica absolves her of inconvenient responsibilities. With Monica around, she doesn't have to worry about her mother. Helen happened to drop in, and immediately wished she could drop straight back out again, but by then it was too late: she was corralled, a witness.

– What's the big idea, Mama? Trying to age me before my time? Imagine what I'd look like pregnant. Gross! Wouldn't I, Helen? Simon would have twenty fits.

– Don't be silly, darling, Colette said sharply. – I'm just trying to think what would be best for you. It's not much fun sitting at home worrying about your work. Any actor knows that. And with Simon being so busy I thought, you know –

Colette sounded uncharacteristically tentative. She knew she was treading on eggs. It's hard to make a living as a painter. Gemma's canvases pile up, unexhibited, *ergo* unsold. But she hasn't yet reconciled herself to the idea that she's going to have to teach if she wants to make a living.

Gemma, of course, heard the unspoken words and retaliated in kind. – You've got too much time on your hands these days, Ma, that's your trouble, she said cruelly. – It always takes you the same way. You start organising people. Have you noticed that, Helen? She does, doesn't she? Gemma laughed to take the sting out of her words (but it remained), rose and gave her mother a kiss. – Got to go now. I'm meeting Simon up West. Bye, Helen. See you, darling. Monica got a cursory wave, provoking one of those martyred downward glances Gemma especially hates.

– She's so unrealistic, Colette said guiltily when Gemma was safely out of the room. You can't win, can you? With one breath I'm accused of being self-centred, and with the next I'm trying to take over her life! Why do we do it, eh, Hel? Don't you sometimes wonder?

Is that what it would have come to between Helen and Laura? Constant sparring, raised hackles, jealousy? Is that what life is like for mothers and daughters when there are sons around? For she can't deny that Tim was always her boy, just as Declan was and is Colette's. And Laura was Benny's, just as Helen was her own Daddy's girl. Perhaps that was why she never worried about Laura's partiality. There was always the memory of her own movement, away from her father, towards her mother and the shared experience of women. Eventually.

She waves, and Tim threads his way towards her. He looks like some exotic wading bird as he picks his way through the armchairs on skinny shanks. He's still faintly tanned from the time in India. Manfully, he allows himself to be kissed. – So how was Declan?

– All right, I suppose. He wasn't telling.

– No, well, there's only one person he'll speak to.

– So who's that? You?

Tim shakes his head. – No. Gemma.

Helen is surprised. – I know she sees him sometimes. But I thought they always got on so badly.

Tim shrugs. – That's the way it is. There was Dad, but he's not around any more. And he gives another shrug.

Tim always wanted Benny's approval. Declan got it. It says a lot for him, thinks Helen, that he never held this against Declan. Or never seemed to. What, after all, does she know of the inside of Tim's head? He's never actually said he dislikes Declan, but then, he's never said much about Declan at all. Why should he? Their paths haven't crossed for years.

A waitress hovers. Helen orders mineral water – she's got to drive to London tonight. Tim orders a beer. – Though God knows what it'll be like here, he says distrustfully.

– Much the same as anywhere else, I expect. Helen has never been a beer-drinker. – D'you know anything about the place he's at? High Leys?

– Not much. It's very expensive, isn't it? If you ask me he just stays there so Colette'll have to keep on paying out.

– What a horrible thing to say.

– What a horrible thing to do. Let's not talk about Declan any more, says Tim abruptly. He's not worth wasting breath on.

He does hate him, then.

Helen thinks, Oh God, how I love you. She says: – Let's get the menu, shall we? You look as though you could use a good dinner.

Driving home that night, she feels nervous and unsatisfied. Of course it was lovely seeing Tim, but for once he does not occupy the whole of her mind. That's still mostly taken up by the brown-haired young woman: now associated not only with Laura, but with Declan, too. And Christopher Clay. Yes, what's *he* doing mixed up in all this? That seedy, untrustworthy figure – and he was hinting that Benny was a colleague, an associate. Which, given Chris's relationship with the truth, presumably means that Benny was in some form his superior – boss, employer? Which leads her back to the nagging question. *How's that possible?* For Benny was never a quack, and if Helen has ever seen a quack establishment, it's High Leys.

She suddenly remembers the video. Did she leave it there? She can't remember what, if anything, she did with it. Put it in her bag? With her free hand, she gropes inside. Yes. There it is. She doesn't really want to see it. But at the same time, she knows she won't resist. As soon as she gets home, she'll rush up to the sitting-room. Though not without a glass of strengthening whisky to hand.

The press of a button, and suddenly Benny fills the room. His face, his voice, his urgency, his unique aliveness. She's hooked, riveted: she couldn't turn him off if she wanted. Which of course she doesn't. For this is not only Benny the guru, the charismatic leader, but Benny her husband, and Helen is enmeshed with him even as she is appalled.

He's in some sort of sunny courtyard or garden, surrounded by vegetation. Synchrony, perhaps, or even Lorraine's little patio – but even the long shots are unrevealing, and he doesn't move: he's standing in front of a creeper-covered wall, speaking intensely to the camera. – I'm Benny Spiro, he says. – I'm a scientist. I was a biologist; now I'm interested in physics. I'm going to tell you about why this is – why I changed my area of interest.

– A few years ago, my little girl Laura died. She was knocked down by a car. I was shattered. I felt that the best part of my life had come to an end with hers. But I didn't question that hers *had* come to an end. I wasn't just irreligious – I was *anti*-religious, and I certainly didn't believe in life after death. I still don't. But now I'm convinced that Laura isn't really dead. What went under that car was just a part of her – and perhaps quite an insignificant part. And physics has given me an explanation of what I know to be true.

The usual sentimental rubbish, the kind of thing which bombards the bereaved from all sides? Helen, hanging on his words, knows it isn't. She knows exactly what he's talking about because she saw it herself. She was right, then. Laura's alive. It was, it was Laura she saw! It must be true – Benny's telling her so.

He's talking now about the Uncertainty Principle, about how an electron occupies every possible position until observation pins it down to one position, and about the hypothesis of parallel universes as one possible explanation of how this occurs. – Suppose these parallel universes exist, he says, – as many physicists much cleverer than me are convinced that they do. There are infinite numbers of them. Every time a choice is made – to do this rather than that, to go here rather than there – a universe is born to take account of the other choice. Because of course the decision we see here was only made here, and all possibilities have to be accommodated, not only for electrons but for more complex structures as well. So you see where this is leading. A universe exists – any number of them exist – where my daughter is still alive. She wasn't killed. The motorist took another route, she decided not to cross the road – an infinite number of possibilities. And I know this is true, because my daughter is alive. I've seen her, and I can tell you. It *is true*.

The camera's tight on his face as he says this. There are little beads of sweat on his forehead. He's rather red, as always happens when he's feeling emotional. As always happened.

He's recovered now, and in long shot again. – A number of interesting questions arise. Where are these other universes? Are they all 'real' – as real as this universe which you and I inhabit? And if they are, is there any way of contacting them? Of getting to them? Physicists approach their subject through mathematics, and using a lot of imagination. But, as I said, I'm a biologist. I'm interested in what I can see, what I can show. And I know from experience that universes intersect. This has happened to me. But how, and why? And is there any way of controlling these contacts?

– Physics says that the way to these universes is through black holes, infinitely dense collapsed stars with which our universe is studded. You can picture a black hole as a tube of rubber with two rims – one in this universe, one in a parallel universe. If we were to enter a black hole and come out the other side, that's where we'd emerge. But everyone agrees that this is physically out of the question. The gravitational forces inside these black holes are so enormous that, even if we could get near them, we'd be torn to pieces as soon as we came within their field.

– So there must be some other way. And I think there is. I think that the secret route is inside us – inside our heads: in our brains.

– Now, one of Einstein's great perceptions was that time is just another dimension. We're timebound, so we find it hard to perceive this; but in fact past, present and future are all there, just like up and down. And of course the same is true of all the parallel universes. And if the future is as real as the present and the past, then all choices have already been made. They were made at the moment when this universe, along with all the others, came into being. So here, I think, we get a clue to a possible line of communication. Because visions of the future aren't unknown. People quite often dream of a future event, and realise, when it happens, that they foresaw it. The obvious explanation is that, in the relaxed dream-state, they've travelled forward in spacetime, where of course the future – our future – already exists. But that's by no means what always happens. Just as often, what we dreamed doesn't take place. We don't think any more about it. But of course that future exists, too: all possible futures exist. Our dream took place in a parallel universe, that's all.

– Maybe, if we can acquire the right mental state, we can learn to become timeless – to travel in spacetime, to surf the intersecting universes. Is this Nirvana, to which the Buddhists aspire? Maybe there are exercises, mental exercises, which can help us attain this state. I believe there are. And if we can travel forwards, as I'm convinced we can, can't we also travel backwards? I think so. In fact, that's what I have done. My life with Laura has begun again, and this time, it won't be cut short.

The camera pulls back, and a little girl wanders into shot. Helen feels numb: the breath drains from her body. For the child is Laura. The video must be quite old, because she looks about two years old, and when Helen saw her she was six or seven. But it's Laura. As on that other occasion, Helen is filled with absolute certainty.

The video ends.

Helen plays it again, and again. But in the end, what is it? Only a piece of magnetic tape. A home movie. If she wants photos of Laura, she has boxes full of them. And that's not what she wants. She wants the real thing.

But how can she get to it? Benny's dead. Laura's vanished. And no-one else will believe her. Pat didn't. Kertes won't: he dismissed Benny's later work as 'off the end', thought he'd descended into pseudo-science, science fiction. Lorraine? But she can't ask Lorraine. It's out of the question.

Who, then? Who might know? Declan? It's obvious he, at least, was convinced – or why else would he be at High Leys? But that's no use, either. Whatever Declan may know, he's not about to share it with Helen.

He talks to Gemma, though. Colette said so. Perhaps she'll go and see Gemma. She could buy a canvas. That would cheer them both up.

Gemma's phone is answered by a man. This, presumably, is

Simon, of whom Helen has heard much. He's a multi-media design wizard, much in demand. He is not Colette's cup of tea.

– They seem very happy, that's one thing, Colette said doubtfully after Gemma had left, the day Helen interrupted them.

– Don't you like him?

– Darling, I don't have to. It's probably just as well I don't, she'd chuck him at once.

Gemma comes to the phone. Helen says, – Gem, it's Helen here. I suddenly felt like buying a picture. Can I come and see some of yours?

– Sure, says Gemma. – If you think you want to. She sounds pleased. – I warn you, she says, – nail your car down and take everything out of it. This is the jungle here. They've perfected a way of taking the wheels off in five seconds. I saw someone doing it, the other day. I called 999, but by the time the police got round they'd been gone ten minutes.

– With the wheels?

– Obviously.

– Didn't you stop them?

– What? And get smashed with a tyre-iron?

– What do you do, then?

– Use public transport, says Gemma.

The outside of Simon and Gemma's house is standard dingy, like the street in which it stands: but this is mere camouflage. The interior is white. White walls, white floors, white curtains. There are a few rugs in primary colours, and some large pictures on the walls, abstract grids and circles, in pastel shades.

– We just finished painting it, Gemma observes proudly.

No wonder she recoils at the thought of babies. A baby would do for all that white in no time at all. The uncluttered look would also disappear. Simon and Gemma appear to have almost no furniture at all.

– There's not much point having a lot of stuff round here, Gemma explains, – it all gets nicked. We keep getting broken into.

– So why not move somewhere else?

– Couldn't find anywhere else so central with this much space. Would you like a coffee?

– No, I think I'd like to see your pictures first. Helen wants a little time to collect herself, to work out what exactly it is she's going to ask Gemma. Not that it's so complicated, really. She just wants to know what's going on, with Laura, with Declan, with Chris, with the brown-haired woman. What was going on with Benny. Of course, there's no guarantee Gemma will know all or any of this.

Gemma takes Helen through her paintings They are large, brightly coloured. Some of them are abstracts, geometrical, like the ones hanging downstairs; some are less formal, with hints of figures. Are they good? Helen wonders, then derides her own uncertainty. *Good*: what on earth does that mean? Is it a sound investment, will it hold its value? Does she like them, that's the only relevant thing. The problem is, she's not sure. At times like this she specially misses Benny. He was always so decided, so certain of his taste. He'd like this one but not that. He'd want to know how long they took, what sort of paints Gemma used, how long she'd been doing this sort of picture . . . But Helen, as usual, can think of nothing to say.

Yes, she likes them. Or some of them. One can't say more. She makes her choice. – How much?

– Three hundred? Gemma sounds uncertain.

– Fine.

They adjourn to the kitchen for coffee. Gemma is relaxed now, smiling: delighted to have made a sale. She shines with pleasure, glowing like one of those Impressionist canvases out of which she seems to have walked. Helen is pleased, too, and relieved to see that the kitchen is a haven of mess. Gemma and Simon are human after all.

Helen says, sipping her coffee: – I went to see Declan the other day.

– Oh, yes? How was he?

– Not being telepathic, I can't say. Disturbed, is the word I'd use.

In that other universe where Laura is now a young woman, does another Declan also take his rightful place, that indefinite but brilliant place which seemed, once, so inevitably his destiny?

Gemma laughs. – He is a bastard!

– You think it's all put on, then?

– Not all. No, it's not. Mostly he just can't help it. You've got to understand, Helen, Gemma says urgently. – We were never given any help. We were just plonked down and told, here you are. Do what you want. Mama and Dad had their minds on other things. I mean, they loved us – well, Mama still does. I was never so sure about Dad. Does he love anyone? Does he have feelings? You see, you're not sure. You don't know what to say. Anyhow, no-one ever told us, You must do this, you mustn't do that. We were just left to get on with it. I know you were there, but it wasn't you we were actually living with in the end, was it? Though I expect it must have felt like it at the time. But when Laura died that sort of came to an end, didn't it? We were on our own. What kids dream of. And actually you can survive. It is possible. I did. I got through. I'm tough, like Mama. That's one reason we don't get on – we're too alike. But Declan couldn't cope. He isn't very strong, and he isn't actually very bright. He hasn't really changed, has he? Not if you think. He was never exactly forthcoming, was he? All I can remember, when we were kids, was him hanging around on the edge looking enigmatic. People looked at him, this great beauty, and wondered what was going on in there. And he was always terrified they'd find out. Because you know what the answer was? Nothing at all. Nobody would believe that, of course. After all, Dad's bright enough, isn't he, and Dec's just like Dad. Another beautiful incarnation for Ma to fall in love with all over again. But that's not what Dec needed. He couldn't cope with all that, all he wanted was to be told what to do. Do this, do that. That's still what he wants. Maybe he should have gone into the army. But only as a private. He doesn't want to be responsible, not even for himself. He can't face it.

Gemma sits facing Helen across the kitchen table. Helen realises she's never known Gemma especially well. She was Benny's friend.

– Tim thinks he's staying there out of spite. Refusing to see Colette and costing her a fortune while he's doing it.

– That's probably part of it. Though Tim's hardly an unbiased observer. He never liked Dec.

– D'you know, I never realised that till the other day.

Gemma does not comment on this. She says, – Why all this interest in Declan all of a sudden?

Now that they've come to it, Helen doesn't know what to say. Should she tell Gemma about the video, about seeing Laura?

Somehow she can't bring herself to embark upon that. If Gemma and Colette have seen it, they never mentioned it to Helen. Perhaps they just thought it was mad, and thought it more tactful to desist. And if they haven't . . . Finally she says, – It's Benny I'm trying to find out about really. He seems to have been linked to this place – High Leys. Did you know that? They gave me a video – he was getting into some strange stuff. I kept out of all that, I just didn't want to know. I was so fond of Benny. We needed each other, and that was a way of staying together. I don't know how long it could have lasted. But now Benny's dead, and I want to know why. I heard he and Dec saw each other in California. That was what I wanted to ask Dec about. There's something about him and Benny I just have to find out. Don't ask me what. I've no idea. If I did, it would be easy.

Gemma looks at her attentively, meditatively. She finishes her coffee, holds out the pot. – Another one? She pours some for herself, sipping slowly. She gets up and says, – I'll be back in a second. Just going to get something.

She comes back carrying an envelope which she hands to Helen. It's a Synchrony envelope. Helen recognises the paper even before she sees the logo. She's received enough of them in her time. This one's addressed to Gemma. She recognises the handwriting, too. Benny's.

– Read it when you get home. Are you taking your picture with you?

The envelope is heavy. It contains several sheets densely covered. Helen, sitting at her desk, the new picture hanging on the wall behind her, feels her heart jump as she extracts them. The sight of Benny's handwriting, these days, always reminds her of that note in the hall. What horrid surprises await her this time?

The letter is dated: July, 1988. He'd have been there a year.

Dear Gemma,

I don't know if I should be writing you this letter. I've promised I wouldn't – tell anyone, that is. But I can't just not say anything. So keep it quiet, what I'm going to tell you, will you? Not a word to a soul, OK? Not your mother, not Helen. This has to be between you and me. It was so extraordinary – I've got to tell someone.

Benny's floating on a sea of impersonality. This is true of all cities – it is the blessed, comforting city characteristic: nobody knows you, nobody cares. Not like villages with their twitching curtains (not that Benny has ever lived in a village, God forbid). But in the league of city impersonality, Los Angeles, in his experience, emerges an easy winner. No-one was born here, there are no oldest inhabitants, no history, no civic traditions. Just a concatenation of egos jostling in the smoggy sunshine. Wandering souls wheeling while they wait, on skate-boards, two hundred-speed bicycles, stretch limos, Mustang convertibles, for the recognition which alone will prove to them that they actually exist.

Existence: a concept about which Benny has been increasingly uncertain since Laura's death. He is. But who is he, what's he for? Why here rather than there? No nationality, no family, no job. Floating, always floating.

He knows who he *was*. Laura's Dad. He can remember exactly, he will never forget it, the moment of emergence, that scarlet, tiny head with its crown of bedraggled black fluff, followed in a sort of slithering rush by the rest of her. He had the grandstand view – Helen, panting and pushing, couldn't see a thing. They cut the cord, wiped her down, wrapped her up and gave her to him to hold while Helen got on with the business of having Tim. And Benny, crying, held his daughter and knew that this was it, he wasn't a free agent any more, Laura's existence would govern the rest of his life. He knew then that he'd been right to resist this, he didn't want to be responsible, tied down, shackled by this terrible love, unlike any other love, which he felt from that first instant. And at the same time, of course, terribly wrong. What was his life, before Laura? Dry bones.

Tim was always beside the point. Why? Who can say? Because that's how it was, that's how it's always been. For Benny, only Laura existed. From the moment of her emergence, there was instant rapport. He knew almost before she did how she would feel, how she would react, what would be her take on a given situation – for were not those his eyes, looking out of that little girl's body? Isn't she like you, they all said. What did they expect? Of course she was like him. She *was* him. There were differences, obviously – of age, of sex. But they were almost irrelevant.

And then she was removed, and Benny floats, unanchored. Not even his work matters any more. Why does he do what he does? Who, in a Laura-less world, could care less about evolution? He had thought the pursuit of knowledge an impersonal thing – it's there, you uncover it: the truth shines through. He's always despised those pathetic weaklings who let their feelings sway their approach to the facts.

But now this certainty has vanished along with the rest. Unrelenting materialism, the visible, measurable givens of biology, no longer chime with his emotional state. Yet what alternative remains? He longs for comfort. Darwin does not provide it.

Synchrony, though, offers possibilities. The new physics opens doors which had appeared unalterably locked, reconciles seemingly irreconcilable opposites. In the singularity before Time and the Big Bang, in the narrow, specific parameters which alone permitted life to evolve and which are (but why?) the parameters of the Universe, in the bizarre possibilities of parallel worlds on the far side of black holes, in the notion of immortality achieved through virtual resurrection in cyberspace – in all these speculative and quasi-mystical musings, Benny finds unlooked-for comfort. He likes to dwell on these notions. And where better to consider them? Is Kertes not – has he not been for thirty years – a leading proponent of such theories? Which, however fantastic they may sound, are based upon experiment, upon calculation, upon reasonable extrapolation. Which are, compared to many creeds routinely adhered to in this city, the merest common sense. In which, therefore, a scientist may let himself believe; by which he may be consoled.

So Los Angeles suits his mood. Lost in thought, he drifts round the supermarkets, along the freeways, and the city drifts with him. No-one hurries. Why should they? Eternity looms.

What made him notice the dog? Perhaps it was the sheer impertinence of its statement that drew his attention. Not many creatures are afoot in this city. You move on wheels. But today

Benny feels like walking. And the dog is so outrageously, so perkily pedestrian: a small poodle, covered with tight, glossy, black curls. Unclipped, naturally. The humiliation of the poodle-parlour is not for this customer. There isn't even a collar round its neck. It's its own dog. Unlike Benny, it does not suffer from uncertainty.

It bounces along the sidewalk, purposeful, directed. Benny is reminded of someone – who? Then it comes to him. Laura. Yes. The dog has her hair, her walk, her manner: questing, intelligent, bold, cheerful. Benny is fascinated by it. He finds himself following it with unwonted urgency. As they trot briskly along, the poodle and Benny, he fantasises that maybe this *is* Laura – if not a reincarnation, then a message. What message? For want of any other: Follow that dog.

From time to time the poodle glances back over its shoulder, as if to make sure Benny is still in tow. Together they traverse intersections, negotiate sidewalks and building-lots. Benny loses track of time and place. He has entrusted himself to the dog, to Laura. Where are they? How long have they been going? He has no idea. As so often when one is led or chauffeured, he finds that his sense of place and direction has switched off.

They arrive at an area of low, pastel-coloured buildings, apparently constructed of plasterboard: fast-food joints, motels, apartments. The dog trots past these and along a brick wall in which a iron gate is set, evidently the last relic of some earlier generation of buildings. The wall is about six feet high, and seems to enclose a garden: greenery spills over the top, there are trees on the other side. When it reaches the gate the poodle stops, wagging its tail. It looks at Benny, then back at the gate. Its meaning could not be clearer. In here. This is the place.

But what does it want him to do? On whose account are they here? Is he to introduce himself? Or pick it up and drop it over the wall? In this situation, virtual speech is no substitute for the real thing. Perhaps he should let them know the dog's back, since it so clearly belongs here. Somebody must be missing it. Benny would, if it was his dog.

He rings the bell. The entryphone crackles. – Who is this?

– I think I've found your dog. It's a little black poodle. It's making as if it lives here. D'you want to let it in or shall I put it over the wall?

– Hold on.

There is a pause, and the sound of footsteps on gravel. The gate swings back. And there stands – Declan.

Declan and Benny stare at each other. Benny bursts out laughing. Declan looks appalled.

– Don't worry, Dec, I haven't come looking for you, I don't know what you're doing, I am not an emissary. I just found myself following this dog for some reason. Does it live here?

The poodle is clearly delighted to see Declan: it's jumping up at him as though there were springs in its knees. – Sheba! he exclaims, petting it distractedly. – It's called Sheba, he adds unnecessarily.

There is a pause while Declan concentrates on the dog, Benny concentrates on Declan, and both try to work out what to do next.

– Well, now Sheba's kindly introduced us, d'you want to come for a coffee or something? says Benny.

Declan looks over his shoulder. He seems worried.

Benny remembers Colette telling him how she spent hours, days, weeks, standing in the road outside the London house owned by the cult to which rumour attached him.

– And what were you planning to do if he appeared? he asked her when she described this vigil.

– I don't know. Kidnap him. Just get him in the car and drive.

– But he's bigger than you. Stronger.

– I don't know, Benny. One isn't rational about these things. Perhaps I just wanted to see him, to know he was still alive.

– And did you? See him?

– No.

Now he spreads his hands. – I promise. Come on, Dec. You can trust me. I haven't even got a car here. Perhaps you could tell me where this is, to begin with. I've no idea. I seem to have been walking for hours.

*

Helen reads and re-reads Benny's letter. Then she picks up the phone and calls Gemma.

189

– Gem, this is ridiculous. Am I expected to believe that some mystical guide directed Benny to Declan?

– *I* don't know, do I? says Gemma, reasonably. – All I know is, he sent me this letter and that's what it says. Maybe it's pure coincidence, he just found himself following this dog because there was something about it which happened to remind him of Laura and it happened to belong to Declan's people.

– It seems very peculiar.

– Well, life is peculiar, isn't it? Gemma falls into the familiar tone of her encounters with her parents' generation. She is the down-to-earth guide, explaining the world's current realities to a hopeless learner. She's so sensible, Gemma. Faced with her relentless common sense, Helen and Colette always feel like a couple of schoolgirls. – Maybe it didn't really happen like that at all, maybe he was just describing something that was going on in his mind. *I* don't know. You can see it how you like, can't you? You know the terrifying thing about you, Helen? You can't bear people making up stories for themselves. You think everyone ought to face life head-on. But people like stories. They're comforting, what's wrong with that? What d'you think Dec was running away from? Undiluted life, that's what. It's too much for him, he can't face it. He wants a story.

– So it was Benny got him back here.

– To this place where he is now, you mean? Yes. Don't ask me for details, Gemma says hurriedly. – I've no idea. I was away on holiday somewhere, and when I got back there he was. Ma said Benny'd found him. Now you know as much as I do.

– You didn't talk to Benny about it?

– I always thought I'd better wait for him to mention it. But he never did.

– And what about Dec?

– He isn't into details. You must have noticed.

How long ago did all this happen? Three, four years? More. The years fly by so fast now. Helen's always so busy. Successful, in demand, rushing here and there when she isn't panicking about some deadline. All she can remember is that, as Gemma says, suddenly Declan was in England. No explanation: just an address. She had no idea Benny had anything to do with it, and he never enlightened her.

Not a word. How could he do that? Perhaps that was the arrangement, Declan's condition. All right, I'll come, but only if . . . A big secret, another of Declan's little games. Colette was away, filming on location in Cyprus, and she came back to find a note saying he'd arrived. And a bill.

– Who's it from?

– This place he's in. High Leys. All those plural English country houses. I always had an ambition to own one called Loggerheads. Don't you think that would be a good name for a house? We're all at Loggerheads this weekend, darling.

– Anything else? Besides the bill, I mean?

– A typed note, saying he doesn't want visitors yet.

– So what did you do?

– Phoned, of course. I assumed it was some sort of scam. A con-trick. They'd seen something in the paper or something.

– But it wasn't?

– No. He's there, all right. Gemma went, just to make sure. He agreed to see her. Won't see me. What can you do? If that's the way it is, that's the way it is. It's his life. I've got mine to get on with.

– What is it, a hospital?

– Some sort of, apparently. When I asked, people did know about it. Detox, getting them to face life again – what do I know? What do I know about Declan these days? I just pay the bills. It's not run on charity, I can tell you that.

– But how did he get there? Who fixed it? I thought he was in California somewhere?

– They won't say. It's all a big secret. That's part of the deal, apparently. Getting their confidence. They won't tell anything unless the patient gives permission, and Declan won't.

The only people he would see were Gemma and Benny. Who, coincidentally, had just come back. Was that why? Because of Declan? Were she and Tim merely incidental? No, that's ridiculous. He even wept, he was so glad to see her, so glad to be back. It wasn't faked. She's as sure of that as she's ever been of anything.

– Why did he pick that particular place? Helen asks Gemma now. – Did you know?

– No idea at all. It's quite well-known, isn't it? For treating people?

They have some sort of system. Surely this isn't the first time you've been there?

– He never wanted to see me. (Didn't want to this time, either.) – And I didn't push that hard, to tell you the truth.

– You make him nervous, Helen, that's what it is. He's probably terrified you'll tell him to stand on his own two feet.

– Well, so he should. Suddenly, Helen can hardly contain her indignation. – What does he think he's doing? Taking whatever it is out on Colette, never seeing her and making her pay these vast bills. What's he punishing her for? Not being there all the time when he was little? You wait till you have kids, see how you feel about giving up your entire life. It's hardly as though you were deprived. I seem to remember you spent half your lives over at our place. You said so yourself. Was that so bad? D'you know what his treatment is? Digging the vegetable garden. For Christ's sake.

– That's just what I mean, says Gemma, and rings off.

*

Benny was very hot on what he liked to call the soul-body problem. He wrote about it in *Immortality and the New Physics*. The same question, she sees now, that he broached in the video, from a slightly different angle. Who, what, is Laura, this new Laura?

Within its own universe, each being is of course corporeal. But suppose an entity finds itself, for a fragment of time, in another, parallel world? What sort of entity is it? What is this self that has slipped across spacetime? It is surely the essence – the soul: and it is experienced as that extra-corporeal state we know as haunting.

Oh, Benny!

Helen thinks: Children. Even when they're alive, they haunt you.

She hears Colette's voice again: *Why do we do it, Hel?*

Because of you, darling. All because of you.

*

Helen knew Colette would be arriving. Twice last week a big, iridescent scarab-like beetle blundered into the room while she and

Benny were eating dinner. Attracted by the light, no doubt. The evenings are warm, and the dining-table stands by the open French windows at the back of their recently-completed kitchen, bathed in the scent of honeysuckle. Helen put that in, with just such evenings in mind, when they first bought the house.

Helen said to Benny, – A scarab! I didn't know we had them in England!

– It's a rose-chafer. They come out at this time of year.

– It looks like a scarab.

– It's a member of the same family.

What could a scarab mean but Colette? She and Patrick still wear those rings, above their wedding bands. This was Helen's first thought when she saw the insect. She did not share it with Benny. Superstition is his bugbear. He is sternly insistent that science holds the answers to the world's questions. Astrology, iridology, reflexology, pyramidology, Nostradamus and the *I Ching* – all those fashionable New Age ologies that go with San Francisco, joss-sticks and flowers in your hair – are for binning. And Helen is with him on this. Nevertheless, scarabs . . . And twice!

Helen glances at her own ring finger. It is bare. She lost her wedding-ring in the garden, not long after acquiring it. They searched, but it was nowhere to be found, and they didn't bother to replace it. Helen never wanted one in the first place. Benny doesn't wear a ring: why should she? But her father insisted. – Really, Dad, she said. – I'm surprised at you. It only marks me out as being owned. I thought you were more modern than that. – You can't have a wedding without a ring, he said sternly.

So they went and bought one. Helen is very fond of her father. She's always been close to him. Daddy's girl. And as it turned out, he was right. The registry office ceremony, instead of being the mere signing of names Helen was hoping for, turned out thoroughly mock-religious, full of homilies and solemnities, and, indeed, requiring a ring. She was appalled, but what could she do? This was hardly the moment to walk out on a point of principle, not with Benny on one side of her and her father on the other, both staring stonily ahead willing her not to giggle or protest. So that when the ring disappeared, far from being displeased, she felt in some way borne out by fate. Friends predicted dire consequences. To lose one's wedding-ring! What could be more symbolic? But Benny and Helen are still married. Three years down, a lifetime to go.

In the case of the scarab, necromancy wins. Colette phoned the morning after the beetle's second visit. She's found a house. She says, – It's just round the corner from you! Will you come and look it over with me?

A house? What's Colette doing looking at houses in London? Isn't she cosily set up in Huddersfield? Perhaps she's looking for a pied-à-terre, somewhere to go when she's up here working.

Benny and Helen's house is in Kentish Town, a flat-fronted terraced slice of grey London brick. It used to be just as depressing as the one Colette is viewing, and remained so, in various different ways, for two years after they bought it. Now the builders have left and only decorating remains to be done. They began with the kitchen and are working upwards.

– They've got such possibilities, these houses, haven't they? Colette enthuses. – You can do so much with them. You could knock this through and make it all into one enormous room. Or perhaps double-height, with a gallery. She spins around, picturing herself against different settings.

Helen agrees. That's what Colette requires. Enthusiastic acquiescence. No intrusion of alien egos or deflating realities. She doesn't want to know about waking every morning to a fresh shower of plaster-dust, picking one's way through the builders to the bathroom (should there be a bathroom), or – even worse – *not* picking one's way through the builders because the builders have failed to turn up and there's just yesterday's plaster-dust, undisturbed. No, Colette's used to being a star these days, and stars get what they want, as if by magic.

Helen, for example, ought really to be at work. She's doing a bit of freelance research for a film about drugs. There's an interview set up for tomorrow: she ought to be confirming it, checking the venue, making sure of the crew . . . – But, darling, Colette insisted, that's nothing but a few phone-calls. You can do it in five minutes, you don't have to go into the office, surely? Do come and see this house, I must know what you think about it, and it's sure to be snapped up if we don't go at once.

It's true, phone-calls can be made from anywhere. Helen sat down at her desk and made them: they took half an hour, while Colette wandered dreamily round the garden. So now the two of them may spend an almost guilt-free hour sipping chilled Gewurztraminer.

– Actually, says Colette, – I prefer red. You don't happen to have any, do you?

– 'Fraid not, lies Helen. She's done enough pandering for one day. She sips pensively. – How often d'you think you'll use the place, then?

– How often? Colette sounds startled. – All the time! We're going to come and live here!

In one way, Helen is relieved to hear this. It will be delightful to be reunited with their old friends. And it was depressing – though naturally she couldn't say so, indeed felt barely able to admit it to herself – to think that Colette already had enough spare cash to buy herself a house in London merely to accommodate the odd weekend. But wasn't she reading only the other week – in the *Observer*, was it? – this big article about Patrick and Colette, English theatre's new dream couple? About the wonderful work Patrick's doing in Huddersfield, how he's making it into a theatrical mecca, far more exciting than anything to be found in London, while she, intelligent as well as beautiful, is the rising hope of stage and screen? About how she loves walking on the moors, just stepping out of her back door into the wild? About how he finds a freedom of manoeuvre up north that would be inconceivable in London . . . ?

– Oh, that! says Colette. – You mustn't believe everything you read.

– But there must be some reason you've suddenly decided to move?

Colette hesitates. – Well, there's a lot of reasons, really. It's all rather complicated.

– Oh? says Helen invitingly. She pushes the bottle across the table.

Colette shakes her head. – It's hard to explain. The theatre's going beautifully. Patrick's done brilliantly with that. They'll be desperate to see him go.

This hardly seems a reason to move.

– But you're fed up with being stuck in Huddersfield, is that it? I couldn't live anywhere except London myself, Helen agrees. – Though I suppose the kind of job he's got doesn't grow on trees, does it? Can he get something down here?

– Oh, it's not me that wants to move. Well, I do, but it's not on my account, if you see what I mean.

There is a pause.

– But if he doesn't want to move and you don't, why are you?

– Oh, it's not that he doesn't want to . . . The thing is, says Colette reluctantly, – Patrick was involved in an accident last year. A child died. He swears it wasn't his fault – I don't really know all the details. He won't talk about it. Anyhow, it was simply dreadful, you can imagine, and he got banned from driving for six months, which made life terribly difficult. It rather put him off the place. And then things got a bit difficult between us. Everything sort of came to a head, you know how it happens, one thing leads on to another. So we thought the best thing might be to try something quite different. A new move, just take a deep breath and begin again. I work a lot in London anyway. And Patrick thought he might have a go at film or television.

*

The train pulls out of King's Cross. Colette sits by the window in her first-class carriage, courtesy of Rosedawn Films. She stares through her reflection at the Regents Canal. Then she gives up the effort. Her face, admit it, is much prettier than the scenery.

Colette Bosanquet is a hot property. She's just finished a film. She was an irresistible call-girl caught up in a murder mystery. The script was terrific, the director loved her, the distributors are delighted. What was more, the call-girl was a lesbian in private life, which ought to help shake off the somewhat over-wholesome image she has felt herself in danger of acquiring. And her agent told her this morning that she's landed the part of Mrs Pepys in a television adaptation of the famous diaries. She's recognised in the street; her views on questions ranging from politics to home furnishings are sought by journalists. She's what a population of envious schoolgirls longs to become. Screen actors are the gods of the twentieth century, and she's entered Olympus. Colette calls the tune now, others dance to hers, not she to theirs. It may not last; but how many taste as much?

So why doesn't she wake every morning buoyant with thankfulness? Why is she filled, on the contrary, with vague discontents and forebodings? On the table in front of her lie a new book, magazines, a couple of scripts. She opens one, then another, but can work up no interest in any of them.

Anti-climax, perhaps. Filming's such a high in spite of all the longueurs. The adrenalin flows, you get caught up in the family life of the unit. And she's fond of this director, he's witty and civilised and flirtatious without going tiresomely over the top. Even so, she still prefers Patrick, her beautiful Patrick. And she prefers the theatre. Film is a director's medium. She's tired of doing what she's told in bite-sized chunks. Film loves her cheekbones, but they're hardly a badge of talent.

They're just going to start a new play. That's part of Pat's plan, to foster new talent, to make Huddersfield a centre of theatrical innovation. With Colette by his side. Her name's a draw now, and her earnings outside mean they don't have to worry too much about his salary – a fortunate chance. Yes, between them they're starting to attract a lot of attention.

She rehearses all this several times in her mind, but still doesn't feel any better.

She saw a magpie on the way to the station. One for sorrow. And the taxi-driver wanted to know if he didn't see her on the box the other night. They were doing Macbeth, and wasn't she Lady Macbeth? She wasn't. She did a guest appearance in a soap recently – perhaps he saw that and got in a muddle. The Scottish play. Two bad omens. Is *that* what's getting her down?

She opens the book and tries to concentrate on other things.

At one-thirty, the train pulls into the Corinthian portico of Huddersfield station. Patrick doesn't know she's coming today. They weren't due to finish until the end of the week, but she's not needed any more, so she snuck off early. She can't decide whether to go to the theatre or straight home. Patrick will almost certainly be at the theatre. He's there night and day. Who would have thought he had it in him to work so hard, to bestow so much concentration upon any project? He always seemed so languid. The result, it turned out, of an English schooling, where to show enthusiasm is to lay yourself open – a fate worse than death. And those luscious good looks that lent themselves so beautifully to lolling. He had to leave Cambridge before he was freed from that spell. Now, at last, he can be himself. She always knew it. She could see the glint of steel beneath the decadent exterior. They've been married four years now. In that time, how many of the stars of their university years have begun the long descent that will last for the rest of their lives? But not them. She knew they'd make a dream team. And it's turning out just as she hoped.

Colette decides to go home. She can't face the theatre yet. She needs a hot bath and a brisk walk, not necessarily in that order. A bit of time to herself. Perhaps tomorrow she'll treat herself to a day on the moors. People can't understand how she can bear to live here, so far from everyone and everything (except Patrick). But Colette likes the idea of dipping in and out of London, of having a secret life of her own. The world's at her feet: she may offer it a toe.

Colette and Patrick have a house on the edge of town, in a suburb that was a moorland village before Huddersfield swallowed the space between. It's built of stone, with walls two feet thick. Magnificent views open themselves before the bedroom windows. Patrick's car is in the drive. He's not at the theatre, then. She lets herself in, drops her case in the hall, shouts: – Anybody in? and, without waiting for a reply, makes for the kitchen. She's been longing all day for a decent cup of strong coffee.

She hears feet on the stairs, and Patrick comes in, followed by Jonathan Godley, a young actor who's recently joined the company. Patrick looks put out, Jonathan, confused and embarrassed. They are both flushed. Patrick says, accusingly: – You didn't say you were coming back today.

– I didn't know. They let me go two days early. Does it matter?
– Why should it? says Patrick. But, quite obviously, it does.

Why didn't she phone? She usually does. See you tomorrow. Getting the ten-thirty. But this time she didn't feel like it. For some reason, she thought she'd rather just arrive. Thought she'd give him a surprise. Which, clearly, she has.

Jonathan says: – We were just going over a part. Pat left the script behind.

– Don't let me interrupt you.

– Oh, we've just about finished. I really ought to be going.

– Have a cup of coffee, says Colette. – It's just made. What's the hurry?

But Jonathan declines. He has some unspecified urgent appointment.

Colette says: – Shall I call you a taxi?

– I'll run him there, says Patrick. – It won't take ten minutes.

– Will you be back?

– Later.

– Aren't you going to ask me how it all went?

But Patrick's already halfway out of the house.

Colette sips her coffee. The unease which was budding on the train now threatens to engulf her in full-blown misery. She wants to cry. Patrick would laugh at her, no doubt. Or, more likely, be irritated. She can hear him now. Oh, God, waterworks again. What is this all about, darling? You can't expect always to be the centre of attention, you know. Other people's lives are almost as important as yours.

Yes, what is this all about? It's about unformulated doubts, distresses that she doesn't want to name. If she does, they'll acquire solidity and swell and swell until they fill the whole horizon. The fact is, she's never really known what he feels about her. There were declarations, naturally. The theatre's a great place for declarations. They sounded convincing enough at the time. He believed them just as much as she did, she'd stake her life on that.

The marriage was her project, though. That's part of their folklore, a joke brought out at parties. She doesn't deny it. Colette's forte: she knows what she wants and makes straight for it. That's the secret of success – her success, all success. Have a plan. It's surprising how many people don't. Patrick was all part of the grand design. He could have demurred. But no: he seemed delighted. And why not? Colette is universally desired: a catch, a cachet. People – her London friends – say he uses her, that it's all give and no take. *Really, darling,*

I think it's quite wonderful, the way you're prepared to hide yourself away up there like that. But that's not the way it is. Their marriage, which includes Patrick's life, is important to her. She wants it to work – she doesn't like abandoned projects. Colette is a stayer. That's another of her secrets.

She didn't expect him back before midnight, but here he is already. Fuming. – Why d'you feel you have to spy on me?

– Spy on you? What on earth are you talking about? Why should I spy on you?

They look at each other. Is this going to be it? Is this small incident going to be the one? Is this the moment when all that hasn't been said will rush uncontrollably out?

Colette sometimes reflects that everything could be traced back to this one missed telephone call. But maybe not. Maybe all that was wanting was an excuse. One would have been as good as another.

The unspoken surrounds them. She hears her mother's voice:
– Always remember, you can never unsay what's been said.

It seemed such hopeless timidity. – Why don't you tell him? Colette urged on one of the many occasions when her father, at two in the morning, had still not come home. – Why don't you show him what he's doing to you?

– Because once the words are out, that's it.

What words can fill their silence now? Small talk? How was the filming? Have you had good houses this week?

Impossible. But the trouble is, only small talk will do. It's either that or very large talk indeed. Can they face that, and everything it will bring with it?

Patrick looks around. He seems at a loss. He looks at his watch. Four o'clock. Having just come in, he says, very firmly: – I'm off out. There are one or two things I've got to do. See you when I see you.

Colette hears the car door slam. Patrick drives off at speed.

Much later he comes back. He's shaking, very white, on the verge of tears. He won't say what's happened. Colette can do nothing to comfort him.

Next day, she notices a small dent on the front of the car.

*

The car is actually travelling quite slowly. Nobody drives fast in a place like this, at this time of day.

As it reaches the big lime tree, a child rushes out from behind a parked van. Virtually under the wheels. Nobody could have foreseen it.

The driver steps on the brakes, but the child is dragged under before he can stop the car.

*

The street is empty, though there's generally quite a crowd at this time of day.

The headlamps catch a bundle of clothes in the middle of the road.

The driver pulls to one side and rushes to see what's lying there.

It's a child. A boy, about ten. He seems very still. Is he breathing? Probably oughtn't to move him in that state. But how can one leave him lying there in the middle of the road?

Didn't anyone see?

A hit and run driver.

If Colette had only rung.

*

– But what happened, exactly? Was there a court case?

Colette will not be drawn. She says vaguely: – Oh, things got a bit out of hand. You know how they do. Helen, she says earnestly, have you thought about having a baby? We ought to do it soon if we're going to. Think what fun it would be. Say Pat and I buy that house, and you and I both get pregnant. They'll be the same age, they'll grow up together – like family, really, only family you like. Not like your real family. We'll be able to help each other out –

Yes, as usual Colette's got it all planned out, down to the last attractive detail. You'd have to be a very old friend, Helen, for example, to recognise the sting in the tail. Help each other out? Helen can see immediately who will be helping whom. But Colette's warmth, her enthusiasm, her panache, carry the audience even so. It *would* be fun. They *should* start thinking about it, if they're going to. Thirty next birthday: she can hear the relentless ticking behind everything she does. Perhaps the more surprising thing is that the subject hasn't arisen before. They've thought about it, naturally; or Helen has, and she assumes that so has Colette, in that sense. The sense that, in looking at other people's babies, one thinks: Yes, I suppose I could be doing that, too. But that's as far as it's gone. Life has been too all-consuming, too full of excitement and ambition. To exchange all this for days spent in the company of people two feet high, washing nappies, bottoms and babyclothes as one waits for time to pass and sanity to return? The prospect is so devoid of temptation (and adult conversation) as not to be entertained. Not, at any rate, until now. If Colette did it too . . .

Helen recounts her day to Benny (not mentioning the scarabs). She says: – Dream couple! What a label to have to live up to! I don't suppose anyone could do it. Colette says Patrick got in some sort of trouble – some sort of accident, she wouldn't talk about it – and they're hoping new pastures'll set them up again.

Benny says: – That wasn't what Patrick said to me.

– Oh? Have you seen him recently?

– We had lunch a couple of weeks ago. He was up in London seeing someone about a job in television.

– You didn't tell me.

– Sorry, it just slipped my mind.

– Slipped your mind! Benny, you're hopeless! How could something like that just slip your mind? But Helen knows that Benny is almost certainly telling the truth. He's perfectly capable these days of having lunch with someone and forgetting all about it by the time he leaves the lab in the evening. He is entirely preoccupied by an exciting piece of research. The self-replicating properties of cells consume his mind to the exclusion of almost all else, even – especially – gossip. It's amazing he remembered to have lunch at all.

– What did he tell you?

Benny plumbs his memory. – He said it was all on account of Colette. Living in Huddersfield's really getting to be a drag on her career, or so she keeps saying. He can't stand the nagging any longer.

– He didn't say anything to you about this accident?

– Not a word. Though he did seem a bit down. Said that actually he wouldn't be sorry to move, in spite of everything.

– What would you think about having children?

– What? Benny, unsurprisingly, is taken aback by this apparently abrupt change of tack. Helen has not broached this topic before. Why should she suddenly start now, for God's sake? How does he know what he thinks? He temporises. – How would you work it with your job?

– If we're going to do it, now's the time. I'm nearly thirty. Perhaps I'd stop working. For a while, anyhow.

In the few hours since Colette planted the seed in her mind, Helen's new train of thought has taken root and begun to germinate vigorously. For the first time she realises, or allows herself to realise, that maybe she doesn't enjoy her work as much as all that. Maybe she'd like to stop; maybe she's only been looking for a good excuse. And what better excuse could one have? She can opt out of the rat-race with full social sanction. It's a woman's privilege.

All she needs is a seed planted in the womb as well as the mind.

She turns to Benny.

8

IT'S LIKE A dream come true. Colette holds out her arms, as so many times she's held them out, and instead of turning away, he rushes towards her. Her lovely boy! Suddenly he's found all those words he didn't have, all those emotions he's been slamming down. She hugs him, holds him tight, tight, inhales his smell, feels him solid against her, storing away these sensations as if she'll never have the chance to experience them again. Which may well be the case.

The house lights go up.

Helen, applauding, feels herself, as so often these days, suspended between two worlds.

The world is the stage,
The stage is the world –

Colette's young man, Nick, is the spit of Declan. She hadn't realised it till she saw him here, acting in his own piece, in which Colette plays out all her fantasies onstage. The play, like so many aspects of her present life, is about a young man and an older woman. She used to be his teacher: now they are lovers. They share some joint destiny, though whether this will involve love or murder, or both, remains uncertain.

Colette, backstage removing makeup, is excited. The play's going to move to the West End. – Though I'm not sure how it'll work in the wide open spaces, she says, apprehensively.

– I'm sure it'll be fine.

And why not? Nick, the playwright, has been greeted as a significant new theatrical find, and Colette is generally agreed to have re-created herself as a significant serious actress. *Many of Miss Bosanquet's admirers have long felt . . . And here at last . . .* The embarrassing soaps are forgotten and forgiven; she has overcome the ghost of the screen beauty she used to be.

Helen is delighted at this success. This has always been the measure of the bond between them: real pleasure in each other's triumphs, failures unsullied by *schadenfreude*. But care must still be taken. Nothing is perfect. And when Colette asks: – What did you think of it? the question is not put in the hope or expectation of unvarnished truth. Their discussions are intricate, a sidestep here, a feint there: when all else fails, a retreat into evasion. Colette wants to hear only that the play is marvellous, that she is wonderful, while Helen, though sympathetic, can't bring herself to tell actual lies.

– Did you see that piece about Nick in the *Guardian*? Wasn't it wonderful?

Helen, as it happens, feels that the play and its author are over-hyped. It's not bad, and nor is he, but people are so eager for the new, the now, the latest talent, that they are apt to kill with kindness. Amid the dross, the faintest glint is a potential goldmine.

– Who set it up? Helen asks non-committally.

– All their idea. They just loved it in Battersea, of course. Nick does such wonderful dialogue.

– Yes, it's terrifically witty. (An acceptable truth.)

– And so subtle, the way he builds the suspense.

Helen does not think subtlety one of Nick's strong suits. – Will you be able to transfer the set? I thought that moment in the second act where the barrier slams down was wonderful. It would be a shame to lose that.

– No probs. You are coming to the opening, aren't you?

– I'm not sure. Helen doesn't like attending social occasions of this sort on her own. Without Benny. The absence at her elbow is too painful.

– Bring Tim.

– Oh, I don't think it's quite his sort of thing, is it?

– Make him do it for you. Hold your nose for Mama day. We'll all be going out to supper afterwards.

Tim groans, as Helen knew he would. – I thought you'd seen it already, Mum. What d'you want to go again for?

– Because Colette asked me. Come on, Tim. Sacrifice yourself. We'll go somewhere nice afterwards.

The theatre is filling up as Helen and Tim take their seats. Second-row stalls. At least they'll be able to see. Helen's been in this theatre before – far from being raked, the floor seems actually to slope downwards in the vicinity of Row H, while the dress circle is set almost vertically above the stage. The two seats on Helen's left are empty, and no-one shows any sign of claiming them. That's surprising on the opening night – you don't want dispiriting gaps where they're too obvious. There's the usual buzz as acquaintances wave and programmes are studied. Then the lights dim and a hush falls: and, simultaneously, a slight commotion as the empty seats are occupied. Helen's neighbours sit. The curtain rises, and once again, fantasy (or reality) reigns.

When the house lights go up for the interval, Helen and Tim prepare to make for the bar and their waiting drinks. The latecomers sit on, interposing their knees.

For the first time, Helen looks at the man who has been sitting next to her. It is Richard Potter, her old heartthrob from *Round-about*. He's still in television: he's become a specialist in savage political interviews. The man politicians love to hate. They queue up to be torn to bits.

There's a moment's silence, then laughter. Richard says, – Helen! *How* long is it? I don't think you've met my wife. Iris. Helen Bartram.

– We're old friends from television, Helen explains. This is my son Tim. I don't think you ever met, did you?

They're all standing now. Richard and Tim are of a height: as they face each other, you can suddenly see what Richard must have looked like in his twenties. Startlingly similar, actually. Perhaps that's why Benny never got on with Tim. He never liked Richard. Even though they worked together for a while, theirs was never more than a strictly professional relationship – and there might well have been some subconscious association.

Iris smiles awkwardly. She's a strange shape, thinks Helen, or maybe she's pregnant. A lot younger than Richard – in her early thirties, perhaps. Alex has been traded in for a younger model. Maybe, indeed, this was not the first such exchange. It's clear that Iris doesn't enjoy encounters of this sort. Faced with Richard's former life, she feels herself at a disadvantage. Who are these people exactly? What do they know that she does not?

– We were just off to the bar. Are you coming?

Iris shakes her head. Richard says, – We'll just stay here. See you afterwards, perhaps.

– I think we're going on somewhere with Colette. She's an old friend of mine, Helen explains to Iris. – Tim's her godson.

– Then we'll see you there, Richard says jovially. – Nick's Iris's brother. I've been following your career, Helen. I like your stuff. We must have a good chat.

Iris looks unenthused by this prospect. Helen smiles and mutters some politesse. Then she and Tim stumble past to the bar.

– I didn't know Richard Potter was a friend of yours, says Tim.

– One of the many things you don't know about me. Helen raises her eyebrows at him, asserting her independence. Two can play at that game.

Afterwards, they go backstage. Colette's on a high. It went well, didn't it? The theatre didn't drown them, did it? Did Helen notice who was in the audience? She chatters on, happy in her natural habitat at the centre of attention. A star once more. And so to supper.

Going to a restaurant with Colette is always the same story. The better she feels, the more of a nuisance she makes herself. It's a sure indicator. This evening, she rejects the long table which has been prepared for them and decides that they will sit at a series of smaller tables, so that more intimate conversations may be conducted. – I hope you don't mind, she coos sweetly at the maître d'. – After all that, I really don't feel capable of shouting loud enough for a long table! He smiles his professional smile and gestures to his minions. Unfortunately all the smaller tables are already occupied, so the long one must be broken up into its component parts. This causes some commotion. While it's being done, they crowd noisily into the small bar. Other diners glare at them. Finally everyone's settled. Menus are presented. Colette studies hers with attention. She'd like extra redcurrant jelly with the wild boar pâté, she wonders if the smoked salmon could be trimmed with little slivers of other raw fish with perhaps a little sharp sauce, the steak here is so wonderful that she'd like it raw, as tartare, with a few gherkins, do they still do that delicious *soufflé glacé*? The head waiter notes all this down impassively and fixes his mind on the final reckoning.

And who will foot the bill for this extravaganza? Helen knows, or rather she knows who won't. She's been here before, in all senses of that phrase. She used to be appalled by these performances, but now she watches with detachment, amusement even, as events take their inevitable course. The answer is: everyone but Colette. Each diner or pair of diners will pay for him or herself or selves, while Colette smiles her charming smile and leaves all that to the man of the moment – in this case, presumably, Nick. Who, being an up-and-coming playwright rather than a once and future film-star, is not rich. He will bite his lip, sign his name and tell himself that this is all part of the deal. Isn't it a price worth paying? Hasn't it got him to the West End?

It's one-thirty in the morning before the party starts to break up. They've had the restaurant to themselves for quite some time. People stumble between the tables in a haze of champagne. Someone brings in the ritual bunch of early reviews. There's only one bad one; two are positively enthusiastic. Helen, giggling at something with Richard, sees Iris glaring from a nearby table. – I like your boy, he says. – Nice-looking lad.

– Yes. The apple of my eye.

– I saw Benny died. I'm sorry. Were you still together? he adds hastily. – You know how it is these days. It's rather unusual, staying married.

– Yes, I notice you didn't.

– No, well, he sighs. – Most people seem to come apart, don't they? I expect Tim misses his father. Not an easy act to follow.

– They didn't get on all that well, actually.

– Didn't they? That's bad luck. He sounds genuinely interested, genuinely concerned. Paternity was always Richard's strong suit. Uxoriousness, on the other hand, was not. Look at him now. Iris is tugging at his elbow, making exhausted little moans. She's dying to leave, to remove him from this gathering of old mistresses (she must know the score there, having almost certainly travelled that route herself), to get him back to their nice safe bed, where none but ghosts intrude. To make the most of their last months of peace. She's five or six months gone. Is that why they married? At any rate, having married her, Richard evidently considers his duty done. He continues exactly as if she were weightless, transparent, inaudible. He'll make a great fuss of the baby, once there's a baby to fuss over, and when he happens to be there to do the fussing. He puts his arm round her, patting her tummy, that visible demonstration of his virility.

– How many have you got? Helen asks naughtily.

– Oh, just the two. They're grown up now, of course. And one on the way. He gives another proprietorial tap.

– It's funny, really, Helen says, talking on regardless of Iris's frantic signals. Why is she being so bitchy tonight? Where's her sense of sisterly solidarity? Lost in the sea of her own troubles, perhaps. And she doesn't much take to Iris. Surely not jealousy, at this late stage? Not as such. She's glad to note that Richard leaves her cold, which is fortunate, since clearly she has the same non-effect on him. Not a lubricious thought in his head. As far as he's concerned, she's well past her use-by date. He, on the other hand, is a man, and men go on for ever. As witness. In these circumstances, she can't resist a little power-play. They may not fancy each other any more, but she's still better company than Iris. – You'd have thought Tim would miss Benny because he was his father, after all, and you wouldn't have thought I would, not so much, because we weren't particularly close recently. We led very independent lives. But I do, horribly. Life's very peculiar without him.

Richard, however, is more interested in Tim than in life after Benny. – What's he planning to do? he enquires. – If he's interested in television, tell him to give me a ring. He nods, and turns – not towards the door, but towards the group surrounding Colette. Iris sighs weightily and flops down on a chair. Waiters pick their way around her, stacking crockery.

– D'you know if it's a boy or a girl? Helen enquires.

– I haven't had an amnio. I'm not old enough to need one. She glares at Helen, and looks yearningly towards her husband. Who is otherwise engaged. A scene, reflects Helen, that will be repeated a thousand times in the course of the coming years.

Next day, on the phone, Colette says: – I'd forgotten Iris was married to your old friend Richard. Did you see him talking to Tim? I couldn't take my eyes off them. They look exactly alike. It's absolutely freakish.

– That's what Englishmen look like, says Helen. – Most of my family look like that. You're just used to associating me with small, dark Jews.

But Colette's attention has already shifted back to the real subject of this call: the reviews. – Well, there you are, darling, she says. – The wonders of genetics. Did you see the *Mail?* All we need is a couple of really good ones on Sunday, and we're away . . .

But Helen's mind is elsewhere.

*

Helen has never felt so happy. From lowest depths to sparkling heights, all in the space of six months. Lorraine and Colette between them have set her free. She savours the pleasure of at last being able to write, of words flowing, of plot and dialogue and character. The play is called *Snookered.* It's a fairly straightforward piece, and not without its faults, but then this is her first attempt.

Anyhow, it's been accepted for production by the BBC. It seems to make people laugh. And Colette, as she promised, is going to be in it, which should ensure it receives a certain amount of attention. She says she loves it, but the truth is more complex: she feels proprietorial, almost authorial. She thinks it was entirely on account of her helpful hints that Helen broke through that absurd block. And who's to say she isn't right? If she hadn't planted the idea (yet another of Colette's ideas – first the baby and then this: it sometimes seems to Helen that her entire inner life is founded upon ideas planted by

Colette) then that sighting of Benny and Lorraine would have led only to anger, directionless resentment. One step nearer the end of Helen's marriage. Whereas at the moment the two of them seem to be getting on better than ever before. Helpless dependency, feminine frustration, do not turn Benny on. Success is what he likes, strength, self-sufficiency. That was the package he bought, and he'd begun to wonder whether the wrapping wasn't deceptive.

What, she wonders, will Benny make of this play? Will he recognise Lauren's provenance? She hopes not. As far as she knows he's unaware of her paranoid feelings about Lorraine. She's never said anything. But is it really necessary to go as far as speech in such matters? Sometimes, when Helen's thinking very hard, feeling very strongly about something, she finds it almost impossible to believe that Benny can't read her thoughts. She imagines thought-carrying particles leaping like electrons across the dividing space between their heads. The quantum theory of telepathy. The empiric evidence, however, is that this does not occur.

Patrick has agreed to direct. It's just a studio piece, which means he will be sentenced to several weeks in the bosom of his family. Quite a sacrifice, as everyone agrees. Nevertheless, he's going to grit his teeth and suffer. Is it because Helen's an old friend, because Colette's his wife, or because he really likes the play? Who can tell? He certainly thinks it needs some work. Helen accepts his advice gratefully. She would happily devote the rest of her life to getting it right, if that were necessary. But it turns out that nothing so extreme is required. There are a few weeks of rewrites and discussions. And then it all starts to roll along, the whole exciting business, casting, design, rehearsals . . . Is this me? she sometimes asks herself. Can this really be me?

She's walking along one of Television Centre's endless circular corridors after one of these meetings, eyes on her script, thinking about some alteration, when she sees a pair of familiar feet approaching. She raises her eyes. It's – her old friend Richard Potter.

She did not have him in mind: it's months since she's thought of him. For once, synchronicity fails.

She's pleased, but also a little sad, to note that her entire inner being no longer somersaults at the sight of him. How many, many evenings she spent at her window, tensely watching for his car, counting the seconds till he rang the doorbell, melting with anticipation! It's hard, now, to connect that scenario with this figure. Not that he isn't attractive still. He's put on a little weight, perhaps, lost a little hair. Well, it's eight years since their affair. She can tell he's thinking similar thoughts. His glance travels swiftly from toe to head and back again. She's getting too thin. And she found a grey hair yesterday. But that isn't what's really changed. Reality was never the perfection they perceived. Simply, it is no longer tempered by a kindly mist of pheromones. The clear view is less forgiving.

They exchange exclamations, establish that each has some time to spare, and repair to Richard's office for a chat. He's recently achieved his own show, a late-night, personalised view of the week's events: something that brings with it not merely an office, but an outer office containing a secretary. *We* are becoming *them*, thinks Helen.

Cups of coffee steam on the desk between them, the door is shut. No calls are to be put through. For the first time since their failed expedition to Brighton, they face each other alone. That, as it turned out, was the end of their affair. There was no quarrel: just a failure to reconnect. Did Richard and Alex rediscover their lost lust on that unexpectedly legitimate bed in the Metropole? Or was it more that Helen's interest transferred itself once again to Benny, there to remain? Perhaps some of both. It is certain that Helen owes her marriage to that chance cancellation. So, very possibly, does Richard.

Yes: he's still married to Alex. In fact they now have two children. Helen, though, has none. She still isn't pregnant. But she doesn't think about that so much these days – another bonus, all part of her rediscovery of the lost Helen, Benny's Helen, that thrusting careerist. In fact, she isn't even sure that she wants a baby just now. Not at this moment. So many new vistas are opening before her. Though, in the contrary way of these things, that probably means she'll get pregnant. She doesn't bother about contraception – given their record to date, what's the point? And Benny, who shrank like a frost-nipped flower at the first touch of Helen's baby-lust, has rediscovered his interest in sex, perhaps because every encounter is no longer burdened by desperation, perhaps because Lorraine has gone back to

South Africa. Or does Helen's new success excite him? Still, however, nothing happens. Perhaps he has a low sperm count. Who's to know? And who wants to? Not Benny. Even at the height of her obsession, they never – it not being a shared obsession – went so far as to find out.

– So you're married to Benny Spiro, says Richard. – Well, well.

– I didn't know you knew Benny?

– Oh, he's a name to conjure with, these days. Surely I don't need to tell you that?

– You know how it is, you live with someone, they're just the person you live with. I've known Benny since we were students.

– I'm looking for a scientist, says Richard. – Someone who can explain the issues so that people will really understand. Someone with a name, someone who can't just do it but who's good at communicating as well. Your husband might be ideal. D'you think he'd be interested?

– Could be. Why not ask him? Shall I pass on the message?

– He could give me a ring. Here's my card.

Benny, when she hands him Richard's card, is delighted. The prospect of more exposure lights his face with pleasure. He was never taught, as good Englishmen are taught, to cloak himself in modesty. He goes for what he wants, and what he wants almost more than anything is fame. Notoriety was no small part of the attraction of student politics, back in 1968, and the same went for the fight against the creationists.

Naturally, this propensity does not endear him to his colleagues. They are suspicious, they are envious; these base feelings make them annoyed with themselves; this, in its turn, renders Benny even less attractive to them. They would like a solid excuse for this disapproval – to be able to point a finger, to show that his work is not all it's cracked up to be. But they can't find one. Benny is painstaking, meticulous, a brilliant synthesist. They have to respect him, even though they don't really like him.

Benny says: – Richard Potter. I didn't know you knew him.

– Oh, he's an old friend from when I was on *Roundabout*. I thought I told you.

– I expect you did. Perhaps I'll give him a ring tomorrow.

How does she feel about her husband working with her ex-lover, Helen wonders. She's supposed to be struggling with a recalcitrant scene, but somehow she can't concentrate. She tries to imagine cosy dinner-parties, the four of them, Richard and Alex, herself and Benny. Just the kind of thing Richard would enjoy. He was always a one for in-jokes and sly glances. And judging by the reputation he had when she knew him, he can probably indulge this predilection at any dinner-party containing a moderately attractive woman. Does Alex realise what's going on? How could she fail to? Alex – the enemy, the wife, the reason Richard could never stay all night. The faceless woman. They never met, Helen never asked for a description, never wanted to see a photo. She didn't want to visualise an actual person: it's easier to bomb thousands from a great height than maim just one face-to-face. Who's the lucky girl now? That there is one, Helen does not doubt.

The phone rings.

– Helen? It's Richard.

– Goodness, I was just thinking about you. Has Benny been in touch?

– Not yet.

– He said he was going to call you this morning.

– Good. That's great.

– Was it him you wanted to speak to? I'm afraid he's not here, he's at the lab. D'you want the number?

– No, don't worry. Well, yes, why don't you give it to me?

Helen does so. But Richard seems strangely reluctant to ring off. The chat meanders on. He assures her he will call Benny within the next half hour. Finally he says, – I don't suppose you happen to be free for lunch? I'm not too busy today, and it was so nice seeing you again.

– Well, yes, she says, surprised. And surprised at herself for being surprised. Are they not old friends now? – Why not?

Why not indeed, thinks Helen, as they sit knee-to-knee in the little restaurant Richard suggested. Here we go again.

She should have known better. She could still know better. She could get up when they've finished their coffee, politely decline Richard's offer of a lift home, say she was just going to do a bit of shopping. She could make herself perfectly clear without even being rude. Without spoiling Benny's chances – and if she did? Would it matter? What's a television programme, set against the kind of career Benny's carving out for himself? Or set against a marriage?

But she knows she won't. It's too late. It was too late the moment she got into the taxi which brought her here. She knows Richard too well not to know what he meant. And (because he knows her just as well as she knows him) he knows she knows.

They finish their coffee. He calls for the bill. They are enclosed in a delightful, wine-hazed intimacy. Old tendernesses need not die – not if someone wants to fan them back into life. Helen feels the familiar bubble of excitement in the pit of her stomach. He isn't, after all, so much changed; it wasn't, after all, so very long ago. He says: – Shall I drop you home?

Helen considers. She could still say no. If she says yes, she knows the house will be hers – theirs – until seven at the earliest: Benny never gets home before then. And she knows what that will mean.

– All right.

They drive across the Heath, past Jack Straw's Castle, into the wilds of north London. They pull up outside her door. Richard says: – That's a pretty house.

– Want to have a look?

– Yes, he says. – I'd like to do that.

Benny comes home extremely pleased with himself and the world in general. – Your friend Richard Potter called this morning.

– Oh, yes? So this, thinks Helen, is adultery. She can remember thinking this once before – also in connection with Richard. She remembers, at that time, thinking: it's exactly like any other sex. What did she expect? That was exactly what it was. Adultery isn't the sex, it's what goes on all around it. All those little deceptions, those casual lies. It wasn't her adultery then: she didn't have anyone to deceive. She does now, though.

This penumbra has its effect upon the sex, naturally. How can what's allowed compete with what's off-limits? She can see that, now. There is no doubt that sex with Benny should be better than sex with Richard. Benny's more energetic, more inventive, more considerate. Better in bed – what a meaningless phrase! Meaningless because it implies objectivity. Who is objective about sex? Richard is forbidden fruit, *ergo* more desirable. As is Lorraine. And, possibly, Colette. Yes, she can't help wondering about that from time to time. They're always talking about each other, Colette and Benny. Mentioning each other's name. Colette told me the other day. I was talking to Benny and he said. A lover's habit: the secret caress, the ritual invocation of the beloved. Is Helen jealous? Not as much as you might think. Not as much as yesterday. Now that she has her own source of guilt, she is almost enthusiastic about these absolving possibilities.

Benny doesn't seem to notice her distraction. He's on a high. He and Richard are going to meet at the end of the week. Television beckons.

Helen is making *oeufs basquaises*, an old standby whenever she can't think of anything to cook for dinner. The peppers and onions are frying gently; the chorizo is sliced; the parsley is chopped ready. She breaks some eggs into a bowl. Two of them have double yolks – something she hasn't seen since she was a child. She points this out to Benny, but he isn't much interested. His mind is concentrated on fame.

Helen finds she keeps thinking about the afternoon's events. Sternly, she wrenches her mind back to the matter in hand. – Will the university mind?

– I don't expect they'll like it particularly. They're all as jealous as hell, is what it comes down to, but there isn't anything they can say.

– You don't mind that?

– Not really. How's the play going? Benny, too, is making a social effort.

– Fine.

The excitements of Helen's day have reduced her to taciturnity. All she wants is to be left to herself and her thoughts. But excitement has the opposite effect upon Benny. He's feeling horny. Helen can tell. He doesn't need to say anything. It's the way he looks at her, the way his eyes follow her. Not unnaturally, she doesn't feel like it. Not tonight, Benjamin.

– Oh, Benny! I'm tired. I've been working so hard today.

Benny is not to be put off. – All you need do is lie there, he says. – No effort required. Just let yourself be fucked.

What can she say? What can she do? What could be more sweetly reasonable?

Two weeks later, Helen realises that her period is late. It isn't really surprising. She hasn't exactly been leading a regular life recently. Over-excitement can have that effect. People are not clocks.

A week or so later, not only has her period still not arrived, but her breasts are beginning to ache.

It can't be. But it is: she knows she's not mistaken. She's been here before, twice. Why should she be surprised? Lots of sex plus no precautions equals babies: basic arithmetic.

Nevertheless, surprised she is. She'd got so used to thinking it couldn't happen, that it never would happen. Never again.

So *whose is it*?

It's got to be Richard's, hasn't it? Not much doubt about that. He's proved that *he* can – he has two children already; and she knows that *she* can. Which leaves only Benny. Who has up till now been completely unsuccessful in this department.

In that case, what's she going to do about it?

She agonizes over this question for a while. Only a short while, however.

She's going to shut up and have it. Quite apart from anything else, she doesn't want to risk another abortion. It had crossed her mind that the ones she'd had might have left her infertile. That does happen. Why not to her? If life has taught her anything, it is this: it can happen to you. But this way, she can stay with Benny *and* have children. A child. She'll just have to resign herself to the fact that this will probably be her one and only. The affair with Richard is not going to be revived. That's another of the day's decisions. She can't keep going back for a few sperm when required.

Just this once, however – why not? Think of it as a surrogate paternity. The fact that those may not be Benny's actual genes in there is really beside the point. All the joys of fatherhood will accrue to him regardless. He'll never know – no-one will ever know. Except, of course, Helen. Benny will see resemblances, family characteristics, and she'll know he's almost certainly mistaken. But she'll shut up. Hardly a unique occurrence in the annals of marriage.

She's seen Richard once or twice since they met for that lunch, but only briefly. He clearly assumes everything is on again, but even before this latest complication, Helen felt less certain. Was it really worth it – the intrigue, the elaborate arrangements, the secrecy, the transformation of the rest of her life into a mere sojourn between assignations? Now she is uncertain no more. The answer henceforth is No. No, no, no. Irresponsibility has done its bit. Thank you, and goodbye. Life is complex enough without optional, added guilts and uncertainties. Benny's just signed a contract: he's going to be appearing regularly on Richard's show. They'll be seeing each other all the time. Just the kind of titillation Richard most enjoys. Helen, in her present condition, wants to put as much distance as possible between herself and such Feydeauesque situations.

– This seems very sudden, says Richard, sounding hurt.

How to explain? Helen would rather Richard did not think this was his child. – It's not personal, she says, giving thanks that telepathy is indeed no more than a psychic's pipe-dream.

– Not personal!

– Wait, let me finish what I was going to say. I'm pregnant.

– What!

– I'm sure it's not yours, so don't worry. Helen crosses her thumbs. Strike me dead if I lie. – But you can see I might just not feel in the mood.

– On the contrary, I should think you might want to make the most of your last child-free months! Believe me, you won't feel much like it afterwards, says Richard with feeling. One who knows.

– Really, Richard. I'm serious. I've got to get in the right state of mind for this, and having you around won't help.

– OK, flower. But remember I'm here if ever you change your mind.

It has to be said that Richard does not sound inconsolable. Even now he's probably riffling through the Rolodex, pulling out new possibilities.

The pregnancy takes its measured and inevitable course. Everyone, even Benny, is delighted. Helen feels supremely fertile. The play is in production, and so is she. Colette says: – Darling, you see, I told you. You were tense, that was all it was. As soon as you forgot about it, Bob's your uncle.

Helen smiles.

The time comes when she must go to hospital for a scan. Benny would like to go with her, but he can't make the appointed afternoon. Anyway, he wouldn't like the clinic – Helen's sure of that. All those enormous women carrying their stomachs before them, all those bored, fractious children, all those embarrassed men. Look what they've done this time!

She enters the scanner room, lies down on the table, flinches as the cold oil is smeared on her naked stomach. The scanner is rolled over her. A green, flickering picture appears on the screen. A little fish swimming inside her.

Two little fishes.

– You've got twins, Mrs Spiro, says the nurse. – Congratulations! Do they run in the family?

Helen is too stunned to reply.

A picture of double-yolked eggs swims into her mind.

It isn't as if she wasn't warned.

*

I am alone, thinks Helen.

It is her first thought every morning now, as she awakes in her Benny-less bed; her last thought at night. When he went off before, after Laura's death, the solitude was in some way a relief. And less complete: there was Tim in the next room, Colette down the road, television colleagues to occupy the day. Now, there are none of these. Only her thoughts, swimming round and round inside her head as once Tim and Laura swam inside her womb. Alone.

She hasn't really faced it till now. There hasn't been time. By accident or design, her life has been filled with frenetic activity. Rushing to Los Angeles to work on the film, clearing up after Benny, trying to find out what happened. And now, suddenly, a pause: the one thing she can't cope with.

Colette's party did for her. Dropped her into a trough, and she can't climb out. What was it? All those people playing games? The sight of Richard with his new wife – his new *pregnant* wife, underlining so unnecessarily the fact that there will be no more babies for Helen? She hears again Iris's voice: *Not old enough for an amnio*. And hates her, and feels ashamed, and hates her some more.

Not that she would want any more.

Perhaps it's just the march of time. Not simply no more babies, but the realisation that more and more holes are going to appear as people drop out of life. First Laura, now Benny. Who next?

In fact it's none of these, or not primarily. No, it's – Colette. Her friend. Friendship with Colette has been the one constant thing. Marriages come and go, children grow and leave. But friends go on for ever. That's been the basis upon which they have built their lives. Or so she thought. And now, suddenly, she's not so sure. Seeing her the other night, Helen felt so *separate*. She's known Colette all her adult life, and suddenly she doesn't know her at all. The usual questions, the usual lack of answers. Who is she really, how does she see life, her own life, Helen's life? Suddenly, Helen realised that she has no idea.

What set this off all of a sudden? Jealousy at Colette's new success? Absolutely not. No, it's something stupid: the fact that Colette met Benny in Los Angeles, and neither of them mentioned it to her.

Ever since, her mind has been filled with it. The question isn't whether they did or didn't go to bed. Perhaps they did, perhaps they didn't. That wasn't what made the difference. No, it's the old sense that, behind her back, without her knowledge, things have been happening which affect *her*. It wasn't just Benny who plunged beneath the surface. Everyone's been doing it. No-one is what they seem. They've all been in collusion. Colette, Gemma, Patrick. Declan, even. All part of that other life from which she is excluded.

This is news? That life is not, is never what it seems? It's a commonplace, an inevitability. Not confined to others, either. If she wants an example to hand, she need look no further than Tim and Richard.

The thought does not cheer her.

They seep out, these hidden things. A drop here, a drop there. A fallen word, a direct question that wasn't expected and can't be evaded. What she needs, what she misses, is a confidant. Someone she can talk to, someone who will listen to her fears, soothe her, reassure her. Colette. But Colette has suddenly changed roles. What part is she playing now? Helen can't be certain.

Who, now, can she trust? Tim? Probably. But his life's his own – she can't burden him with hers. Her mother, Frances. But sharing this particular load with Frances would be no relief. At Helen's age, at Helen's stage, it's hard suddenly to switch roles and become a daughter again. It might be easier if Frances had liked Benny more. But she didn't. She thought he was arrogant. Couldn't stand the way he treated the domestic help when he visited the Bartrams. Speaking to Mrs Shergold the daily, the Bartrams' friend and helpmeet for twenty years, as if she were a servant. Carrying on conversations in the same room as if she didn't exist. The way he was brought up, no doubt, said Frances. That's the way things worked there. She was probably right. He did it to Monica, too, one couldn't help noticing. And Lorraine, with that girl at Synchrony, was just the same. Whatever the reason, Frances could never really take to him after that. The way he treated Tim didn't help, either.

Helen lies in bed and wonders why she should ever get up. What's on the menu, today? Anything? Nothing. Not even Mrs Martins, who finally quit last week – hardly unexpected, but depressing nonetheless. It's not so much the fact of having to clean the bathroom herself – is her time so precious, is her life so exhausting? But it's another piece vanished from the jigsaw. Nothing and nothing and nothing. Nor ever will be, unless she pulls her finger out and does something about it.

A reason for getting up: she has to pee. She lies inert, fantasising a tube reaching from bed to bathroom. Rises, pees. Pulls on a dressing-gown. Down to the kitchen, make tea. Look at the diary in case she's forgotten something.

Miss P. 11.00.

Christ! Today's the day when Miss Parrinder's finally got to be paid off. How could she have forgotten? She looks at the clock. Ten to ten. An hour to get ready, get dressed, collect herself. Thank God for bodily functions. The doorbell would have rung, and there she'd have been, in her dressing-gown, frowsy, unprepared. Terminally disadvantaged. The forces of reason fall at the first fence.

Mostly, Miss Parrinder's conducted her operations in Helen's absence. Another good reason for all that activity in Oxfordshire, Los Angeles and points west. They haven't had to face each other since that day just after the funeral. One of them would surely have cracked – and it wouldn't have been Miss P., secure in her conviction that she, alone, understood and appreciated Benny. The poor Professor! Such an unsympathetic home environment! No wonder he gave up. *She* knew, though of course she would never say such a thing out loud. All that resentment, all that terrible loyalty – how could Helen have survived it?

Meanwhile, Miss P., ensconced in self-righteous rectitude, has been through all the papers, classified, indexed, arranged the files in order, Astrophysics through Zoomorphs. Including, of course, correspondence, filed alphabetically under the correspondents' names. Excluding Lorraine. Did she notice that box was missing? Probably. Helen can't imagine that there's a corner of those files, a documented millimetre of Benny's life, with which she is not intimately acquainted. That's the source of her power, that's what Helen can't forgive her. One of the things. She knows more about Benny's life – about *their* life – than anyone. Much more than Benny did. She knows stuff he forgot years ago.

Perhaps she's still hoping that Helen will suggest her as a suitable editor to Collinge and Pearson. She'd be the logical choice. Well, Lesley's welcome to make it – not on Helen's recommendation, though.

Miss Parrinder has her own key, but she's punctilious about not using it when Helen's in the house. The bell rings and there she is, standing on the doorstep. Rosalinda. Neatly suited as always, hair pulled back, spectacles glittering. Antipathy is strength.

Helen shuts the door behind her. They go up to Benny's study. They sit at his desk, Miss Parrinder in his chair, Helen on a small chair pulled up at the side. Miss P. takes Helen through the index, through the filing system. Everything's on disk, backed up, printed out. A summary of the contents is pasted to the back of every box. What's she thinking, as together they travel through Benny's life, so neatly parcelled up? Who's to say? Not Helen. Miss Parrinder hides between files and printouts. Singularities and synchronicities reduced to alphabetical entries: File under S. Does she for a moment consider the *stuff* behind all these entries she's made – this world into which Benny retreated, whose paths he mapped for a multitude of eager followers? And if so, does she believe it? The question is otiose. Of course she believes it. Benny said it, ergo it is.

They come to the end.

– Well, Miss Parrinder. What can I say? I'm so grateful. How much do I owe you?

Miss Parrinder mentions a figure. Helen doubles it, tears off the cheque. Conscience money. – How about a drink? She rises and heads for the door.

– I'll be down in a minute, says Miss Parrinder delicately, making for the bathroom. She, too, has bodily functions. One forgets, which is as she would wish. Or has emotion overcome her?

Waiting, Helen ponders this gut loathing there's always been between them. One doesn't have to like everyone, but this? It's far deeper than any of their personal exchanges could justify. Relations between Helen and Miss Parrinder have never been less (or more) than businesslike. Is it that sense, again, of hidden lives, hidden currents? Of attempts at manipulation – perhaps failed, perhaps not, who's to know?

Maybe it's Helen's old sceptical dislike of the moony-mystical, the impatient scorn she has always felt for those pathetic persons who can't, who won't, face up to reality. And the myth-weavers, the gauze-wavers, who cater to them: of whom Benny, in his new incarnation, became one. (Or was he, too, just one of the poor deluded?) He used to tease her about this. – Admit it, Hel, the Spanish Inquisition had nothing on you. You talk about rationality, but what's so rational about foaming because people don't see the world the same way you do? Aren't you supposed to be the great artist? the one who gets into other people's skins?

She didn't argue. It was too painful. In a situation such as theirs, you don't deliberately push the other person off the ledge to which he so agonisingly, so effortfully, clings. What would be left? No satisfaction: just awful solitude. But what she still thinks is only what they both thought. Before. And then he abandoned her for the enemy.

What Miss Parrinder can't forgive is that, despite all this, he returned to Helen in the flesh. Let the next world do its worst – in *this* one Benny was Helen's still, despite all blandishments, all discouragements. A puzzle to many, not just Miss P. What did they still see in each other? What was left in common? Why, after all that, did he return, did she accept him?

Helen's thought about it, often, both since he died and before. Calamity does not bind. Did not bind. His leaving was no surprise. But his return? What was he hoping for? Why did she agree?

Naturally, she can't speak for Benny. For herself, it came down to what it always came down to, since the day they married. Liking. She enjoyed his company more than anyone's – and found, somewhat to her surprise, that this had remained true despite everything. Benny was still her preferred companion. Being without him did not suit her. He had to go, that was obvious, but she was glad when he came back.

Evidently, however, what remained – what he was hoping for as he shut the door behind him and hugged her to him – was not enough for him.

Helen sets two glasses on the table and places a bottle of Irish whiskey beside them. Jamesons is Miss Parrinder's tipple. After a few minutes, she descends. She looks composed. If tears threatened, they threaten no more. She declines ice. Helen pours a couple of stiff tots. They clink glasses.

Miss Parrinder leaves.

9

THE FRONT DOOR slams. Helen falls back into her chair. Inertia reclaims her.

She sits in the silent house and contemplates the dust and the whiskey. They complement each other. As there can be no question of doing anything about the first, now or possibly ever, should she not have some more of the second? Blot the dust out? It's very tempting. She looks at her watch. Two o'clock. So late! Well, they went through a lot of stuff. No stone unturned. Both of them intent upon making this the positively final goodbye. (Though isn't anything, even dealing with the enemy, better than this nothing?)

She should really have offered Miss Parrinder lunch. That way, she'd have got some herself.

But she didn't.

She pours another whiskey in the end, a small one. Stoppers the bottle, replaces it in the cupboard, mounts the stairs glass in hand. The door to Benny's study is shut. Did she shut it? Either that or Miss P. did. It's of no account. The shutness is the thing. She's not planning to reopen it, now or . . . But never say never. In the foreseeable future. Is that better? Once again she's filled with that anger that sometimes visits her. Why should she think about him any more? He was, he chose not to be. Finish.

She turns her back on the shut door and, still fuming, enters the drawing-room. It's filled with agreeable ways to pass the time:

shelves full of books, varied and copious sources of music, drawers full of playing-cards, a television, VCR, two sofas, a large armchair, a piano. Helen ignores them all.

There's a small writing-table by one of the windows, a delicate little piece of country Sheraton they picked up years ago, before the children were born. She wanders towards it: it's as good a place as any to sit, sip whiskey and stare out into the street.

On the table lies a folder she doesn't recognise, a cardboard wallet in a dispiriting shade of mid-urine. It wasn't there last time she was in this room – yesterday, was that? Not that she cares. She's in no mood to care about anything, let alone some stupid folder. But it seems she is no more able to control her own body than any other aspect of this wilful world. Of their own volition (the action certainly has nothing to do with Helen) her fingers wander towards the folder and flip it open.

It's filled with letters. Letters to Benny. All from the same person – at any rate, all in the same handwriting. Just as her fingers, unwilled, revealed them, so her eyes unwillingly scan through them. And, having begun, are quite unable to stop.

The letters are from someone named Saffron (though sometimes she just signs herself S). She's American: that's clear from her handwriting, that loopy American script. And female? Helen assumes so. Why? Because boys aren't called Saffron. Because boys wouldn't be writing to Benny (she thinks – but what does she know? Less and less, it seems). Because there's something about the handwriting, the style . . . And although there's no address, none is needed. They're written on Synchrony paper.

Helen's fingers flick through the letters, her eyes scan them. And, willy-nilly – or rather, nilly: there's no will in this at all – she finds herself taking in the messages they seem to hold.

They appear to have been stuffed in the wallet as they arrived. They're not dated, but to judge from the contents, the earliest ones are at the bottom, the later ones on top. The story they tell is both clear and unclear, at once banal and unnerving.

The clear, the banal part, is that Benny was conducting an affair with Saffron, perhaps living with her. If that were so, then the letters must date from his unlooked-for and abrupt return to London, that return whose cause she so carefully did not seek to know. If he wanted to tell her, he would; if not, she was happy not to hear. And he did not. When did Benny ever volunteer anything? Especially about himself, his feelings, his private affairs. In that way, he remained supremely un-Californian. The book was never entirely open. You knew what he chose to reveal.

– Missing you, Saffron writes. That was in the early days. – Come back soon.

Later, there seems to have been some disagreement. – How can you ask me to do this? You know how I feel about this. We've been through it all so often. We'll talk again when you come back. You know I hate writing letters, especially about important stuff.

Whatever his response, it was unsatisfactory. A tone of desperation set in. – Are you trying to ignore me? It's six months since I heard from you. *Six months!* Don't you care what happens over here? Cherry sends love.

Cherry? Who's Cherry? A friend of Saffron's, presumably. All these 1960s nature names. River. Rose-petal. Sunshine. Saffron and Cherry are restrained by comparison. Nevertheless, they carry the stamp of a particular time and place and mindset, turning on, dropping out, going with the flow. Just the kind of thing Benny once hated. Pot, which was the key to all that, never had much effect on him. He remained obdurately level-headed when everyone else was reduced to giggling helplessness, a state which when viewed from outside is sublimely irritating. Perhaps if he'd liked pot he wouldn't have been so hardline. Helen would take bets that Saffron and Cherry's parents more or less lived on pot. This of course does not mean that Saffron and Cherry do likewise.

Benny clearly felt under some obligation. – The money's fine, writes Saffron, – but it's a lousy substitute. Her tone becomes shriller. Why did Benny avoid her last time he visited? The money is no longer sufficient – will he increase it? – I enclose a photograph. (But there is no photograph. Where is it? What did he do with it? Would it mean anything to her if she saw it?)

And then the tone changes again, and becomes threatening. The threat, however, is never spelled out. Presumably it was well enough known to need no clarification. – What would your wife think, if she

227

knew? Have you thought about this? You think you can just keep your lives separate. Well, you can't. I shall tell her – how can you stop me? What's she given you that I haven't?

Yes, what? wonders Helen. What?

She shuts the folder, and looks down at it in a sort of despair. What is all this? How did it suddenly arrive on her table?

That at least is obvious. Miss Parrinder put it there. That's what she must have been doing while Helen thought she was in the bathroom. She extracts the folder from its hiding-place, wherever that was – a drawer? a cupboard? a shelf? that enormous bag she always carries? – creeps in and dumps her load. Then, cleansed, refreshed, she descends. Takes the ritual whiskey and departs in triumph, knowing that soon, soon –

Or is this the paranoia of grief? It might have been mere awkwardness – the act of a woman who is socially inept, who can't handle difficult situations. She finds this possibly compromising stuff, and what's she to do? File it, list it with everything else, for anyone to find? Lesley Collinge, for example? That would be grossly irresponsible. Obviously, she should point it out to Helen. I found these, I thought perhaps they should be kept separate . . . But she can't bring herself to do that, either – can't face so personal a confrontation, given the awkwardness between them. The embarrassment factor is too much for her to face. In desperation, she dumps the folder where it's sure to be found, and leaves.

It's possible. But it's not what happened. More than once during their meeting Helen raised her eyes to find Miss Parrinder staring at her. It was an oddly unnerving gaze, steady, unfriendly, cool. Not mad – nothing like that. Confident. Yes. The confidence of superiority – but stemming from what? What's Miss P. got that Helen hasn't?

Knowledge. Miss Parrinder has known about Saffron all the time.

Saffron, and what else? What secrets remain to be divulged, as and when she chooses? Will Helen ever be sure she's laid Benny finally to rest? What ghosts still lie in wait? Only Miss Parrinder can say. She knows. She knows everything. She was Benny's confidante, he opened his heart to her, spilt worries into her lap that couldn't be shared with Helen. And now he's dead, leaving her, if nothing else, this little piece of power.

The only drawback is that she's not present to see the effect of her bombshell. Involuntarily, Helen glances through the window. Can she espy a familiar figure, lurking in the street, behind a lamppost, inside a doorway?

Don't be ridiculous.

Helen leaves the drawing-room. She notices that the door to Benny's room is now slightly open. It must be the wind.

There's no wind.

Did she think that he would be dismissed so easily? By the mere shutting of a door? That she knew, even, what there was to dismiss?

Fair's fair. They were married twenty-five years. And would she say that *he* knew *her*?

*

– Darling, it really isn't at all convenient, says Patrick. Aren't you tired of all this toing and froing?

– I'm sorry, says Helen. – I've just got to come. I'll tell you when I get there – it's not something I can talk about over the phone. Look, don't worry. I can find somewhere to stay. A motel or something.

He sighs. – Don't be silly, you can't come here and stay in some motel. It's just – oh, never mind. Give me a few days, OK?

It's George, thinks Helen. And why not? He has his rights. He won't stay in the house when she's there. She asked Patrick, last time, why not. It isn't as though they're in competition.

– Ah, but you are, aren't you, darling? You have such a narrow idea of competition! He's got me now, but what about all the rest of my life? That's what you represent.

It's funny, she thinks, as once more she unpacks her bag in Patrick's guest-room. Patrick: the one person I didn't expect to end up close to. Though close is a relative term in this context. When was Pat ever close to anyone? Always inside his own world. At a distance, even (to all appearances) from himself. That conversation they had, last time she saw him. Why did he marry Colette? All that stuff about drifting into it, not being a strong person. Everything but the main reason: that he was trying to pretend, to himself as much as everyone else, that he wasn't really gay.

229

She leaves the room and makes her way to the pool. It's dinner-time. When he sees her, Patrick removes the wine from the ice-bucket, opens it, pours it with a flourish. Once he got used to the idea of her arrival, he became, as she knew he would, charm itself.

– Sit down, darling, he says. – I expect you're bushed. What you need's dinner. Something to eat and drink and a nice fairy story to go with it. So I thought I'd just fill you in on *Joseph Elroy*.

*

The dinner-table. A metaphor, a symbol of the intimate pleasures – eating, drinking, talking together. And security: the diners make their forays into a hostile world, and return to the certainty of sustenance, corporeal and social. The life-giving bosom of the family.

Which is, of course, a more complex matter. The dinner-table is wholly benign, but the family? Everyone needs one, but not necessarily the one they were born with. Patrick's father owns a tannery and cares nothing for art; Benny's parents represent a bourgeoisie he despises; Colette's father goes his own way while her mother maintains appearances; Helen's mother has vanished servic-ing her father. This is family? Not for them. They have become each other's family. Together, they are safe.

Sometimes, though, even surrounded by this loving surrogate family, Helen feels depressed. Sibling rivalry claims her: they've all made it, they're all famous. Except her. What has she achieved? One measly play. Who knows if she'll ever write another? From time to time she tries, but she's drained. The ideas won't come.

Benny points at the twins. Nine months old. – Isn't this enough to be going on with? Give yourself a chance. What are you, a machine?

Tim and Laura. Her little bonuses. Her unexpected present. Guess who from?

Studying them, in the long hours spent *à trois* since the twins emerged one dark November morning, she has concluded that the answer to this question is by no means as simple as she had assumed it might be. Obviously they're not identical: they're different sexes. Fraternal twins, two eggs activated in the same cycle, a freak of fertility.

But they aren't just non-identical: they're not alike *at all*. You could not imagine two more different babies. They are an object-lesson in spermatozoic caprice. Tim is long, placid, blue-eyed, with wisps of straight light hair; Laura, little, round, mercurial, with round brown eyes and a dusting of black curls. – Just like her daddy! they all exclaim. – What lovely curls! They're so different, aren't they? So interesting, the way they all turn out different!

Yes, the arbitrary marvels of heredity could scarcely be more clearly demonstrated. Arbitrary, but (as Benny's life's work points out) significant, often in quite unlooked-for ways. Blond, dark, tall, short. Suppose Napoleon's chromosomes had allowed him just a little more height. Unassailed by the short man's compulsion to prove himself, would he have needed to command, to control, to go on and on in the teeth of the odds until he had conquered the world? Four centimetres in the right place, and what a different world *that* would have been!

Surveying her twins, Helen is nonplussed. But her thoughts are not filled, as Benny's are, with wonder at Nature's infinite permutations. She is more concerned with Mendel's laws, the laws of heredity, which are not infinite at all. On the contrary, no boundaries could be more clearly defined. She looks at Laura; she looks at Tim. And she wonders.

Just like her Daddy, eh? But which Daddy?

Helen and Richard both have blue eyes. So does Tim. Benny has brown eyes. So does Laura.

Brown eyes are dominant, blue, recessive.

Does this mean Tim couldn't be Benny's child? Not necessarily. If either of Benny's parents has light eyes, then he may have one blue-eyed gene and one brown-eyed. This will mean that although he himself has the dominant brown eyes, he can pass on a blue-eye gene in the great genetic lottery of fertilisation. And it meets one of Helen's two blue-eyed genes, resulting in a blue-eyed child. Tim.

Helen tries to think back to Mr and Mrs Spiro's last visit, when the twins were a couple of months old. She seems to remember they were both brown-eyed, but that may simply be because she associates brown eyes with dark colouring. She could ask – Benny might know, though she wouldn't bet on it – but somehow she doesn't want to be the one to bring the subject up. At the time, she didn't think to look. The twins both had blue, or bluish, eyes, as very young babies do. Laura's changed later.

So Tim could be Benny's son. But Helen knows he isn't. For he, too, looks just like his daddy. He's the spit of Richard, the living image. The same nose, the same slow grin. And no problem at all about blue eyes.

On the other hand, two blue-eyed parents can't have a brown-eyed child.

But that's impossible. Isn't it? For Benny is infertile. Isn't he? All these years, fucking regularly, several times a week, he and Helen failed to conceive. Why should he suddenly succeed on this particular occasion? All that was different was that Richard had been there first.

And quite apart from anything else, twins, identical or fraternal, are conceived at the same moment. On the same occasion. Aren't they?

Helen looked up *twins – fraternal* in the medical dictionary. But, not surprisingly, this particular set of circumstances was not discussed. So she asked a friend of hers, a doctor. Not directly, of course. She made a sort of joke of it. – Honestly, Timmy and Laura, they're so different you'd hardly think they were related. It set me wondering, you know, one's always thinking about possible plots. Would that be possible? I mean, could you have twins with two different fathers?

Her friend considered. – I suppose you could. The mother'd have to have sex with the two men pretty close together, of course. On the same day, probably. He looked at her closely. Helen changed the subject.

She thinks back, tries to recall. Richard left around half past five. He didn't want to risk meeting Benny in the hall. And they'd actually got out of bed (it was the spare bed – easier for both practical and aesthetic reasons) about half an hour before that. Then Helen had a shower, and Benny got home about seven, as usual. Following which she and Benny went to bed quite early – around eleven, it must have been – because he had to be up early the next morning, he was going to a conference in Sheffield (a proper zoology conference, for once). And she said, – I'm tired. And he said –

Does Benny suspect anything? It's noticeable (to Helen, at least) that he seems much fonder of Laura than of Tim. Are these the eyes of guilt? No: just eyes. It's Laura he makes for, Laura he always holds in his arms. Blood instinct? Perhaps not: it's well-known that cross-sex bonding can be very strong, especially when the children are young. Her own attachment to Tim is certainly different from the bond she feels with Laura. With him there's already a certain alien glamour, while her relation with Laura is, even at this young age, one of familiar friendship, fellow-feeling. But there's something else, too. For Helen, Tim represents aspects of herself which marriage and motherhood might otherwise have buried: privacy, subversiveness – the hidden life. She holds him in her arms and thinks: My little cuckoo. Not entirely coincidentally, she's meditating a play about William the Conqueror, known during his lifetime as William the Bastard. Son of William, Duke of Normandy, and Arlette the tanner's daughter. Good, strong bastard blood. Result: a much-needed injection of civilisation into these benighted islands. Which would otherwise have remained a sub-Teutonic outpost, entirely lacking in refinements. Probably not a good place for persons named Spiro.

Mummy's boys; Daddy's girls. Colette (who knows nothing of all this: there are some details to which even Colette is not privy) says she and Patrick feel the same way about Declan and Gemma. Except that poor little Gemma isn't really even Daddy's girl. Babies of either sex bore Patrick. Sometimes, when Helen's visiting with her two, and he comes home to find a crèche in progress, it's all he can do to force himself to stay in the room, or even the house. A new man he is not. His idea of parenting: to be shown his nice clean babies for half an hour before bedtime, in the Edwardian manner. Perhaps he'll like them better when they're bigger.

*

– They're thinking, says Patrick, – of making Joseph Elroy Josephine.
– What are you talking about?

– What I said. They thought it might make a wonderful part for Meryl Streep.

– But this is an *old man*.

– Well, if you remember, he'd already become a younger man. So why not a younger woman? Not a *very* young woman, you understand, drawls Patrick, – but young enough to be box-office. Then you can cut out the daughter, and what we have is Meryl Streep going to the conference –

– But I thought the conference was *on* Elroy?

– That's right, but the new idea is, she goes as it were incognito. And falls in love with the guy organising it and so on and so on. The thing about Meryl Streep *is*, she brings a hundred per cent financing. No questions asked.

– But I thought the money wasn't a problem these days, with *Gurdjy* doing so well?

– Darling, says Patrick, – financing is *always* a problem. Unless you're Spielberg. Or Meryl Streep. He sits back, takes a sip of wine, and looks across the pool towards where the moon is rising above the cypresses and Greek columns. – Remember Italy? That holiday we all had? I always think whoever did all this must have just come back from there. Create your very own poolside Italy.

– Greece.

– Greece, shmeece. Hollywood, don't you love it?

– So whose idea was all this?

– The work of many hands, he assures her. – That was one reason I wasn't sure about you coming out. I thought you'd be too horrified.

– I'm beyond being horrified by that sort of thing, says Helen, and reflects that she is probably telling the truth. Life is too short. Twenty years ago, she was more shockable.

Patrick goes over to the barbecue, where a fennel-sprinkled sea-bass is gently spluttering, pronounces it done, dishes it up, hands the lemon, tosses the salad and lights the candles. Helen sniffs appreciatively. – You should have said. I'd have made you my special cream sauce.

– Cream sauce! Darling, d'you want to kill us both? Imagine what that would do to our cholesterol counts!

– I've no idea. I've never counted mine.

Patrick looks at her incredulously. – It's no good burying our heads in the sand, darling, he says severely. – At our age, we have to take care of ourselves. I for one have no intention of leaving the set until the very last possible second. Expertly he dissects and serves the fish. – Well, now. D'you feel strong enough to tell me why you had to come over so absolutely?

Helen takes a deep breath. – What do you know about a person called Saffron?

– Ah, sighs Patrick, gazing at the moon. – Saffron. I wondered if that might be it.

– You know her?

– I wouldn't say *know* –

– Who is she? I assume she was Benny's mistress when he was out here. But who *is* she?

Patrick spreads his hands. – You know as much as I do, then, darling. The bare facts. Benny was always so secretive, wasn't he? God, it seems so strange, talking about him in the past tense. But there you are. He was. I always put it down to early political training. He doled out the minimum of information, strictly on a need-to-know basis. Didn't you feel? I frankly don't know how you stood it all those years.

– We led rich fantasy-lives, Helen says drily. – It's funny, you know, I always assumed there was someone, but I thought it was Lorraine.

Patrick eats in silence. Either he knows nothing or he is, like Benny, disinclined to share the contents of his mind.

– I found some letters. They seemed to come from Synchrony. Is she at Synchrony?

– Synchrony, says Patrick dreamily. – I believe she may have been. I've no idea whether she's still there. He looks relieved, as though once again he had braced himself for something which has not after all transpired.

*

The Synchrony Institute has changed little since Helen's last visit. The Master's harmonious forms are eternal, the California sun beats down as it always did. What, then, has happened to the beholder's eye? For now the house, which seemed so open and lovely, fills her with foreboding. As she shuts the door of her car and walks towards that stately Egyptian entrance, her knees buckle and her heart is pounding.

For God's sake! So Benny had a girlfriend! Is that such a surprise? Is she really about to play that hackneyed old chestnut, The Wronged Wife Confronts? Get real, Helen. Let's enter into the spirit of things here. Spirit being the operative word. The man's dead. These are stale scandals, yesterday's news. Why this compulsion to scratch old itches? It isn't even as if she's married any more. What's left to destroy? Only illusions.

A boy and a girl are working in the garden, clearing weeds and watering. They take no notice of Helen, but weed on relentlessly. They avert their eyes, pretend she isn't there. She thinks: Like the kids at High Leys. And shivers. But this is no English winter's day. Today's temperatures will hit the eighties. Students, maybe, paying their way through college on piecework: Weeds, a dollar a ton.

Helen pushes the door, but it does not swing open as it did the first time she came. Perhaps that was a mistake, or more likely they've had some trouble since and been forced to take the usual defensive measures. She rings the bell, identifies herself, hears the buzz of the door unlatching. It clicks shut behind her, and she stands in the stillness of the entrance-hall.

– I've come to see Dr Kertes.

There's a different receptionist today, a fat girl with long green fingernails. She surveys Helen impassively. – Do you have an appointment?

– I'm a friend of his.

– Can I have your name?

– Helen Spiro. Helen Bartram Spiro.

The receptionist picks up the phone. – There's a woman here asking for Dr Kertes. A Ms Spiro. Helen Spiro. She listens, replaces the receiver. – I'm sorry. Dr Kertes is in a meeting.

– How long will it go on?

– All day, I'm afraid. Can anyone else help you?

Saffron. But she doesn't know Saffron's other name. – Is Ms Margulies around?

– I'm sorry? I don't think there's anyone of that name here.

Has she gone mad? Or has there been a management shake-up since Helen was here last?

– Lorraine. Isn't her name Margulies? I thought she was the administrator here.

– Oh, *Lorraine*. Sure. The girl lifts the phone. – I'm sorry. What was your name again?

– Spiro. Helen Spiro.

It's clear that this means nothing to the girl. Not much of a memory-span there, thinks Helen. You'd think Spiro would ring a bell. Though I suppose it's years since Benny was actually around much. She was probably still in high school.

– Hi, Lorraine. It's Angie again. Ms Spiro would like to see you . . . Yes . . . Sure. She turns to Helen with a perfect toothpaste smile. – If you'll just take a seat?

Helen sits and waits. Silence surrounds her. The tap of green fingernails hitting Angie's keyboard echoes through the Pharaonic space. Once again she's reminded of High Leys. The silence, the waiting, the sense of thick impermeability.

There's a click of approaching heels, and Lorraine enters the hallway. Perfectly groomed as always, in a cream silk shirtwaist. Her face is a mask of impersonal amiability. – Hi, Helen, she says briskly. – I didn't know you were paying us a visit. She keeps her distance, awaiting enlightenment.

– I'm doing some more work on that film I told you about, Helen says. Her voice is calm, and it seems that no-one else can hear her heart beating. Ker-thud! ker-thud! Have they all gone deaf? Perhaps the sound's drowned out by the seamless tattoo of those long nails. – There was a free morning, so I thought I'd call by to see Stefan, but I gather he's busy.

– Well, there you are. Lorraine smiles. She doesn't say, Was there anything particular you wanted to see him about? She doesn't move. She isn't about to prolong this encounter. Her posture says: This was not a good moment. I'm a busy person.

The silence is broken by a soft pattering, sprightly, allegro. At first

237

it's barely audible, but it's getting louder all the time. Something's approaching. And here it is! They all watch, fascinated, as a small black poodle trots bouncily into the hallway. Lorraine says, – Sheba! Where did you spring from? At the same time the receptionist, with evident pleasure, calls: – Hi, Sheba! and holds out a hand. The dog trots towards her amd jumps onto her lap.

Sheba! How is this possible? Helen's heart, which had subsided slightly, resumes its agonised thrumming – still, apparently, inaudible to the others.

– Is she yours?

Lorraine shrugs. – Oh, she kind of lives here. The Synchrony dog. She's Stefan's really, but he's away half the time.

– Has she lived here long?

Obviously Helen's taken leave of her senses. Testily, Lorraine turns to the receptionist. – Angie, how long has Sheba lived here?

– She's been here longer'n I have, Lorraine.

Lorraine is bored by this dog-discussion. – Was there anything special you wanted? she asks, in the tone of one expecting the answer No. What's happened to her? Last time they met, she wasn't like this. Helen hears her voice again: *I used to really envy you your family life.* An admission of weakness! The person before her would never permit such a thing. That was on her own ground, of course, she set the parameters. Perhaps she doesn't like being taken by surprise, caught unprepared. Or maybe that was just a test-run – getting to know the enemy. And now the relationship is revealed for what it's always been: adversarial. Fighting over the corpse? Fighting over something, at any rate.

– I'd really like a talk. Helen is meek, unrefusable. She doesn't trade punches: she slides beneath them. – Is there somewhere we could go?

Lorraine the executive glances at her watch. – I don't have that long right now. Any moment, she'll start to tap her toe on the floor.

– It won't take a minute. Helen, too, can be forceful when she puts her mind to it.

– OK. Lorraine heads back out of the hallway at speed, heels clicking testily. Helen follows. Down corridors, along the loggia. All the doors are shut. Synchrony's activities are not revealed today.

They round a corner and Lorraine opens the door of a small room, plainly furnished with a desk and two chairs. Perhaps it was originally a pantry, or a maid's room. Is this her office? This cubby hole? Impossible. There are no files or papers, not even a telephone. Who can administer without a telephone? No, this room was selected with a purpose. The medium is the message. It reads: a convenient site for the briefest of impersonal encounters.

Lorraine sits. Helen sits.

– I'm interested in Sheba, Helen says.

– Is that what you came here to ask me about? The *dog*?

– It wasn't, actually. There was something else. But first I'd like to know about the dog.

The dog is on her side. She knows it, just as Benny knew it.

– What about it?

– The thing is, I've been finding some stuff out about Benny.

Lorraine says nothing.

– He wrote a letter. Describing how he came across Declan, here in LA. Didn't he ever tell you about it? You said he brought Declan to see you.

Still nothing from Lorraine. She waits, impassive, behind the desk.

– He was led to him. By – a little black poodle named Sheba.

Helen's voice dies away. Suddenly, she feels ridiculous. Her words echo in her ears. Led by a poodle? Lorraine is studying her fingernails. Like the rest of her, they are a model of unspectacular good style: unpainted, but perfectly shaped and buffed to a high shine. Finally she raises her head, takes a breath and plunges into speech.

– Helen – I don't know quite how to put this, but perhaps you didn't realise quite what a state Benny was in when he came over here after Laura got killed.

– What on earth are you talking about? Of course I realised. Naturally he was in a state! We both were. How could we not be?

Lorraine shakes her head. – I meant mental state. He was – quite unreliable.

– Lorraine, says Helen steadily, – I'm not talking about figments. I saw a letter in which he described how he ran across this dog and it led him through the streets to Declan. Who had disappeared. He was lost, no-one had seen or heard of him for months. That much I can vouch for. And Benny found him because he followed this dog. It was a small black poodle called Sheba. And living here I find a small black poodle called Sheba. So I'm curious. Wouldn't you be? I assume it's the same dog. How did it get here? Benny implied Declan was living with some weird cult – I don't know, they're two a penny here, aren't they? Benny persuaded him to come away. The dog was apparently living there, wherever it was. So what's it doing here?

Lorraine sighs. – Sheba's always been here. As long as I have, anyhow.

– But –

– Listen, Helen. What do you know about Declan?

– You mean over here?

– Over here.

– What I've been told.

– So what were you told? Apart from Benny and the dog.

Helen tries to remember. It's a long time ago, and she had her own preoccupations. – He ran away. Disappeared. Colette – his mother – was frantic. You can imagine. Then there was some sort of possibility he might be over here. So she came over, partly to try and look for him. She saw Benny then, I think. And Benny found him.

– Helen, he was here all the time.

– *Here*? At Synchrony? Helen stares at her.

Lorraine nods.

– But how could he be? Declan isn't interested in physics. He doesn't know the first thing about it. He probably thinks Heisenberg's a brand of beer.

– I told you before. Synchrony's not just about physics. It's a whole outlook on life. Lorraine's tone is explanatory, patient, confident: these are words she has recited many times. – Based on the physical world, of course, as Stefan sees it. But as you know, that implies a great deal more than most people realise. The new physics opens the way to the intangible. What we're evolving here is a whole new science of life. There are physicists here, but not *just* physicists.

– You mean Stefan's set himself up as another California guru?

– What's so wrong with that? Lorraine sounds nettled. A definite

240

hit – the notion of Stefan Kertes as *just another* anything. – People need what Stefan has to offer.

She's a formidable woman, Lorraine. Helen always thought she and Colette scored fairly high on that scale, but beside Lorraine they come nowhere. If the secret is knowing what you want, she divined it in the womb. Her life is lived according to plan: this year, next year, ten years' time. The plan is flexible, naturally. But the goal is never lost sight of. Each step is considered, a means to the end. Which is? To rule the world. *Her* world, naturally – are there any others? Lorraine's got to be the one who gives the orders.

So who's in charge here at Synchrony? Kertes? Once, maybe. But no more. He seemed – he *was* – so intimidating, larger than life, all-knowing, all-manipulating. But now he's old. The bald pate, the white fluff fringing it. And inside, the machine running down. He still speaks the words, but who has the power? And *what is it*?

Helen thinks of the boy and girl in the garden, the averted looks, the silence, the deference. Of the servant-girl she glimpsed in Lorraine's house last time she was here. Of the girl who brought the tea at High Leys. Where Declan now lives and digs the vegetables. Where Benny brought him. What have they to do with the majestic concepts of astrophysics?

– What is this place?

– What d'you think? It's an institute.

– Yes, but what for? Is it academic or, I don't know, some sort of church or cult?

– Helen, it's worldwide.

– But worldwide *what*? What d'you do to all these people?

– We don't do anything *to* them. We give them a philosophy, a way of coping. I can't explain it just like that. It's complex. If you want to find out, you should enrol.

– Did Benny know all this when he came here? First of all?

Lorraine shrugs. – That was years ago. It's developed, it goes on developing all the time. You see –

– And Declan? How did Declan come here? Helen asks abruptly, cutting Lorraine off in mid-sentence. It's like when she talked to Chris Clay. She can feel that mist of words again, lapping her round, enveloping her in fuzz, a wrapped fly ready for the fatal injection. Of what? Passivity, acceptance, dependence? It would be so easy to let herself float away on that warm tide, to let go – to go with the flow –

– I believe his father brought him. Hoped it might do him some good, I suppose. He was not in a good way. The father's a friend of yours, right? Perhaps Benny told him about our work.

– But he described finding him – I saw the letter –

– Helen, he was a sick man. His mind at that point . . . He was very fond of Sheba, it's true. He'd take her out for walks. Perhaps he and Declan went together. Who knows? The mind makes its own metaphors. When a child dies, you're pushed to extremes, I guess.

*

The medium is a comfortable matron in her mid-fifties, amply bosomed, grey hair neatly permed. – Mrs Costelloe? And this must be your friend.

Her name is Mrs March. She looks keenly at Helen. She ushers them inside: a beige-carpeted hallway, with mountainously Artexed walls and ceiling. – Have you brought something, dear?

Colette warned Helen of this. The medium needs something that belonged to the dead person. – For the vibrations, Colette explained. Helen produces a sock. She put her hand in Laura's drawer and took the first object it lighted upon. She could not bear to look.

Mrs March leads them through into a back room containing a round table and four chairs. She lights two candles and draws the curtains against the speeding clouds and blue sky of April. In the flickering half-light, the three of them sit around the table and, on Mrs March's instructions, join hands. The small white sock lies before them. They stare at it in silence. Mrs March sits with her head sunk on her chest. Then, all of a sudden, she throws back her head and, in a strangled, rasping voice, says: I'm getting – a child!

Helen, who has promised herself that she will remain impassive whatever may transpire, feels her body jerk. She is angry at this betrayal – can't she even trust her own body any more? – but Mrs March remains impassive, motionless, head thrown back. She rasps: – It's a dark child – short hair – I think it's a girl, yes, a girl. Not long arrived. I'm getting Anna – no, Sarah – an S – is that right?

To Helen's fury, she hasn't been able to stop herself raising her head. S is for Spiro, isn't it?

The medium gives no sign that she has noticed this reaction, however. She remains rigid and motionless. – I see an S there somewhere, she intones. Though names have no importance up there, they've left our world behind – she says, Mummy, you mustn't worry. I'm so happy, it's so beautiful here! The sun shines all the time! I'm just waiting for you here, Mummy, I can see you, and I know that soon we'll be together – time passes so quickly here – I'm sending you my love, Mummy – Can you feel it? It's a warm wind around you! I love you so much! There is a pause. Then the hoarse voice again: – Goodbye, Mummy!

Mrs March's head flops back onto her chest. Silence returns to the room. After some minutes, the medium gives a little sigh and drops her hands. They all sit back. Mrs March draws back the curtains, blows out the candles. She says: – Did someone appear?

– Oh, yes, says Colette in her deep actress's voice. – We're so grateful. Thank you so much.

There is a murmured confabulation between Colette and Mrs March; money changes hands. Helen and Colette leave the house. As they walk towards Colette's car, Helen bursts into tears.

– You cry, darling, says Colette. – You'll feel better. You see, she's there.

Helen says: – For Christ's sake! You believe that awful dingy stuff? You really *believe* it? It's an obscenity! She could see it was a little girl's sock! And I'm quite dark, and my hair's short – isn't it likely I'd have a dark child? There was nothing personal there at all! It's nothing to do with Laura! It's nothing to do with anything! It's just guesswork and experience and *rubbish*!

– Well, if you don't want to believe it, I can't make you, Colette says huffily.

*

I'm sorry to upset you, murmurs Lorraine. Maybe you'd like to sit here a little while? Take as long as you need. She gets up. She's on her way.

– Oh. Abruptly Helen re-enters the real world. This small office. Lorraine across the desk, poised for flight. And she hasn't even got around to asking . . . She got diverted. Always, a diversion. Lorraine is moving towards the door. She's turning the handle –

– But that wasn't what I wanted to ask you about.

– Helen, I'm busy. I have work to do.

– It won't take long. I just wanted to ask whether you know a person called Saffron?

Lorraine freezes. All movement ceases. Helen's scalp creeps. She notices that her arms are covered with goose-bumps.

– Saffron?

– I found some letters from someone called Saffron. Going through Benny's stuff. They were written on Synchrony paper.

Lorraine says: – Helen, I think perhaps you don't realise what kind of place this is. People trust us. They come to us for help. We have to act with discretion. I can't just discuss personalities.

– Then don't. I'll see Stefan. At least he doesn't treat me like some sort of semi-criminal halfwit.

– Stefan's busy, says Lorraine, tight-lipped. – I'm in charge.

– You? How can you be in charge of a place like this? You're no more a scientist than – than I am!

Lorraine says: – I don't need to listen to this. She leaves the room, and Helen rushes after her. They retrace their steps, back through the loggia and the corridors towards the Egyptian atrium, Lorraine walking fast, eyes front, resolutely maintaining silence, while Helen runs, yelling, at her side. – What is it about this Saffron, anyway? she shouts. What are you trying to hide? What is it you can't tell me? Haven't I got a right to know? I'm Benny's wife – his wife! And now he's dead, and I want to know why. Why did he kill himself? Why did he do it?

Doors fly open as they pass, revealing, as when Helen was here last, circles of chairs surrounding symbol-covered blackboards: today's text. Faces peer out.

– Was it because of Saffron? Was it? Who is she, anyhow?

On her left, Helen sees a group turn towards one of their number, involuntarily, as people do when they hear a particular name. Helen stops, and follows the direction of the group gaze.

She is looking, presumably, at Saffron.

She is looking, of course, at the brown-haired young woman.

Their eyes meet. Saffron opens her mouth. Helen takes a step forward. But before they can speak or otherwise make contact, the door slams shut. Lorraine says loudly: – I don't know what you think you're doing. I told you. You can't just walk in here and talk to people. We have responsibilities. People get upset.

Lorraine takes Helen's arm and propels her along the corridor towards the entrance-hall. Helen cries: – But she wants to talk to me, you could see that!

– I'm sorry. If you want to talk with one of the students here, the rule is that you must make an appointment.

Helen breaks away and runs towards the door. She throws it open. The room is empty. A French door on the far side is open. It gives onto a terrace. But that, too, is empty.

*

– Is it true? Helen demands. – Was it you that took Declan there?

Patrick shifts awkwardly. He's in the middle of doing a new storyboard. Meryl Streep, a.k.a. Josephine Elroy, is addressing the conference. The other conferees are not yet aware of her identity. Her ex-lover, who has claimed the authorship of the books for himself, is leaping out to try and silence her. – It's hard to remember exactly what happened. It was all so long ago, darling.

– Come on, Pat. Stop flannelling. You remember perfectly well. You must have realised Colette was going mad with anxiety.

With a sigh, he puts down his felt-tip and turns to her. – You've got to realise, Helen. I was in an impossible position. I was living in this tiny apartment, with a man I'd known for a few weeks, and who should arrive on my doorstep? Declan, looking like hell. I can't imagine what he'd been doing. Or rather, I can. Too well. I didn't ask, though. What would have been the point?

*

It's a beautiful morning. Joggers and dog-walkers are going through their paces on the firm sand along the sea's margin. Patrick and Pietro are having breakfast on the deck. Every morning begins with a little light furniture-shifting. It's a nuisance – but if you leave the table and chairs out overnight, they're liable to get stolen, and that's even more of a nuisance. It's worth the effort, though. What's the point of having a beach condo, otherwise?

Patrick met Pietro in Brazil, filming his Amazonian epic. Now Pietro's come back to help on the edit. Though the truth is, there isn't an awful lot for him to do. He's getting bored: it's hard to know how much longer he'll stay. But breakfast is a good time. Relaxed, not too hot, and there hasn't been time to get bored yet.

The doorbell brays.

– Who on *earth* is this? Shall we ignore it?

But Pietro is still a boy, still excited at the thought of the outside world. He's already at the entryphone. He presses the button.

– Dad?

– What?

– Is my Dad there?

– You Dad? Who you Dad?

– I thought Patrick Costelloe lived there, says the voice. It sounds young, and desperate.

– Wait a minute. Pietro returns to the deck, where Patrick is placidly slicing a pawpaw. – Someone asking for Dad.

Patrick jumps up as if all the bees in Brazil have suddenly stung him. He rushes to the entryphone. – Declan? Is that you?

The person at the door is hardly recognisable as Declan. He's emaciated and bedraggled; his golden hair is lank and dull and dirty; his skin is grey with grime. His shoes have holes, as do his jeans – and not the fashionable holes Pietro sometimes affects: they're falling to bits. There's a sore on his ankle. Patrick might have passed him on the street without recognising him. Perhaps that's exactly what happened. Perhaps that's how Declan knows he's here. That's not what he says, though. According to Declan, he just got off the plane.

– You don't look as if you could pay for a meal, let alone a plane ticket.

– Well, I did.

– Where did you get the money?

– Out of the building society.

– I don't believe you. Patrick stares at his son in horror. Then he remembers Pietro, who is staring incomprehendingly at this incongruous pair. – Pietro, this is my son Declan. Dec, Pietro. Christ, Declan, what are we going to do with you?

– I hoped you'd let me crash here for a bit.

– Not before you've had a wash. And some clean clothes. And something to eat. Does your mother know you're here?

– No, and you're not to tell her. If you tell her, I'll go.

– But she must be going crazy!

– Serve her right.

Declan seems near to tears. Any further interrogation had better wait, or he'll collapse. Patrick takes him to the bathroom, hands him soap, towels and shampoo, finds him some clothes, and sits down to wait. Pietro leaves for the editing suite. Patrick wonders if he'll see him again. He's a beautiful boy – nearly as beautiful as Declan promised to be, once. He's been attracting some covetous looks.

Finally Declan emerges. He seems dazed. He eats an enormous breakfast, sits back and smiles sweetly. – Lucky you were around, Dad.

– But Dec, what are we going to do with you? You can't stay here, not for long. There's not enough room. Anyhow, shouldn't you be at school?

– I've left.

– What did your mother say?

– She didn't know.

– So what did you think you'd do?

– Bum around.

They look at each other.

– I thought you might be able to find me some work.

– That's not so easy.

– What does that fag do, then? I bet you found some for him.

Patrick looks at him. Reunited for an hour, and already they're getting on each other's nerves. Just like old times. And then Declan will run off again, and – (but Patrick prefers not to pursue this line of thought). Instead, he says: – Maybe Benny could think of something.

– Benny?

– He's in LA, didn't you know? At that institute. I was speaking to him the other day. Would you like to see him?

– OK. Declan makes no difficulties about this. Is Patrick pleased? He's relieved, anyway.

Patrick dials. – Benny. Guess who just turned up? Declan. Yup, just arrived on the doorstep. No, she doesn't. Look, d'you think you could come over?

*

– You know how close he was to Declan, says Patrick. – He said he knew the right place for him, a good place where he could rest up and calm down. So we went. All three of us. Dec and I didn't need to be together long for us both to realise *that* wasn't the answer. I wasn't cut out for parenthood.

– You only just realised. But what was supposed to be going on at Synchrony? I always understood it was strictly academic.

– Oh, Kertes has been attracting this huge following for years now. They seem to see him as a sort of latter-day Messiah. I suppose if you've always thought you're God, you're not going to disagree when the world finally starts to catch up with you, are you? Actually, according to Benny, he tried to laugh it off at first, but then I suppose he thought he might as well make the most of it. Or someone did.

– Lorraine.

Patrick shrugs. – That's the gossip. I've barely met her myself, but they say she's a forceful woman. And Stefan's not getting any younger. Synchrony's still a learned institute, but there's a sort of therapy centre, alongside the original think-tank. A practical extension of Kertes' ideas, was how Benny put it. A way of approaching life and death. A Jungian synthesis. I quote. Apparently it helped him after Laura died. That part of it's run by Lorraine.

Helen does not comment.

– Anyhow, says Patrick. – Benny said he'd deal with Colette. I don't know exactly what he told her. That he'd run into Declan somewhere, wasn't it?

– Why didn't he just stay? Dec, I mean. Why did he move to England?

– I believe there was a sort of falling out. Benny decided Synchrony was no good – that side of it, anyhow. So he persuaded Dec to move to some place in England, run by someone he knew. Actually, the impression I got was that it was Benny's place – that he'd branched off in some way from the Synchrony line and set up on his own account.

– I went there.

– Did you? Then you know more than I do. What's it like? Is Declan still there?

– He's there. He looks pretty much a fixture to me. I thought maybe he'd been brainwashed, you know, like the Moonies. There were some other kids there in the same sort of state. Casualties. It's run by – do you remember Christopher Clay?

– The name rings a faint bell, but I can't really put a face to it.

– He's a sort of plausible crook. He used to be in politics. I knew him at Cambridge. Helen looks at Patrick. – Does Colette know about all this? She's never mentioned it to me.

– No. I hope you're not proposing to tell her. What would be the point, now?

– All right, I won't. But only if you tell me about Saffron.

– I told you, says Patrick. – That's it. I met her a couple of times.

– Lorraine doesn't want me to talk to her. D'you know why?

– No idea. He looks at her blankly, blandly. – Are you sure you want to find out?

– I've got to, now.

– Ask Kertes, then. He can hardly refuse you.

– I tried. He's in a meeting that's scheduled to last all day.

– Let me have a go, says Patrick. He picks up the phone. – Got the number? Okay. Hello, is this Synchrony? I'd like to speak to Professor Kertes, please. It's Patrick Costelloe. Thanks. He sits back and waits. – Yes, I'm still here. Stefan, is that you? Hope I'm not interrupting your meeting? Oh, I thought . . . Look, I've got Helen here. She'd like a word.

*

He's waiting for her at the front door. He looks almost furtive, or

249

maybe that's just her imagination. This visit is taking place strictly without Lorraine's permission. For the first time, Kertes seems old. He's nervous, he looks over his shoulder, his step's uncertain, his voice trembles slightly. Has this just happened, or is it simply that we see what we're looking for? Or maybe it's a function of context. Amid his equations, surrounded by adoring acolytes, he's reconfirmed in his godhead. Elsewhere, power has seeped away. What's going on in his name, under his auspices? Things are sliding out of control.

– Believe me, Helen, you do not want to see Saffron. It is not a good idea.

– Believe me, Stefan. I do. Why shouldn't I? What can she possibly do to me?

– My dear Helen – His voice fades: evidently, whatever the reason for keeping Helen and Saffron separate, it is not easy to put into words. – It is for your own good. Why make yourself miserable?

– I'm miserable already. I can take it, whatever it is. What I can't take is not knowing.

– Please, Helen. I beg you. Don't.

– But I must. I have to. How can you stop me? She wants it, too. I know. I saw her.

– Lorraine told me. He sounds tired.

Age overtakes him.

IO

HELEN AND SAFFRON are to meet on neutral ground: a restaurant not far from Synchrony.

Entering, Helen feels strength ebb from her knees. She looks around: her heart beats wildly. Can she be real, the brown-haired girl? After all this time, all those hauntings, Helen can't yet believe it's true.

And perhaps it isn't. Saffron isn't here. Helen takes a deep breath. She'll arrive, of course. Soon enough. Meanwhile, Helen can collect herself. She needs to.

She sits back in the gloom. She's often wondered why Americans prefer to eat and drink in semi-darkness, but this particular occasion would not be improved by bright lights. She orders a coffee, glances at her watch. They arranged to meet at eleven. It's ten past. Perhaps, in the end, Saffron won't come. Her courage will fail. Lorraine will get to her. She'll be beamed back up to her home universe . . .

The chair opposite is pulled back. Someone sits down. A young woman with brown hair, not that you'd guess it in this purplish dusk. Helen experiences a sudden shock of recognition, and no wonder: it's herself, twenty years ago. There are differences, of course, but in the gloom you'd hardly notice them. Yes, it's like talking to a ghost: her own.

– Hi, says Saffron. She smiles brightly, nervously: orders a coffee.

The voice, at any rate, is quite different. Helen speaks quietly and very fast; Saffron, in a high, edgy drawl.

– Won't you have something else?

She's very young.

What's she seeing, what's she thinking? For years Helen has been her faceless adversary, as Alex once was Helen's. The legal wife, that figure of power, to whom the errant swain reluctantly, but invariably, returns. The enemy. A view of things less easily maintained across the table from a tired, middle-aged woman. Helen, looking at Saffron, sees her past, but it's unlikely that Saffron, from the other side of the table, perceives her own future. She sees a slight figure, expensively dressed, but whose hair, though well-cut, is visibly greying. Why doesn't Helen dye it? Shouldn't she be on HRT, get a makeover, a facelift maybe? Saffron would, in her place. But Helen no longer has the strength, the will, to fend off mortality. Why bother? Mortality is a fact of her life.

– No, thanks. Saffron's voice is sulky. Nerves, probably. She keeps biting her lower lip. Her fingernails are bitten, too. In this city of manicures, these are details you notice.

– You wanted to see me, she says.

– Yes. That's to say, I have seen you. What I wanted was to speak to you.

– You've seen me? Oh, yeah, at Synchrony.

– Before that. At Benny's funeral. And at High Leys – it was you, wasn't it? But the first time was here. In a shopping mall. In a shoe-shop. You were with a child. That was why I noticed you. I thought it was my daughter Laura. But Laura's dead, Helen affirms angrily.

– I know.

– But the child was real.

– Yes.

– Who is she?

– She's my daughter, says Saffron. – Her name's Cherry.

Cherry sends love.

– And Benny was her father, Helen states, knowing as she speaks that, of course, this has to be the truth.

Saffron nods.

– Where is she?

– She's in school.

– I'd like to see her.

– Sure. You want to go now?

– In the middle of the day? Won't they mind?

– No, says Saffron. – We can go. That'll be OK.

*

Benny sits in the labour room. He holds her hand, offers encouraging words, watches dumbly as the contractions peak, and finally retreats to the seat with the grandstand view. The midwives take up their final positions. He watches, rapt, as the tiny scarlet head with its covering of bedraggled black fluff makes its very first appearance. As before. All, all as before.

It's a girl, of course. He knew it would be, even though she didn't take the test. How could it be anything else? As the baby's cord is severed, as she's cleaned, wrapped and handed to him, as he blinks back his tears, he knows that the impossible has happened. His dreams have come true. The reel's rewound. A parallel universe has opened before him, where all's still to happen. Another bite at the –

This time, it will be all right. This time his daughter will have her chance, like all the other children.

*

It's a short drive to the school, through steep, leafy streets. They pull up outside a spreading, pastel, one-storey building, set in a pleasant garden. There are swings and slides and sandboxes, and a few children playing by themselves. Cherry is one of them. Helen spots her instantly. She's about eight years old: the image of Laura at that age, although now there's more time to look, and Helen's vision is less clouded by shock and emotion, the differences are also visible enough. Laura was stockier, less fragile-looking. And livelier: always in motion, always (like Benny) full of vivid change. The little girl on the video wandered abstractedly into frame, where Laura, at that age, rushed and danced. Yes, Cherry is different. She sits very still, unnaturally still, studying grains of sand as they trickle through her fingers. When her hand is emptied, she picks up more sand.

Saffron goes up to her. She says, – Hi, Cherry! Hi, sweetie!

Cherry concentrates on her sand. She studies each grain minutely, then lets it drop, grain by grain. Her mother's presence doesn't register.

– Here's a friend come to see you. This is Helen.

Cherry puts down her sand, rises, and walks into the building. She hasn't looked at them once. Surely something's wrong? But Saffron seems to take it all for granted. She doesn't, as Helen would in her place, try to offer any explanations (she's tired today, out of sorts, shy with new people . . .)

Saffron and Helen follow the child. As they enter the building, sound assaults their ears. Someone is playing a piano. In another room, a child is banging a drum. Someone, somewhere, is having a screaming, heel-drumming, ear-bursting tantrum. But something – what? – is missing. Helen tries to identify it, but it eludes her.

Saffron makes for a small office where a young black woman sits at a word-processor.

– Hi, Amy. Do you know where Cherry went?

Amy looks at a clock on the wall. – To the dining-room, I guess.

– OK if we go find her?

– Sure.

Saffron leads the way. The familiar, universal school smell, of polish, chalk, children's bodies, envelops them. Mostly, the doors they pass are shut. Inside one or two rooms children can be seen, some sitting vacantly, some engaged in minutely concentrated activity.

In the dining-room, Helen suddenly realises what she's been missing. Conversation, the buzz of speech: that deafening, urgent, high-pitched clamour which dominates every school day. These children do not talk. Speech means that you register the other person, which they don't. Each of them is alone. Some are eating, some not. Some just sit and stare, or rock back and forth. A boy flaps his hands. Another begins to scream piercingly. The rest take no notice. They go on with whatever it is they're doing. They don't look at each other. They don't look at anyone. There are also a number of adults, women of various ages and a young man, who move among the children, trying to get them to eat, to respond, to acknowledge the presence of other people: to behave, in short, like human beings.

Cherry is sitting at a table on the far side of the room. Before her is a plate with a hot dog and some coleslaw. She's intent on eating, cramming the food into her mouth, taking absolutely no notice of the young woman who is sitting beside her. As Saffron and Helen approach, the helper says: – Why, Cherry, here's your mommy. Say hello now. Come on, you can do it! She taps the child's shoulder.

After a while Cherry says, – Hello, Mommy. How are you. The words are blank: without emphasis or inflection, learned by rote.

Saffron says, – Wow, a hot dog! Your favourite. She uses that tone of exaggerated enthusiasm with which adults try to coax a response from a recalcitrant child.

Cherry stares indifferently ahead. Suddenly, she bursts into tears. And what tears! She screams, she rages. The world is too much for her, this jumble of voices, colours, movements, that she can't escape, that she can never escape, that she can't understand. She gets up and runs away, out of the room. The helper, a girl with a long yellow plait, runs after her and hauls her back, howling. – No, Cherry, you sit right there! You eat at the table. Not doing so good today, she says to Saffron, who looks understandably distraught.

– But it was going so well last week.

– It comes and goes. She's improving, though. She's getting a few more words.

Saffron says to Helen: – She's autistic. You probably guessed.

*

Benny goes to pick up his daughter. But Cherry won't meet his look. She arches away, wriggles out of his arms and screams. She screams for hours, and nothing will comfort her. She doesn't want to be held. She can't bear human contact: he can't bear its absence. She's something from another planet.

She's two and a half. She had a few words once, but they've disappeared. Now she just screams and grunts and makes animal noises. Animals, she can cope with. She knows what they're feeling.

255

Not her parents, though, nor other children. She won't meet their eyes, won't admit their existence. They remain a terrifying mystery. She sits by herself in a corner for hours, fixated upon a snailshell she found.

At this age, what was Laura doing? Speaking? Non-stop, it sometimes seemed. – Do shut up, Laura, they pleaded in self-defence as the verbal barrage rolled inexorably on. Her first word came at eight months. – Tat, she said, pointing at the cat. They were sitting in the garden. It was a sunny June day, and the babies were rolling around on the grass. Must have been a weekend, if he was there. She had no teeth yet, and almost no hair – the black frizz she was born with soon fell out or rubbed off. He couldn't believe his ears. Did she really say it? That toothless mite? Benny fetched the cat, and sat down with it by her side. – What is it, Laura? he said. – Can you tell me what it is? – Tat! she said. – Tat! And gazed up at him triumphantly.

In the two euphoric years which followed Cherry's birth, before the words began to go, Benny wrote his book and recorded his video lectures. He *knew* he was right. All was not, all will not be lost – this was what millions wanted to read, wanted to hear. But how do you do it? How can you be sure? Benny had the secret, the knowledge, the absolute assurance they sought. Allied to the scientific weight of his name, it was irresistible. His agent saw that at once. When she rang with news of the offer (– Are you sitting down, Benny? she said. Now, just listen to this!) she told him she'd never been in the slightest doubt.

He couldn't write it now.

He can't bear it. He can't bear to be here with Cherry. It's much worse than if it had never happened, than if he'd never had that illusion of a second chance. It's a caricature, the figment of some madman's fancy. So like, and so terribly different. And those words he wrote, those words he spoke – escaped beyond recall. What's said can't be unsaid, much less unwritten.

Benny says, – Saffy, we can't go on like this.

– So what are we supposed to do? Ditch her? Throw her out the window? So she's difficult. So? Babies aren't just conveniences. Cherry can't help it if she isn't like your other little angel. She's herself! And Saffron snatches up her child, who recoils from her touch while her screams redouble.

– There must be places –

– You want to put her in an *institution*?

– Man, she's not normal. Something's wrong.

– What can be wrong? Look at her. She's beautiful!

– Yes, but impossible. We should take her to a doctor.

– Some children are just like this. I don't want to take her to any doctor.

– Well, unless we do, I'm leaving.

Saffron looks at him. – OK, then, so leave! I don't want to live with any man who can just walk out on his own child because she happens to make a lot of noise.

How many times did they conduct this exchange? Ten, twenty, a hundred? Saffron would never agree, never give in; and, in the end, he stayed. Until it happened once too often, until the screams, the tantrums, the obdurate refusal to accept what was so obvious, so apparent, was finally too much for him.

– You might have given me a bit of warning, says Helen.

– Sorry, says Benny. Couldn't face it, long explanations over the phone and all that. I just suddenly felt it was the right time.

The silence, the peace, the familiarity, are too much for him. He falls into her arms and sobs.

*

– So what was I to do? says Saffron. It's not easy. You need support. I guess that's why I stay at Synchrony. It's kind of like family.

– You finally took her to someone, then?

– After he went, I was in despair. Can you imagine? I had to get help somewhere. And of course as soon as I took her to a doctor, they could see what was wrong.

– Wouldn't Benny see you at all, after he left?

– He'd visit with us a little. Never for long, though. Being with Cherry freaked him out. He helped financially, there was never any problem with that. I guess that made it easier for him to justify not staying with us. Cherry has an income from a business venture he started. It's doing real well, I'm glad to say. That's what pays for her school. We certainly do need all the help we can get.

Business venture? It must be High Leys. Is that why Saffron was there, to check it out?

– Were you both at Synchrony when you met? Do they have couples? I didn't notice any children there.

– No. I'm in therapy there now – I don't believe I could carry on otherwise. But Mrs Kertes introduced us. She taught me at college.

Helen stares at her, thunderstruck. – *Mrs Kertes*? I didn't know Stefan was married!

– Lorraine.

– *Lorraine* is Mrs Kertes?

– Yeah, it's no secret. I don't know how long they've been together, but as long as I've known them, for sure. They finally got married three, four years ago. I met her when I was in college. She teaches psychology, and I majored in that.

Saffron is still speaking, but Helen isn't listening to her any more. She's thinking about Lorraine, how she *organises* her life. That's the only word: not one that Helen would apply to the concatenation of chance occurrences which have characterised her own trajectory, that headlong zigzag dance. A nudge here, a nudge there, and all would have been different. She'd assumed it was the same for everyone. Apparently not, however. Did Lorraine's pupils realise what an adept they'd got teaching them? She's an expert course in applied psychology all on her own.

How long has she been planning all this? Or does she simply seize her opportunities, take fortune by the throat? How did it happen? Did she meet Stefan through Synchrony, or vice-versa? Did she see at once that this was her road to power? To reclaim Benny and, failing that, to ensnare the old man and take over his institute? What does she offer, what do they do together? Is she the one, the one he's been waiting for all his life, the one who sets him free in his old age? And then, spotting Saffron, knowing what had happened, did it suddenly occur to her: *The game's not over yet* . . .

– She fixed for you to meet Benny?

– She asked some people round. This was before they married. Stefan was there, of course. She said, I have this old friend, he's a little sad right now, so I'd like you to be real nice to him. And we just hit it off. I guess she realised we might.

*

– Just a small party, says Lorraine. Come on, Ben. You can't spend the rest of your life moping. You need to get out of yourself more. Meet some people.

Benny sighs. Why is Lorraine so obsessed with his social rehabilitation? It's not like her. Lorraine, as he well knows, doesn't usually devote much time to other people's welfare. She must have some scheme in hand, some plan she's pursuing. Lorraine's life is an artefact, painstakingly shaped and contrived. It's terrifying but true: and he can't help admiring it, never could, even though it's a little scary. She forges ahead, along her chosen path, and the weak world churns helplessly in her wake.

Then he sighs again, for of course he's forgetting the first rule of science. The simplest solution is the most probable. Why search for ulterior motives when such an obvious one is staring him in the face? It's guilt, sheer guilt. She feels she's failed him, and she wants to make up for it.

And, in a sense, so she has: but it wasn't her fault. He knows as well as she does that that was all a fantasy, wishful thinking to the nth degree. Suppose she'd said yes? What would have happened then? More than likely nothing at all. How long is it since he and Lorraine made love? Years, anyhow. And even then, the lustful children *they* once were had vanished as certainly as Laura has vanished now. Laura stopped, marooned forever at ten years old; they metamorphosed. But in both cases, their moment passed. Lorraine's right: life does not offer a rewind facility.

She's wrong, however, about his immediate needs. He came here for the work. He'll bury himself in work. From now on, that will be his life.

– I know what I need.

– Oh, well, let's not argue about that, says Lorraine soothingly. – Think of it this way. You've got to eat, or you'll just fade away. You do eat, I've seen you. So why not eat at my place? You don't have to stay any longer than you want to.

Here he is, then, in Lorraine's little garden behind the Institute, watching the shadows lengthen as the sun sets behind the Pacific horizon and fragrant smoke rises from the barbecue. People are drifting in and out, hundreds of them, it seems to Benny, although he knows in fact that there's only about twenty, and that his perception merely reflects the smallness of the space plus his current aversion to social occasions of any sort.

There's a bottle of chilled wine at his elbow. He pours himself a glass and glances (since one must glance somewhere) towards the barbecue. And feels the goose-bumps rise. For there, framed in the doorway, clutching a glass, stands Helen. Not Helen as she is now, but Helen as he first knew her, when they were students. His nut-brown girl: leafy brown hair, blue eyes, rosy cheeks blushing through clear brown skin. And not just the hair and complexion: the stance, the set of the head: the same slight figure, the same – oh, just *the same*. Quite simply, it's her. The movements, the quick smile . . . He's transfixed, he can't take his eyes off her.

Now here's Lorraine in the doorway, tall, elegant, authoritative. She's saying something to the girl, and now they're both looking at him, and they're coming towards him, Lorraine and Helen. He clutches his glass: he feels slightly dizzy, as though maybe he's going to faint. And now Lorraine's saying something. He forces his attention towards her, towards her words, although really all he wants to do is look at Helen, at Helen reborn, at this embodiment of all he had dismissed as impossible. At life rewound.

– my oldest friend, Lorraine is saying. – Benny Spiro. I expect you've heard his name. We knew each other when we were kids. Benny, this is Saffron. Saffy Russo. One of my students.

Saffron. So it's not Helen after all.

Well, of course it isn't, dumbo! What did you think? That Lorraine can summon up ghosts?

Does she realise, he wonders. She must, of course. He was right: she had something in mind, she always has something in mind, and this was it.

When he looks more closely, there are differences. Saffron's face is wider, her eyes are grey rather than blue, her movements are slower, her manner less sharp than Helen's. But the fact still remains. He can't take his eyes off her. And how can he help feeling that it's somehow *meant*? That this is some sort of message, directed at him?

And Saffron? What does she feel? What does she suppose is happening? She knows Benny, naturally. That's to say, she knows who he is. Doesn't everyone, around Synchrony? He's an object of awe, of fascinated speculation, especially among the women. Everyone knows he's recovering from some terrible tragedy, though as to its details, nobody is entirely certain. Some say his entire family was wiped out in an accident, some say his wife has gone mad and had to be locked up. Whatever it was, he's out of it. Never with you, never entirely present at any conversation. Not like he used to be. Everyone says how he was always so intense and energetic: so *present*. So attractive! All those ideas, all that bursting enthusiasm.

But that was before she came to Synchrony. It's only recently that the Institute has opened its doors to people like Saffron – to, as it were, congregants as well as priests. And these days, no-one ever sees Benny Spiro. He doesn't give lectures or seminars – just sits in his room and thinks. He's rethinking his entire subject. Or that's what they say. Who's to know? Saffron's always had this theory (insofar as she's thought about him at all) that the fabled Benny Spiro is just that: a fable. If you go into his room, all you'll see there is a cardboard cut-out.

So meeting Benny, in the flesh, is an unreal experience for Saffron. Is this how Beauty felt, when first she came upon the Beast? Or Leda, realising just who that swan really was? He's transfixed, can't take his eyes off her, and she meets his gaze steadily. Without a word being spoken, he asks and she agrees. Why should she resist? It's just as they said – he truly is tremendously attractive. Plus, she's always liked older men, that compact, curly-haired type.

Ben Spiro! She can't get over it.

And she won't.

*

It's getting clearer now, thinks Helen. What he wanted when he left for California. A new life in every sense, to replace the old.

– *Shall we have another?*

When Helen wouldn't, he turned to Lorraine – who else? But she wouldn't, either. Couldn't, very likely. *I can't do it. I'm sorry. Part of me would like to, more than anything. But I just can't . . .*

It was too late for us one way in London. And it's too late again now. For all sorts of reasons, too late. I don't imagine I need to spell them all out. This is painful enough without that.

I just can't. It's too late. Read it how you like. In any case, a statement of fact.

Clinging to fantasy isn't going to do it for you. No, indeed. Poor Benny.

But if Lorraine couldn't, or wouldn't, oblige, then she'd do the next best thing: find someone who would. That way, she could keep her eye on things, feel they were under control. Who's the one with power, the madam or the working girl? The puppeteer or the dancing doll?

How did she feel, though, when it all worked out so swimmingly, just as she had planned? Pleased? Maybe. But only on an experimental level. She didn't allow for feelings, that was the thing. Even Lorraine has feelings. And how must she have felt when Cherry was born? On the outside looking in, all over again.

So she married. Looking at Benny over her shoulder, no doubt. She's trumped him with Kertes. Now he'll be sorry.

– So you threatened to tell me about it all.

– He told you that?

– No, I found your letters.

Saffron hugs her knees and wriggles her toes crossly. She drove to the ocean after they left the school: now they're sitting on the beach. Perhaps she hoped the sea would calm them. Joggers pound, as ever, along the firm sand at the water's edge. Far out, white-sailed dinghies bob in the blue Pacific.

She's taken off her shoes and is digging her toes into the sand. She won't look at Helen, or anything else – not the joggers, not the dinghies, not the infinite line of the horizon. Instead, she keeps her eyes fixed sulkily on her feet. It's all too much, this confrontation. On top of everything else. Why does she just sit here? What's keeping her? So why doesn't she leave?

Ah, but who else can she talk to? Who else will understand so entirely?

– He gave me this story when we met, I guess it's the usual thing, she mumbles. – How he was married, but it was finished. He was going to get a divorce. He and I would start over. Why shouldn't I believe it? It was the truth. That was what he really felt. I loved Benny. I just loved him. He was the most exciting man I ever met.

Oh, Helen can see it, just as Lorraine saw it. What chance did anyone stand against that relentless will, that driving enthusiasm? – Poor Benny, is all she can say.

– Poor Benny! How about Cherry and me?

– That too.

– He wouldn't talk to me. I called and called, but he just put the phone down. I thought, I'll come over. If I'm there, he's got to talk to me. If not him, then you. I've got to speak to *somebody*. But when I came, he was dead.

In her short blue cotton dress, with the sea breeze blowing her hair, she looks about sixteen. Sounds it, too. What happened to all that psychology Lorraine taught her? Unlike her mentor, she evidently did not connect theory with practice.

– What did you think would happen if you spoke to me? That I'd throw him out and send him running back to you?

– I thought, if you knew, maybe you'd persuade him.

– You were wrong there.

Saffron flinches before this brutality. Helen goes on angrily (but who is she angry with? Benny? Saffron?): – But anyhow he wouldn't have come. Cherry wasn't what he bargained for.

Saffron shrugs. What is there to say?

– Oh, I suppose I'd have done something, Helen finally allows. – Though I'm not sure what it would have been. It's too late now, anyhow. It looks as though you pushed him over the edge.

– Fair's fair, I guess, Saffron says.

She gets up, walks to her car, and drives away.

Helen lets herself into her house. She shuts the front door behind her, and leans against it, taking in the silence and familiarity of this space. Her own space. She switches on the hall light. It's getting squalid. The dust builds up, there's never that pleasant sense of the whole place being clean all at the same time. She must find someone to replace Mrs Martins. An agency, perhaps. No more uncertainty – will she come this week? Is her knee playing up, or her back? Agencies don't get the flu. It needn't even be every week. Once a fortnight would do fine.

Peace of mind, that's what she wants. When Benny was alive but (as so often) absent, there was always a niggle in the corner of her brain. *Where is he? What's he doing now?* He dominated her consciousness, but the converse was not true – a fact she resented but could not escape. Why? Because. It wasn't fair. Life is not fair. The finality of death, in that sense, is oddly relieving. Amid the grief, compensations may be discerned.

She wanders upstairs. She'll have a bath, then bed. She bought a new novel this morning.

The door to Benny's study is, as always, shut. But the thought of Schrödinger's Corpse no longer oppresses her. She fancies there's a crack of light under the door, but even that doesn't worry her. It's her imagination. Yes. Or the moonlight coming through the window.

She flings the door wide. For a moment, she imagines that Benny's at his desk, working by the light of the green shaded lamp. But when she looks again it's a trick of the light. Nobody's there.